Electrifying Praise for the Novels of

DAVID POYER

THE THREAT

"Plenty of action, plot twists . . . frenetically paced . . . [an] engaging pot boiler."

—*The Virginian-Pilot*

"Poyer remains the most thoughtful of the military-thriller set and a master of authentic detail."

—*Kirkus Reviews*

"Poyer's forte is storytelling, and *The Threat* delivers a masterful tale that leaves the reader dazzled."

—Steve Berry, *New York Times* bestselling author of *The Third Secret, The Templar Legacy,* and *The Romanov Prophecy*

"[Fans] of *The West Wing* . . . and political novels will enjoy the author's revealing portrayal of the backroom goings-on at the White House. . . . Recommended especially for fans of Robert Ludlum's political thrillers (although Poyer is a superior writer)."

—*Booklist*

"Terrific suspense . . . perfect authenticity . . . powerful storytelling and compelling characters . . . David Poyer is our finest military novelist and *The Threat* is simply superb."

—Ralph Peters, author of *New Glory* and *Never Quit the Fight*

THE COMMAND

"[An] explosive climax . . . the reader takes a well-informed cruise on a U.S. destroyer. Poyer knows the ship intimately. Vivid descriptions cover everything from knee knockers to combat information center, radar to computers, wardroom to enlisted quarters. Battle scenes in particular come alive with authenticity . . . and all that, and more, is in this latest chapter of Commander Daniel Lenson's contentious career."

—*Proceedings*

MORE . . .

"Absolutely riveting. David Poyer has captured the essence of what it is like on long-range patrols. His book is distinguished by quick action and continuing suspense that will keep the reader on edge until the very end."

—Maj. Gen. H. W. Jenkins, United States
Marine Corps (Ret.), Commander of the
Marine Amphibious Forces in the Gulf War

"One of the strongest books in an outstanding series . . . the remarkably vivid portraits he draws of the variety of men and women drawn to serve their country merit high praise."

—*Booklist*

"One of the best . . . action fans will be rewarded."

—*Publishers Weekly*

"Poyer's close attention to military practice and jargon will . . . suit those looking for accurate detail."

—*Newport News Press*

"A thrilling and suspenseful fictional piece . . . you won't be able to put the book down."

—*Roanoke Times*

CHINA SEA

"Poyer's characters are as good as ever, and the action scenes lively."

—*Library Journal*

"The battle scenes are scintillating and satisfying . . . Poyer displays a fine sense of pace and plot."

—*Publishers Weekly*

"Action, realism, and exotic locales . . . an absorbing, exciting, and thought-provoking experience."

—*Chesapeake Life*

"An exciting story . . . The author's vivid descriptions of life on a ship show us not only the 'Anchors Aweigh' honor and dedication, but also the boiler-room sweat and frustrations of naval life."

—*Virginia Times*

"Poyer springs plenty of action on us . . . his narration and dialogue ring true."

—*Jacksonville Times-Union*

"Poyer brings the courage, honor, and commitment of sea duty to life in this vivid portrayal of life aboard a Knox-class frigate . . . the details describing life at sea are captivating as the action is continually rolling along, and each page pulls a new twist into the architecture of the story. In the end, the reader is treated to a fantastic battle that pulls each of the story threads together as a tightly woven yarn . . . the scales of intrigue, from murder, piracy, and battle to international diplomacy, capture the imagination with lifelike characters of heroes and villains most naval readers can link to real people met during their own world travels . . . *China Sea* belongs in the library of avid fiction readers."

—*Shipmate*

TOMAHAWK

"There can be no better writer of modern sea adventure around today."

—Clive Cussler

"An absorbing narrative that whips along at the author's usual firecracker pace . . . *Tomahawk* is very much a book of today."

—*The Virginian-Pilot*

"Poyer's characters are well-developed and frequently complex. His description is vivid. And he certainly knows the navy."

—*Jacksonville Times-Union*

"Sharp-edged . . . [a] tense tale."

—*Florida Times-Union*

"*Tomahawk* is a book of many levels. On the surface, it is a book of suspense—spies, secret missile strikes, murder . . . Dig a little further, and there is an officer who is troubled deeply by the effects of the weapons that he is developing."

—*Proceedings*

"The intrigues of bureaucracy have a ring of authenticity . . . if you're into military thrillers, you'll like this book."

—*Wisconsin State Journal*

"A gritty thriller."

—*Microsoft Network*

THE
THREAT

DAVID POYER

St. Martin's Paperbacks

This is a work of fiction. All of the characters, organizations, and events portrayed in this novel are either products of the author's imagination or are used fictitiously.

THE THREAT

Copyright © 2006 by David Poyer.
Excerpt from *Korea Strait* copyright © 2007 by David Poyer.

Library of Congress Catalog Card Number: 2006040591

ISBN: 0-312-94854-9
EAN: 978-0-312-94854-2

Printed in the United States of America

St. Martin's Press hardcover edition / November 2006
St. Martin's Paperbacks edition / August 2007

St. Martin's Paperbacks are published by St. Martin's Press, 175 Fifth Avenue, New York, NY 10010.

10 9 8 7 6 5 4 3 2 1

*For Vince Goodrich and the
other heroes of the Greatest Generation*

ACKNOWLEDGMENTS

E*x nihilo nihil fit.* For this book I owe thanks to Morgan P. Ames Jr., Richard Andrews, John Ball, Eric and Bobbie Berryman, Rob Cole, Mark D. Culpepper, Vesna Dovis, Parker Dooley, John M. Fedida, Marie Estrada, Dan S. Hope, Bill Hunteman, Deborah James, Marty Janczak, Terry Lawrence, Deborah Loewer, Will Miller, Robert "Buzz" Patterson, Al Petersen, Laura Plattner, Naia Poyer, Daniela Rapp, Charle Redinger, Sally Richardson, Sandra Scoville, Matt Shear, Leighton W. Smith, Robert L. Starer, Jay Towne, Bill Valentine, Davor Zidovec, and many others who preferred anonymity. My most grateful thanks to George Witte, editor of long standing; and to Lenore Hart, best friend and reality check.

The specifics of personalities, locations, and procedures in the White House, National Security Council, Joint Interagency Task Force, other executive agencies, and the theaters of operations described are employed as the settings and materials of *fiction,* not as reportage of historical events. Some details have been altered to protect classified procedures.

As always, all errors and deficiencies are my own.

THE
THREAT

To whom shall I hire myself? What beast must I adore? What holy icon shall I attack? What hearts shall I break? What lies shall I believe in? In whose blood shall I walk?

RIMBAUD, Une Saison en Enfer

231440Z AUG
AMICABLE:
//Anybody here?

231440Z AUG
SCHOLAST:
//Been logged on since 0900. Where you?

231440Z AUG
AMICABLE:
//Reporter in office. Gone now.

231441Z AUG
SCHOLAST:
//How's your day?

231441Z AUG
AMICABLE:
//Totally certain this wire secure?? Security monitoring? NSA?

231441Z AUG
SCHOLAST:
//They don't have access.

231442Z AUG
AMICABLE:
//They have access to everything!!

231442Z AUG
SCHOLAST:
//Not time-critical point-to-point strategic communications.
The phone system goes first. Then the Internet. Then GCCS.
But this stays up. That's why it's text only. Low baud rate.
But it'll always be there.

231442Z AUG
AMICABLE:
//I don't feel comfortable discussing this issue.

231443Z AUG
SCHOLAST:
//It's only a contingency plan. In case P gets totally out of
hand.

231443Z AUG
AMICABLE:
//So what's the intent?

231443Z AUG
SCHOLAST:
//As G described it when you saw him at the 30th.

231443Z AUG
AMICABLE:
//That's a pretty fucking vague concept of operations, cow-
boy.

231444Z AUG
SCHOLAST:
//Really want to know details?

231444Z AUG
AMICABLE:
//Point taken. Who's got the op end? Do you have a candi-
date?

231444Z AUG
SCHOLAST:
//Still in the search phase.

231445Z AUG
AMICABLE:
//Just for the record, let me add this. The only reason we're
talking is to have it for, like you said, the contingency. Which
I have a real problem envisioning ever being needed.

231446Z AUG
SCHOLAST:
//That's right.

231446Z AUG
AMICABLE:
//And you'd need the go-ahead from Two to implement it. It
would all have to go according to the—. All perfectly legal.
Looking at it from outside. Anyone who knew otherwise??

231446Z AUG
SCHOLAST:
//Would not be available to testify.

231448Z AUG
AMICABLE:
//I want to say again I have no intention of agreeing that
anything like this be carried out!!

231448Z AUG
SCHOLAST:
//What, you want that on the record? I keep telling you
there's no record. There will never be a record.

231449Z AUG
AMICABLE:
//***Null response***

231449Z AUG
SCHOLAST:
//Remember to log out at end of chat. I power down my ter-
minal too, just to make absolutely sure nothing left any-
where. Out.
LOGOFF

231450Z AUG
AMICABLE:
LOGOFF

I
WEST WING

1

WASHINGTON, D.C.

The corner of Seventeenth and Pennsylvania, early, but the Starbucks across the street was already walled in by secretaries, interns, lobbyists, and Hill rats. The air smelled of exhaust, perfume, latte, and fresh croissants. It was the end of summer, and the morning heat promised a scorching afternoon.

Dan Lenson glanced at his watch as he paced along the black wrought-iron fence. On the other side, camera crews were setting up satellite feeds on the putting-green smoothness of the North Lawn. His gray two-button suit felt loose, baggy, after so many years of wearing a uniform.

He straightened his back to ease what felt like high-voltage shocks shooting up his arms. The year before, he'd intercepted a nondescript trawler in the eastern Mediterranean. The nuclear weapon in its hold, intended for Israel, had instead detonated a mile away from his ship.

He'd hoped for another command after USS *Horn*. Instead, an office in the Pentagon had called with an offer he'd thought hard about before accepting.

He checked his Seiko again. Early, as he was for everything. A habit that didn't drive his wife as nuts as it might, since she was the same way. A woman holding a camera in one hand and a Doberman's leash in the other asked him to take her picture in front of the White House.

Finally it was time. He straightened his tie and went up to the gate house. Tapped his ID on the little shelf. "Yeah?" grunted the guard.

"National Security Council staff," Dan said. "Reporting in for duty."

I'll take him from here," Jonah Freed said. "Commander. Come on in."

Freed, a CIA detailee, was the Defense Directorate security officer. He'd walked Dan through the nomination interviews, and taken care of the special clearance for White House duty, Yankee White, which was even more demanding than the top secret/compartmented clearance Dan already had from the Navy.

They checked in again at a second post in the lobby of the Old Executive Office Building. The gigantic pile of pillared granite was enclosed by the same wrought-iron fence as the White House. Part of the "Eighteen Acres"—the White House complex—it held the agencies that made up the executive office of the president: the National Security Council staff, the office of the vice president, Management and Budget, and so forth. The lobby smelled faintly of fresh manure. He wondered why, but decided not to ask.

He followed his guide through cavernous corridors that receded to infinity. The building was much larger than it appeared from Pennsylvania Avenue. Grandly conceived nineteenth-century moldings arched overhead. The floor was a checkerboard of white marble and black limestone, all well worn. Here and there fossils lay frozen, remnants of an age long past. Over them scurried hundreds of men and women, each intent on his or her fragment of the national security policy of the sole remaining superpower.

Someone called from behind them, "Okay, hold it right there. Who's tracking the damn dog shit all over the floor?"

He turned to see a disgusted janitor pointing at the tiles. At footprints, traced in brown, that ended . . . at his feet. He lifted his shoe to examine the sole. "Sorry," he told the man.

"Lady had a Doberman out front. Guess I wasn't looking. If you've got a mop, I'll take care of it."

"Never mind, mister. Just pay attention where you step next time, okay?"

"Sorry," Dan told Freed. "I wasn't looking where I was stepping, I guess."

"Don't worry about it," Freed said. "There's paper towels in the restroom."

With his shoes cleaned, they climbed a bronze-railed staircase to a cubbyhole admin office. Dan got a check-in list. He signed in-briefing sheets. Signed for a safe combination, again for usernames and passwords for both "high-side" classified and "low-side" unclassified e-mail networks, and yet again for a pager.

Back to the first floor, and a photo booth in the Secret Service office. "That's a blue-gold pass," Freed told him as Dan adjusted it. The stainless-steel chain felt heavier than it ought to around his neck. "In a couple weeks we'll get you one with two gold stars on it. That'll get you full access. Not to say you just stroll into the Oval Office. But if you're told to go, you're cleared in." Freed looked at his watch. "Remember where your director's office is? Third floor?"

Dan said he thought so. Freed gave him the room number, just to be sure, then vanished down one of those labyrinthine corridors.

The first name on the check-in was General Garner Sebold.

The senior director didn't have as large an office as Dan had expected. He supposed the 1600 Pennsylvania address made up for it. Sebold removed half-moon reading glasses as Dan came in. His eyes were pouchy. He had white bristly hair. He wore a regimental-style tie and polished cordovan wingtips with a gray suit. The only military note around was a print of an Abrams tank charging through a sand berm as shells burst around it. Dan got a quick handshake and an invitation to sit. Sebold said to the admin assistant, "Ask Bry Meilhamer to come up." To Dan, "You said you were buying here, right?"

"We found a place in Arlington. Closed last week." The price had taken his breath away. But with Blair's salary added to his—and she made more than he did—they'd manage the payments.

"You're coming off sea duty, right? Remind me."

"Commanded a Spru-can." Seeing the general's blank response, he went generic. "A destroyer, sir. Interdiction operations in the Middle East."

"Oh, yeah. I remember now." Sebold looked at Dan's lapel. "Don't wear your congressional?"

Dan had pondered that question before the mirror that morning. The Medal of Honor came with a small blue bar with white stars that you could wear with a civilian suit. He'd held it at his breast. Then left it on the dresser.

"It attracts too much attention. Plus, I don't feel right wearing it."

"Or the Silver Star? The Navy Cross?" Sebold had a file folder out now, was turning pages.

Dan didn't answer. As far as he was concerned, the ones who deserved the decorations were the guys, and girls, he'd served with. Some of whom had never come home from Iraq, and the Gulf, and the Med.

The general cleared his throat. "What's your medical status?"

"Recovering from injuries, sir. I'm approved for light duty."

"I've got you headed for the counterdrug office, director of interdiction."

Dan blinked. "Something wrong?" Sebold said.

"I understood the billet was director for threat reduction."

"Director, yes, but counternarcotics. Not threat reduction."

Dan sat forward. They'd told him he'd be working to reduce the number of nuclear weapons in the states of the former Soviet Union, and secure them against the kind of theft and misuse that had killed so many of *Horn*'s crew. That was why he'd decided to take the job. He fought anger. Since Iraq, since being captured and tortured by Saddam's Mukhabarat, he'd had to second-guess his emotional reactions. "I don't understand. Does Ms. Clayton know about the change?"

"The national security adviser signed off on it," Sebold said. He smiled, glancing at a wall clock.

Dan got the message, but decided to push the button once more. "I was under the impression she wanted me in the threat reduction billet. My missile-development background. And the . . . operational experience with loose nukes. I've got some ideas. To get ahead of the curve instead of behind it."

"Let's get one thing straight, Commander. You're hired to the NSC staff. What you do when you get here's up to us," Sebold said. "If it's that important to you, maybe I can get you some of the action on threat reduction. And maybe a seat on the Iraq working group. But we need to make things happen in counterdrug. Tony Holt wants this initiative pushed hard this fall." Holt was the White House chief of staff. Dan had heard him called the president's personal nut-cutter. "It's a joint mission, and a huge effort, force-wise."

Dan rubbed his mouth. Cutting down the number of nukes in the world ranked high on his list. But fighting the flood of illegal drugs was important too.

"Orders change, Commander."

"Yes sir, I know that," he said at last. "I'll do my best."

Sebold slapped the desk with eight fingers and rose. "Mrs. C will be back in town tonight. Morning conference in the Sit Room at 1000 tomorrow. Take one of the wall seats. Introduce yourself when it's your turn, but keep it short."

"Yes, sir." Dan stood too as another man came in without knocking.

"Bryan Meilhamer. Bry's been here a long time, knows his way around the halls of power. Bry, your new boss, Dan Lenson," Sebold said. To Dan he added, "We go pretty much on a first-name basis around here."

Meilhamer was in a sport coat and a sloppily knotted tie. He looked to be at least ten years older than Dan and thirty pounds heavier. His shirt was pulled out from his slacks on one side. Sebold said Meilhamer was civilian permanent staff, and would be his assistant director in counterdrug. Dan took a chubby soft hand, looked down on graying strands combed over coral pink.

"Give him the talk yet, General?"

"I was about to." Sebold clasped his hands behind him, stood front and center before his desk. Like Patton, in the movie, Dan thought.

"We say around here, the Hill's where they talk about things; the Eighteen Acres is where they get done. This won't be like any assignment you've had before. For one thing, the hours are going to be longer. And every minute you're not physically here, you'll be on call.

"You'll be asked to take on heavy responsibilities, in different areas, at very short notice, depending on the demands of the moment. The legal limits are spelled out in the read-ins I sent you. Conflict of interest. Financial disclosure. But the requirements go beyond that.

"We exercise the power of the presidency. Because of that, and the trust it implies, even the appearance of impropriety here *is* impropriety. Not only do you not favor anyone's interest, you can't appear to do so, even in the most innocent way. Did you vote for Robert De Bari?"

The question was so unexpected Dan almost answered it. "I'm not sure that's really—"

"No, you're right; it doesn't make any difference. We're here to further his objectives. Not ours, or our individual service's. If you've got any agenda of your own, put it aside.

"As a National Security Council staff member, you'll be working with full generals, agency heads, the most powerful people in government. But as far as the Constitution goes, we don't exist. If you want your name in the papers, you're in the wrong place. If you have any criticism of the president, or anyone around him, keep it to yourself. Or bring it to me, if you absolutely have to."

"I know what loyalty means, sir."

"I hope so," Sebold said. "A lot of what goes on inside

that iron fence never goes public. The people who matter know how to keep their mouths shut."

"I keep classified information to myself," Dan said. "If that's what you're talking about."

"Good. Because you're going to be working with some who it will sometimes seem aren't playing on the same team as we are. Before you assume they're being mendacious, or willfully ignorant, pick up the phone and talk it through. Nine times out of ten it's just someone protecting his turf. If that doesn't fix the problem, call me. I'll take it to a level that'll settle it."

Sebold reflected. "Don't be surprised when people you expected more of turn out to have feet of clay. And when things get chaotic around here, remember, you get to see only one little piece of an issue. There's a bigger picture, but you most likely won't see it till a lot later . . . if you ever do. And don't get the idea you're at the center of things. We may work here, but we're not the banana. We're actually more like that white pulp on the inside of the peel."

Dan was ready for more words of wisdom, but that seemed to be all. The senior director slid past them. "I'm due in the West Wing. If you want to come along, I'll drop you at the DNSA's office."

Meilhamer murmured that it had been nice to meet him.

Outside, a small lot was parked solid with freshly waxed black Lincolns. Sebold said this was West Executive Drive. The white awning ahead, flanked by small evergreens and flower plantings in heavy cast-concrete pots, was the staff entrance to the West Wing. A blue-carpeted lobby was hung with framed art. Dan recognized a World War II battle scene by Tom Freeman. A vase of roses stood on a side table, their perfume mingling with the odors of frying pork and coffee. Keyboards rattled in the offices they passed.

At the corridor intersection of the Roosevelt Room, the Cabinet Room, and the steps Sebold said led up to the Oval Office, the general grabbed his arm. "Just a minute. Some-one's coming."

Dan saw them, young guys in suits, walking purposefully

abreast. A hefty black man with round, babyish cheeks examined him as they neared. His look was impersonal, yet observant. His eyes flicked to Sebold, but they didn't exchange any greeting. Dan looked after them as they went away down a corridor which had, he noticed, suddenly gone empty.

His mind formulated a sentence along the lines of "What's going on." But when he glanced back, mouth open, he was looking into the president's eyes.

Robert De Bari looked much as he did on television. Only the screen didn't convey how tall he was, nor how blue his eyes were. He wore a beautifully tailored suit, gleaming, wedge-toed cowboy boots, and a sky-blue silk tie. Two more agents flanked him; another, a compact and expressionless young woman in a gray skirt and blazer, trailed the swiftly moving party.

Beside him Sebold said, "Good morning, Mr. President."

"Hello, G-man. Who've we got here?"

"New staffer, sir. Dan Lenson. Going to counterdrug."

The president stopped, braking his entourage, and put out his hand. Dan flinched as a static spark zapped between their meeting palms. "Good to have you with us, Dan. I need somebody to shake things up in that job."

Dan couldn't seem to think very well. But looking into De Bari's eyes, feeling the strength in his grip, he suddenly felt both totally known and completely accepted by someone he could trust. It was the feeling you got sometimes with a brother, or a best friend.

He felt he should say something back, but couldn't get the words out. Having the Secret Service basilisking him didn't help. Despite himself, his eyes dropped to the president's right hand. The famously missing fingers. De Bari had lost them years before, as a firefighter, carrying a black child through the broken window of a burning apartment building in Carson City. The president nodded in a friendly way, as if he understood how Dan felt. He slapped his arm and bounded up the carpeted steps, taking them two at a time.

He got a breath at last. He said to Sebold, "Sorry—should I have said something?"

"You could have, but don't worry about it." The director waved him off. "Don't forget. Sit Room. Ten tomorrow."

2

ARLINGTON, VIRGINIA

The house was within walking distance of a new Metro station, down a street that still had maples and elms and an afterglow of the sleepy peace of the 1950s, when most of the homes along it had been built.

Blair had found it while he was in the hospital. The tan brick colonial was surrounded by flagstone walks and the yellow poplars the locals called tulip trees. Three bedrooms and a family room in the basement with floor-to-ceiling shelves he planned to fill with the hundreds of books he'd accumulated and had never been able to winnow down. Oak floors, and a kitchen where two could sit for breakfast. Blair had brought her furniture from her apartment in Crystal City, pieces from the country antique stores she made him stop at when they drove out to visit her parents. Azaleas burned like sunset under the front windows. There were tulips and peonies too, and butterfly bushes and lavender. There wasn't a lot of yard, which was good. He could polish it off in half an hour with the Snapper. At the end of the street was an assortment of shops, including a German delicatessen. One of Virginia's oldest churches was a mile away. George Washington had served there as a warden, and the gravestones had been used as targets by Union cavalry.

It was enormously more comfortable and spacious than the house, the town, the life he'd grown up in. He felt like an intruder. That didn't mean he wasn't happy things had turned out this way. Just that he didn't always feel he belonged.

He figured some of that was posttraumatic. The same reason he couldn't sleep without a weapon within reach. But knowing why didn't change the feeling.

When he swung up the walk it was almost dark, but the next-door neighbor, Mrs. Brawridge, was still out. They exchanged waves and smiles. She was in the yard every day, trimming plantings or tending a decorative fish pond in shorts so abbreviated he could see the bottoms of her cheeks. Which were on the decorative side too . . . The garage doors were closed, so he couldn't see if Blair's car was there. She had a government sedan and driver, but drove herself in and back. When she wasn't on travel. But the lights were on in their bedroom and the paper wasn't on the lawn. They should probably cancel it: They both got the *Early Bird* at work and read the *Post* and *Times* there. When he threw his briefcase on the couch he could smell dinner.

"I'm home," he said, wondering how it could sound so commonplace and yet so nice.

She came out of the kitchen for a garlic-flavored kiss. "I figured you'd want something good after your first day at work. Then we can go look at beds for the guest room. How'd it go?"

Blair Titus was almost as tall as he was, with shining blond hair and the rangy relaxed way of moving so many people had who'd grown up with horses. He'd met her in the Persian Gulf, back when his career was in the tank and she'd been adviser to the chairman of the Senate Armed Services Committee. Blair had been asked to brief De Bari, elected but not yet in office, before he addressed the annual meeting of the National Guard Association. He'd invited her to serve on his transition team, then appointed her undersecretary of defense for personnel and readiness. This was the first time they'd actually lived together, and he was still getting used to it. Even in his first marriage, he'd never spent more than a couple of weeks home at a time.

"All right, I guess . . . but they switched me from threat reduction to drug interdiction."

A metallic crash from the kitchen, and a curse. He went in to offer help. His skills were limited to casseroles, chili, burgers. Guy cooking. She tended to attempt dishes that were beyond her actual level of skill. Usually they turned out okay. When they didn't, you saw her temper. Blair looked passionless but wasn't. She intimidated a lot of men. Not with anger, but with a probing intellect. She did the same thing with him. Forcing him to examine his motives. Confront his self-questioning.

"You can peel those. But I thought they promised you TR."

"Not exactly promised." The frustration he'd felt in Sebold's office came back; he bit his lip as he scrimshawed a potato. "He said he'd try to get me on a working group, though."

"That's where things get done. How's your neck doing?"

"Okay." Actually he was feeling some pain again, but he didn't want to get dependent on the pills.

She slid a pan into the oven and sighed, pushing back damp hair. "Boy, I hope this comes out the way it's supposed to. Anything else I ought to know about?"

"Ran into the president." He told her about their meeting.

"He zeroes in on you, doesn't he?"

"The charisma thing. He's got it, all right."

"We were prepping him before the debate. Midnight session. We figured he'd get zinged on the conscientious-objector issue. Like, how could he send men to war if he wasn't willing to go himself? He said he'd answer it when the time came. Then the mike failed, remember that? And he made that quip that made everybody just sort of laugh and shake their heads.

"And when Ted Koppel hit him with the question, he said he'd thought long and hard about what to do. Fight in a war he didn't believe was right? Go to Canada, desert his country? In the end, he'd told his draft board that if his number came up, he'd just have to go to prison. He stood by that choice now. No teleprompter. No prepared remarks. And it came across."

Dan remembered the coverage, and remembered wondering at the time whether it hadn't just been a clever evasion. And whether a guy with an attitude like that should even want to serve as commander in chief. But the incumbent had been no hero either, snuggled into a deferment his wealthy daddy had arranged. De Bari was the first Italian American to make it to the top, as remarkable in his way as John Kennedy had been. "Bad Bob" (a nickname from his firefighting days) had scored with ethnics, Catholics, fellow Westerners, and the unions. But the recession—punishing, endless, grueling—had put him in office. The other candidate had seemed embarrassed about it, but not really concerned—an impression that had doomed him at the polls.

"So what's going on across the river?" he asked, admiring her long bare legs as she bustled here and there.

She told him about her ongoing feud with the comptrollers. "The force just isn't getting the money they need. I don't mean for weapons or force levels. I mean what keeps people in—health, housing, the no-glamour issues."

"So put it in the budget."

"I tried to, but what we keep getting back is 'We're already putting too much into defense.' I wish the service chiefs were focused on the issue. Or just more responsive when you point out that a sizable percentage of our junior enlisted are on food stamps."

"They ought to listen to you," Dan said.

"Why should they? A woman. Never served in uniform. Working for a president who didn't either." She frowned into the distance. "But it's not just me. They've never liked the fact civilians get to tell them what to do. I just have to get used to that."

The phone rang and she answered it while he set the table. When they sat down it was full dark, and kids were rattling down the sidewalk on skateboards. The salmon was just right, the young asparagus tender.

After dinner they went to look at beds. He saw pieces he could live with, but they all seemed flimsy and overpriced. Especially considering his daughter was starting college that fall. Finally Blair asked him what he thought of one suite. He said he didn't have an opinion.

"Dan, this is your house too. You've got to have some idea what you want."

"It's *furniture,* hon. As long as it keeps your ass off the carpet, who cares what it looks like?"

Which only seemed to irritate her more. They left without buying anything. It occurred to him that they usually did. As if she too wasn't sure and had doubts about the life they were trying to build.

B ut they made up on the way home. That was one thing he liked about her—she didn't hold a grudge.

That night they made love in the new queen-size for the first time. Or, more exactly, tried to. But cervical injuries didn't help erectile function.

At last he gave up and rolled off. They lay facing away from each other. His neck burned. His arms pulsed as if he were gripping a power line. He smelled her scent and hair spray, his own stale sweat . . . He wondered why women even bothered with men, exactly what they got out of it.

When she turned back her fingers slipped around him, dropped between his legs. But it was still no good.

"I'm sorry," he told her. "It's just not going to work. I can do something else, though."

She didn't answer. His fingers traced the curve of her hip, of her cheek.

"What's wrong?"

"Nothing. I'm sorry too. I thought it was supposed to come back."

"Well, it did there for a while."

"You said the doctor told you things would improve. The nerve pathways, or whatever."

"That's what she said. But it just sort of . . . it's there, then . . . it isn't."

"Well, don't let it get to you." She groped for the sheets. "I married you, not your dick, okay? It's not a big deal. Just give it time."

In the light that came through the blinds he could see her face close as she kissed him good night. Some might say her nose might be a little large. But not him. He put his hand against her cheek. "You're so beautiful."

She murmured, "But there's something else going on, I think."

"What do you mean?"

"I mean: I thought you'd like living together. But sometimes you don't seem to. Like that remark at the furniture store."

"I didn't mean anything by it."

"Then why'd you say it? It's as if the harder I try to make things nice, like a home, the more it threatens you."

"Well—I'm here. Aren't I?"

"But are you committed to it? Sometimes I'm not sure you are, Dan."

He told her he was, but actually he was trying not to groan. The pain felt like augers drilling down all the way to his wrists. He rolled out at last and took a pill. Drank some water and came back to bed.

He lay waiting for the drug to work. Or for her to say something else. But she didn't. He wondered if he ought to apologize again. No, fuck that. He felt angry. Then frightened. He felt things trying to come into his mind. Instead of letting them in he visualized the pistol in the nightstand. Remembered how it fit into his hand. It was loaded. He took a deep, slow breath. Let it out. Then another. Not thinking about Iraq, or the way the flash had lit the faces in *Horn*'s pilothouse, or anything at all. Not thinking of anything at all.

Without quite meaning to, at last he fell asleep.

3

THE WEST WING

The next morning he filed with others whose names he didn't know yet down a blue-carpeted corridor narrow as a frigate's passageway. It ended in a windowless conference room. He'd thought from *Dr. Strangelove* and *The President's Plane Is Missing* that the Situation Room would be far underground, paneled with sophisticated terminals and displays. And much, much bigger.

But it wasn't belowground, though they called this the "basement" of the West Wing. Their living room in Arlington was bigger than this cramped, damp-smelling space. And as the lead-lined door sucked closed, he didn't see any screens at all. Just polished cherry paneling. A folding easel. And the table, with eleven leather-upholstered chairs.

He found a seat along one wall, balancing his briefcase on his knees. Not much in it yet. Reports Meilhamer had given him to read. A Brookings book. He shrank back to let more men and women crowd in. The air started to get stuffy.

Sebold noted his presence with a nod and settled in halfway up the table. Dan recognized the deputy national security adviser. Brent Gelzinis wore rimless spectacles. His jet-black hair was slicked back like Robert McNamara's had been. The rest were the deputy assistants, the regional and functional senior directors, other directors like himself, and a few twenty-somethings he guessed were interns. The room quieted. He glanced toward the door, started to his feet. Then sank back, catching an amused glance from Sebold.

Mrs. Nguyen Clayton was slight, with a close bowl of dark hair. The assistant to the president for national security affairs had been evacuated from Saigon as a child; her native accent was overlaid now with Harvard and New York. Her tailored blue suit had filigreed gold buttons. Heavy bracelets and earrings pushed the envelope of Washington taste. Still young enough to be attractive, she brought with her into the room something most of those there found far sexier: the consciousness of power. She'd made a hundred million dollars in Silicon Valley before meeting Robert De Bari, when he was still governor of one of the emptiest, most crooked states west of the Rockies, and managing his campaign. The deputy adjusted her chair, and she descended among them.

"Let's get started," she said.

Gelzinis cleared his throat. His low-key briefing was so packed with acronyms Dan was lost from the first sentence. When he was done the deputy assistants had their turn, then the senior directors. Clayton said little as she listened. Occasionally she asked if they'd checked with State, or Commerce, or the CIA. Once she said sharply, "No, we're not letting it lie. They have to have access to that technology. I'll speak to the appropriate people about it."

When his turn came Sebold said, "We've got a new join at counterdrug. Dan?"

He got to his feet. Some looked up; others didn't. "Commander Dan Lenson. Navy," he said, trying for terseness. "Glad to be here. I'll try to get up to speed as fast as—"

"All right, thank you, everyone," Clayton said, rising. They all got up with her and followed her out. Leaving him looking around the empty room.

Room 303, in the southern wing, third floor of the Old Executive, was one of the "split-level" suites, so called because to shoehorn more bodies in, the nineteenth-century's fifteen-foot-ceilinged offices had been divided with a false floor at the seven-and-a-half-foot level. This and gray cubicle partitions made a two-story suite out of what had been several very tall rooms. As an added benefit, the false floor included ductwork for central air. The effect might have been claustrophobic for someone as tall as Dan. But it wasn't as tight as the cable-overheaded passageways of the typical destroyer.

His people were gathered at a table behind the receptionist's desk. Meilhamer had explained that given counterdrug's limited manning and worldwide responsibilities, he'd divided them up among the assistant directors by geographic area. Asia/Europe was Marty Harlowe, major, Marine Corps, a rail-thin blonde Dan trusted on sight. He noticed she didn't wear a wedding ring. South America/Caribbean was Luis Alvarado, a Hispanic Coast Guard lieutenant commander. The continental U.S. belonged to Ed Lynch, an Air Force major. Interagency liaison was Miles Bloom, Drug Enforcement Agency. Bloom was younger than Dan, fit-looking, with a heavy black mustache and leathery skin that testified to a lot of time in hot climates. The staff assistant, Elise Ihlemann, was an Army Guard sergeant. At the moment she was at the waddling stage of pregnant. All were in civilian clothes, suits or sport coats, corresponding office attire for the women.

Marty, Luis, Ed, Miles, Elise. Plus Bry Meilhamer, of course. The temptation was to think of the career incumbent as the exec and himself as the skipper. But permanent civilian staff might not have the same goals as those who'd return to the field, the fleet, when their tour was up. They looked impressed by him. Perhaps even afraid of him. The grapevine would have given them their new boss's background. Even if it just hit the high points, he supposed it'd be an earful.

"Want me to summarize what Mrs. C put out this morning?" Meilhamer asked him.

"Thanks, Bry, I'll give it a go." Dan went over what he thought pertained to them, then flipped his wheel book closed. "I'd like to get briefed on what each of you has on his plate. What packages you're working. What events we have to prepare for. I need someone to explain this counter-drug intelligence-plan initiative. That's going to change how we do business. Miles, that fall into your area?"

"I can brief you on that, Dan."

First names, right. "Come on into my office and we'll talk. Bryan, you too. Marty, you available this afternoon? Talk about the Taliban and poppy production?"

The major said quietly that she'd be there.

M eilhamer and Bloom briefed him in a long two-on-one interrupted by many phone calls. Dan's office was so small their knees bumped. The view through his half window was of construction vehicles down in the central courtyard. GSA employees in green uniforms were free-throwing bags of trash into blue Dumpsters. If he bent low and looked up he could catch a sliver of sky.

"We're basically walking point for the administration's initiative. That's what's coming down these days from the chief of staff," Meilhamer said, looking down at the carefree janitors, not at Dan.

"I read something about us being a coordinating agency."

"We're not an agency, but yeah, we coordinate."

"Which means?"

Meilhamer said patiently, "Getting military and law enforcement and State to work together to reduce interstate drug flows."

"Interstate?" Dan said, puzzled. He'd thought their charter ended at the national border.

"He means international," Bloom put in. He was sprawled back, clearly not impressed by having to brief his new boss. He also didn't hew to the suit-and-sport-coat code. He was in shirt sleeves, collar open. His gray silk shirt was more stylish than what the others wore. "But we also keep tabs on the grass growers in the national parks."

"So we coordinate military, law enforcement, DEA, and State?"

"And CIA, Customs, and Justice, and Commerce, and sometimes Agriculture. Whoever we need to reach out and touch." Meilhamer wiped his glasses. "But let me make one thing clear: We coordinate, but we don't command."

"Who does?"

"Well, that gets fuzzy above the task force level."

Great, Dan thought. He frowned at his notes. "Who exactly is our customer? And who's our boss?"

"Boss and customer are the same guy: the president, through Mrs. Clayton. But there's a lot of congressional involvement."

He looked at his notes again. "NDIC?"

"National Drug Intelligence Center. Justice Department. Strategic intelligence fusion."

Dan said okay, and what was the linkage to the military? Meilhamer said it went through three task force headquarters, in Key West, Alameda, and El Paso. "But Defense doesn't really want to play."

"Why not?"

"It's not a traditional mission, they look at it like a tar baby. But the national estimate's fifty-two thousand drug-related deaths last year. Like Castro invaded and wiped out Galveston. You think we wouldn't declare war the same day? But it's sprinkled here, sprinkled there. And the corruption's oozing in along with it."

Dan frowned, trying to get his head around why the military didn't want to participate. That didn't make sense.

As soon as Desert Storm wrapped, everyone had expected that peace dividend. The Republicans wanted lower taxes. The Democrats wanted to fund social programs. The idea of being ready for war seemed like an anachronism. A lot of people saw the military-industrial complex as a blind and hungry wolf, swinging its muzzle to and fro as it searched desperately for the next threat.

Sometime he saw it that way too. But at other times, his

complacent, tolerant, unsuspicious country looked more like a staked-out hog, around which predators circled in a threatening night.

He said, "I read the presidential directive. Sounds like he thinks this is the new big threat."

"There's a case," Bloom said, his attention engaged at last. "The Russians and Cubans used to fund all these terrorist organizations along the spine of Central America. Now that teat's gone, the producers, the traffickers, and the terrorists are doing a mating dance. These are not a bunch of barefoot boys from the barrio doing things on a whim. They've got technical training, the latest weapons and equipment, and strict operational security."

"Their interests interlock," Meilhamer said. "The armed groups can undermine and eventually overthrow the governments. The traffickers fund them in exchange for protection. And the producers, well, the weaker the government, the freer they are to operate. Right now the relations are local. The Shining Path in Peru. FARC in Colombia. But if they start coordinating operations . . ."

"We've got a fucking war," Bloom finished for him.

Dan had read the speculation in *Defense News* and *Armed Forces Journal* about the next threat. He had personal reasons for disliking China, a country that would soon have the industrial horsepower to present a serious challenge. There was also the possibility of a resurgent Russia. And the fanatical Muslim terrorists who'd attacked *Horn.*

But maybe this was the real menace of the future. Ruthless multinational criminal syndicates, with their own banking, logistics, intelligence, armies.

"Right now," Meilhamer said, "they're on the defensive. With the aerostats and patrols we've just about got the cork in in the Caribbean and Gulf. And this new guy in Colombia—"

"Tejeiro," Bloom put in.

"—Edgar Tejeiro, the new president, he sounds serious about clamping down. If he'd cooperate, root 'em out on the producer end, that'd be a double whammy." After a moment he added, "Of course, it'd be dangerous for him too. You make these people mad, the default is to blow you away."

"We could actually make some progress then?" Dan said. "With this Tejeiro? I'd like to find out more about him."

"You want Luis for that. He does most of the interfacing with the host governments down there."

L uis Alvarado brought in a PowerPoint brief on his ThinkPad. The Coast Guardsman said trafficking via the Bahamas and the Caribbean had gone up and down since importation started in the sixties. Fought to a trickle in the late eighties, when the product had been mainly grass, flown in to dirt airstrips, it had rebounded once traffickers got their hands on Global Positioning Systems. Now they precision-dropped cocaine at night. Intercepting them took a cruiser to track aircraft out of the Barranquilla Peninsula. When that net got too tight, he predicted, they'd fly at low level up Central America, land in Mexico, and jump across the border by road, with local cops paid not to notice. There were signs traffic was rerouting already.

"How about Tejeiro?" Dan asked him. "Is he serious in these promises he's making to move against the traffickers?"

"It might cut down on the coke supply," Alvarado said. "But the meth suppliers will just pick up the slack. The only real answer to addiction is to cut down the demand side of the equation." He glanced at Bloom. "Education. Awareness programs. Maybe even partial decriminalization."

"Then the pusher goes for the fifth-grader instead of the teen," the DEA agent said. "Ever go into a ward, see the babies addicted to crack? Do that, you won't talk about legalization."

"I'm not talking about legalizing crack, Miles."

"You remove the stigma, you'll have ten times as many fucking addicts."

Dan sensed a long-running argument and stepped in. "Thanks, Luis, Miles. I'd like to have a few minutes with Major Harlowe now."

• • •

Dan laced his fingers, listening to Marty Harlowe's oral brief on Asia. Like every marine he'd ever met, she projected perfect self-assurance. Unlike the others, she also looked very good in patterned stockings. She said the rate of initiation for new heroin users in the U.S. was climbing again, and typical age of first use was down to seventeen. In Burma, the United Wa State Army, what Harlowe called a "narco-insurgent group" linked to the junta, was trafficking methamphetamine and heroin into California. Dan asked her if there was a link to China too.

"Definitely. They provide Wa with ephedrine, a methamphetamine precursor. Along with weapons, computers, software, communications . . . The drugs go through Chinese shipping channels to Canada, and into the U.S. through motorcycle gangs."

"How do we know all this?"

"The royal Thai government. Operation Tiger Trap. I can give you chapter and verse if you want it."

One of the items of discussion at the meeting that morning, in fact the one Mrs. Clayton had spoken so sharply about, had been approval of what Dan understood to be the export of satellite stabilization technology to China. Now he asked, "What's the State Department's take? Do they ever put Beijing on report?"

"Not a good idea," Meilhamer put in. "Commerce is powerful in this administration. They're pushing hard to get access to the Chinese market."

"Yeah, but they can't have it all their own way. Importing our technology, exporting us drugs."

"I'd run anything like that past the senior director first," Meilhamer said firmly. "Really. Commander . . . you've just taken over this ship, remember. That's deep water where you're headed."

Dan thought of pointing out that shallow water was what a skipper worried about, not deep, but decided that would sound like nit-picking.

When they were gone he swiveled his chair and looked down into the creeping gloom in the courtyard. Rolled his head around, trying to work out the kinks, though it actually didn't feel that bad today. Some people—his previous commanders—had accused him of having a hair trigger. But what was the point in gathering the intel, finding out where the shit came from, if you didn't try to close the spigot?

He knew this much by now: It was better to come out of the gate bucking. Start off as a chair warmer, it was too easy to stay one. But if you charged off in the wrong direction, you might end up stampeding over a cliff.

Thank God there was one enlisted around to serve as a reality check. "Ihlemann!" he shouted.

"What?" she yelled back, just as loud.

"Grab yourself a cup of coffee, Sergeant. Then get in here and tell me how things really work around this friggin' place."

4

Over the next weeks, he began to find his way around.

He went to the Indian Treaty Room for a retirement ceremony, some old-timer gold-watching out of Systems and Technical Planning. This was a majestic space, with green marble, encaustic tile, bronze sconces with shield-bearing cherubs, opal glass chandeliers, and a glorious view of the Jefferson Memorial. Less splendid was the Old Executive cafeteria at 0630, with its high-school steam tables and no place to sit. The gated courtyard where the Roadrunners were parked, mirror-black Econoline vans that acted as command centers when the president went on the road. The pressroom, with the worn folding seats of a 1940s movie theater, filled day and night with bored, unshaven reporters and cameramen. The White House mess, where you could order a burger on the tab, and pick it up at the window outside the Sit Room.

Connected to the West Wing by a short corridor was the White House itself. Wandering through the public rooms on his lunch hour, looking at paintings, china, exquisite antiques, it felt to him more like a museum than a residence. The first family lived on the second floor, with the most private and informal areas on the nearly invisible third. Beneath everything lay a noisy, smell-filled basement that was

busy at all hours, like the kitchen and scullery of some
great hotel. A concrete-walled ditch in front of the North
Portico let staffers cross from the West to the East Wing
without going through the ceremonial spaces. A basement
archway still showed black smudge marks the British destruction party had left in 1812. To the south lay the
clipped and fragrant rectilinearities of the South Lawn,
glistening in the mornings with the rainbows of spray irri-
gation on the Rose Garden; a running track; and the heli
pad for *Marine One*.

   The political staff, who seemed to Dan very youthful, operated in a different world than the military. He sensed
standoffishness from the permanent staff too. They were polite, but had the air of residents watching the transients pass.
The Secret Service were like Terminators in business suits,
as if the radios plugged into their ears had taken over their
brains. His only unpleasant encounter was with a young female staffer he'd asked for directions to the East Colonnade.
She'd glanced at his haircut and turned away without a word.
There certainly seemed to be a lot of them about—young,
good-looking women.

   But he didn't spend a lot of time thinking about it. Work
sucked him into its vortex. He read interagency approvals.
He spent a lot of time on the phone. Meilhamer told him to
go to all the meetings he could, to get his face known.
Sounded reasonable, but sometimes Dan wondered if his assistant preferred to have him out of the office. He'd gone to a
session of the Iraq working group, which discussed Saddam's defiance of the inspection regime. When an attendee
from Commerce had questioned the embargo, Dan had been
able to make some points about its effectiveness, based on
his time in the Red Sea and the Gulf.

   This afternoon he was due at the National Photographic
Interpretation Center. For something that close, he took the
Metro, a three-block walk through downtown to the Farragut
West station. When he got off at the Navy Yard stop it was
another two blocks to the west gate. The last time he'd lived

in D.C., this had been a dangerous section. Now it showed signs of gentrification.

A CIA counternarcotics specialist asked the attendees not to make notes, then began explaining how multispectrum overhead imagery could do crop estimates in Peru. Find individual pot plants in national forests. Show upturned faces on a boat being loaded at a Guajira pier. Unfortunately, it was less useful above triple-canopy jungle, where the processing took place. What Dan found interesting was the ability to eavesdrop on phone calls. The briefer said if assets were requested in advance, and the environment was radio frequency–quiet, they could provide real-time relay of cell conversations. "Given, of course, that they're not scrambled," he added. "And that this administration doesn't cut the program, along with the rest of our high-technology assets they're throwing out."

Dan raised his hand. "We can't decode?"

"Year before last we could. Now companies are marketing systems we can't break."

When the brief was over he checked his watch. He'd already told Meilhamer he wouldn't be back in the office. He had an appointment out in Fairfax. One he'd made weeks before, and wasn't about to break.

"Dad! Over here!"

His daughter leaped and waved in front of a new-looking redbrick dorm. Her legs were brown in shorts. He swallowed, dizzied by how much she looked like her mother.

Nan gave him a quick hug. Said into his ear, "Boy, Dad, I almost didn't recognize you out of uniform."

He tried to smile. "They don't like 'em where I work."

"The White House, right? My roommate was so impressed."

Strolling around a huge lawn where the students were tossing Frisbees or lying together on blankets, she told him about her courses. She didn't have to decide till sophomore year, but thought she'd try for a bachelor's in life sciences and maybe a master's in molecular medicine.

"Holy smoke," he said. *"Molecular medicine?"*

"I know, but they've got a world-class biotechnology program." She wanted to take economics and Japanese too. She was already on the tennis team. Did he want to play a game? He said he was out of practice, hadn't brought his racket. Instead he proposed a snack at a café overlooking the campus. "So, what's new with your mom?"

"She's the dean now. She does yoga these days. Says it helps with the stress."

"I can imagine. How's Ted?"

"Oh, the same. How's Blair?"

"She's good. Really busy, but we'll take you out to dinner. The Four Seasons, maybe."

"So who's more important, her or you?"

He had to grin. "She swings a lot more weight in this town than a Navy commander."

"You know, I met a guy from the Navy once. In an airport. I asked him if he knew you. He said everybody did. You were a . . . what did he call you . . . a warfighter. Like, you'd really done stuff. Dangerous stuff."

"Most people don't have that positive an opinion."

"He said you got the Medal of Honor. You never told me that."

He looked away. "It's not something you make a big deal about, Punkin."

She frowned. "Why not?"

"Because the guys who really deserved it didn't make it out."

"Didn't make it out of where?"

"The Middle East. Actually Iraq."

"And, what—you don't deserve it, because these *other* guys got killed?"

He remembered a man's head on fire, and closed his eyes. "Right."

She reached across the table for his hand. "Oh, Dad . . . I

know I was a brat sometimes growing up. I was mad at you
for not being around. Hearing stuff from Mom didn't help.
You know, what an asshole you were. But you know what? I
never quit loving you. And I'm proud of you, for not drinking anymore, and I like Blair, and . . . anyway, thanks. For
not giving up. On me, or anything else."

"Your mom's a good person, Punkin. We just couldn't get
along."

"Want to know a secret? That's why I picked this school.
To be near you."

"Are you serious?" he said. "That's great. That's really
great."

"I thought we could do something together. Go sailing or
something . . . I've never been on a boat."

"I know a guy in Annapolis who runs charters. Pick a
weekend."

"Oh, look! There're my friends. Over here!"

She immediately began telling them about the boat trip,
inviting them along. This was disappointing. He'd conjured
a picture of the two of them sharing memories and dreams
out on the bay. But he put it aside. Just being in her life again
was great.

Just then something like a trapped roach buzzed against his
flank. He flinched before he remembered. He'd set the pager
on vibrate. The White House number, but he didn't recognize
the extension. He excused himself and found a pay phone.

"Sit Room," a voice said. Female. Businesslike.

"Lenson from counterdrug, returning a page."

"Lenson? Jennifer Roald. I understand you're the go-to
guy on Tomahawk targeting."

Captain Jennifer Roald was the director of the Situation
Room. Dan said, "I've done some in the past, ma'am. It's
not my current assignment."

"Firing? Or targeting?"

"Well . . . both. I was on the development team, and—"

"Can you come in? We need some in-house advice."

He hung up and stood there for a moment. What the hell
was going on?

"I'm sorry, I've got to go back to the office," he told Nan, back at their table. He gave her friends a smile, patted her back, and said good-bye.

Walking back to the car he cupped his hand to his face, breathing in the scent of her hair. It smelled like the freshness from an opened window, when a room has been closed too long.

5

Full night. Outside the Sit Room windows, past the nodding petunias in their kitschy boxes, a salmon glare backlit the limos on West Executive. Columns of text scrolled down screens. The clatter of keys rose to a cicada drone as the duty officers processed another wave of messages. The phones were ringing. Illuminated numerals glowed the time in Tokyo, Baghdad, London. Dan hadn't expected rosewood cabinetry in a watch center. He hoped his car would be okay. Sometimes they got broken into out on the Ellipse, tires slashed.

There didn't seem to be any official nomenclature for having all hands on deck, like "general quarters" or "red alert." But the analysts were at their desks, the call-ins were working in the executive secretariat area, the deputy and director were in their cubicles, and the coffee machine was doing a steady business. The mess had sent in trays of brownies and sandwiches. Now and then one of the watch staff would take a paper plate and eat quickly at the comm desk, or leave for a smoke under the awning outside. Five, six quick puffs, then he'd slide back into his seat, like a gamer addicted to the flickering screen.

• • •

Captain Jennifer Roald turned out to be small-boned, older than Dan, with a piquant face and a chin pointed as a McIntosh apple. She'd explained the situation while standing before a display. "The North Koreans have announced they're abrogating the nonproliferation treaty. There's a meeting at midnight in the videoteleconferencing room to prepare talking points for a 0300 call to South Korea."

"De Bari will call from there?"

"No. That will be Mrs. Clayton to Mr. Kim, to set up for the president's call. Which right now we think will be around 0900. We place the calls from here, then connect to the Oval Office."

"Okay. What do you want me to do?"

"I want you to work problem number two. The joint task force in northern Eritrea. Providing security for civilian relief organizations after the earthquake and famine. Several of their helicopters have been shot down."

"SA-7s?" The Russian version of the Stinger antiaircraft missile.

"Apparently not, but they've developed antihelo squads. A tactic of massed RPG fire to bring them down at low altitude."

All he knew about Eritrea was what he'd gleaned from CNN and the *Post*. But this hadn't been in any of the papers or on TV. "That's not good," he said, reflecting on how heavily U.S. forces relied on choppers for logistics, fire support, transport.

"The militias withdrew into the mountains under coalition pressure. The SecDef authorized the on-scene commander, an Army one-star, to send Special Forces teams and local allies in after them. Now that force has been ambushed at Kerkerbit, near the border. They're getting Sudanese military aid and pushing south. This could be an attempt to destabilize the Eritrean government. Make it another terrorist enclave, like Afghanistan or Sudan."

Above their heads Wolf Blitzer came on the screen, face grim. Behind him spread the South Lawn, the lit facade of the White House. Dan could just make out the West Wing over Blitzer's shoulder. Was the reporter out there now?

"Government radio says the relief column has been ambushed. Heavy casualties are reported to American and allied troops. A portion of the city appears to be on fire."

They watched shaky handheld footage of sooty smoke rising over littered, dusty streets. A crackle of automatic fire, punctuated by thuds Dan judged as light artillery. Or . . . tanks? The Sudanese had T-76s. Women in rags wailing, shaking fists at the sky as an SH-60, the model the Army called the Black Hawk, whacked overhead.

"Rumors are a senior deputy of elusive al Qaeda leader Osama bin Laden, suspected of several attacks on U.S. forces in the Middle East, was engaged in the planning of the elaborate trap."

" 'Trap,' " Roald repeated drily. "Damn it—they're going to want to put out a react. A statement. Along with Korea . . . and no matter whether we've actually had the time to think it through. Anyway. They tell me you know strike plans."

"I've done my share."

"CENTCOM's been proposing for some time that instead of fighting the rebels in Eritrea, we hit their base camps and weapons dumps inside Sudan. Now they want to do it to relieve the pressure on Kerkerbit. Mrs. C wants us to evaluate their plan."

Dan tried to focus. Lethality analyses. Vulnerable dimensions metrics. Roald was still talking. "Is what they're proposing reasonable? Short term. Long term. We don't have time for a paper. Just talking points. Any hard spots you see."

He hesitated. It took a master conductor to orchestrate subordinate commanders to achieve surprise, shock, and overwhelming force while keeping one's own troops out of the enemy's lethal envelopes as long as possible. The finished plan could run twenty single-spaced pages. Hours of analysis lay beneath every digit. If one got changed in the wrong way as it ascended the chain of command, people could die who didn't deserve to. Innocent civilians. Friendly troops. Pilots. He'd seen what could happen if too many fingers got stuck into that pie.

But he wasn't being asked for an opinion on just the strike plan, but on the whole idea of going over the border into Sudan. Maybe even whether they ought to be in Eritrea at all.

"Got a problem?"

"I don't think we should be screwing with what the force commander wants to do. The last thing they need is us second-guessing them."

Roald put her hand on his shoulder. Bent his head close, so the watchstanders couldn't hear. "I know you're a new gain, but you'd better reorient your thinking. Crossing that border will extend that war. If the situation goes to shit, there'll be diplomatic and political fallout. As well as maybe a lot more troops dead. Understand?"

"I hear you, but—"

"Our job's to advise the president. That means: not blindly accepting what the Chiefs hand us. Second-guessing the generals is our *job*. And think ahead: effects on allies and neutrals and, yeah, on the domestic constituencies—though that's more De Bari's political people that'll be bending his ear on that. Clayton's on the line to Nelson Mandela's office now."

"Uh . . . why Nelson Mandela?"

"It's a joint U.S.–South African task force."

While Dan contemplated this, Roald's short nails hit the keyboard. A message flashed on the screen, displacing the mountains, trails, villages of a distant country. "Okay . . . that's the preliminary execute order to evacuate Seoul. Pacific Command wants us to posture to Defcon Three to warn the Chinese off. I can't give Eritrea another minute. Tell me if this strike plan is smart, and if it isn't, what you recommend. Stoneman here'll help you. J.T.'s from State. He put in three years in Eritrea before he came to us."

For the next five hours, CNN carried speculation by "military experts" on the deepening emergency in Korea. Hundreds of messages streamed in from Pacific

Command, Central Command, Strategic Command, and the joint task force commander in Eritrea and the strike assets in the Red Sea. The assistant national security adviser, Brent Gelzinis, argued with Roald in the teleconferencing room.

Hunched at a terminal, Dan and the State analyst made sure the attack aircraft and Tomahawks would arrive on time, and that as few as possible friendly forces, economic assets, and local noncombatants would be endangered. They worked on paper maps a courier brought over from the National Imagery and Mapping Agency. Western Eritrea and eastern Sudan were not yet e-mapped. Here and there, through Stoneman's vivid vignettes, Dan got a heartrending glimpse of the ancient Baraka Province, and what was happening as the drought worsened, as crop failure, famine, and now war began to erase its long-suffering but incredibly brave half-Christian, half-Muslim Tigrai and Agau peoples.

He had no doubt that in the bowels of the Pentagon and in Riyadh and at the various combatant and supporting CINCs, others were doing much the same thing. But Roald was right. If the buck stopped with the president, he had to know what was going on. He needed someone who could answer hard questions and, perhaps, now and again, recommend decisions without waiting for responses from commands in different time zones, at the far end of comm pipelines that were shaky, to say the least.

They finished just in time for the midnight meeting.

Roald had said Gelzinis was working Korea, but apparently he had the ball for Eritrea as well. Looking like a tired family lawyer, the assistant adviser convened a tense meeting in the conference room. The execute messages had gone out. Halfway around the world, destroyers and the carrier in the Red Sea were moving toward their launch positions. Mrs. Clayton listened, as tastefully dressed as she'd been that first morning, when she'd cut off Dan's self-introduction.

Dan knew the next briefer. A CIA Mideast specialist

named Provanzano. They'd met at a desert base called 'Ar'ar, before the deep-penetration mission called Signal Mirror. Provanzano recognized him too, and winked as slides came up on a large-screen display that had lurked behind the paneling.

Operational intelligence sources reported that significant figures in the obscure organization that had targeted USS *Cole* and USS *Horn* might be involved in the fighting around Kerkerbit. General Wood recommended extending the strike into a second day, hitting four more training camps.

The senior directors tossed questions. Then Mrs. Clayton took the floor back. On the whole, she said, she agreed with where CENTCOM was going. The president was wary of committing forces, but this seemed like an opportunity to win time for the new Eritrean regime. The same strategy the South Africans had used against SWAPO in Angola, and Nixon had used in Cambodia. "Not that I'm Henry Kissinger," she said, to chuckles. She told Gelzinis to make sure the Chiefs got that word. She'd call the secretary of defense after she briefed the president. Provanzano would backchannel advance warning, so the planners could keep ahead of the decision makers.

One of the directors asked if he should start calling his Saudi and Egyptian counterparts. Clayton said no, that could leak to the press.

When Provanzano left, Dan followed him out into the watch area. "Commander Lenson," the CIA guy said, shaking his hand, though Dan hadn't offered it. "Glad to see you made it out of Baghdad. No hard feelings? That I was right?"

"I wish you hadn't been. What are you doing here?"

Provanzano jerked his chin toward the lead-lined door. "Nobody here pays much attention to Eritrea. But Afwerki's the closest thing to an ally we've got on the Horn. If he goes down it's solid hostiles on the west bank from Egypt south."

"What do you think about going across the border?"

"Time somebody punched the Sudanese in the nose." He grinned at Dan. "The Great Game, buddy. You're playing it now too."

"Mr. Lenson." A brittle voice from the conference room. "Do you happen to have a moment for us?"

He and Stoneman presented to a smaller group: Mrs. C, Gelzinis, and Dan's immediate boss, General Sebold. Clayton asked tough questions. Dan felt nervous but managed to answer everything she asked. Actually he felt they did okay, considering they'd started only a few hours ago. "All right," she said at last. "Then, we go. I'll let you know as soon as the president approves launch."

Just then a phone rang. She flinched and looked away, seemed to go somewhere else. Then groped under the desk and brought the handset to her ear.

Listened, gaze remote. Then snapped to a hovering Gelzinis, "Clear it out."

"Let's go, folks," the assistant said, herding them with outstretched arms toward the door. As it swung closed Dan heard her tone go angry.

She came out ten minutes later with lips set. The assistant stood with head bent as she spoke rapidly, laying her finger in her palm.

Without looking at the analysts and watch personnel, the enlisted people who'd been called in to help with the cable traffic, she whirled and left. Leaving Gelzinis contemplating the ceiling. He coughed into his fist before looking down. Dan thought again how much, with his glasses and slicked-back hair, he resembled McNamara. The apologetic yet still smug smile was the same too.

"The strike package is canceled," Gelzinis said. "Orders are going out now from the national military command center at the Pentagon. I know you've all worked hard on this tonight. But there you have it. Thanks for your help."

Lenson?" One of the watch team, leaning away from the endless stream of priority messages and cables rolling in from every command and embassy on the planet. "Weren't you working Eritrea?" He pointed to a secure phone, lit and blinking.

Dan was sitting at the desk he'd spent the night at, feeling as if he'd just vomited. The strike plan had been sound. As far as he could see, there was nothing else to do, if they didn't want more trouble from the bandits and militias that had already massacred hundreds. Yes, there was a crisis in Korea too, but none of the forces tabbed for Eritrea were on call for a Korean response. "I was, till they scrubbed it," he said.

"Can you take this? It's from Camp Cougar. Isn't that in Eritrea?"

"Who is it?"

"Guy named Wood."

The joint force commander in Eritrea was named Wood. But why would he be calling here? Bypassing the National Military Command Center and his unified combatant command? Dan glanced toward Roald's office. He could see her through the window; she was talking earnestly to someone out of his line of sight, drawing shapes with her hands for emphasis. He remembered how much he'd always hated being put off when he'd called headquarters, being fobbed from hand to hand.

Someone called across the room as he picked up. "Remember, don't use your rank. And there's no need to identify yourself beyond the Sit Room."

The set synced, and an angry voice crackled out. "This is Lem Wood, in Keren. Who'm I talking to?"

"This is the Situation Room." He choked off the reflexive "sir" at the end of his sentence.

"Sorry for the call, but I can't get any consistent response from higher here and I can't wait, my people are under fire. I'm standing by for support here—"

Dan said, "Your strike's been canceled. You'll get the word any minute now via your chain of command."

The eight-thousand-mile-away voice went baffled. "*Calling off* my strike package?"

"That's right."

"But . . . the CINC signed off. NMCC signed off. What the fuck's going on up there?"

Dan felt his feet go numb, as if the impetus of his heart no longer pushed blood that far. "That's the decision, General. Sorry."

"You people don't understand. We need support here. I've got—"

"The issue was discussed at the highest level," Dan interrupted. He was fighting to keep his voice level. Because everything he'd ever seen told him the furious, bewildered man on the other end of the line was probably right. So that now he said through a constricted throat, "There are other considerations involved." Though he didn't know what, so it felt like a lie before it was past his teeth.

"What's higher than protecting our troops? We let these people keep pushing us back, this whole piece of the planet's going to slide right back down the shithole."

"This is no place for a debate," Dan told him. "Your orders are on their way. The strike's off."

"Leaving people to get massacred? This is . . . goddamn it, I've got five KIAs now, fifty-plus wounded. Goddamn it. God *damn* it! I want to talk to the president. That . . . conscientious-objector son of a—"

This was getting out of hand. He still hadn't found words when a calm, emotionless voice cut in. Roald's gaze met his through the glass wall.

"General Wood?"

"Yes?"

"This is not an appropriate call," the Sit Room director told him in even, clear notes. "Under the Goldwater-Nichols Act of 1986, the secretary of defense has full authority, direction, and control over all military forces. Military action must be directed by the national command authority. If your combatant commander disagrees, there are ways for him to make his disagreement known. And if you dissent from his action, you can tender your resignation as a serving officer. You know all this, General. Therefore I suggest you hang up and obey your orders."

"Listen here. We've put up with enough of this . . . lack of support . . . this . . . *backstabbing,* when my guys are dying out there. I want to talk to that lying, cowardly son of a bitch—"

"I don't want to continue this conversation. And I don't think you want to either."

Silence on the far end, the crackle of scrambled microwaves. A sucked breath that told Dan what the other was feeling. He knew that desperate rage. The kind that made your career worth throwing away. That rage at those who *didn't understand*. Who *didn't want to hear*.

The warble of a disconnected line.

He hung up too. Sweat trickled under his shirt. He understood now why they'd told him not to use his name. Why none of the watchstanders used their military ranks.

He dragged his hands down his face. The surge personnel were leaving. They looked subdued, but not as overwhelmed and guilty as he felt. They nipped out under the awning for a smoke, or went back to their offices, or down the street for the early *Post* to see what had leaked.

0600. Just another dawn in Washington.

H e was so exhausted and furious that any thought of going home was out of the question. His neck felt tight as iron. He looked at his watch, then sprinted across West Executive between arriving sedans.

In room 303, Harlowe was already at her desk. A dozen e-mails were in his queue. By the titles, nothing that couldn't wait. He grabbed his gym bag and went back downstairs.

The Old Executive had been built sixty years before anyone thought of exercising at work. A grimy washroom on the ground floor, 18-M had the fiberglass shower stalls you found in cheap hotels, blue-tile walls, and a busted ceiling he could see asbestos-crusted pipes through. And five vertical gray steel lockers. He pushed through the morning crowd and got the last one. He didn't know the guys undressing, clanging locker doors, but judging by their haircuts, they were military like him.

Which they must have figured too, because one said, "Mike Jazak. Army." Looking at Dan. "You West Wing?"

"NSC. Dan Lenson."

They shook hands. Jazak said he was one of the military aides. "You a runner? Up for a couple miles? Not too fast?"

"I guess so," Dan said, not catching anything in the glances the others exchanged.

"We suit up every morning and wait around for Mustang. If he comes, we go."

"Mustang?"

"POTUS. President of the United States." He asked one of the others, who Dan now saw had an earphone, "Okay if this guy comes along? We're supposed to have four on the track." The Secret Service guy ran an eye across Dan and nodded.

He followed them to the South Lawn and a glare of sun more suited to July than September. Did a few push-ups, sucking in his breath as pain lanced up his arms. "You all right?" the Secret Service agent asked. Dan said he just needed to warm up.

He was still stretching when the president came out in gray cutoff sweatpants and a baggy T screened with what seemed to be a cherub. It might have been an old rock concert T. Out of a suit De Bari looked less impressive than he had in the corridor. More like somebody who got into the ice cream more often than he should. He tousled Jazak's hair and poked the other runners in the ribs, joking about how much dust they were going to eat today.

The aides and agents eased into motion like a destroyer screen escorting a carrier out of port. Shoulder holsters printed under the protective detail's track suits. Across the lawn Dan caught sight of a guy watching them, in full uniform, a black briefcase at his feet.

It wasn't much of a track. Maybe a fifth of a mile, a resilient-surfaced loop. They started fast but the pace dropped off quickly. Dan lagged back, letting the agents stay close to their charge. They shambled along together in a close scrum meant, he supposed, to protect the president if someone took a potshot from the fence line. As they rounded a turn he saw tourists pointing. Taking pictures, though at this distance they wouldn't get much.

"Whew . . . take a breather," someone muttered. They slowed to a walk. The chief executive's layer cut sagged over his forehead. He rubbed his side, blowing out ruefully. An intern or press relations woman was walking along the colonnade. De Bari eyed her yearningly.

He muttered, "You know, I had a good ole boy working for me in the governor's office. He always had the best-looking women around. I asked him one day how he managed to do that. Know what he told me? 'I tell 'em to walk over and face the wall. If their tits hit it before their nose, I hire 'em.' "

The agents laughed dutifully. Dan didn't, and caught the president's glance.

They jogged another slow lap, then walked again. The air was sultry. Everyone was sweating now despite what Dan found to be an undemanding pace.

A hand with two fingers missing came through the press and grabbed his arm. "Hey there. Who's this?"

He'd thought De Bari might remember him from their encounter that first day. But face-to-face with flushed cheeks and blue eyes, Dan realized he didn't. Well, as many people as he met . . . He introduced himself and said where he worked.

"Counterdrug," the president said, looking toward the colonnade again. No one there Dan could see. "Need to make some waves there. What do you think? Are we doing all we can?"

"Mr. President, I'm not sure we are. Especially in Asia."

"That's what I thought. Damn it! Look, anything I need to see, anything to shake things up, put it in a paper and send it up. Tell Mrs. C I said so."

He sounded so concerned and eager that Dan felt eager

too. Even if this was just a job to bureaucrats like Meilhamer, the president cared. "Yes sir, I sure will."

They came abreast of the Mansion, and though Dan had
thought Jazak had said two miles, and they hadn't gone that
far yet, the president broke off and headed across the lawn.
The detail stayed with De Bari, as if welded by invisible bars.
The aides didn't. They kept walking till the president was
hidden by the shrubbery, then broke into a run again. Someone said something Dan didn't catch, and they laughed.

Suddenly he felt energetic, optimistic. There were those
who said Bad Bob wasn't particularly bright. But close up
the guy seemed very intelligent. Dan put on a burst of speed,
catching up with the aides, then cut off the track and kept
going, walking now, sweating, not meeting anyone's eyes,
through the West Wing.

6

His first meeting the next morning was at the New Treasury Building, south of the Mall, listening to a senior Treasury investigator touting a new weapon against trafficking. So sensitive he didn't even want to describe it over the "high-side," or classified, government Internet. The theory sounded good: a cell that traced money.

The investigator said the U.S. twenty-dollar bill was the currency of choice for drug dealers from Oakland to Karachi. Every Andy Jackson not fresh from the presses carried traces of coke from being on the same tables with it. The Federal Reserve had maintained records of bills' movements to their first destination. The Secret Service had traced them to defeat counterfeiters. The FBI and DEA had recorded the serial numbers of seized currency to frustrate diversion. And the Argonne National Laboratory had used gas chromatography and mass spectroscopy to identify finely milled organic substances on permeable substrates. Not just cocaine, but precursor and process chemicals.

Now Treasury was bumping all the databases together, and a subterranean river was rising into view.

"We see drug-related movement in three directions." The investigator slid a graphic in front of him. It was marked "Top Secret LIMDIS" and looked like a chart of ocean currents. Only this ocean was the world economy and its currents were cash flows. "The first goes from refiners and distributors in Colombia to Peru and Bolivia. Not well known, but very little coke's actually grown in Colombia. It comes from farther south, via the Cali and Medellín networks. They pay the growers and paste manufacturers in U.S. dollars, because that's what the farmers demand. The scale's consistent with that interpretation."

"Okay," Dan said.

"The second movement's out of the U.S. to Central America, as payment back to the cartel. Again, consistent with our model. There's also what we call the peso exchange system. They buy luxury goods here and smuggle them into the receiving country. But most of that goes as cash too."

Dan nodded again. The Treasury agent leaned to place a pencil point on a smaller arrow angled northeast. "The third's unexpected. This vector into Europe. We don't have full cooperation there. Also, most of the capital shifts to Western Europe are handled by electronic funds transfer. That makes it harder to trace. Though not impossible."

"Investments? Escobar and Gasca and Nuñez's retirement fund?"

"We thought so at first. We've been trying to make the financial system more transparent. If we can confiscate their profits, that'll get their attention. Give us more resources to prosecute the war with too."

Dan didn't know if he cared for the sound of this. Governments raiding drug cartels for their profits? But the investigator was still going. "However, when we checked with Swiss authorities they were firm in their denials. What we came up with is *purchases* from France and the former Warsaw Pact countries. Given that those are not major drug-producing areas, we're tabbing it as arms and equipment buys."

"Big ones," Dan said. If he was reading it right, they were talking sixteen billion a year.

"Significant links between the cartels and arms dealers in Europe." The investigator paused, then said with a satisfied air, "But that's not really news, is it? What I wanted you to see is this." He slid another graphic and sat back.

It looked like a who's who of the European defense industry. Major producers of jet aircraft, advanced avionics, small arms, artillery. One he recognized as a French company that produced some of the most advanced electronics in existence. The Navy was evaluating its masking equipment, designed to conceal ships and aircraft from hostile radar.

He rubbed his mouth. "You got all this from tracing dollar bills?"

"It's more complicated than that. And as you can imagine, some governments don't want us looking into their financial systems. I have to say, the president's economic adviser could be more helpful in pressuring international banks to open their books." He paused, as if waiting for Dan to defend another part of the executive staff. When he didn't, the investigator sniffed and continued. "But we're reaching a point where we can trace some payments direct from the cartel to its suppliers."

H is second appointment was at Foggy Bottom. The State Department.

He'd realized by now the government didn't work like the military. Agencies didn't respond to orders. They were separate circles of power. He was used to having everyone work together. The machinist's mates didn't have a different policy from the fire control technicians. But this was the opposite of a ship. Even a presidential directive might not mean much would happen. To get anything done, you had to work through persuasion. That meant meeting people, finding out what they wanted, what their agency's interest was, then crafting an approach that benefited everyone.

So he'd set up an appointment with Dr. Dina White, who held the counterdrug portfolio at State.

Lanky as a heron, White met him in the enormous 1960s-modern lobby. Around them people of every color were speaking every language he recognized and dozens he couldn't guess at.

Her upstairs office was less impressive, the cubbyhole of an untenured academic. Binders sloped off metal shelves. The brown leaves of a long-dead pothos rustled in the blast of an air conditioner. She shuffled papers off a chair so he could sit down.

Over Taylors Yorkshire from an electric kettle White told him how optimistic State was about the new administration in Colombia. Senator Edgar Valencia Tejeiro had campaigned on a platform of reducing cartel violence, restoring justice, returning the country to normalcy. It was important to encourage him. That included the usual way America expressed friendship, with helicopters and other weapons. Congress was considering a $1.2 billion supplemental appropriation. The actual transfer would be a Defense responsibility, under the Foreign Military Assistance Program. Dan said he knew people in that office. Perhaps he could help expedite it. White said she'd appreciate anything he could do.

"The point I want to get across, that our people in country are telling us, is that this is a dangerous time for President Tejeiro. The cartels have assassinated newspeople, police, even high officials in the Justice Ministry. He could be a target too if he presses them too hard."

He told her, "Yeah, I'd heard that. How can we help over at NSC?"

White said she'd drafted an attempt to persuade France and Germany to put the same financial and legal controls in place that the U.S., Britain, and Japan had. The European Union should enforce heavy penalties for laundering money and supplying arms and technical assistance to the cartels.

"All right," Dan said. "Our shop will support that, and I have a contact at Treasury who's thinking along the same lines. Maybe a meeting? To look at your draft?"

"Set up a time and I'll be there."

"Now let me shift to a different issue. Threat reduction."

"Um, I do work some of that, but Dr. Sola has the lead in that area. Dr. Umberto Sola. Director of the Office of Nuclear Affairs. Unfortunately he's speaking at the Middle East Center in Michigan today."

Dan tried to find out exactly what State's plan was for expanding operations in Kazakhstan. White grew vague. She said the effort was underfunded and not well coordinated. He asked whom she dealt with at Defense. She said as far as she and Sola had observed, Defense displayed little interest in threat reduction. "The undersecretary's tried to push it in several venues. With nothing in the way of concrete results, manning, or even transport. Destroying a weapon by negotiation's not *manly*, I guess. Or maybe, the more warheads the other side has left, the more Defense gets to keep. Regardless of what the president's promised."

"That's a pretty cynical attitude," Dan told her.

White looked as if he'd just told a joke. "You think so? The Chiefs pooh-pooh *anything* from us. They might respond to White House direction, though."

"I have some of the action on threat reduction," Dan said, though so far he hadn't actually seen his name on anything. "Maybe we could coordinate a paper. Or ask for a supplemental?"

White said it would be good if he could get it into one of the president's speeches somehow. Just a line or two. "Funding's what makes things happen, but it's not the whole story. We can have teams out there, but if the leadership, on both sides, isn't serious about securing the weapons, the situation on the ground's not going to change. De Bari's personal attention, that could move it to the top of everyone's agenda."

Dan reflected grimly on the damage one loose nuclear shell had caused. He'd lost ten people topside to the burst itself, forty blinded or injured, and who knew how many to cancer in years to come. Maybe it wasn't where Sebold and Clayton wanted him to put in his time, but he was determined to get involved somehow. And hadn't De Bari said, while they were jogging, that he wanted his ideas? "Well, I can't promise anything, but there might be a chance of getting the president to go on the record. If you and this Dr. Sola think it'd help."

"That would be *great*," she said, and knocked a binder off

the desk. It hit a pile of papers and publications, and the tower rocked alarmingly before she grabbed it. "The last administration blew us off whenever we tried to do *anything*."

He tried one more question. "Has anyone over here given any consideration to how somebody could get nukes into this country?"

White looked surprised. "Well, that's not our area of expertise. I'm sure your military and intelligence people have *that* covered. On threat reduction, let me talk to Dr. Sola when he comes back. Let's see if there's *something* we can do to move this issue forward. Are you going to Leningrad? I mean, Petrograd? The conference?"

"I'd like to, but I'm not sure they'll send me."

"I might be able to do something. To make sure you get invited."

The Pentagon. He had a turkey sub and soup in one of the cafeterias off the Concourse, with two colonels. Then, though it hadn't been on the agenda, they told him their boss would like ten minutes. Dan followed them through polished sunlit corridors around to the Army staff spaces in Wedge One.

The sign on the door of 3D389 said Lieutenant General Thurman Knight, U.S. Army, was the Army's operations deputy. Most civilians thought the Joint Chiefs directed military operations. But that was actually the job of the combatant commanders, four-stars who controlled all forces, from whatever service, within their geographic area. But the old terminology lived. Each service chief appointed a deputy who worked with the director, Joint Staff, to form the body known as the Operations Deputies, or OPSDEPS in milspeak. They met in sessions chaired by the director, Joint Staff, in his office, or in the Tank, to review major issues before they went up to the Chiefs and then the SecDef.

Knight welcomed him into a better-appointed and larger office than either he'd been in earlier. The general's dress

greens matched his eyes. Huskier than Dan, he moved with
the deliberation of a trainer of wolves. The diplomas on his
walls were from the War College, the School of the Ameri-
cas, and the Command and General Staff College.

Dan had looked up Knight's bio before he came over. The
general had been a first lieutenant in Korea, served as an adviser with the Vietnamese and Peruvian armies, and commanded first an airborne brigade and then the 101st Airborne
before commanding the Special Operations Command South
in Panama. Looking at his chest, Dan read the Distinguished
Service Medal, the Purple Heart, the Superior Service
Medal with an oak-leaf cluster, the Legion of Merit with an
oak-leaf cluster, the Bronze Star with a V and three oak-leaf
clusters, the Meritorious Service Medal, the Air Medal, and
the Army Commendation Medal. He had the rifle and wreath
of the Combat Infantryman Badge, a parachutist's badge of
some sort, and Ranger and Special Forces tabs.

For the first time, Dan wished he'd worn his lapel decoration. Knight's gaze moved as slowly as he did and, when it
settled, was hard to meet directly. His grip, complete with a
gold VMI ring the size of a handball, was hearty, but his
manner warned this might not be a pleasant call.

In his inner office, settled on a sofa so close Dan smelled
lime aftershave, Knight didn't want to discuss the issue
items Dan had brought with him. He wanted to talk budget.
Specifically, the line items the president's budget reduced.
Dan said he wasn't on the budget side. The general asked if
the president had any idea how hard he was stressing the services. Dan said he presumed De Bari was getting that word
during the lunch he had every week with Jack Weatherfield,
the secretary of defense, and General Stahl, chairman of the
Joint Chiefs of Staff.

This didn't seem to be what Knight wanted to hear. He lit
a cigar, toasting the cut end with a chrome lighter in the
shape of a Maxim gun. Almost as an afterthought, offered
one. Dan shook his head.

"Now, correct me if I'm wrong, Lenson. Let's not make

this on any kind of record, all right? But you're military staff over there, that right? What—an O-6?"

"O-5, sir."

"Army? Guard?"

"Navy, sir."

"Well, you're uniformed service. Academy too, I see."

"Yes, sir." Dan wondered if he should quit wearing the ring, since he wasn't supposed to be in uniform.

"We're getting concerned over here. It started with this 'no further discrimination' bullshit, which wasn't the way to get on our good side. And it's gone downhill from there."

One of De Bari's first acts on taking office had been to end the services' exclusion of gays. And part of his platform, responding to the recession, had been what he called a "tailored" cutback of 10 percent per year in military expenditures, down to a 40 percent reduction in the Pentagon's budget by the end of his term.

Knight said, "This guy's tuned to the moon, if he thinks what he's doing is enhancing our national security. Pulling back from Germany, the Horn of Africa, now Korea. Korea! It's quieted down some now, but now Pyongyang's out from under the inspection regime, God knows what they're up to. This is all between us, by the way."

"Yes, sir."

"We've got civilian appointees without the faintest idea what they're doing. No prior military. Well, you know what I mean. Working with them every day. What do you hear over there? What kind of atmosphere readings are you getting?"

Dan didn't like this question. He wondered if the appointees Knight was talking about included Blair. She couldn't drive a tank or assemble a bomb. But he didn't know anyone in uniform, from flag rank down, who could drill as deep into a manpower issue as she could. He cleared his throat and shifted on the sofa. "If you mean, is this a military-oriented administration, I guess the answer's 'not very.' But it's still early."

"I've been over there twice talking to Garn Sebold and what's her name, the Asian woman. I understand campaign promises. But once the election's over, you expect some movement toward reality. The fact of the matter: We have defensive boundaries around the world. A lot of guys, some I knew, gave their lives to put them there. We keep backpedaling like this . . . it's like you live in the projects and you put a sign on your door, 'Break in my house, rape my wife, and steal my shit.'"

Dan didn't believe a three-star couldn't remember the name of the national security adviser. It was a put-down, though subtle enough it couldn't be quoted against him. "Well, sir, like everywhere, I'd say some are professional, others less so."

Knight shook his head, scowling. "I'd rather have them over there than over here. But cutting our readiness, manning, the procurement accounts—that's a no-go. Let me tell you a little story.

"Back in '32, '33, this country was in a worse depression than anyone remembers now. FDR wanted to cut the Army budget to practically zero. Douglas MacArthur was the chief of staff back then. He went to Roosevelt's office and put his resignation on the table. He said that when we lost the next war, and an American boy was dying in the mud with a bayonet in his belly, he wanted him to die cursing Franklin Roosevelt, not Douglas MacArthur."

Dan wasn't sure whether this was a historical reflection, a message he was supposed to take back, or just the general blowing off steam. As far as he could see, he was pointing the finger in the wrong direction. "General, I know this administration's committed to reductions in defense. It was in their platform from the start. But what actually gets appropriated isn't an executive branch call. Congress sizes the accounts."

Knight picked something off his lip. He examined it, then put it carefully in the ashtray. "We've been talking to our friends on the Hill. Sonny doesn't think any further reduction's wise. Neither does Strom or Mike."

Dan rubbed his eyes. The cigar smoke stung at close range. "Then it seems like the appropriate steps are being taken, sir. Maybe I'm oversimplifying here, but that's my understanding of the process."

The dull green irises came to rest on him like twenty-pound weights. "I don't need you to tell me the process, Commander."

Dan said, "Sir, nobody over here, or over there, can stop the president from putting in whatever budget he comes up with. If he thinks it's what the country needs."

Knight watched cigar smoke rise, silent. He seemed on the cusp of saying something else. But got up abruptly instead and walked Dan to the door. A handshake, briefer than the first, and he was on his way.

The car idled, crept forward, idled again. A Metro cop stood with hat pushed back and hands in his pockets. A marine guard bent to glance inside the Bentley ahead, then straightened and waved them on. Dan saw it had diplomatic plates.

He was in blues, and it felt good to be back in them, but the marine still wanted to see his ID. He also managed an appreciative glance at Blair's legs. Dan couldn't blame him. She looked great in a short black cocktail dress. She knew what her legs looked like, and occasionally used a strategic glimpse of thigh to fluster and confuse.

The vice president's residence was a white Victorian with mansards. Dan thought it looked like a battleship, with its porch as a prow and the cupolaed turret as the bridge. More marines directed them where to park on a clipped lawn. Dan held Blair's door. It wasn't Halloween yet, but mist eddied from the porch as they approached, and creepy music. A skeleton twinkled with electric lights.

"Good evening, how are you, thanks for coming . . . Oh, Blair, thanks for coming. And who's this? Mr. Titus?"

"Dan, meet Geraldo B. Edwards. And Mrs. Edwards. Dan Lenson, Mr. Vice, currently serving on the NSC staff."

The vice president was short and peppery, with gray hair brushed straight back like Spiro Agnew's. A former Disney executive, then junior senator from Florida, Geraldo B. Edwards had cratered on Super Tuesday after a bitter nomination fight. De Bari had picked him at the convention to balance the ticket. The office of the vice president was in the Old Executive, but Dan had never seen him there. Early in the term, Edwards, appearing on *The Capital Gang* with Al Hunt, had challenged the president's decision to reduce troop levels in NATO. Since the First Commandment of the vice presidency was "Do not publicly disagree with the president," Edwards hadn't spent much time around the Eighteen Acres since. The president kept him on the road with trade delegations, fund-raising, and foreign funerals. The word was that Edwards was "out of the loop," and there was no more scathing dismissal. The second lady was padded, powdered, and pleasant, and said absolutely nothing as she shook his hand with a slow, sweet smile that plainly conveyed *Inside my head I'm far away.*

The house seemed empty, though guests were still arriving. They looked down into a tented annex set up in the garden, facing a back lawn and a wooded ravine. The guests were already deep into the drinks and buffet. Most were elderly or middle-aged. Many seemed to be foreigners, judging by the dashikis and thobes and saris among the black ties and long dresses. Dan even saw one tiny woman in a kimono.

"See anyone you know?" he asked Blair. She was fiddling with her earrings, a wrinkle between her eyebrows indicating mild annoyance.

"I'm more interested in those I don't know. Is that Milton Obote?"

Dan wasn't sure who that was. But the intellectual-looking officer by the garden exit was certainly the new deputy CNO for training, Admiral Contardi. Dan remembered briefing him in the cramped flag officer's quarter of USS *Cochrane* before a strike into the littoral of Africa.

In the foyer, shaking hands with the vice president, Mrs.

Clayton sparkled like a garnet set in gold. Behind her Dan recognized Alicejames "Mokey" Revell, the secretary of state, a political general who'd served four presidents with steadily decreasing competence. So he'd be Dina White's boss . . . "Big Jack" Weatherfield, the secretary of defense, the only African American in the cabinet. He was a former trial lawyer and, according to the whispering gallery, a left-handed nephew of one of the Dulles brothers, Allen or John Foster. There was an aging columnist whose picture Dan had seen in the papers since his childhood. A laughing woman surrounded by admiring men; he recognized her as a hot star.

"Halle Berry," Blair whispered. She had a gaga smile he'd never seen before, and he realized she was starstruck. It made him grin. Who'd have thought?

She started to move, towing him behind her like an energetic tugboat with a balky barge. She introduced him to senators, floor assistants, the assistant commandant of the Marine Corps, the SecDef general counsel. He strained to remember names, but didn't obsess. He remembered when he'd hated parties. This wasn't so bad. When she excused herself to use the ladies' room he stood absently swirling the ice-melt in his glass, watching Berry and wondering if he should go over and make pleasant.

"Why, is it Daniel V? I think it is. Is that you?"

He took a tighter grip on his OJ and tonic. He'd wondered when and where he'd run into her again. "Sandy. What a pleasant surprise."

Sandy Cottrell had been in his postgraduate class at George Washington. There'd been something there, but not romance, despite Cottrell's frictioning his crotch with her bare toes on the dais of the Ways and Means Committee hearing room. With her flushed cheeks—she sweated even when it was cold out—her over-the-edge manner, her spacy laugh, he'd always suspected she was on something stronger than the hand-rolled cigarettes she chain-smoked.

A decade had not been unkind. But she'd gone glossy, as

if sealed over with some transparent lacquer. Her blond hair was expensively cut. Her perfume was even stronger than it had been years before. She wore a diamond-studded Rolex and was smoking, but now it was a filter tip.

He gestured at it. "What's this? You used to smoke that ragweed stuff—"

"Douwe Egberts. But smoking hand rolls isn't good for the image."

"You never worried about your image before."

"You've got to be the most unobservant son of a bitch I've ever met," Cottrell deadpanned. He saw that, as usual, she gave the impression of being three sheets to the wind.

"Whatever happened to you and Professor F?" he asked her, trying to crack through the gloss.

"I know you thought I was fucking him for the grade. But that actually turned out okay. We even still like each other."

"I never thought you were fucking him for a grade, Sandy."

"What *did* you think I was fucking him for?"

"So, what are you doing now?"

"I'm in Congress," she told him. "Remember the guy I used to type for? The guy who tried to put rubber in the asphalt? He got caught buying ad space for a citizens' committee that didn't exist. They had to come up with somebody fast, from a district that breeds more farmers than lawyers. Who better than his campaign committee chair? And the name's not Cottrell anymore. It's Treherne. That's my man, over there talking to the guy in the sheet. He had a million to spare. The rest is mystery."

Her gaze shifted and Dan realized Blair was back. The two women traded evaluating looks. He said hastily, "Blair, this is an old friend of mine, Sandy Cottrell, I mean Sandy Treherne, recently elected to Congress from Tennessee. My wife—also undersecretary of defense for manpower and personnel."

"Oh, yes. I'd heard . . . I won't ask you what the difference between manpower and personnel is, if you won't ask me if I ever bonked your husband," Sandy said.

Dan had thought absolute zero impossible, but Blair's smile proved him wrong. "I'm so glad to meet you, Mrs. Treherne. Tennessee? What district?"

"Seventeenth."

"Then you're one of Newt's new hires."

"Oh, Sandy," Dan said. "KISS, Garth Brooks, Metallica, and the Contract with America?"

"It's the same me," she said, putting her empty glass on a passing tray and snagging a full one in the same motion. Dan concluded she wasn't with AA anymore. "What people who aren't in politics don't realize is that it's like casting an actor. You fit the role, you sell the donors, you get hired. I look at people like Zoelke and Mulholland and Dwayne Harrow and *your* old sugar pop, Bankey Talmadge," she said, fluttering her lashes at Blair, "and I figure, why not little ole me? Dan, you never said what you're doing." She fingered the lapel of his blues as if she were thinking of buying it. "I see you're still in the Navy. You an admiral yet?"

"A commander."

"Shit, you were one of those when we used to get blitzed after class at Mister Henry's, weren't you? Aren't you supposed to get promoted once in a while?"

"I was a lieutenant commander then. A full commander now."

"Yeah, you were always full. Of something."

"I'll let the two of you catch up," Blair said, with the no-tone that meant somebody would be doing some explaining after the party.

"*Cute* girl," Treherne sneered after her retreating back, loud enough that even in the party noise Dan knew Blair must have heard.

"She's my wife."

"Yeah, you said. Where are you working now?"

Dan told her he was on the National Security Council staff. Treherne looked incredulous. "God help us. *You're* at the White House, and *I'm* in Congress?"

He smiled. "That's how I feel."

"I wonder if everybody here does."

Dan wondered too. How many of those at the apex quailed at where they'd arrived, and what power they wielded. Others, though, probably didn't. For some reason Knight's scowl came to mind. The lieutenant general he'd met that afternoon. The disdainful assumption that he knew better than his civilian masters, better than the voters . . . no, that didn't seem to signal much self-doubt.

But wasn't his own flaw the opposite? To distrust himself, and what he was told to do? Wasn't that the key to his fatal ability to complicate the simple equations of command and obedience, to bring chaos out of order?

The emperor Vespasian moved stiffly past holding a Scotch. Or at least it appeared to be his broad face, wide, bony head, and iron gray buzz cut. The rest was clad in Army green. Dan recognized General Ulrich Stahl, chairman of the Joint Chiefs but rumored by the columnists unlikely to be asked to stay for a second term. He'd briefed Stahl once too. A small gray woman followed the stately general, tottering slightly. It was often shocking to see the spouses of senior military men. On the other hand, maybe that was a positive. At least they'd stayed with their first wives.

Treherne's Salem-flavored breath in his ear brought him back. "So what are you doing over there? At the NSC?"

He told Sandy about counterdrug and threat reduction. "They're serious about reducing the number of loose nukes. If you can vote in favor of that sometime, I wish you would."

Past her Dan saw another familiar visage sharpen out of the blur; Knight himself, as if conjured by his recollection. The OPSDEP was on an intersecting course with Stahl, moving steadily through the crowd toward the chairman.

Treherne's cheeks hollowed around a fresh filter tip; her eyes searched over his shoulder as more guests handed wraps to servants and joined the receiving line stretching ever longer in front of the Edwardses. "Let's see. Threat reduction. That's where we pay the commies to say they destroyed what they said they didn't have in the first place, right? Cut checks to their army, keep them in shape for the next time they decide to fuck with us?"

"I guess we're not on the same side on that one."

"I don't know about you, but the people I represent want to keep some of what they earned."

Dan said, "We buy weapons for security against a threat. Why not spend a hundredth that much to reduce it? Too many people seem to be looking around for the next enemy so they can keep everything the way it is. I see a window instead. Nobody knows how long it'll be open. Maybe now's the time to say, 'Let's get these things off our backs.'"

She cocked her head, interested, or maybe just acting it. "*What* are you talking about?"

"Put the genie back in his bottle. Isn't that what Reagan tried to do? One on one with Gorby? We made having nukes the mark of a superpower. Why don't we make not needing them the mark of a postnuclear superpower?"

"You're so cute when you get serious." She took his arm and he felt the soft pressure of her breast. "So cute I *could* be on your side. But give me a reason, Dan—because I absolutely cannot afford to do something for nothing. A PAC check. A swing bloc. A hot issue, if that's all you've got. If you can't . . . then hasta la banana. It is that cutthroat where I live. If I don't claw and scheme every minute I'm awake, I won't keep playing."

He had to admit she'd always been up front about exactly what she thought or wanted. Unless, of course, that too was one of her games. Did she play it with the older man who was weaving between couples toward them, smiling fawningly at her?

"It may be a long shot," he said. "It's the right thing to do, though."

"So tell *him* that," Sandy said, as if she were sucking something bad. "Your wop boss. The Firefighting Cowboy."

But her husband was taking her arm, presenting Dan with what might pass for a smile but looked more like a territorial display, a monitory baring of teeth. Sandy was turning away.

"Stay in touch, Dan," she trilled. A whiff of Guerlaine, and she was gone.

He went over to Admiral Contardi, who was still standing alone, and introduced himself. Reminded him of the Arroyo Gold operation, when he'd briefed him on a then-untested missile. Contardi's eye lingered on the blue-and-white ribbon. He said he remembered Dan and was glad to see him again. Then started talking about something he called a smarter, nimbler military. It involved "networks" and "nodes" and communications and satellite surveillance. It sounded very high-tech, but after a few minutes Dan wasn't sure he was following. Maybe that showed, because after a quizzical pause where they stared at each other Contardi said gently, "Well, I'm still sort of bouncing these ideas around. We can talk about it some other time if you want."

Dan took the hint and excused himself for the buffet. Held a plate and nibbled, looking around for Blair but not finding her. Then he saw her talking to the actress, her face flaming, her eyes sparkling. He smiled again at how excited she looked.

"Commander Lenson, I presume?"

He turned from the table to a swarthy, smiling man whose silver hair gleamed in the candlelight. He was in a tux, with some sort of foreign order in his buttonhole. Dan took his extended palm.

"You are Lenson?"

"That's right. Have we met before, sir?"

"No, sir; you don't know me. And there's no reason you should. I happen to be in the service of the state of Israel."

Dan said he was glad to meet him. "Perhaps it's best that way," the man said, keeping his voice so low amid the hubbub Dan had to bend to catch it. Still holding his hand—he'd not released it after shaking it. "A certain distance must be maintained. Especially with this administration, it seems. But we know you. Yes, we do. And I have something for you."

"I'm sorry, I don't—"

"When you were in command of USS *Thomas W. Horn.* I don't believe you have ever been officially thanked for your service. For what you risked, and what you suffered."

Dan cleared his throat. "Oh. Uh, that wouldn't be necessary, I was actually—"

He was interrupted in midsentence. "Good, because we do not intend to do so officially. *Lo hayu ha'dvarim miolam.* We are not supposed to know what took place off our shore. But rest assured we appreciate your—acts." He squeezed again, the hand he hadn't let go, and with the other slipped a slim case of dark wood from inside his jacket. "If you would do me the honor?"

Dan clicked it open, and blinked, dumbfounded at what lay within.

The silk ribbon was red as fresh blood. The heavy, dull silver medal, nestled in dark blue velvet, resembled no American decoration he'd ever seen. Swords, entwined by an olive branch.

"What's this?" he muttered.

"It's the Tzalash. The Medal of Courage. I do not think it has ever been awarded to a foreigner before."

"Well, it's very handsome. But I, uh, I can't accept this. We can't accept foreign decorations—"

The Israeli raised both hands. "Unfortunately, I cannot take it back. We are in your debt, and always will be. If ever we can return the favor, please—just ask."

The little man bowed, smiling faintly, and moved off.

Dan frowned after him, trying to sort out what had just happened, as Sebold hove into view, smiling like a benevolent lord. He closed the case quickly, a small snap in the party noise, and slipped it inside his shirt. The director's arm was around the shoulders of the assistant secretary of defense for international security affairs, a Carter-era retread Blair said made a copperhead look like a model of forthright goodwill.

He looked around for his wife again, but this time saw neither Blair nor the actress. A door was open, letting cool air into the overheated atmosphere. He headed for it, taking his glass along, hoping for a moment alone.

Outside the air was almost frosty. Lights glared on a beautifully manicured putting green. Guests moved slowly across it, talking in low voices. A heavy man mimed a putt for two companions; Dan caught the words "Dan Quayle" and "pool house." He saw the pool house and strolled toward it.

"Dan? Dan Lenson?"

A man his age, in a dark suit, with a boyish, winning grin. A cowlick behind a haircut so short the guy had to be a marine or Special Forces. When he lifted his glass Dan recognized him. Thirty-fourth Company; they'd played lacrosse together. But he couldn't recall a name.

"Good to see you, classmate."

"You too, uh—"

"I left a message for you. You must not have gotten it."

"It's been busy as shit. All kinds of incoming."

"Not a problem."

Dan tried hard, but nothing was coming. Jake? Jack? Skip? Chip? "What are you doing these days, man? You got out, right?"

"Yeah, decided to make some money instead. Outfit here in D.C. We represent issues over on the Hill."

"Lobbying?"

"Just trying to get the right message across. How about you? Getting any face time with the poster boy for the gay generation?"

"I've seen him exactly twice."

"Never a day in uniform. Too fucking two-faced to wear one."

He seemed to assume they shared the same contempt for De Bari that Dan had heard on the talk radio programs that played nonstop in most Pentagon offices. "Did you read the *Times* article on how his wife got her winery land exempted from taxes? The land-easement scam? And then how convenient, the attorney who actually had the records died in the same fire that destroyed them. Her whole family's Family. They don't leave witnesses."

There'd been a lot of rehashing of the De Baris' reputed Mob connections and state-lottery manipulations during the campaign. Dan didn't know how true they were. Like single men in barracks, few politicians seemed to be plaster saints. Truman and the KKK. Kennedy's bootlegger father. Nixon, in a class of his own. But the shrill chorus of Daily Hate left a bad taste. He said, "He's probably as slippery as the rest of them. But at least he's trying to get something done. Considering the zero cooperation he's getting."

"Heard this one? Jimmy Carter, Dick Nixon, and Bob De Bari are on the *Titanic*. They hit the iceberg. Carter yells, 'Women and children first,' and gives away his life jacket. Nixon snarls, 'Fuck the women and children,' and shoves his way into the lifeboat. De Bari looks at his watch and says, 'You think we have time?' "

"Funny."

"He's driving this country down the highway to hell at eighty miles an hour," the man told him. "And I love this country. Do you love it, Dan?"

"This some kind of joke?"

"It's no joke, classmate. Remember a piece of shit named Martin Tallinger?"

Dan stiffened. He'd spat in the journalist's face when the law gave him no hold on him. Tallinger hadn't pulled a trigger. But he was still a murderer. "What about him? How do you know him?"

"Keep your eyes open where you work."

"I haven't seen Tallinger where I work. Just what the hell do you mean?"

In return he got a contemptuous, pitying grin. Dan was stepping closer when a thrill brushed his skin. His pager. As he reached for his pocket he noticed the same abstracted pursing of lips elsewhere in the crowd.

When he lifted it to the light it was the Sit Room again. Bracketing its number in the little display were the asterisks that meant *urgent*.

7

KEY WEST, FLORIDA

He peered down on islands green as corroded brass set within infinite turquoise shadings. They reminded him of the reefs and jazirats of the Red Sea, and the memory was tinted dark with remembered danger. He was being jerked from one crisis to another, too fast to really get a solid fix on anything in the murk around him.

Well, Sebold had said it would feel this way. Would he see the big picture someday? He rubbed his mouth, then checked his seat belt as the order to prepare for landing came over the cabin announcing system. Right now, it didn't seem likely.

He'd boarded at Andrews before first light. It was the first time he'd flown in one of the executive jets high-ranking officers traveled on. Miles Bloom sat beside him, the DEA agent deep in an Alan Furst novel.

It was a week after the canceled strike on Sudan. Since then Kerkerbit had fallen. The enemy forces, which were coming into focus as the same brand of fundamentalist killers as the Afghan Taliban, were still advancing. The other party had called for hearings in Congress. The crisis with North Korea had escalated again, with the Pyongyang government now offering ballistic missiles for sale to all comers unless guaranteed oil aid and free food. The Chinese seemed unable to bring their unruly client to heel.

Tony Holt had received Dan and Bloom in his corner office on the second floor of the West Wing. One window observed the cabana and pool on the South Lawn. The other
looked out over Executive Drive. Three years before, Holt
had been a state lottery director. Now the president's chief of
staff was in shirtsleeves and a green plaid bow tie. He
seemed to know every detail of what was going on in the
counterdrug office. Including business Bloom had told Dan
about only days before, with the warning that this was the
kind of operational top secret that could get agents killed.
Now Bloom was updating him, information Holt took in
with head cocked back, brushing his lips lightly with the tip
of a finger.

"It's a guy we had deep in the cartel. Unfortunately he
lost his cover and got whacked. In Bogotá, having a double
vodka in the airport bar. Five nine-mils in the chest and one
in the head."

"Too bad."

"Yeah. He was a good guy," Bloom said, without the least
trace of actual regret. "Four kids and an ex-wife. But he
managed to make a phone call before he went to the bar.
They're setting up a top-level meet."

"All right, go on." Holt swiveled his chair as if bored.
"This is Cali, right? The new heavies?"

"Sounds that way. They're scrambling their cell chatter,
but this new circle-of-contacts software is giving us an idea
who's invited. Also, the guy who got shot in the airport, he
wasn't our only guy inside. The Bureau's got a mechanic on
Juan Nuñez's aircraft team."

"Nuñez. This is the one they call Don Juan? The one who
picked up all Pablo Escobar's trade?"

"Yeah. They call this guy 'the Baptist'—everybody who
gets on his bad side ends up underwater. FBI says he's getting his plane prepped for a long flight with a full cabin. Including Francisco Zuluaga, the biggest money mover in
Colombia, and other names you'll recognize. They're also
installing some kind of hot-shit electronic gear our mechanic's never seen before. It's French, he says."

"What's the destination?" Holt wanted to know.

Bloom looked at the closed door. "This is a secure location," the chief of staff said.

"Miami," Bloom told him.

"*Inside* the *United States*?" Dan said.

"No, in Miami," Bloom told him straight-faced. "The perfect place, if you think about it. Not one we'd suspect. Latin types to blend in with. Good restaurants. A stone's throw from Customs headquarters, and not that far from JI-ATF East."

"So. We going to Appalachin 'em?" Referring, Dan realized, to the raid on a Mob conference in New York State back in the fifties.

"Absolutely not," Bloom said. "That'd be terrible PR. Bullets flying around, dead bystanders . . . Some of the secondary figures we'll vacuum up there. But we'll take the principals en route. That's the no-mess picker-upper. Without a pack of bodyguards and collateral damage."

"Specifically, who? Lehder? Nuñez?"

"We'll take Don Juan Sebastiano Nuñez's plane in the air. AWACs will follow him from takeoff to intercept. At the appropriate point in his flight path, our fighters join up. They force him down on a military-controlled airstrip, and the arrest team moves in."

Dan couldn't keep quiet any longer. He sat forward in his chair. "Uh, Miles. I know Mr. Holt holds the highest possible clearance . . . but does he really need to know all the plans, the times? Even who our informants are?"

Holt looked as if he'd just been slapped. Bloom coughed apologetically. "The commander hasn't been playing in the majors long," he told the chief of staff. To Dan he added, "Tony here's kept the lid on a lot of stuff. If you can't trust Tony, you can't trust me either, okay?"

"I didn't mean I didn't trust you, sir. Just that—"

"Not a problem," said Holt, waving it away. "Who's going to be lead for the bust?"

"DEA. But it'd be good press to include the Dade County cops. Only at the last minute," Bloom added. "No advance word. These *narcotraficantes* are sharp. The only way this'll work is if we surprise them. And I think we've got a chance to."

"It sounds good. Decapitate the cartel. Do you need the president's go-ahead?"

"No, sir. This is within our charter."

"It'll be international news. We'll need a robust staff presence."

Bloom cocked his head. "Meaning . . . what, Tony?"

"Both of you on scene, and General Sevinson does a press conference in Washington." Sevinson was a retired two-star, acting head of DEA. "We can't let Dade County take the credit when we've done the work."

Dan had figured what the chief of staff meant was he wanted the administration to get credit for the bust. Well, he wasn't averse to letting them hog the limelight. Or even to standing in for them if they wanted him on scene.

And now the runway of Key West International stretched ahead, streaked with the black crayon of hundreds of landings. With a thump and a shriek, they were down.

T he sea breeze was warm. An Air Force colonel was waiting with an official car. Dan was wearing what he was starting to think of as his NSC uniform: gray suit, white shirt, subdued tie. Bloom had changed into boots, jeans, and a black windbreaker with "DEA" on the breast. He was also toting a holstered Glock now. But the suit and tie seemed to work better. The colonel called him "Mr. Lenson" with great respect, and opened the car door for him. While they listened to Rude Girl on the WAIL morning show Dan reflected on the advantages of being from Washington.

Tourists in bright shirts and funny hats were taking pictures of each other next to a concrete buoy. A sign marked it as the southernmost point in the United States. Just past it was the JIATF fence, barbed wire, palm trees, then the Coast Guard piers. The operations center was low, gray brick, isolated on a spit of land. The colonel introduced him to the director, a recently arrived Coast Guard two-star named Quintero. Then it was up a flight of stairs, and through a steel door with card-controlled entry.

In the joint operations command center four leather command chairs faced computer-driven back-projection displays. The command duty officer and the watch team, mostly uniformed but with intelligence analysts from Customs and DEA, sat around a four-armed table crowded with computers. The beeps and murmurs of voice circuits kept on as the briefing began. Fifty-one brain-numbing PowerPoint slides, narrated by a nervous young lieutenant commander. Dan sat beside Quintero, only partially tuned in.

"JIATF East, originally Joint Task Force 4, was established when DoD became the lead agency for providing detection and monitoring throughout the transit zone. Our mission is to integrate the military's C3I capabilities to assist law enforcement agencies. We now include representatives from DEA, DIA, NSA, FBI, and the British and Dutch Royal Navies. Our area of responsibility encompasses a region comparable in size to the triangle bounded by the cities of Miami, Seattle, and New York, and includes the airspace of eighteen nations. We detect and monitor air and maritime trafficking activity in the transit zone, hand off this information to appropriate law enforcement agencies, and deconflict non-D&M counterdrug activities occurring in the transit zone."

"D&M?" Dan muttered to Quintero. The admiral whispered back, "Detect and monitor."

Dan was saying "Thanks" when the next slide came up.

Labeled "National Counterdrug Organization," it showed the operational line running from the president, through the NSC, down to the cabinet secretaries: Defense, Treasury, Transportation, State. From there it went through the secretary of defense to the Joint Chiefs, where it split three ways: to JIATF East via the Atlantic Command, JIATF West via the Pacific Command, and JIATF South via the Southern Command.

Of course it didn't mean Dan Lenson was about to give

any direction to the secretary of defense. But it was a beautifully clear wiring diagram, and he contemplated its elegance
before leaning again. "I've got to have that slide."

"Hey, I'll send you electrons on the whole brief."

The rest was boilerplate—interdiction assets, baseline
force laydown—but he paid attention when the ground-
based-radar information came up. The main coverage was
from ionospheric backscatter arrays. They could detect
air targets two thousand miles away. Smaller radars on
aerostats—tethered balloons—passed their pictures to the
Caribbean Regional Operations Center, the room they
were in. The rest of the brief was on a classified data link
and the tactical analysis teams and local coordination centers that fed intel into the system.

"If there are no questions, we'll take a break," the lieutenant commander said, obviously glad it was over. "After
which we'll describe Operation Hot Handoff."

Hot Handoff was the code name for the interception
of the major players en route to the meeting in Miami. DoD was the lead agency, and assets would be
coordinated from Key West. Cold Handoff was the stateside
piece of the operation, run by the DEA Miami Field Division with assistance from Dade County, the U.S. Marshal's
Service, the FBI, and Customs. Admiral Quintero briefed
from his chair as the slides came up.

Usually the trackers applied sorting criteria to determine
if a given aircraft was "suspect." That meant off a legitimate
air route, not filing a flight plan, not squawking a valid code,
or flying an erratic course near shore. But they'd lock up
Nuñez's new twin-jet Falcon the moment it popped above
five hundred feet over Palonegro Airfield. The over-the-
horizon radar in Texas would hand off to a Perry-class
frigate, USS *Gallery*, loitering off the Venezuelan coast.
Gallery would add its track data to the information flow. At
this point the Falcon would be designated an "air target of

interest," or ATOI, and handed off to a Navy E-2C command
and control aircraft as Air Force fighters launched to intercept and identify.

By the time Nuñez's pilot realized he was getting special
attention, he'd have F-16s from the 125th Fighter Wing to
port and starboard. They'd escort him to Homestead Air
Force Base, where an arrest team from the FBI, DEA, and
the Florida State Police would be waiting.

Dan got the impression of a showboat operation, involving as many agencies as possible. But it sounded workable.
Unless he aborted before he left Colombian airspace, Don
Juan Nuñez—the biggest trafficker in Cali, kingpin, locus,
famed for years for his slipperiness, ruthlessness, and im-
placable vindictiveness—was American meat.

He checked in at the combined billeting office at the
naval air station, showered, shaved, and tried to
close his eyes for a couple of hours. Instead he
stared at the popcorn finish of the ceiling. Wondering now if
Hot Handoff was as airtight as it had sounded.

Considering when Nuñez's plane was scheduled to leave
the ground, the intercept would take place well after dark.
Would that be a problem? He didn't think so, considering
the radar and ELINT assets that would be tracking him. On
the other hand, he'd never seen an operation where everything went down as planned.

If it worked it would be an enormous coup. If President
Tejeiro was serious about rooting out drug-based corruption
and violence in Colombia itself, taking Nuñez down now
could wreck the whole cartel.

The phone woke him minutes after he'd finally dropped
off.

The sun was going down in flames over the Gulf.
Lights popped on above the barbed wire. Armed sen-
tries patted him down before letting him into the op-

erations center. He approved. This headquarters would be a prime target for a bomb or raid.

The duty officers, analysts, operations specialists, sat absorbed at their consoles. The air was icy. Quintero was stretched out in one of the big elevated chairs. He pointed to the one beside him. Dan looked around for Bloom, and located him headsdown with another agent over some printouts. He checked his watch against the wall clock—2115—and tried to relax.

The big flat-panel display showed the whole transit zone, with air routes and boundaries of national seas and airspace. Dozens of aircraft flowed down the airways, each tagged by a data readout. The western boundary was the coast of Yucatán; the eastern, the scattered arch of the Lesser Antilles, Grenada, Barbados, the Grenadines, Martinique, on up to the U.S. Virgins. Colombia and Venezuela pushed up from the south, the tip of Florida down from the north. It was a godlike view of two million square miles of continent, island, and sea.

Quintero probed as to the administration's plans for the aerostats and the Customs boat fleet, since seizures were declining. "It's easy to quantify seizures. Impossible to quantify deterrence."

"We can put numbers on it," Dan said. "That's what I'll try to do."

"But it doesn't give you the public support. You can't take pictures of cargos of cocaine not being seized because they're going overland."

"The classic dilemma of deterrence. But if we can take down Nuñez, that'll give Tejeiro a chance. What about control? Any hard spots there?"

"Tactical control here works pretty well. We've got the joint bugs worked out and we're smoothing things out with the Brits and the Dutch. But nobody coordinates activity between me and JIATF West or South."

"How much attention do you need? Hourly? Daily? Weekly?"

Quintero said he didn't need hourly coordination. Handoff procedures were established for tracks and intel that crossed the JIATF boundaries. But there were issues it would be nice to pass to a higher level, rather than trying to negotiate with his opposite number.

"We're going to start running those out of my office," Dan told him. "I don't want to set up another command center. We've got enough command centers. But somebody's got to have the big picture."

Quintero seemed about to say something, but didn't. Instead he started describing the data, secret Internet protocol, and covered voice circuits they were guarding. He was saying the primary coordination voice net would be UHF satellite voice link 409, when Bloom came over and cleared his throat. "He's off the ground."

"Nuñez?"

"None other. They don't know we're listening to their airport communications. Over-the-horizon radar should report them any minute now."

They sat watching the display. "Flight profile match," one of the console operators called.

Quintero said, "This is terrific intel. Usually all we get is rumors, vague locations. This was spang on the money."

An aircraft symbol popped up on the screen, west of Bucaramanga. Simultaneously they got confirmation from a Customs Service–modified P-3 patrolling off the Mosquito Coast of Nicaragua. Dan was impressed. Dozens of icons winked and crept over Colombia. Somehow they'd plucked Nuñez's out of that welter and mountain return, and locked on it as it headed north.

"Subject TOI's gone black," a grille at his elbow reported.

"No transponder return," Bloom explained. "He's turned it off. Hoping if we're tracking him, that'll shake us off."

"Will it work?"

"Not a chance," Quintero said.

An hour later *Gallery* reported in. She held a small business-type jet, transponder off, no radars or other emitters active. It was traveling at 240 knots at forty thousand feet, northbound across the Gulf of Venezuela for the open sea. Quintero told the command duty officer to launch the ready E-2C, the plane that would control the air assets that would carry out the intercept. They'd need time to get into position in the Straits of Florida.

Dan was surprised to see that the Colombian's intended flight path, outlined in orange, led across eastern Cuba. After the overwater leg, he'd make landfall at Montego Bay, then turn slightly west for Ciego de Avila. Quintero said Castro had no problem granting flight clearance to civilian aircraft. It meant ready cash—five thousand dollars just to cross the island from south to north—and the Cubans were desperate for foreign exchange. The intercept would take place just south of point "Ursus," where Miami-bound traffic split off from the stream continuing north to Bimini. Far enough north and offshore so that the surprised pilot, and his no doubt enraged passengers, would have too little reserve fuel to duck back into Cuban airspace.

Over the next hours Dan and Quintero drank coffee as the orange pip crept north. The F-16s launched. The E-2 vectored them. At midnight pizza came in. ATOI 3 was holding a steady course at flight level 410. Forty-one thousand feet, Quintero explained, the most economical altitude for a light jet. "A direct flight from Colombia to Miami, he's operating at the extreme limit of his range. Usually the coke flights, they come in over the Bahamas and air drop."

"The Air Force does your interceptions?"

"Strictly speaking it's Air Guard. Usually we have either Customs Citations up with them, or sometimes the Marine OV-10s out of New River, for identification. To make absolutely sure you've got who you think you've got. But a corporate jet like this is too fast for the turboprops to catch. We're just going to have the F-16s identify. They've got night vision now anyway."

The display showed the various aircraft closing steadily. Two moving southwest, the fighters; from the south, their quarry boring along straight and level. "Put it on the speakers," Quintero said. A chief flicked a switch at the comm panel.

Minutes later they heard an unhurried voice. "Hawk One, contact bogey. Bull's-eye 360, thirty miles track north. Hawk One flight unplug, Hawk Two cleared fluid. Bogey course three-zero-five. Throttle back . . . let's take this slow. He's traveling without lights. Appears to be twin-engine private jet. I can just make out the winglets."

"That's our boy. Can you get a tail number?"

"Not from astern. Stand by as I move up on him."

Dan could close his eyes and see them sliding into position. Staying on the bogey's six, the blind spot on almost every aircraft ever built. Quintero said that typically the interceptors identified a drug aircraft, then returned to base while the slower, longer-legged tracker bloodhounded it to the drop point. But tonight the fighters would visually ID with night vision goggles, and escort this bogey all the way to touchdown, and the open arms of U.S. law enforcement.

The pilot again, tin-can hollow as what Dan assumed was a satellite relay bounced his signal over hundreds of miles. "Okay, there he is . . . got a nice glow off the engine. Throttling back to 250 knots. Hold him now bearing 295. Hawk One weapons safe." The wingman must have rogered, though it didn't come through the speaker. "Confirm arming switches off. Initiate lock-on . . . lock-on."

The command duty officer glanced their way. "Permission for close pass and visual ID?" Quintero eyed Dan, who nodded. The admiral gave a thumbs-up.

"Hawk One, this is Clear View. Shadow VID," came over the net.

"Roger, beginning phase two. I'll pitch up and throttle back to match speed while I call him on thirty-two eight."

An interdiction display flickered up on the right-hand display. It showed the target aircraft and the interceptors. The fighters were covering the last mile to the Falcon now. No way it could escape the much faster, more maneuverable military jets.

"Closing . . . closing . . . you're edging ahead, lose ten knots . . . Yeah, that rattled his drawers. Okay, Hawk One is now going Christmas tree." The same voice seemed to move about five feet, to directly above Dan's head; emerging from a different speaker, slower, speaking to someone who might not understand English well. "Unlighted aircraft bound three-zero-zero at 240 knots, approximately twenty-three degrees north, eighty-five degrees twenty minutes west. This is U.S. Air Force interceptor off your starboard wing. Over."

They waited: Dan, Quintero, the pilots, the men and women around them at consoles. But no answer came.

"Settle back in . . . ," the pilot was saying over his cockpit-to-cockpit, to his wingman.

"Light in the cockpit. Flashlight, looks like. Guy's waving at us."

At the same moment another speaker between Dan's and the admiral's chairs hissed to life. "Clear View, this is Hawk Two. That's not the right tail number."

"Say again?"

"What's he mean by that?" Quintero snapped. "What's he reading? Have him read back what he's seeing."

The tracker pilot read off six digits, using military phonetic code. Dan jotted HK 4016 on his palm with his ballpoint. On the command center floor an analyst called out, "He's right. That's not Nuñez's tail. I can go into the database here . . . stand by."

"What, he's altered his tail number?" Dan asked Quintero. "Repainted it?"

"The Viper has a spotlight on the port side of the nose," someone put in. "He can illuminate."

"Not necessary," Quintero said. "Who else is it going to be, flying dark out of Bucaramanga?"

"Negative radio contact," said the flight leader. "All right, blinking our lights, waggling our wings. As soon as he confirms, will commence a slow level turn to . . . Holy shit!"

The controller's voice: "Say again?"

"Oh my holy shit. He just *fireballed*! Fuck, fuck, that hurts! Did you see that? . . . Clear View, this is Hawk flight leader, our A-toy just fireballed."

Every head in the command center snapped around. The controller said, "Flight leader, say again your last."

"He's going down now . . . there's a tail surface coming off. He's on fire. Bright orange, fuel-type flame. I'm turning to port to follow him down. Stay clear of me . . . still falling."

Quintero was on the circuit now, voice taut. "Flight leader, Clear View actual. Did you shoot him down?"

"Negative. Arming switches were off here. Confirm— off. Frank, confirm you didn't fire."

The wingman attested to it in a voice as shocked and puzzled as his flight leader's. Dan rubbed his mouth, shaken. If neither fighter had fired, who had? The only other aircraft on the plot was seventy miles away. Could a vortex from the fighters have jarred a fuel line loose? Struck a spark, where a spark could not be afforded?

"We need more details here," the command duty officer was telling the flight leader. Who was breathing hard, apparently in a tight turn.

"Frank, stay clear of me to the west. . . . You getting anything here?"

"Negative, flames too bright, blanked my display."

"I'm following him down. Clear View, take a fix on my posit . . . that will be crash datum. Doesn't look like there'll be any survivors. There's the wing . . . a fuel tank or something. It's just a fireball. There . . . impact. I have no idea what happened to this guy. It wasn't anything we did. Flames on the water . . . We did this *right*, goddamn it. That's all I can see now. Flames on the water."

The words hung in the cold air. Beside him Admiral Quintero was, Dan thought, as pale as he must be himself. Of course Don Juan Nuñez was a bad guy. If anyone deserved death, it was the chief of the Cali cartel. But still the voices leaping across space had conveyed the horror of watching men fall, burning.

"Everybody with wings, in the conference room," Quintero said, swinging down from his seat.

He was halfway across the JOCC when one of the analysts beckoned. The admiral bent. They conferred in tones too low to overhear.

Quintero put out a hand to steady himself. He stared at the printout the man held out.

Dan stepped up. "What is it?"

"This could be bad," Quintero muttered.

Tail number HK 4016 was a twin-engine Lear 55 owned by a company called Central Charter de Colombia, SA. It was roughly the same size and type, with the same engine location and control surface conformation, as the jet Nuñez flew. Another watchstander handed them photos of both aircraft, still damp from the printer. Dan looked from one to the other. At night they'd be indistinguishable. But he didn't understand. What was this other aircraft doing en route to Miami, without clearance, without IFF, without radio, without lights?

In the conference room, the two pilots who happened to be on duty at the command center, one Customs, the other Air Guard, were telling Quintero it was impossible for the F-16s to have knocked such an aircraft down with only a close pass, when the same analyst who'd come up with the tail-number list knocked. He closed the door behind him.

He'd contacted Medellín air traffic control. They said HK 4016 was under contract to Ecopetrol, the Colombian state-owned oil company. Then he'd called the duty desk at the U.S. embassy in Bogotá, who had managed to contact Ecopetrol.

"All right, tell us," Quintero said.

They were still trying to confirm, the analyst said. But it looked like the aircraft that had just disintegrated had indeed been on its way to Florida. But not to Miami, and not to a drug conference. The embassy trade rep, routed out of bed, said it was probably en route to a meeting with the Tampa Export Association on behalf of the Corporación Invertir en Colombia, the Colombian National Investment Promotion Agency.

"Who was aboard?" Quintero asked after a reluctant moment. Dan saw that the analyst no more wanted to tell them than they wanted to hear.

The traffic controllers and the night desk at the embassy weren't entirely sure yet, he said. They were still checking. But early word was that the primary passenger had been the eldest son of the new president of Colombia.

8

The phones began ringing, and mounted to a discordant crescendo.

Quintero ordered a cutter dispatched to the crash site. Even at flank speed, it wouldn't arrive till midmorning, but it was the closest rescue asset between Miami and Nassau. Then he sat like a brooding gargoyle, watching the wall display as if he could by sheer will make onrushing time rewind. He took a call from Atlantic Command in Norfolk. The handset clattered when Quintero put it back in its cradle. It rang again instantly. "You take it," he said to the duty officer. "If it's JCS, I'll talk. Otherwise I'll get back to them."

Bloom said, "This is a disaster. A fucking disaster. Who's going to tell the Colombians?"

"I'd say that'd be the White House," Quintero said. "Right, Dan?"

Dan tried to think. "Well . . . it really should be State, since the initial notification will come through the embassy. I'll let my boss know, though, so Mrs. Clayton can tell the president. He'll want to make a consolatory call."

Right after he fires me, Dan thought. He didn't think he was to blame. But you didn't have to be responsible to be guillotined. Only junior enough.

"It's the CINC, on the conference room speaker," the

deputy interrupted. "The public affairs officer's in there already. He's getting together a release, to get our version on the street first."

Quintero closed his eyes. When he opened them again he looked resigned. He nodded to Dan. Then went into the room and closed the door.

Unwillingly, but knowing he had to, Dan placed the call to Sebold's home number. The director came awake instantly. No doubt over the years he'd been roused many times with bad news. He asked how they could be sure the fighters hadn't fired. Whether their gun cameras were being checked. What Quintero and Dan were doing to get help to the crash site. He closed with the unadorned remark that there'd be repercussions. What they'd be, he didn't say.

When he hung up Dan kept the handset against his ear to get a moment to think. He broke out sweating as the reality of what had happened penetrated another layer, like molten metal thawing its way through successive deposits of ice. By some unimaginable chance, they'd managed to kill the son and heir of the first leader who'd shown the inclination to rein in terror in the largest exporter of cocaine in the world.

By *chance* . . . but even as he thought it, he knew that had to be wrong. This was no coincidence. *That* night, of all nights. *That* aircraft, out of all the hundreds in the sky. No. It was too horribly perfect.

Some malevolent intelligence, some malign *strategy* must lie beneath.

His fists were clenched. His jaw hurt. He felt as if he ought to, no, he *had* to do something. He was only here as an observer, true. So a press release could mention White House participation. But he wasn't used to being surrounded by panic, confusion, and *not doing anything*. Command meant you gave orders, took action. Any action! That was Navy doctrine. Any action was better than none. Even the wrong move could confuse the enemy, blow his timetable, screw up his plan. Sitting on your hands, waiting for the situation to clarify itself—that was the freeway to defeat.

When he looked up everyone in the center was looking at him.

Of course they were. Wasn't he the guy from the White House?

He slid down, past two people holding up phones in his direction, and bent over the comm console. Glanced at a tote board with frequencies and call signs.

"I'd like to talk to CTG 4.3 . . . belay that . . . where's the frigate now? The one that confirmed the track, took the handoff from the radar in Texas?"

The operator said *Gallery* was off station, headed east.

"They still in satcom contact? I need a level-three voice channel."

The operator hesitated, glancing toward the closed door of the conference room. But finally nodded.

Dan took the handset. Keyed, and waited. When a note signaled they were linked, he said, "USS *Gallery*, this is the director of drug interdiction from the president's staff. Present in the Carib Ops Center. Request to speak to *Gallery* Actual."

When the commanding officer came on Dan explained who he was again, once more without using his name or rank. "This is in reference to ATOI 3, track 930, detected approximately 2200 last night when you were on station off La Guajira. I want you to replay your raw video data on that contact."

"Roger, understand you want to revisit the acquisition. And do what?"

The problem was he wasn't really sure. Just that he was remembering a conversation with a Treasury agent. "I can't tell you exactly what to look for, but I need you to reconstruct the air plot," Dan told him. "Not just track acquisition. Before that. And have your shit-sharpest air intercept controller eyeball it very closely."

Gallery didn't ask why. Just said he'd have his ops specialist chief look at it too. Dan signed off. It most likely wouldn't pan out, but he had to try.

Quintero, back from the call to the combatant commander. Sweat glittered on his forehead. Dan told him, "My boss wants the cameras on the fighters checked. To make absolutely sure they didn't fire. And the film or whatever they use as a recording medium sequestered as evidence."

Quintero told the command duty officer to make it happen. "What else do we need to do?"

Dan reflected on the irony of an admiral publicly asking a commander for advice. But he was the Suit from Washington now. Here to help? More likely to get himself tacked up on a cross between Quintero and the pilots. "What else?" Quintero said again.

"Well, I had one idea," he began, when the console operator waved, holding up the red handset. He told the admiral he'd be right back.

"This is *Gallery* Actual. Captain Starer here. We went over the plot again for the initial acquisition. Ran it through the point it went off the screen. Over."

"Anything out of the ordinary? Over."

"No. Nothing." Dan's heart dropped. Then the voice added, "Something funny before that, though. We didn't have one aircraft come on the screen at 2210. We had two."

"Can you put this on speaker?" Dan muttered to the chief. He crooked a finger to Quintero and Bloom to come over and listen.

The frigate's skipper explained that by running the tape slowly and tweaking the display, they were able to make out not one but two aircraft approaching the coast. At the same speed and nearly the same altitude, but on converging courses. Just before meeting, one had vanished from the screen.

"Which one?" Dan asked him.

"Can't tell. Blip meld; too close to distinguish."

"But one just . . . disappeared?"

"Right. Two contacts, then there's only one."

Dan tapped the handset against his shoulder. His brain felt like a generator with too much power demanded of it. Two contacts—then one. The frigate, and no doubt the more distant AWACs and over-the-horizon radars too, had continued to track the plane that continued north. "What happened to the other one? Over."

The distant voice sounded puzzled. "Like I said, from one sweep to the next we go from two contacts to one, proceeding to seaward. We passed it off to the E-2. Oh, and it goes dark—the target's radar and IFF snap off."

"They snap off *after* the two contacts merged? Or whatever they did?"

"Correct. That was what we were supposed to look for—right? A nonsquawker. IFF off."

A possibility took shape. Still murky, but it might explain at least part of what had happened. "How long after the first aircraft drops off the screen does the second one go black?"

The CO said to wait. A moment later he was back. He said no more than a minute.

Dan signed off, and found Quintero and Bloom both frowning at him. "What've you got?" the admiral said.

"*Gallery*'s skipper says there were originally two aircraft," Dan told them.

"What?" said Bloom. Quintero just blinked.

"One must have been Nuñez's. The other, Tejeiro's. Converging courses. Nearly the same altitude. Same speed."

He tried to think through what was still only a suspicion while he illustrated it with his hands, aviator-fashion. "Call them N and T. Let's say . . . N takes off from Nuñez's airstrip in Bucaramanga. Heads north. T takes off from Bogotá. It heads north too. But since they're both headed for the same way point, their courses gradually converge."

"Okay," said Quintero.

"Obviously they're at different altitudes, but maybe there's not that much separation at their closest point of approach. For a few seconds the contacts merge. Especially to an ionosphere-scatter radar, lower frequency, thus lower resolution, than the frigate's SPA-60. Then N disappears somehow. Making us think plane T is really plane N. Texas tracks T and hands off to *Gallery*, telling them it's Nuñez. *Gallery* hands it off to the E-2, telling him the same thing. And everyone just buys that identification, no questions asked, from there on."

"Okay, two questions," said Bloom. "What made Tejeiro's jet blow up? And how does plane T just 'disappear'?"

"And why was the Lear flying without IFF or lights or radio?" Quintero added.

"I don't know how they blew it up," Dan told him. "Maybe put a bomb aboard?"

"They do that in Colombia," Bloom said. "Judges, senators they don't like."

Dan took a breath, aware that he was skating on thin ice. "But the second contact . . . assume Nuñez's plane has some kind of spook gear that vanishes it from radar." Quintero frowned. "I know, I know . . . but bear with me here. Once they figure we've merged the tracks, they turn it on for a few seconds. Long enough for us to miss the track split. Maybe it dives away till it's below the radar horizon. So intel fusion comes out with one bird. Which we then track across the Caribbean."

"And vector our fighters onto, at which time they trigger the bomb." Bloom looked impressed. "But how could they make it disappear from radar? You mean like stealth?"

"Not exactly. Stealth is just very low radar reflectivity. We're talking something different . . . transmitting a negative image of the returned radar pulse, which effectively erases it as far as the receiving station's concerned. It takes sophisticated computers," Dan told him. "But it can be done. Given the money. Which I happen to know has been going to a French electronics company that's been trying to sell that technology to the Navy."

"This is all new to me," Bloom said.

"I heard about it from a guy at Treasury who tracks cartel cash flows. I called the CIA division chief in Europe and checked it out. Turns out they've been trying to sell the same gear, or at least the technology, to the Chinese, too."

"What about the lights, the IFF?" Quintero asked again.

Dan said, "I can only guess at that. Maybe a radio-controlled relay in the electrical system. They'd be close enough to make it work if they transmitted the signal as the planes passed. Tejeiro loses transponders, radio, radar, lights, everything. A black airplane, like you called it. So we read—drug smuggler."

"Beautiful," Bloom said. "Not only does it get the top people out of the country right under our noses, it ruins us with President Tejeiro."

Quintero said, "It's also a message to Tejeiro from the cartel. 'Your son first. Then you. We can screw you anytime we want.'"

Bloom said no, it would be that only if it had cartel fingerprints on it. "Which it doesn't. To all intents and purposes, we shot down the president's son. Oh, it's beautiful. And it hurts."

Quintero said, "It's impossible to prove. And even if we do, his son's still dead."

"We can't bring him back," Dan said. "True. But I don't think proving we didn't do it is impossible. Not if we can find out where the second plane went. You archive your track data, right? If we can come up with a Falcon going north, that's going to be our boy."

They found it eventually, though it wasn't heading north. The Falcon had headed to Port of Spain instead, far to the east, then landed to refuel before striking out along the island chain at dawn. USNS *Capable* picked it up there. Its flight plan was properly registered. It was squawking a proper Mode III IFF. Quintero pulled in Dutch assets to keep tracking it up the Antilles chain: a Fokker Friendship, a ground-based radar on Sint Eustatius. "Why doesn't he just leave this masker thing on?" Bloom wanted to know. Dan explained that if the cartel had a way to make its planes invisible, it'd be smart to actually use the capability as little as possible. Once you knew such a device existed, there were ways to minimize its advantage.

Meanwhile he fielded calls from Sebold, Gelzinis, and Tony Holt. He explained to each exactly what had happened, what he thought was going on, and what he hoped to do.

Holt cursed Dan as if he were personally responsible. Even-tually, though, the chief of staff grudgingly agreed that De Bari had to call President Tejeiro personally. But he wasn't going to mention the fighters, or that the leased Lear had been under U.S. surveillance. Just that it had exploded over the Straits of Florida, and a cutter was on its way to the site.

Dan pleaded with him to present the whole picture. The networks were already carrying the crash. So far no one had implicated U.S. drug interdiction, but that was only a mat-ter of time. Holt cut him off angrily, saying he'd make that decision.

At 1000 the AWACs reported that the Falcon had turned northwest, to pass through the airspace of the Turks and Caicos. Later it altered course again, to a southwesterly heading. Then it faded from the plot.

Dan didn't know if it had turned on the masker again, or simply dropped too close to the wavetops to pick up. By this time, though, he'd managed to get NPIC on the line, and persuaded them to redeploy satellite assets to follow it. They picked it up again a few miles off the coast of Hispaniola. Then lost it again. But Quintero had traced out a cone of courses on a chart. They looked down at it.

"Get me Colonel Desrolles," Quintero said.

Desrolles was the Haitian liaison. Very dark, very tall, he listened courteously as they described the aircraft, the de-ception plan, and what seemed to be its destination.

When they were done he cleared his throat. "Absolutely," he said. "I know your media present my country as ever so poor. But there are also very wealthy families. They do not live in the cities. They have estates in the hills." He pointed here and there above Cap-Haitien. "They are beautiful, and well guarded. These men will fly in, have their meeting, and fly out. If you like I can call someone I know. See if he has noticed any air traffic into the north."

Dan got on the phone again. He was using his contacts, reaching out to the people he'd met at interagency confer-ences and working groups. He didn't have the authority to do some of the things he was doing. But if he could come up on the other side of this shit pond with whoever had arranged Emiliano Tejeiro's fiery death, much would be forgiven.

If he failed, he'd be out of a job.

T wo hours later the satellite images came in over the data link. They showed eight aircraft parked about a grassy strip. Trucks and groups of men formed a security perimeter. It surrounded a large gated house with gardens, pools, courts, a tiled roof, and what looked like guardhouses set around it.

By this time Bloom had pulsed the DEA's rapid reaction team. Scrambled immediately, it could be in Haiti that afternoon, but with only three helicopters and ten agents. Counting heads on the perimeter manning and the airfield guard, and adding the personal security that was probably within the villa, they agreed the mismatch was too great to commit such a small force.

But one of the marines on Quintero's staff remembered that the 3rd Battalion, Eighth Marine Regiment, had troops in country with the Multinational Interim Force. Dan's call to the Combined Joint Task Force–Haiti brought the information that a motorized patrol was out forty miles south of the compound. He half persuaded, half ordered them to redeploy as an anvil, lay fire, and pin down anyone in the villa long enough for the Haitian National Police to mobilize.

The clock was ticking, though. They didn't know how long the meeting would last. Not overnight, Bloom said. Don Juan never slept in a location he didn't control. The essential thing was to block the airfield. Once their line of retreat was cut off and the compound was surrounded, negotiations for surrender could proceed.

They worked this through the late morning into afternoon, and were rewarded by reports of a more or less coordinated descent on the airstrip a little after 1500. A few cannon rounds from a Cobra dispersed the guards on the airfield. The patrol reported both roads from the villa blocked.

Then nothing. The circuits hissed mute in the cold conditioned air. Quintero looked strained. He went outside for a cigarette. Bloom, nervous as a cat, went with him. Dan sat in the leather chair, drumming his fingers.

G elzinis called again late that afternoon. "Lenson? Mrs. C's getting pissed-off calls from agency heads. All sorts of end-arounds. What in Christ's name do you think you're doing down there?"

"We've captured Don Juan Nuñez," Dan told him, weary but exultant. "The Baptist himself. Along with the cartel's host in Haiti, the biggest drug banker in Medellín, and four other kingpins and twenty-two high-ranking staff."

He told the deputy adviser that along with the prisoners, the DEA team had seized notebook computers, forty-five kilos of documents, and six aircraft, including a Falcon Ten with infrared flares, drop tanks, and sophisticated electronic masking equipment. "Intel's still going through everything. But you can call President Tejeiro now and tell him we didn't shoot his son down. It was a cartel bomb."

"You'd better be able to prove it."

"We can," Dan told him. "I'm sorry his son had to die. But this could cement his determination to cooperate with us. We've got video, too."

"Video?"

"There was a cameraman with the DEA assault team. Good stuff, they tell me."

"I want a personal report," the deputy told him, but the accusatory tone was gone. "Get back no later than dawn. Be ready to brief the press secretary and Mrs. Clayton. Make absolutely sure that tape and a list of the documents are on a flight to D.C. tonight."

Dan said he'd get back as soon as humanly possible.

When he hung up he felt wrung out, yet fairly pleased. They'd managed to retrieve the situation. The administration would come out looking resolute and effective.

It occurred to him then, though only fleetingly, that the cartel might not be quite so happy.

II
SPRING WIND

281221Z OCT
SCHOLAST:
//Logging on. Who's here?

281221Z OCT
AMICABLE:
//Here.

281221Z OCT
BLUE DANUBE:
//Been here awhile.

281222Z OCT
HELLGOD:
//Here.

28122Z OCT
SCHOLAST:
//Sorry I'm late. Greetings all. Hellgod, love your handle. Any problems?

281222Z OCT
BLUE DANUBE:

//Is this a secure site? For a discussion like this? And why so
early?

281222Z OCT
HELLGOD:
//Same question.

281222Z OCT
SCHOLAST:
//Have already assured Amicable of airtightness of this site.
No records will exist after power down. Not like your VAX
system, or whatever it's called now. Check the indicator,
lower right of the screen, for who's in the room. Should be
just the four of us, that's what I show.

281223Z OCT
AMICABLE:
//Let's get to it. The less time we're online the better I'll feel.

281223Z OCT
HELLGOD:
//On the security issue: I'm going to have one of my people
backcheck that. For peace of mind. Will not tell him why.

281223Z OCT
SCHOLAST:
//Fine on the backstop on security.

//All right, an update. We've made progress. Brought concerned citizens aboard. All good guys. This is not for anyone's personal gain or advancement. Correct?

281223Z OCT
BLUE DANUBE:
//We all have more to lose than to gain from even dis-
cussing this.

281223Z OCT
HELLGOD:
//What's the code name? Valkyrie?

281224Z OCT
AMICABLE:
//?? You lost me there, cowboy. Meaning what??

281224Z OCT
SCHOLAST:
//There is no name for this plan. Officially it will never exist.
It is prepared solely in case P gets out of hand. A lot of guys
have given their lives to draw certain lines in the sand. I won't
stand by and let a sleazy politician, a—Sorry. Out of rant
mode now.

281224Z OCT
AMICABLE:
//Continue report??

281225Z OCT
SCHOLAST:
//Overall concept of operations is G's. It required a contact
on the inside. Blue Danube is now with us. Welcome again.
There is also another, who declines to participate in e-mail
exchanges. G will handle him personally. All this very close
hold. No printouts, no penciled notes. You do not discuss
with others in the picture, other than by face-to-face conversation, or this channel. Nothing written down. And with no
one else—not wife, not your aide, not your COS.

281226Z OCT
HELLGOD:
//Has an Oswald been identified?

281226Z OCT
AMICABLE:

//No, but I have a Ruby. ;)

281226Z OCT
SCHOLAST:
//Ha ha. Now, what we need: BD, take a close look at your junior people. Go back and review your organizational security guidelines to identify those at risk. Those = our candidates.

281228Z OCT
BLUE DANUBE:
//Assume this person is to be expendable.

281228Z OCT
AMICABLE:
//The cartridge is fired, then disposed of.

281228Z OCT
SCHOLAST:
//Now you're getting with the program. Felt some misgivings/reluctance in our last "conversation."

281228Z OCT
HELLGOD:
//No doubt here. I vote for executive action today.

281228Z OCT
AMICABLE:
//My vote is no, if we're voting. I'm no admirer, but this Republic has survived bad leadership before. Don't pull the pin till you're ready to throw the grenade!!

281229Z OCT
SCHOLAST:
//This is not an election for third-grade president, gents. G will make decision to implement, if such a decision is necessary. But A is correct—this is backup measure only.

281229Z OCT
AMICABLE:
//Is Two officially aboard?

281229Z OCT
SCHOLAST:
//Friendly but in deniable mode.

281229Z OCT
SCHOLAST:
//Continuing to BD: we need an operator who will be motivated to act for reasons external to us, not attributable to
us. Someone already close to the breaking point, or would appear to be, in retrospect, to an outside observer/investiga-
tor/historian. Our role only creating conditions for him to act.
Then stepping aside.

281230Z OCT
HELLGOD:
//We have resources over here we could help out with. My
question: how ENSURE he acts? We can facilitate, but how do
we push him to move?

281230ZCT
SCHOLAST:
//All excellent questions, Hellgod. Let's discuss offline. BD,
research and report back. Nominate direct to me with as
much detail as possible.

281230Z OCT
SCHOLAST:
//Good, but no nominations off the top of the head. Everything about this has to be airtight. Even looked at twenty
years down the road.

281230Z OCT
BLUE DANUBE:

//Will work up package.

281230Z OCT
SCHOLAST:
//Basically it for now. Remember to log out at end of chat.

281230Z OCT
AMICABLE:
//If we're done I'm out.
LOGOFF

281230Z OCT
SCHOLAST:
//Out here.
LOGOFF

281230Z OCT
BLUE DANUBE:
//Out Here.
LOGOFF

281230Z OCT
HELLGOD:
//Done. & GHMOUA.
LOGOFF

9

OVER THE NORTH ATLANTIC

Weeks later Dan strolled down the aisle of another aircraft, holding the orange juice that was supposed to stave off jet lag. This plane was much larger, much more spacious than the one he'd taken to Key West. It was the best-known aircraft in the world.

Air Force One was more than a plane. It was a microcosm of the political universe. It cocooned politicians and press, network people, guests and major donors, the staff, and the aides and agents and aircrews that enabled them all, thirty thousand feet up. The sea, drawing his eye through a window, seemed to belong to another planet, which they were transiting far above, in some separate dimension.

He'd come to feel that way often in the past months. That he was leaving his old life behind. Rising above the Navy and even the military. Toward new prerogatives and new challenges. Like the one ahead: a seat at the first international threat reduction conference, in St. Petersburg. Sebold had assigned him as the Defense Directorate's rep.

The Tejeiro incident seemed to have started something. Maybe something good. He felt like a fully engaged gear in an engine running at full power. His work days started at six, the only time he could read without the phone constantly interrupting. He didn't get home until eight, nine, even ten.

After Key West, Sebold had called him in. The general had told his assistant to hold his calls. Then read Dan the riot act. He'd arrogated authority. Bypassed the chain of command. Ignored interagency coordination procedures.

Dan had tried to point out that without a hand on the helm, nothing would have come out of what had looked like a ham-handed shootdown except bitter publicity and probably the ruin of the whole Central American drug initiative. Sebold had waved this away. "Positive action? What I expect from my staff. But you can't operate on your own, Dan. The last guy to try that here was Ollie North."

"They gave him a mission. He tried to accomplish it."

"And damn near brought down the government. I like Ollie. Who doesn't? But like Bud McFarlane said, a can-do spirit but not a lot of brains." The general paused. "See, the actual issue is, there really *isn't* any limit to what we can do from here. The black funding. The compartmentation. Just the fact we operate in the president's name. So we've got to regulate ourselves, or there'll be more Watergates, Irangates—and others I might mention, but we got the blanket over them in time. Am I getting through? Or am I wasting my breath? This isn't the bridge of a ship. Or a cockpit, or a company of infantry."

"No, sir. I'm getting the picture."

"You'd be walking now if you hadn't nailed Nuñez at the end of the day. That's how serious I am."

"Yes, sir. And I appreciate your taking the time to counsel me."

"You're on the fast track to flag, they tell me," Sebold told him. "You wouldn't want to screw that up."

Dan nearly laughed in his face. The only reason he'd made commander was the congressional. And that hadn't been the Navy's idea at all. But he'd kept his mouth shut and his face straight, and eventually the director had warned him one last time and let him go.

∙ ∙ ∙

But nothing ever happened the way you expected. Certainly no one he talked to on a daily basis had predicted Don Juan Alberto Mendieta Nuñez-Sebastiano had a Get Out of Jail Free card in his pocket.

The uproar after the raid had been immense, the signals out of Colombia contradictory. The foreign minister had excoriated the United States for interfering with innocent passage of Colombian nationals. The justice minister had taken credit for the intelligence leading to the raid, and insisted that his country's most famous criminal be extradited for trial at home. *Time* and the *Wall Street Journal* praised Emiliano Tejeiro as a wunderkind who'd have driven the business renaissance of his country. De Bari was on the line with the elder Tejeiro for an hour, and left the teleconferencing room blowing his nose.

The press called Dan at the office, at home, waylaid him on the street. On Meilhamer's advice he said nothing, not even "no comment." Thank God the Air Guard tapes showed neither interceptor had armed its missiles, and that all the AIM-7s and AIM-9s checked out for the mission had been signed back in.

But as far as anyone knew, the Haitian operation had been legally flawless. Until Bloom stuck his head into Dan's office and said, interrupting him while he was on the phone to Marty Harlowe in Burma: "They let him walk."

"What? *Nuñez? Who* let him go?"

"Aristide. The Haitian government."

He said into the phone, "Marty, gotta go. Keep pushing this Wa Army thing. And find out where the Red Arrows are coming from. Okay? . . . Yeah. Bye."

Bloom said, "Get this: We didn't dot all our T's and cross our I's going in to get him. Their judge said it's a bad bust. The Don left this morning. Private jet to Honduras."

"That's *bullshit*," Dan shouted, clutching his head. Ihlemann, at the front desk, looked startled. She was due any day and spent most of her time with her feet up on a chair, alternately cranky and dazed. "The colonel, the police guy—Desrolles. What the hell *is* this?"

Desrolles, reached after a couple of calls, was smoothly regretful. Yes, he'd thought all legal requirements had been taken care of, all responsible officials notified. That was his job as liaison. Unfortunately some preconditions to the raid had been overlooked, both in the Ministry of Justice and in Key West. Haitian law, like that of the United States, did not permit troops to kick down doors. A tainted arrest could not proceed to prosecution. True, Colombia had requested extradition. However, Don Juan did not hold a Colombian passport. He was a naturalized citizen of the Cayman Islands, which had obtained a court order in Port-au-Prince for the release of their national. His government, the delicately accented voice imparted sadly, had no alternative.

"How much did he pay Aristide?" Dan wanted to know. Bloom covered his hands over his eyes, mouthing *Hang up, hang up.*

"I don't believe I heard you correctly, sir. Are you speaking about the democratically elected president of Haiti? Which your administration has urged to respect the rule of law?" When he didn't answer the colonel went on. "You achieved your goal, Mr. Lenson. You caused Don Juan and the other leaders to lose much respect. As well as increasing their costs of doing business. They are very angry now with the U.S., with your president—possibly even with you. I would step very carefully in pursuing these men."

Dan slammed the phone down. Bloom said, "That was pretty goddamn unwise. Insulting him."

"They took money to let him go."

"Absolutely. Shook him down and waved bye-bye. But it wasn't Dickie Desrolles's decision. And look at the plus side—Haiti needs the bucks."

Something else occurred to Dan. "The mechanic—the guy who worked on his plane, gave us the flight plan. Brave as hell—"

"Found him this morning. In Bucaramanga." Bloom looked back to where Ihlemann was eating at her desk again. Eased the door closed. "Head, arms, and legs severed with machetes. Suicide, the local cops say."

"Oh *no*. How did they find out about him?"

"Somebody talked who shouldn't have. But Dickie's right about them being mad. Now they have to make things right. But again, look at the plus side."

"There's no *plus* side to this, Miles."

"Sure there is. Now Tejeiro wants the cartel's balls on his rearview. He fired the guy at the Foreign Ministry who protested, and replaced him with a hard-liner. And another thing: One of the boys we picked up in Haiti's starting to sing."

Bloom told him again, as if he still had to, that this was totally close hold and shoe-shakin' secret. "One of the second-rankers broke under joint FBI-DEA interrogation. He's giving chapter and verse on operations. He also mentioned something about Washington."

"As in, D.C.?"

"He heard Nuñez talking to Francisco Zuluaga—his moneyman—during the flight. *'Habrá un viento muy caliente en Washington este primavera'*—'There'll be a hot wind in Washington this spring.' And they both laughed."

Dan turned that over. "What's Zuluaga say it means?"

"Zuluaga's not talking. According to the agenda it was what the heavies were getting together to discuss. *Viento de la primavera*—spring wind. Or maybe metaphorical, like a springtime wind."

"If it's on the agenda, there'll be supporting documentation."

"Not in the documents or on the hard drives. Believe me, we looked. Had the best computer forensics guy in the business go through them. He found evidence about the flight plans and so forth, though. That helped back up our presentation to Tejeiro about how his son died."

They'd discussed it for a while, then called the office of the White House counsel to see if there was anything they could do after the fact. A staffie was happy to pee on their hopes. Once the Baptist was out of Haiti, he was in the clear. The U.S. had no extradition agreement with the Caymans, but that didn't mean Nuñez was limited to that country. Taking advantage of the slowness of Latin American legal procedures, using cover identities where he had to, Nuñez could stay on the move indefinitely. Bloom suggested putting a price on his head. The staffer said that might be possible. He'd look into it. Sooner or later the guy would go back to Bucaramanga. Until then, he was at large.

Dan tried to tell himself Bloom was right. They'd embarrassed the cartel. Cost it money, and the cloaking device. You couldn't obsess over a loss. Not at the pace the Eighteen Acres operated at. The cookie had crumbled, and it was on to the next battle. He wasn't happy. But he couldn't think of anything else he could do.

W hich brought him to now, over the distant blue Atlantic. The president was up front. Then came the senior staff compartment, the medical compartment, and so forth. Dan was in the middle, between the actual VIPs and the media gang aft. Blair was up in the conference room, a Defense prebrief, she said. There were no dining rooms on *Air Force One*. You got your meals on trays. So he was sitting down to catfish and garlic green beans and whipped garlic potatoes with Telfair Freck in an otherwise empty row of high-backed luxury seats.

Freck was the chairman of the House Military Caucus. Sandy Treherne had come through on her promise to put him in touch with somebody willing to talk about stepping up funding on threat reduction. She'd warned him Freck was no admirer of De Bari's. He was one of the most conservative members of the House. A perfect voting record as rated by the Christian Coalition. But if Dan wanted to mobilize support for his ideas, he had to talk to as many people as possible, on both sides of the Hill/Executive divide.

Freck was ponderous, grizzled, an athlete long run to fat. Like most everybody else on the plane, he was dressed casually, in his case canvas slip-ons and a lavender velour track suit the size of a small concession tent. He gestured at the seat beside him. "So, you're the fella from the NSC."

"Dan Lenson, sir."

"Navy man. Old flame a' Sandy's. Nice to meetcha."

"Not a flame, sir. Just went to school together."

They both said how great Sandy was, straight-shooting gal, the usual cautious prelude to a Washington conversation. "I'm really glad you agreed to talk with me," Dan opened.

"I'm not one of those who thinks everybody over there's evil personified. Though I'll say this, between us: I've never known Bob De Bari to actually give a hoot about another human being."

"He knows how to create that impression, though."

"Course; that's how he got where he is. An' I know you folks who work for him probably think even less of him than we do on the Hill, all that woman chasing, the cocaine thing, the organized crime. His wife more than him maybe on that last—but tar rubs off."

Dan said, "We serve the office, not the man."

Freck sniffed the fish on the end of his fork, then rammed it home. Said around it, "Knew him back when he was in the governor's mansion. Exactly the same. Secretaries. Staff girlies. Anything with titties and ass, after it like a dog in heat. And the way he's failed to support the boys who defend our country, that's a shame too."

"Well, sir," Dan said, "I wanted to talk to you about something along those lines. About helping to make America safer."

Freck ate with the tolerant air of a man who'd listened to thousands of lobbyists make their cases. When Dan paused he said, "The Cicero Foundation did a study on that. Said State, Bert Sola, I think, really fucked that program up. Wasted millions and got nothing back."

"Well, they never actually got the funding that was—"

"I been thinking the way to make something happen there might be to set up some kind of private foundation, private outfit. Let folks loose on it who're used to getting results. Sort of privatize it."

Dan couldn't see how such a thing could be done but was willing to give it a hearing. The old man had been in government a lot longer than he had. "You think so?" he said, playing wide-eyed.

Which Freck seemed to respond to; he leaned forward. "Know a bunch of fellows who take on things like that. I forget what the outfit's called. BSA, PSA something. Forget what it stands for."

"It's like a think tank?" Dan said, still trying to figure out how you could do it privately. Did Freck mean with foundation funding? "Like Rand? SAIC? CNA?"

"None of those," the congressman said. "BSA, that's it. Major General Froelinghausen. Skip. He retired four-five years back."

"Well, I will check that out, sir. Now let me try one more thought on you."

Dan told him about his idea for a close-hold group to try to guess where the country was vulnerable, to envision unconventional means of attack or disruption. "I call it the 'Threat Cell.' To try to game out in advance how enemies could hit us in ways we don't expect."

Freck sounded encouraging. He wanted to know who would run it, Pentagon, CIA? Dan said to be effective, it had to break the "stovepipes"—the vertical channels through which data went from the field to the respective agencies.

"It's got to be independent of the military and intel communities. Otherwise it'll get coopted by whoever's peddling the next glamour program." He kept going, pulling ideas out of the air, playing to where he thought the congressman might want to go. Maybe it *shouldn't* be part of government. Maybe it should have futurists, screenwriters, people who were more comfortable with using their imagination than retired generals. "You want people who can think outside the box. No offense, but that's not something that gets rewarded in government work."

Freck was going through banana pudding like Godzilla through downtown Tokyo, but he was nodding, seemed to be with him. Dan was getting excited. If he could get Freck to back it in Congress, the Threat Cell could be up and running in a year.

The fat man said, "It might be worth funding for a cycle, see what comes out of it. And you know what? You might be just the fella to head up something like that."

"Me? Well . . . thanks," Dan said. Taken aback, but pleased. Maybe it wasn't impossible to get something done around Washington after all.

"You must run or something," Freck said. "What is it? Gymnastics? Play tennis? Pretty buffed up."

"I work out," Dan said. "Not so much since I got to D.C., but when I can."

"Look like you're in shape. Good chest. Good arms. But you carry yourself stiff. No looseness there, like you see with most men in good shape. You know, we might get together sometime," Freck said.

Surprised someone with so much power on the Hill could be so approachable, Dan said, "Sure, we could do that. You mean run?"

"No, no . . . been a long time since the knees were up to that! Just hang out. Just spend some time together. You like to swim? Come over to my place, we could swim. See what develops."

To his utter astonishment, Dan felt Freck's hand sliding up his thigh. He jerked away. Freck's face didn't change, not an iota, still the grave mien of the rectitudinous statesman. Dan started to get up, felt his face burning. Freck was folding his napkin, blotting his lips, perfectly comfortable. Past him Dan saw two of the crew members grinning at him. As if they'd known all along.

It was dark when they landed, though only 3 p.m. local time. They left Pulkovo Airport in a motorcade, limos, but without the pomp and security that would have accompanied them had the president stayed. But De Bari was off again, en route to the emerging central Asian states. Actually he'd only landed here to pick up people he wanted to speak with en route to central Asia and perhaps on the way back as well. Or so Blair had said. Which was why they'd gotten to fly in *Air Force One* instead of the more usual military or commercial air.

Dan had never been in what had so recently been the USSR. In fact security regulations had still required him to get clearance to enter the country. Blair was in another car, with the other Defense people; they'd had time for a hug-and-peck coming down the jetway, but no more. . . . He looked out curiously. They were heading down a broad avenue, six empty lanes of concrete lined with apartment blocks like some enormous, badly funded prison. Between them stumpy figures pushed snow around with brooms. As they passed a polished granite pylon, huge bronzes of soldiers, workers, women, their driver called back that this was the monument to the blockade during the Great Patriotic War. The main line of defense against the Germans had been two kilometers away; the monument marked where the relief forces had broken through to the jubilant Leningraders in 1945.

As they neared the heart of town the buildings sank, grew lower, became stone and plaster instead of preformed concrete. Dostoevsky's city. Dan remembered Raskolnikov stalking the slums and bars of the Haymarket, his crime gnawing at his sanity. The overcoated people, the babushkaed women, looked ground down and afraid, as if even after the fall of the Party so many years of state terror had milled deep into their souls. The only spots of color were advertisements for Western liquors and cigarettes. They crossed bridges, islands, more bridges. A golden spike jabbed the sky; the Admiralty Tower. A turn-of-the-century cruiser he guessed was *Aurora*. Spaced between the palaces, glimpses of lead gray sea. White-gloved policewomen waved them through barricades. Trucks filled with troops idled on the side streets.

Their hotel was a Scandinavian-style aluminum-sheathed central block with two even taller wings. The limos deposited them before a reception table marked with the U.S. flag, one among dozens cracking in the chill wind. It overlooked a shingle beach and then the Baltic. He didn't see any ice yet, but to judge by the temper of the wind, it would be forming soon. Blair smiled at him over bent heads.

Dan was working his way toward her when he bumped into Dina White. The State staffer was supporting a bent senior with a fringe of cottony hair. He looked feeble and, without even a topcoat, was seriously underdressed for the windchill. White said, "Dr. Sola, this is Commander Lenson, National Security Council. Dr. Umberto Sola, director of the Office of Nuclear Affairs."

They shook hands, but the old man dropped his grasp as a dark-eyed woman in a business suit and fur hat whacked her clipboard against the table for attention.

She said her name was Larissa Fyodorovna. She worked for the Russian government, and her assignment for the next three days was to make the U.S. delegation comfortable, welcome, and happy. Which she sounded determined to make happen come what may. Dan leafed through his welcome packet as they trailed her through an entrance hall.

He caught up to Blair as they climbed a staircase in blond wood and mauve carpeting. Larissa, chattering explanations in English and for some reason French too, took them into a business center. Yet another area held "technical facilities," library, dining areas. . . . Only gradually did he realize how huge the complex was.

Behind them the press peeled off to a media lounge. Everything was new but already worn around the edges, and the staff, except for Fyodorovna, didn't seem all that interested in their guests. The two-room suite a bored escort showed him to was adequate, no more, with a sterile air that made him uncomfortable. It was icy cold, too. He turned the thermostat up and stood before a casement window. It overlooked a cruise passenger terminal, with a small ship flying Dutch colors.

When he turned around, he was alone, though he'd thought Blair was behind him. He went back to the elevators, looking for her blond height. Instead he caught sight of Larissa again, who was waving her clipboard and screaming at a porter.

Somehow they'd been booked in separate rooms. The desk people were uncooperative and belligerent. They insisted the reservations were correct. The Defense people had a separate block from State and the White House. Dan was frustrated, but assumed they'd get it straightened out. They'd talked about getting away together. He wanted to see the Central Naval Museum; she wanted to see the Hermitage, though she'd been before on other jaunts.

He finally found her room. When she said, "Hey, come in," he rotated, looking up, and whistled. Three big rooms, with a knockout sea view and a curved steel staircase leading up to a loft.

"You should see the bathroom," she said.

"You live nice up here."

"Up here?"

"They've got me in the other wing. Nothing like this."

"Well, go back and get your suitcase," she said, smiling. He held her off to look at her. She was so slim and honed the air around her seemed to glow. She met his lips in a kiss, then kneaded his neck. "How is it today?"

"Not too bad, actually."

"I have to have dinner with my people. To get our positions straight."

"Need company?"

"Sorry, honey, this'll be a working meal. Why don't you just get some rest?" She gave him another quick kiss and patted his arm. "And I'll be back, and we can go down to the bar or something before it gets too late."

But as it turned out he slept through the afternoon and night, more tired than he'd realized from the stress and long hours. He was vaguely aware of her sliding in next to him, sometime late, but didn't come fully awake. The next morning she had to shake him into consciousness to make the limo shuttle out to Tsarskoye Selo for the opening ceremonies.

The space was unashamedly opulent: a massive ballroom

at the Catherine Palace, half baroque fantasy, half barbaric nightmare; the walls seemed to be made of solid gold. Three speakers kicked off: a UN diplomat from a Geneva-based center, the colonel general in charge of the Twelfth Directorate of the Ministry of Defense of the Russian Federation, and Dr. Sola. The old man still looked wilted, but lectured with messianic fervor on the need to secure both nuclear weapons and nuclear materials.

Dan listened with rapt attention. Probably alone among all those in the magnificent room, he'd experienced a nuclear detonation close up. He could put faces to the dead. Had seen men and women he was responsible for blinded, flesh roasted on their bones by the thermal pulse. He got letters from them every week, telling him about their recurrent nightmares, their white blood cell counts, and most poignant, thanking him for saving the ship.

He wished again he hadn't taken *Horn* in so close. No one had told him a nuclear weapon might be aboard the trawler. But he still felt guilty, and figured he always would.

Sola said, "At Princeton I was privileged to work with Dr. J. Robert Oppenheimer, the scientific director of the Manhattan Project. Before he died he said to me, 'The genie won't go back into the bottle, for me. But maybe he will in your lifetime.' And ever since, that is what I have worked toward.

"The theft of one nuclear weapon, or of fifteen kilos of enriched metal, would inflict suffering never seen on the face of the globe since 1945.

"This is not just a problem for the United States, or Russia, or the European Union. It is a problem for every country that harbors a dissatisfied minority, an insurgent group, possibly even one madman with enough resources and helpers.

"When I wonder why this nightmare has not taken place yet, I have only one answer. We have been fortunate beyond our deserts. Humanity has not been granted a pass from catastrophe. We have given our very existence into pawn."

The ballroom was silent when he bowed his white-maned

head. His audience dispersed with uneasy coughs, clearings of throats, to the labor of the day.

That afternoon Dan sat in on a breakout panel on nuclear-materials protection, control, and accounting. Mainly it focused on which tracking software to buy. He was standing in the lobby afterward hoping for the coffee break noted in the program, though no one was setting up for it, when Dr. White grabbed his arm. "Dan."

"Present."

"We have a problem. Umberto's taken ill."

Dan said he was sorry to hear that, then blinked as she asked him to substitute the next morning on a panel titled "Disposal of Legacy Nuclear Components." "We don't have anyone else who can step in," she told him. "The moderator's the deputy minister of atomic energy of the Russian Federation. We have someone from the UK, a representative from the Chinese State Science and Technology Commission, and one government rep each from Ukraine, Kazakhstan, and Belarus. What we don't have is an American."

"I don't even know what 'legacy components' are," Dan said. "Maybe Dr. Sola'll bounce back by tomorrow."

"Umberto's dying. The only reason he came is because this is more important to him than his comfort, maybe his life. I can't do it, I'm on another panel. The White House is on board with this push, isn't it?"

Dan said unwillingly, "Well, yeah. But I—"

"So you'll sit in? I have some papers you can read tonight. To get familiar with the various alternatives."

Dan thought that over, making sure he was covering not just his own druthers but his direction from the assistant national security adviser. Gelzinis had told him the administration policy was to push hard on both threat reduction and further arms reductions. Reducing the weapons the other side held would give the president chips to keep trimming the defense budget. "If that's what you need me to do."

"Our official stance, State favors return of all weapons

still held by the successor states to the USSR. I mean, the CIS. But you don't have to say much. Just be there, and fix the little U.S. flag in front of you so it comes out clear in the pictures. Can you do that?"

"I guess so," he told her. "On one condition."

"Which is?"

"Find me a cup of coffee."

She looked taken aback, then put out. But at last muttered, "I'll see what I can do."

That evening he and Blair finally got away. Neither to the Hermitage nor the Naval Museum, but a reception at Petrodvorets. Peter the Great's "Great Palace" lay west of the city, on a range of low hills overlooking the sea. As their limo trailed its headlights down the coast road he could see out in the black the distant twinkle of Kronstadt, a Russian and then a Soviet and now a Russian naval base again. He thought of all the neglected, poorly guarded reactors over there and shivered.

He was going to have to look intelligent tomorrow, at a mike with some very savvy people. He'd barely had time to glance over the studies and monographs. "Legacy" systems were nuclear and missile components stranded in the various republics when the Soviet tide had receded. Those in the earliest states to go—Latvia, Lithuania, Estonia—had been pulled back in good order. Those in the "Bubbastans," Statespeak for the Muslim-populated republics, had not. Which was where the device that had devastated *Horn* had probably come from, according to the findings of the board of inquiry.

"You're quiet," Blair said.

"So are you." She was wrapped in a heavy coat. He put his arm around her in the backseat. "Do any good today?"

"Maybe we did."

She told him about her committee meeting, on tactical nuclear weapons. He was about to say he'd be on display tomorrow when the heavy Chaika wheeled uphill and there was the palace, a kilometer of shimmering light: windows, arches, cornices, balustrades, cascades, fountains, statuary groups. As the car glided to a stop soldiers sprang forward to open their doors.

He was in uniform: the formal white gloves, blue short jacket, white shirt with studs, bow tie, gold cummerbund, and high-waisted trousers of mess dress blue. He left his cap with a bowing soldier on the way into the Chesme Hall. He patted Blair's arm and said to stay put, he'd get the drinks.

But as he'd started to notice, in Russia no one drank anything nonalcoholic. Finally he talked one of the soldier waiters into opening a bottle of *voda gazifie*. He took Blair her wine and found her deep in conversation; she accepted the glass without looking at him.

Taking the hint, he circled off on squeaky parquet, sipping the sparkling water as he inspected huge paintings of forgotten battles hung so high it pinched his neck to look up at them. Each canvas was huge enough to serve as the topsail of one of those long-vanished men-of-war.

He felt both out of place and perfectly at ease. It was like a formal dance in Memorial Hall at Annapolis. He slipped among diplomats, officers, consular personnel and their elegantly dressed ladies. A few even of what he guessed were the new *biznessmen*. Larissa was speaking rapidly with her flat expression to a man in gray. Solas, looking cadaverous, sat in a carved chair with his back to a painted door as another elder statesman gesticulated.

A group of soldiers in 1945-ish baggy uniforms and high boots took center stage, singing Red Army songs that the Russians roared out along with them. Gradually, like diffusing isotopes, the guests parted into separate groups. He found himself near a group in the dark blue naval-style uniforms of their respective countries. Englishmen, Dutch, many Russians. A Britisher was drawling out a tale of sailing the Baltic in the seventies when Dan felt a tug on his sleeve. He turned to confront an unfamiliar face, a shock of blond hair.

"I think I know you. No?"

Dan studied him. Slavic cheekbones, clear blue eyes. Buttoned-tight formal blues.

"Gaponenko. Grigory Vasileyevich. And you are . . . Lenson, no? Lenson. Daniel, right?" He pronounced it *Den-yell.* "Ten years ago now. No, more. I was captain lieutenant then. *Politruk,* on *Razytelny.*"

Dan remembered then. Recalling a leaky, sinking skiff bobbing in the blue clear of the Windward Passage, and a shape pushing up under the topaz haze of turbine exhaust. The reluctantly recognized silhouette of a Krivak-class destroyer.

"Den-yell. Yes? You recall me now?"

He said he did, and they pumped hands with more warmth than had been present, Dan thought, when Gaponenko's frigate had pulled him out of the water after a night of hurricane seas. He wondered if the Cuban woman and her baby had ever made it to shore.

Gaponenko was chattering away in a lubricated amalgam of languages. He told Dan he was a *polkovnik kapitan* now, captain first class. When Dan told him where he worked now, Gaponenko's eyes widened. "*T'chort vozmi!* The White House? I am much impressed. Hey, you have 'dark eyes' with me."

Dan had a lot of trouble convincing him he didn't want one, he didn't drink anymore. Finally the Russian desisted, though he went on marveling at how young Dan looked. "*Americanyets,* they don't age like us. Especially the women. Oh, you see that over there? Look at that fucking blonde. How fucks-able, no? How old you think she is?"

"That's my wife," Dan said. Blair was wearing a deceptively casual silk ensemble. The blouse was black and the pants were sheer, with lace cutouts at midthigh and silver heels with starbursts of glittering gems. Her hair was up; simple but elegant turquoise earrings played off her eyes. Her skin glowed like vanilla ice cream beneath the ruddy spectrum of the chandeliers, and an admiring circle surrounded her as she laughed, almost spilling her wine.

"*Sik'in sin!* She is your wife? You are damn lucky sailor."

"That's true," Dan said.

A soldier held out a tray of vodkas, brandies, sliced cheese and sausage, and caviar. Gaponenko grabbed greedily. Dan rubbed his mouth, smelling the booze up close.

"You here for conference? What you think of our average Russian house?" His former captor hooted, waving his glass at the masonry and chandeliers and architecture.

"Very impressive."

"Germans destroyed it all. What could not evacuate, they destroyed. Blew up palace. Blew up hydraulic works. Melted statues. What you see here"—he swept a paw, and Dan saw he was quite drunk—"twenty years, but we build all again. Did you *Americanyets* really think we wanted another war?"

"You were building a lot of missiles, too."

"Ah, only defend, only defend. Russians peace-loving people. There's my boss. Let's go meet my boss."

Grabbed around the neck, Dan was dragged willy-nilly into a ring that lurched unevenly to let him in. All as bombed as Gaponenko. The "boss" had three stars on his shoulder boards. Gaponenko called him *viz admiralya.* Dan caught his own name. Their eyes snapped to his when Gaponenko said, *"On naznatye na White House tep'yer."* The boss— Yermakov—asked something. Gaponenko replied placatingly, but it didn't seem to work. He shook his head at Dan, looking chastened.

"So, you think you have defeated us," the admiral said. He didn't sound happy.

"I think both sides have defeated war," Dan said.

The other officers guffawed when this was translated. But they sounded hostile. He was beginning to think this wasn't a good idea when Yermakov snagged his sleeve. Dragged him close, and said in English better than Gaponenko's, "You think you have defeated us. That there is only one great power now. But alone, you will become everyone's target. This is the dialectic of history."

"We'll be smart enough to tread lightly. But I don't want to argue with you, sir."

"Don't want to argue? Then listen! De Bari thinks he can threaten Russia. Make us destroy arms. Well. You can tell your people this president will not be so for long. *Then* we will step back into the light. Regain all we lost. We will not bow. We will restore the might of our armed services. Tell that to your people, so they do not make further mistakes."

Dan was confused until he realized that by "this president" the three-star must mean not De Bari, but Yeltsin. An aide put a restraining hand on the admiral's arm. The senior officer shook it off. Raised his voice. "He will not be there! It is us you will have to deal with. You will learn this soon."

Gaponenko pulled him away. "The *viz admiralya* is very potted," he said. "Too much *khanyahk o eysse*. Sorry to subject you to such no-culture behavior."

Dan said that was all right, but the captain begged Dan not to report the conversation. He didn't want his boss to get in trouble. Dan nodded, half agreeing, and Gaponenko, looking worried, moved off.

He caught up to Blair and pried the hopefuls off her. It was getting late. But they were in one of the great palaces of the world. "Let's go for a walk," he pressed her. "See the gardens."

"It's awfully cold out there." But at last he got her into her coat.

They walked beside a long pool, drained except for black ice at the bottom. The fountains were shrouded with canvas. The sea wind breathed of the imminence of Russian winter. He looked up and halted, watching gauzy draperies of delicate light ripple against the unwinking stars.

"The aurora," she said, and he made out her face, up-turned, just barely visible in the unearthly fire.

After a time he said, "I just had an interesting conversation."

They walked on, the wind buffeting them as he told her

about it. "That sounds like something you should report," she said.

"I don't think so. Some disappointed admiral shooting his mouth off?"

Blair said she meant the reactions of the younger officers, the colonel types, when he'd threatened Yeltsin. "There've been rumors. Some of the bureaucrats are trying to persuade the generals to turn back the clock. Restore their privileges. That's why I'm not sure De Bari's going in the right direction, trying to downsize."

He blinked. "That's administration policy, isn't it?"

"Just because it's policy doesn't mean I don't have my doubts. Gerry Edwards thinks maybe it'd be better to wait a few years, make sure they've really changed."

"The veep? I hear he's kind of out of step with the rest of the party."

"He's out on the right wing, if there is a right wing. But that doesn't necessarily mean he's wrong."

Dan wasn't really paying attention. He slipped his hand under heavy cloth, discovered within a velvet warmth. He nuzzled her ear. "Let's go back to the hotel."

"You feel like it?"

"Yeah."

"Really?"

"Well, we have to try to find out."

"I don't mean just that," she said quietly. "I've been trying to bring this up for a while."

"What does that mean?"

"The worse things get, the less you say. Maybe that's good at sea, but between two people, it's counterproductive."

"Guilty."

"It's not funny. We don't have much time together. When we do, and I try to talk about something important, you dismiss it or change the subject. As if you're embarrassed. Or don't really care." She looked out over the darkness. "I guess I'm just losing my illusions about us. And that's not easy to deal with."

That hurt. "What's *important* to me is you and Nan, and

my duty to my country and the people I lead. Those are my priorities. If you're talking about my career again, that comes out at around item five or six. It's just not that all-fucking-important to me."

"You think it's easy trying to close bases? Keep the machine running on less and less money, and the brass fighting me every step of the way? But since what happened on your ship . . . you're someplace else. I've tried to not add to your problems. But there's something going on I don't understand."

He wanted to punch the stone wall. She didn't understand *at all*. "I'm just trying to *hold myself together*, Blair. I have to control what I think, what I say. I feel guilty. I feel angry. If I just let it all hang out—"

"I'm trying to allow for that. I know you're trying not to take the drugs, and I respect that. And I guess not being able to . . . get it up, can't be that great for a guy. Though obviously I have no idea. I certainly won't find out from *you*."

"You want to dissolve the partnership, fucking tell me. Okay? I don't want to be the last one to know."

"Yeah—you sound angry now. At least that's real."

"It's all *real*. It's just that it's not stuff you have to chew over and over."

"I just believe in talking about things instead of ignoring them. So, when you want to talk—well, come back and we'll talk. But till then—there's not much point to it. Is there?"

Then she was gone. Gone from the sea-cold and silent shifting aurora, back toward the earthly glittering inside. Her heels tapping across stone laid back when Russia had been an autocracy. The property of one man. Before it had become the property of all.

"Testing. Testing. Can you hear us in back?"

The conference hall at the Pribaltyskaya was not exactly crowded, but there was enough of an audience that he felt nervous. Then thought: Get real. After all you've been through, what's a little public speaking? He and the other conferees took their seats, eyeing each other like strange dogs shoved into the same cage. The Ukrainian adjusted his little tricolor. Dan remembered White's instructions, and adjusted his own banner so it was clearly visible. The reporters and photogs in the front row were focusing on him. The hot lights felt good.

The heating in Blair's room hadn't worked very well, and the wind, whistling and buffeting the warped casements all night long, had made him dream of the sea. He'd been on some ship that was no ship he'd ever served on and at the same time all the ships he'd ever served on. He'd been the skipper. Running, for some terrible but unknown reason, at full speed through the fog. Filled with dread, waiting for the crash, the impact . . .

Blair had been gone when he woke. He'd made it through another few pages of the briefing materials over a skimpy breakfast. The coffee was water-weak, and when he asked for more the waiter snorted in disbelief. So he felt both jumpy and not very alert. Two men were setting up a slide projector that looked as if it had been designed to bolt onto a tank.

"I had expected Dr. Solas . . . ?" offered a cultured Oxbridge accent from the seat next to him.

"Not feeling well," Dan said.

"The czar's revenge? I hear it's going around."

He didn't elaborate, not knowing if Solas's affliction was public knowledge or not. "Dan Lenson. Stand-in, at short notice." They shook hands.

The chair opened with a long statement, which Dan was able to follow in simultaneous translation through earphones. Droningly factual, detailing what had existed and where, what had been destroyed or deactivated, what had been agreed on and what deferred to a later date. All nuclear weapons had been removed from Eastern Europe, the Baltic republics, Azerbaijan, and Armenia. Unfortunately, Russia was undergoing a period of insecurity and economic instability and could offer little in the way of resources to her former republics.

Dan had been stunned, reading through the materials, at how much the Soviets had left behind, and how little attention had been devoted to its security until very recently indeed. There'd been finger-pointing, but no action. The second speaker, from Belarus, was in that tradition. He sounded by turns apologetic and belligerent. The new republics had pressing challenges. The Russians had treated them as dumping grounds. The international community owed them recompense for their suffering.

The chairman put his oar in here. Weapons had been based in the republics not to "protect Russia," but to defend the entire state, which had then included the Belorussian Soviet Socialist Republic. The other answered angrily; his country had been *occupied*, not defended. Nor had the Russians honored their promises to permit Belarus to monitor the destruction process, to guarantee weapons were really being destroyed.

Dan cleared his throat, exchanging glances with the Briton, who interposed himself, attempting to move the discussion past recriminations. After muttered imprecations both sides subsided.

Time for the U.S. statement. Which he had in front of him, in fourteen-point caps. Apparently Solas was nearsighted. The chairman got his name right introducing him, though someone had finessed his title to "Mr. Daniel V. Lenson, U.S. National Security Council, Liaison for Threat Reduction." He read out eight minutes of bland assurances of how important reducing the nuclear threat was. Unlike the old man's impassioned declamation the night before, this read like oatmeal. Still, it felt good, putting it on the record. It ended with the announcement that Washington was pledging $12.5 million to the destruction and removal program as part of the president's Threat Reduction Initiative.

The representative from Ukraine spoke next. She said serenely that all nuclear weapons would be gone from Ukrainian territory by the end of the current year. The quadripartite U.S.-Russian-Kazakh-Belarusian declaration to be signed as the capstone to parallel negotiations to this conference would underline that commitment.

The tone changed when the delegate from Kazakhstan got the mike. He shouted directly at the chairman, in a threatening snarl. Dan watched faces alter as the translation filtered through the earphones.

Kazakhstan had acquiesced in the Lisbon Protocol to relinquish all strategic weapons over a seven-year period. It had also agreed, in principle, to the removal of hundreds of tactical nuclear weapons on its territory. The Kazakh government had implemented robust security. Rumors of unguarded weapons were false. However, aid promised by Russia, the United States, and others had never come. Extensive areas of radiological contamination from tests and accidents remained, especially around Semipalatinsk. Thousands of citizens suffered from radiation-induced cancers. The materials in the warheads were valuable property. Nor had Russia honored promises to allow Kazakhs to ensure that evacuated weapons were really being destroyed. As had also been pointed out by his friend from Belarus.

Therefore, President Nazarbayev had decided not to authorize the removal of the remaining R36M missiles from Kazakhstan. The country did not intend to use the weapons, but had to keep in mind its own security in an unstable region. Kazakhstan needed assistance and compensation, and a public apology for Russian actions there as well. Until these conditions were met, the missiles would stay. He spared a glare for Dan and the Chinese panelist too.

Flipping through his references, Dan saw that the R36M was known in the West as the SS-18.

With that knowledge came dread. A huge fourth-generation ICBM with ten one-megaton warheads, the R36M was bigger than the U.S. Peacekeeper and housed in deep, hardened silos. The M2 was a late-eighties variant, which meant they'd be both accurate and in decent shape.

Kazakhstan had been left with 104 of them at the breakup. If it kept them, a poor, Islamic, and increasingly

corrupt and authoritarian country would wield a massive and
invulnerable nuclear arsenal for many years to come.

He didn't think this was a good idea, and judging by the
silence after the Kazakh's speech, no one else did either.
The chairman looked furious but wasn't saying a word.
Looking along the table, Dan didn't see anyone else reaching for the mike.

Reluctantly, he pulled it toward him, reminding himself
to speak calmly and to accuse no one of anything. To feel
his way forward, the way he'd seen the State people doing in
the other panels. They usually started off by rephrasing
what somebody they disagreed with had said, in the passive
voice.

"The, uh . . . distinguished delegate from the Republic of
Kazakhstan has advanced several reasons for abrogating his
country's obligations under the Lisbon Protocol, which was
signed by President Nazarbayev signed"—he glanced at his
notes—"three years ago. If I can summarize. They are, that
assurances of foreign help in cleaning up contamination and
to bring medical assistance to those ill as a result of testing
activities have not been followed through on; that turning the
weapons over would be divesting Kazakhstan of valuable resources; that they were not confident that weapons turned
over were actually being destroyed; and finally, that retain-
ing the weapons would enhance the republic's security."

"And an apology," murmured the Brit.

"And an apology from the Russian Federation, successor
state to the Soviet Union."

The Kazakh nodded briefly, arms folded.

"With the chairman's permission?" Dan glanced at the
Russian general, who was sitting with arms folded too. No
apologies from that quarter.

He cleared his throat, wishing they had water to sip, to
stall with, while he figured out what the hell he was doing.
"Uh, addressing those issues one by one. First. Far from
ameliorating the situation left behind by previous regimes,
maintaining a nuclear force will soak up funds needed for
those very tasks of decontamination and health care. Far

from being valuable resources, though the fissionable materials may have a certain economic value, these advanced missiles and associated systems will probably prove a liability, not an asset, over the long run, because of maintenance costs.

"Holding back weapons is not the way to assure yourself that those taken out of service will be destroyed. Working with the UN and other concerned agencies may be a better way to move toward that goal.

"Finally, the idea that nuclear weapons bring 'stability' in some form may be a misapprehension. Certainly both Russia and the U.S. can testify to that outcome. Twenty thousand—plus warheads on either side didn't seem to bring any more stability, or security, than when there were a hundred. Or maybe, none."

He didn't know how well the translators were keeping up. He couldn't tell from the expressions in the front rows. His fellow panelists looked interested, though. So he took a breath and plunged on.

"Yet the concern about security is real. It seems to me the way forward may be to address the delegate's concerns in this area. Maybe we need to discuss a joint guarantee of his country's security. Perhaps by the U.S., Russia, and possibly China as well."

After a moment of silence the Kazakh said something, which Dan got a moment later through the headphones: "A guarantee? From exactly what?"

Dan referred to his briefing materials, having found a sentence he liked. "Against threats of use of nuclear weapons, threats of conventional force, threats of resort to force, and economic pressure."

He was not quite done with this sentence when he caught undisguised horror on the faces of both the British and the Chinese delegates. The Brit was whispering, "Not on your Nelly." The Russian had gone white. The Kazakh was still sitting impassively, listening to the translation.

Dan sucked in his breath, realizing he'd done something wrong, but not knowing what.

Both the Chinese and the Kazakh were beginning to speak when his Oxbridge neighbor put in, having wrestled the mike out of Dan's hands, "Of course, this is offered on a speculative basis, for discussion by the appropriate authorities. I believe that is all the United States' participant is placing on the table. And Her Majesty's government would no doubt be glad to assist in such discussions, in the interests of fostering mutual understanding. Should the responsible principals desire our participation."

Dan wasn't stupid, so when their eyes switched back to him he said meekly, "Uh, that's right. On a . . . speculative basis. For discussion by the appropriate authorities."

"The record should show that," the Brit delegate prompted. Dan said into the mike, "The record should show that: on a speculative basis only, no commitments by the United States or any other government."

He was sweating by the time the discussion broke. Seeing the punji pit he'd almost stepped into. As they stood to polite applause he muttered to his new friend, "Thanks for saving my can there."

"We must all help one another," the Briton said quietly, and limped off the platform. Dan, watching, realized he had an artificial leg.

It took twenty minutes after the panel ended for Dr. White to catch up with him. In fact she was lying in wait for him outside the men's room. Her mouth looked as if it had been drawn with white chalk. "Tell me you didn't make a public commitment to a security guarantee for Kazakhstan," she hissed.

"Uh, it might have started out that way. But the situation got retrieved."

He told her about the British diplomat's skillful pullback of his gaffe. White fitted a hand over her eyes. "But the transcript. What'll the *transcript* say?"

"I got to the woman who's producing it. From the Carnegie Endowment. It won't be in there."

She wavered, caught between further anger and, he saw, the knowledge that she'd asked him to sit in; chewing further on him, or passing the ding up the line, would be admitting her mistake. At last she said he had to watch everything he said. Even a hint that the U.S. was considering a security commitment in central Asia would trigger every immune system left in Russia, and send the Chinese to the battlements as well.

But maybe he'd succeeded in retrieving his misstep, because he hadn't heard anything since, no calls from a livid Sebold or outraged cablegrams from the president's personal son of a bitch, Holt. And the parallel negotiations must have gone all right, because *Air Force One* landed again that afternoon, back from central Asia with De Bari and the presidents and other plenipotentiaries from the region. Blair was invited to the signing ceremony for the protocol or whatever it was, Dan hadn't gotten a clear picture exactly what, back in the Catherine Palace. But he thought he might as well make himself invisible for a while.

H e woke suddenly in the icy dark, clawing for the bedside light. Gusts rattled the windows, shrieking. This time he'd heard them screaming, behind the wind. The ones he'd left behind, while he went on. But the dark presence was with him. He couldn't see it. Only feel its paralyzing closeness, as if it were lying next to him.

When he reached out, her side of the bed was empty.

The bedside phone beeped again. He realized it was what had woken him. As he lifted it even the memory of the dream faded, leaving only a lingering terror. Black outside the window. The sea crashing far below. "Yeah?"

"Lenson?" An unfamiliar voice. Male.

"Yeah. Who's this?"

"You might want to check on your wife."

He tried to focus. It felt as if he were still in the dream, or maybe in another one, a follow-on, the way dreams ca-boosed from one scene to another. "What? What'd you say?" He wasn't sure if that was exactly what the guy had said. It wasn't the hotel desk—the accent was American. "*Check* on her? Is that what you said?"

"Try the third floor."

"The third floor . . . wait. Who *is* this?"

The rattle of a handset.

Squinting at his watch, he couldn't tell whether it was 4 a.m. or 4 p.m. Anonymous calls . . . nightmares . . . But where *was* she? He called out, but got no answer from the loft. She wasn't in the bathroom, either.

At last he pulled on pants and shoes and went out into the corridors. They were cold as meat lockers. When he saw his breath in the air he wished he'd put on a shirt too. But he kept going, though he wasn't sure what he was looking for. The third-floor elevator was locked out. He got off on the fourth and walked down.

He was coming down the hall when he saw them waiting. For a moment he didn't recognize them, or realize what they were there for. He wondered again if this was all part of the dream. The cold. The loneliness. The voice on the phone. The stocky men in sport coats, just standing around. Relaxed yet alert, heads cocked as they stared at him. As if listening to voices that whispered on and on through the wires that led to their ears.

WASHINGTON, D.C.

Back in counterdrug, two days later. Exhausted, jet-lagged, he gripped his skull in both hands as Meil-hamer ladled out every item of minutiae that had gone through the office since he'd left. But he wasn't listening. He was back again in that moment when he'd realized what the Secret Service agents meant. Whose suite Blair must be visiting. At four in the morning.

And, no, he hadn't made the first motion toward that door. Not only because it would have been futile to try to force his way in. He didn't want to face it, or her. Not feeling the way he did.

Because he wanted to kill them both, then himself. Tear her, and the man she was with in there, into bloody, palpitating fragments with his bare hands.

Instead he'd gone back to the room. Waiting, awake in the dark, for her to come back. But she hadn't.

He'd watched *Air Force One* take off from the air lounge at Pulkovo, where White and Solas and the rest of the U.S. conference team were waiting for the other 747, the backup. The central Asians and their entourages had taken up so much space there wasn't any left for lower-ranking staff. And then it was delayed. So he hadn't seen her there, either, and had gotten in at five that morning eastern standard time, without a wink of sleep en route, and come straight to the Old Executive because he couldn't think of anything else to do.

". . . and you might want to sign this card. Ellie Ihlemann had her boy. Seven pounds eight ounces." Dan stared at a Polaroid of a wizened, scarlet humanoid. Scribbled his signature. Added *Get well soon,* which he realized too late didn't jibe with the sugary printed sentiment, or even make sense.

He cleared his throat and tried to concentrate. On anything . . . "Tell me about the Baptist, Bry. He popped up yet?"

"I try to stay clear of the operational side. You should too."

He ignored that. "Who's in?"

"Bloom and Ed Lynch. Oh, and Marty's back from Burma. Alvarado's down in Miami trying to help pick up the pieces. That boy's a real hard worker. Always volunteering. Always the last to leave."

"What do you mean?"

"I mean he's always the one who locks up," his assistant said. "Don't know what he's working on—it's always in Spanish. But he's always there, beavering away."

Dan was asking him to send Miles Bloom in when the DEA agent poked his head around the jamb. Dan beckoned him in, saying to Meilhamer, "Okay, then what's on my plate on the administrative side?"

"Nothing."

"Nothing?"

"You gave me signing authority when you left. Remember? Copies of everything that went out are in that blue folder. You've got a chance to catch up, next couple of days. Mrs. C'll be out of town with the president. Manila this time. It'll be quiet around here."

Meilhamer smoothed his shirtfront, smiling and bobbing on his toes. Dan gave him the compliment he so obviously wanted and nodded to Bloom again to come in.

The DEA liaison brought him up to date on the fallout from what was looking more and more like a fiasco in Miami. The raid had netted lots of bodies, but either has-beens, blasts from the past, or with no discoverable connection to drugs at all. Local consuls, political donors, media figures whose arrests had embarrassed the cops who made the tags. "It was a setup," Bloom said. "Same as with the shoot-down. The only single thing we did they didn't expect was bust the Haiti meet."

"Which we ad-hoced at the last minute, from Key West." Dan eyed the door Bloom had closed. "What you're saying is, we have a leaker."

"Either that or they're reading our comms."

"Is that likely?"

"It's never *likely,* but ordure occurs. I'd suspect a human source, myself."

"Somebody in this office?"

"Could be one of a long string on this one. All the way from the top on down to the foot soldiers."

Dan remembered how much Tony Holt had known about the operation. The rumors about drug use among the civilian staff. De Bari supposedly blowing coke in the governor's mansion. His wife's ties to organized crime. He blinked, shook them off. The administration had counted on this bust to prove it was hammering the drug trade. Giving it away wouldn't have been in its interest.

What about his own people? Everybody in his office had known about Hot Handoff. Should he start suspecting them? Lynch, Harlowe, Sergeant Ihlemann—she saw a lot, heard a lot, at that front desk. Alvarado—could the cartel have gotten hold of one of Luis's relatives, squeezing him that way? Certainly the Coast Guard officer was closely associated with South American operations. The banal, cunning little Meilhamer? Bloom himself? He cleared his throat, watching Miles watching him and knowing he was thinking the same thing about him. "So . . . where to from here?"

"On the cartel? I'll pass along DEA's view. Smartest thing we can do right now is to let the silt settle. Know how when you're spearfishing, you go for a big langouste and miss, he kicks a lot of sand up into the water? We still picked up some heavy players in Haiti. A clear gotcha. Let's see how things shake out with Tejeiro, and where Nuñez pops up next."

Dan swiveled, looking out and down a hundred feet into

the loading area. The GSA guys were playing b-ball with trash bags again. One scored a two-pointer as he watched. Unfortunately the bag broke, showering documents all over the asphalt. Yeah. Great security.

He was struggling with the old craving. But getting drunk wasn't going to help with Blair, or Nuñez, or with anything else that was wrong. He needed sleep, and to get things straight with her, one way or the other. "Okay, I guess we can let it ride awhile," he said at last. Glad Bloom was here. Behind the breezy facade, the guy was sharp.

"Another issue, if we're done with that, boss."

The first time one of them had called him that. He leaned back. "Shoot."

Bloom cracked the door and yelled, "Ed! Get your ass in here." The Air Force major took the last chair, and they all three sat uncomfortably intimate, knees bumping.

"Here's the picture," Lynch said. "Remember, you told us to keep an eye peeled for anything pointing to a linkup of terrorists and druggies."

"Right."

"Well, the FAA's surfaced something."

Dan told them to go on, and Bloom started. "Kind of a weird indicator; we're not sure what it means. Aviation Administration called it in. Has to do with someone who might be trying to penetrate the cargo-handling setup for UPS."

Lynch told him that United Parcel Service, which most people thought of as the guy in shorts who came to your door in a brown truck, was actually one of the biggest airline operations in the world. "Six hundred airplanes, making it, like, the tenth biggest. That's how the package gets from the truck that picked it up from you, to the truck that delivers it. The Office of Transportation Security/Civil Aviation Security service—that's the part of the Transportation Department that does security on air cargo. They put out a bulletin reporting inquiries by a group in Pomona, California, called International Blessings. They were importing empty containers from Mexico."

"Wait a minute." Dan rubbed his face. "I missed that. What'd you say was in these containers?"

"Nothing."

"I meant originally. When they were shipped."

"There was never *anything* in them. As far as Aviation Security could tell."

"That's illegal? Shipping nothing?"

"Course not. That's why they got bulletined, not charged. There's a write-up, you want to read it?"

"Maybe later. What kind of containers?"

"The usual air cargo boxes. They load up ramps into the plane. Like sea containers, only smaller."

"So they're coming in from Mexico, you think it's drug related? Dry runs for shipping drugs by air cargo? Illegal immigrants? Or what?"

Bloom said, "That's why they liaised up. We put a warning out, thinking yeah, like you said, it might be a new wrinkle on transporting stuff. Using the air cargo system, which is admittedly pretty loosey-goosey security-wise."

"Is it? A new wrinkle, I mean."

"I talked to the guys who looked into it. They X-rayed the containers, put sniffer dogs in and everything. No secret compartments. No traces of coke, opiates, cannabinols. Nada," Bloom said. "That's kind of the universal conclusion."

Dan said, as patiently as he could, "So these idiots were shipping empty containers. Why are you telling me?"

"Because you asked us to pop a flag on links with any kind of terror organization. And this International Blessings is an Islamic outfit. The guys who contracted for the delivery say they're a humanitarian nonprofit, trying to put together a rapid-reaction package to go to Mideast countries suffering natural disasters."

"So it *might* be up and up. Like Catholic Relief, United Jewish Appeal."

Lynch said, "Except what kind of humanitarian supplies would they be importing from Mexico? The guys I talked to over at Transportation were thinking charter fraud, money laundering, some kind of reshipment. But they still haven't gotten a lock on anything actually illegal."

"What about it, Ed? You think this could be terror-related?"

The major said he thought it was more likely drug-related. He couldn't speak specifically to UPS, but as Bloom had said, the international air cargo system was definitely porous. There was no accountability or tracking procedure for consignments. Customs was undermanned, so they didn't actually look inside more than one in a thousand containers, and ramp security—of aircraft at the gate, being loaded and unloaded—was lax.

"There was a drop in theft when containers came in, but the crooks have figured out how to get access. The stats on drug shipments via air container are rising too. A lot of coke moves by air. You see it in walls and ceilings of containers. Shipments of concentrated pineapple juice, fresh asparagus, cut flowers, chocolates. They found some once in teeny plastic bags inside the stomachs of live tropical fish."

They sat digesting that last one, so to speak. Dan remembered the consensus in Key West that now that they had a handle on the seaborne traffic, it would shift west, to air routes over the Mexican border. He shook his head, feeling that sense of sweeping against a rising tide with a busted broom everyone in counterdrug had to come to terms with. "Okay, you mentioned money laundering. How would that work?"

Bloom took that one. "That can run either with the smuggling or on its own. First you collect the currency. That comes from your local distributors, gangs or whatever. You run it through the legitimate banking system first. The cover's gambling profits, or real estate. A lot of the run-up in real estate in L.A. is laundering profits. Shuffle it through wire transfers and cutouts a couple of times, to add smoke. Then it goes overseas."

Dan said, "An aid agency, they're going to be shipping things overseas, not importing them."

"That's why we were checking out the money angle. But we came up as empty as those containers."

"Okay, whichever it is, it sounds like the kind of between-the-cracks stuff we want to keep everybody comparing notes on. Ed, why don't you dig into it a little more, Miles has been putting in a lot of hours lately. Due diligence. Liaise with FBI, DEA, and Transport. Anything else?"

Bloom told him President Tejeiro had asked for a conference in Bogotá in one month with top U.S. and Central American officials, to coordinate a major movement against the cartels, possibly involving military force. General Sevinson, now confirmed as head of DEA, would lead the U.S. delegation. "It's not billed as revenge for their blowing away his kid, but there's not much doubt where Tejeiro is coming from," the agent said. "Even among the Latins, he's known as a guy who keeps score. Help him, you get rewarded. Cross him, he'll fuck you up, no matter how long it takes."

"That's good—from our point of view. But in Bogotá? That's going to take tight security," Dan said. The cartel was wounded, and wounded animals were dangerous. "Does the White House need presence?"

"That's up to Bony Tony. Sevinson might be enough of an executive-side marker. Aside from that, we got this hearing coming up on the the High-Intensity Drug Area program. That's gonna be our big budget Donnybrook. You ever testified before?"

Dan said he'd seen it done, though he hadn't been the guy on the hot seat. He remembered reading about HIDA but didn't recall the specifics. Bloom said Meilhamer knew about it, he'd been fighting for it for three administrations. Dan blinked. Having that come out of left field made him wonder if the grubby little administrator might not be more of a mover and shaker than he looked. It also made him wonder why his second hadn't mentioned that this morning. "Okay, I'll ask him. Get back to work, you guys."

Meilhamer hauled out an immense binder and pointed to two more behind his desk. He said HIDA was the only appropriation that went directly through the counterdrug office, $107.5 million that got allocated to various agencies over and above their operating budgets. Dan saw the idea. A pot of money to throw at emergencies until the dinosaurian budgetary process could lumber around and charge. "I didn't know we had that much cash to play with, Bry. And Miles said you drove getting it?"

Meilhamer smirked modestly. "I had a role."

"Where does it go?"

"It's driven by each region's needs. Like, see this table? It lists where and for what we wrote checks the second quarter. The Drug Squads Initiative in Houston. A Black Ice Task Force in L.A. Tactical monitoring system for the Border Patrol."

"Who decides who gets what?"

"I chair a round table twice a year. The appropriate-level administrators. We hash it out, try to keep a geographic balance, and generally that gets approved pretty much the way we send it in. We try to keep the Hill out of it. Keep it responsive to what the agencies need instead of just porking."

Dan flipped through the binder. He'd have to know it almost cold before the hearing, but his guys would be sitting behind him; they could pass notes if anything tough came up. He wondered if there was enough slack in it to fund something like the Threat Cell.

Meilhamer said, peeling open a Kit Kat, "So how was Leningrad?" Using the old name for the city. And that reminded him all over again. He was back in the corridor looking at the Secret Service agents.

He put the binder down, muttered something, and went out to the hallway. The high corridor echoed. The black stone slabs were cracked. He rubbed his shoe over a tiny misshapen thing that had wiggled in ooze and died a billion years before man had walked the earth. He wasn't ready for this. Not two marriages in a row. But could he really blame her?

What mere mortal could compete with the most powerful man on the planet?

• • •

He thought about calling her at work, having it out over the phone. But it seemed better to do it face-to-face. So he kept at it until after rush hour, then took the Metro home. Stood watching the other riders as they huddled, each in his or her shell of loneliness.

But when he let himself in, the house was quiet. The oak floors shimmered. He found the note anchored on the kitchen island by a bottle of cumin.

> Dan,
>
> I'm headed to the Philippines this afternoon. We need to talk when I get back. It's not something we can do long-distance. There's frozen stuff from Schwan's in the fridge, the turkey mignon and other things you like. Gloria will be in on Tuesday. Her check's on the hall tree.
>
> You need to take better care of yourself. Remember how this was supposed to be a time for you to unwind and get your bearings? But you just seem more and more stressed.
>
> Take care of yourself. We'll talk when I get back.
>
> Yours,
> Blair

He stood holding the note, looking out into the little yard. A black bird hopped around on the bare parched winter ground. Checking it over, inch by inch. It saw him at the window and cocked its head, evaluating him as a possible threat, before going on with whatever it was doing. He stood watching it for quite a while before he went up for a shower.

11

SARAJEVO, BOSNIA

Another plane, but this one a noisy, unheated transport, high-winged and strut-legged, lurching down through bursts of rain into a mist-shrouded valley. Dan sat strapped in beside a whey-faced Dutch major from Amsterdam. Probably, he figured, on the same kind of mission he was.

He was even more exhausted than he'd been back in D.C. three days ago. But getting shot at had a way of jolting you into alertness. Tracers had just come up for the second time, looking like hot wires reaching up for them. The compartment was crammed with troops in light blue helmets. Folded litters were stacked by the rear ramp.

"So who's firing?" he shouted.

The major shouted back, "Who knows? They see a plane, they shoot at it. Just saying, 'Welcome to the former Yugoslavia.'"

It was hard to believe how fast you could go from the Old Executive to a beaten-up, bullet-holed Spanish Army "Aviocar," letting down through a rainstorm toward what might be the site of the worst massacre on European soil since World War II.

Or so some sources said. Others, that it was the biggest hoax since the Man Who Never Was.

Finding out which was going to be his job.

• • •

He'd gotten his orders from Mrs. Clayton, in her office on the main floor of the West Wing. The ceilings were higher there, the decor more impressive, than in the worker-bee cells beneath. Sebold and Gelzinis had been there when the secretary brought him in. "Mr. Lenson," the national security adviser had said, with barely a glance at him. "Ready to do some traveling?"

"Ma'am?"

She'd taken off her reading glasses. And for the first time he'd seen the marks of fatigue on her face. She said slowly, kneading her eyes, "News organizations are reporting that Dutch peacekeeping troops have let Bosnian Serb forces carry out a huge massacre of Muslims."

Gelzinis said, "The UN disarmed them. Made the town what they called a 'safe area.' So they couldn't fight back."

Clayton gave him a cool look, for what reason Dan couldn't guess. "But other sources say the reports are hoaxes. They say the townspeople are hiding out in the woods after evacuating the town during an attack by Ratko Mladic. The UN's holding secret discussions about pulling out of Bosnia. Meaning, we have to come up with a position, a recommendation for the president's response."

Mladic was the Bosnian Serb military leader. "What's the CIA say's happening?" Dan asked.

She frowned. "There's not much coming out of the Agency. I'm not sure why. They just keep saying they're 'preparing a report.' The embassy's lost its usual contacts. Of course, we have imagery. But it doesn't give us what we need. We've got to find out what's going on on the ground."

Gelzinis elaborated. The Bosnian Muslims were begging the UN not to abandon them. The Saudis and Turks wanted to know what was being done to protect the Muslims. The Bosnia working group had just broken from a meeting. They needed a fast, objective opinion, from someone outside State and the other diplomatic and intel stovepipes, on (1) whether there'd actually been a massacre, and (2) whether air and Tomahawk strikes could retrieve the situation.

When he finished, Sebold jumped in. "We know this is outside your current taskings. But this thing's blindsided us. Mrs. C asked who I thought had the smarts and gumption to get in there, with the experience to give us a trustworthy opinion on the missile-strike question. The pointer stopped on Daniel V. Lenson."

They hadn't asked if he wanted to go. But he figured that was because it didn't actually matter.

He'd left D.C. via a Military Air Command flight to Joint Task Force Provide Promise, a U.S. operational headquarters in the NATO compound in Naples. Dan had flown over in khakis, but they told him everybody went in-country in BDUs, the camo battle dress. He drew fatigues, cap, field jacket, socks, and boots. Uniform issue was followed by an update on Bosnia and the UNPROFOR, the United Nations Protection Force.

He'd tried to concentrate, but right now all he retained was seven points. He'd watched so many PowerPoint briefs he was starting to think in bullets:

- Bosnia and Herzegovina, formerly one of the six republics of Yugoslavia, was made up of Bosnian Serbs, Bosnian Croats, and Bosnian Muslims.

- All Bosnians were racially identical and spoke the same language.

- Bosnian Croats were Catholic.

- Bosnian Serbs were Greek Orthodox.

- Bosnian Muslims were Muslim.

- Slobodan Milosevic, the president of Serbia, was grabbing as much land as he could in Bosnia to build a Greater Serbia.

- The whole place was coming apart at the seams.

Or as the briefer, a reserve Navy captain, had put it more succinctly, "Terrible shit's been happening in the Balkans for a thousand years. They took forty years off. Now they're at it again."

Maybe that was flip, Dan thought, peering down between towering mountains. Below their wings a village passed in which every house was roofless, in whose dirt streets no one moved. But what else could you say about a country disintegrating into tribes? For the past couple of years a skin-thin UN contingent supported by NATO air power had kept the lid on. Now it was off again.

The briefer had shaken his hand good-bye. "You know they won't want you there," she'd said.

"The Serbs?"

"Well, them too. But I'm talking about the UN. The chief of staff, Cees Nikolai. Watch out for him."

"He hasn't signed off on me?"

"UNPROFOR isn't a U.S. operation. We have units down along the Macedonian border, but they don't work for Nikolai."

"They don't?"

"No, they're under a Finnish dude who works for the UN commander in Zagreb. But that's separate from the UNPRO-FOR structure. Confused yet?" Dan nodded. "Good, then you're going out oriented properly. Anyway, we've got a liaison who'll meet you, but we most definitely do not have the stick up there. If we told Nikolai you were coming, guess what? You wouldn't go."

"So . . . you didn't," Dan said, getting that sinking feeling again.

"Exactly right, Commander." The captain had patted his back fondly, like an older sister. "You have a *great* time now. Hear?"

For some reason the UN had put its headquarters for the whole Bosnian protection effort in a besieged city under shellfire. Sarajevo lay along a thin blue-and-white lace of river. On the final approach, Dan made out the Olympic stadium, left over from '84. Housing blocks. A sizable downtown, with ten-story buildings. A haze of woodsmoke. Minarets, and church spires, and the needle-and-globe television towers you saw in Bahrain and Saudi. The turboprop, wings groaning and hold-downs rattling, sideslipped precipitously toward a strip that suddenly came into view between steep hillsides. The folded, rounded mountains didn't look too different from those he'd grown up among. That was the creepiest thing of all, how much like home it looked.

The pilot came back and spoke to the Dutchman in Spanish. "Approach control has problems with the runway," his seatmate told Dan. "Let me give you some advice. Wear your flak jacket whenever you're in the open. Be aware of mines. Be especially alert around the cemeteries. They like to plant them there and get the people visiting their dead relatives.

"That's a two-thousand-foot mountain," the major added, pointing off to the south. "They're not supposed to shoot, but we'll still do evasive as we come in. If you look down, you'll see something interesting."

They roller-coastered past the mountain toward the shortest runway he'd ever seen. And there they were, tucked under the trees overlooking the city whose lights were sparkling on here and there down in the shadows of the hills. Artillery. Troops shading their eyes up at them. The drab green, knobby turrets of T-54s. Campfires. Tents. Pickup trucks with what looked like ZSU-44s in tow.

"JNA. Yugoslav Army," the Dutchman said grimly as the fuselage bucked, throwing them together. They grappled like wrestlers, off balance. He pushed Dan away. "The fucking Serbs."

Now and then during the trip, Dan had wondered darkly why Clayton wanted *him* for this. Surely State or CIA could confirm a massacre. Blair was in the Philippines. So it couldn't be that. Or could it? Sending the inconvenient husband off to vanish? Playing Captain What's-his-name . . . Bathsheba's husband . . . started with a U . . . to De Bari's King David?

Or was he going over the cliff, into post-traumatic stress, disorientation, madness? He'd been told before he was prone to imagining more was going on than met the eye. On the other hand, in the China Sea, in the Caribbean, in D.C. years before, more *had*. Like the wisdom scrawled in the ship's heads: Just because you were paranoid didn't mean they weren't out to get you.

Now he took slow, deep breaths as the landing gear shrieked on wet pavement. He tried to divert his apprehension by lacing the too-big boots tighter around two pairs of socks.

Uriah, he thought then, fear settling in his bowels like an impacted turd. The dutiful, unsuspecting Hittite. Who'd snapped off a salute, barked, "Aye aye, sir," and marched off to Rabbah, never to return.

S arajevo International looked like an airport in West Virginia that had been shelled and looted. Battered concrete-block buildings. Barbed wire. A rusty truck loaded with gravel. More gravel lay piled along the runway. Shell holes pocked the tarmac. The French seemed to be running things. At least there were French flags flying. The blue UN banner too. The plane emptied fast, blue-bereted noncoms shouting the troops out. A swarm of hungry-looking handlers clawed at the cargo. A forklift snarled away with the palleted stuff, trickling rice as it jolted over craters.

The mountains looked much higher than from the air. A turbulent river foamed along south of the airstrip. Past it a blue-gray escarpment towered like a barrier between worlds. It was capped with snow. Valleys opened to his left, to his right; ahead loomed an even more enormous peak, so high his neck flashed a twinge as he looked up at it. He remembered watching skiers tear down its flanks on television, years before.

"Let's go," said the Dutchman. "We need to get off this strip."

Dan flinched. Ducking, he followed at a jog through air that was warmer than he'd expected toward the largest building. A huge black U and N were painted on its roof.

He sat nursing a paper cup of Nescafé in a cold office that smelled of piss with Captain Manuel "Buddy" Larreinaga, U.S. Army. The American liaison was dark and short, and his border twang sounded strange in the split heart of Eastern Europe. He and the Dutchman sat on opposite sides of the table in their different green-and-brown camo patterns and did not look at each other. Both smoked, though, and Dan's eyes stung as they went over the route and what might ambush them along the way. He kept expecting the captain to ask exactly why Dan was here, but he never did. As if there was no point questioning anything from Higher.

The hulking armored car Larreinaga called a "transporter" was painted a white that looked dingy at close range. Its cramped interior stank of sweat and cheese and diesel fuel, but Dan felt more secure with steel around him. He clicked open a firing port as they growled and lurched into a city that had undergone a siege almost as long as that of Stalingrad.

The liaison officer told him he was going to have to be alert in the open. It wouldn't hurt to beware of windows too, especially facing south. The city was surrounded, and everyone in it was a target. Bridges, crossroads, streets that weren't masked by buildings, were areas of increased risk. If you had to cross them nobody would laugh if you broke into a jog. The residents had put up signs in the most dangerous areas. He should obey them and cooperate if someone grabbed him to pull him back into cover. "Remember, if you can see a mountain, whoever's on that mountain can see you," Larreinaga said.

The signs were daubed on plywood or plastic sheets or chalked on the walls. In English, French, and what must be Bosnian. The streets were pocked with shellbursts. Some of the black ripped-out stars had been filled with gravel. Others hadn't. Every window had been blown out or shattered. The streets were lined with shipping containers, burned-out buses, wrecked cars, sections of levered-up sidewalk. Two old men huddled over a chess table close under high-school lockers stacked with sandbags. Dan realized they were cover from snipers.

They passed a huge nineteenth-century building, smoke trails like black eyebrows above the empty windows. "That's from the shelling three years back," Buddy said. "These people have been through it. War One, War Two, this is War Three for them. That corner—see the bridge? That's where Gavrilo Princip shot the duke and the duchess. Where World War I started."

Some streets farther on, the transporter slowed. It wove between giant jacks of rusty I-beams and stopped at a checkpoint. Troops with automatic rifles exchanged shouts with the driver. The transmission whined.

Headquarters was a multistory office building that hadn't been spared fragment damage. It was ringed with concertina wire, sandbags, parked transporters, and stacks of rusty containers decorated with large-caliber-bullet holes. Women hoed onions in garden patches no bigger than bedsheets. A desert tan French tank aimed its main gun down the street.

"Keep moving, remember," Buddy said, and they went inside, Dan careful to keep as much metal and concrete between him and the mountain as he could.

The United Nations Military Observers headquarters held Swedes, Turks, Italians, French, Portuguese, British, Belgians, Japanese, Dutch. The UNMOs wore blue berets and all seemed very busy. Larreinaga did what he could, but Dan didn't get much attention. Shunted from office to office, he ended up on the fourth floor. The office was on the north, the safe side, and he could look out over the city.

"Commander Lenson. I trust you had a fast and safe trip in. Cigarette?" said a slight, poised officer whose name tag said B FEVRIER.

"*Non, merci.*" Dan declined the proffered Gauloises bleues.

"We were, I very much regret to say, not prepared for your arrival."

He'd thought about how he should handle this, and decided on low-key first. He also thought it might help to try it in French. "*Je regrette beaucoup d'entendre cela, mon colonel. J'espere que ce sera possible de visiter la site des evenements recentes, en poursuivant les orders de ma gouvernement.*"

Fevrier made a half-concealed grimace, as if tasting a bad peanut. "You will excuse me, but perhaps we should conduct our business in English. I have taken the opportunity of calling the chief of staff, Brigadier Nikolai, about your request. I am sorry to say that though it is our desire to help, it is not possible at present to transport anyone to Srebrenica." He pronounced it *Sebreneetsa*. "We are as you may have observed in the middle of a war. A confused and ugly little conflict. It is not a time for fact-finding missions."

"Nevertheless I must insist. The president wants the situation clarified. It would be very desirable if transport and a small escort—"

Fevrier inclined his head politely, as if being introduced to the dignitary Dan had just invoked. He seemed to be listening. A moment later a heavy, close-by crack rattled the windows. Dan stopped speaking, interrupted not by his courteous interlocutor but by the shell.

Fevrier gestured, leaving a trail of smoke in the air. "A 120 mortar . . . We too would very much like to have the situation 'clarified.' Unfortunately we are attempting to police a state of five million people with seven thousand troops, while both Croats and Serbs are trying to tear it in two. Envision two starving wolves, and a tasty piece of fillet. We simply cannot get you to Srebrenica. The peacekeepers there have been ejected. Local resistance has collapsed. Which means Ratko Mladic is in control. We would like to know what is going on there as much as you would. Naples may know more than we. That is where your Predators are controlled from. Have you checked with them?"

Dan had gone over the pictures the remotely piloted surveillance drones had taken. They showed crowds. Detainees. Then empty fields. But no graves. No clue where they could have gone. *That* was the mystery. But he just said, "May I speak with this Nikolai?"

"Impossible. Far too busy. It might just have been possible to get you in last week. The various factions would let an occasional truck through with supplies for UN Bravo. The Dutch unit there. But now—no. I am so sorry."

"What happened in Srebrenica, Colonel Fevrier?"

The Frenchman blew out and scratched his scalp hard. "The local commander had seven hundred fifty men to cover the perimeter around the enclave. The Muslims refused to disarm. Went out at night raiding. Burned people alive, in their homes. These people are not as helpless as they portray themselves. Nasser Oric—ugly piece of work. Videotapes his victims. Both sides sniped at Bravo. Then three days ago the BSA—Bosnian Serb Army, Mladic's troops—began to push in the perimeter. To try to stop the raids. The Dutch tried to call in air strikes, but they could not be provided until the town had been overrun."

So far every account Dan had heard differed. Sebold had said the UN special representative had refused to give permission for the air strikes, from the on-call carrier force in the Adriatic, until after the town fell. The reserve captain in Naples had said NATO air had actually been aloft, staged out of Italy and orbiting over the Adriatic; but by the time the request was approved in Zagreb, they were too low on fuel to go in. The Dutchman on the plane had said bitterly that his country's contingent had requested support repeatedly and never gotten a reply. And Larreinaga had said the Dutch had cut and run, but admitted they had no heavy weapons, while the Serbs had tanks.

He could see why Clayton wanted eyes on the ground, an unbiased report, if such a thing was possible.

"I'm not here to assign blame," he told Fevrier. "I don't care who's responsible. That's a UN matter. All I want to do is get out there and see what happened."

"Once again, I can't help you." Fevrier stood. "We'll fly you back to Naples tomorrow. Be ready an hour before dawn. That is the safest time. Before they have enough light, on that mountain over there, to aim."

L arreinaga, encountered again downstairs, told him the only place to find a bed was the Holiday Inn. Dan walked over, staying close to the wrecked trucks and buses. The hills reverberated now and then to a falling shell or exploding mine. No one shot at him on the way, though.

"You get one of the good rooms. No view," the clerk joked. In the corridors he saw most had been wrecked, burned, their windows shattered. Some lay open to the wind, and all were unheated. The hallways smelled of shit. The few other guests who passed him wore coats.

He was hungry and realized he'd missed a bet. He should have eaten at the headquarters. He had an MRE pack and a Snickers from his briefcase instead. Tried the faucet, but nothing came out. He changed into civvies, jeans, and a down-filled jacket. Looked at himself in the cracked mirror. Thought about shaving, then figured he'd blend in better if he didn't.

The electricity was out in the first-floor bar, but somebody had an accordion, and candles flickered on the tables. It felt like a bunker in Stalingrad. He got fruit juice that tasted as if it had been canned under Brezhnev. There were a lot of customers, all smoking harsh-smelling local tobacco and talking very loudly above the Polish-sounding music.

He'd thought about this as he was changing, and decided he wasn't going to be on the plane back in the morning. He wasn't going to give up just because the French wouldn't give him a ride. Or because he was scared, though he was. Somebody else must want to find out what had happened. He asked several people if they knew anybody who was trying to get to Srebrenica. They looked at him as if he were nuts and waved him off. Except the last, a gray-haired old man with one eye. He muttered, "The Gypsy bitch. See her? The one drinking shots, in the corner."

She was small-boned and fine-featured, with black shining hair that fell in ringlets. Pale lipstick, and kohl pencilled around the eyes. A worn brown leather jacket, open just enough to show a zip-up blouse the color of plums. Black jeans. She and the mustached, ponytailed guy with her watched Dan approach. They were smoking. A bottle of clear fluid glowed in the candlelight. "Hi," Dan said. "Speak English?"

After a minute the guy with the ponytail said, "Some." He didn't sound welcoming.

Dan pulled out a chair. He perched on the first two inches, to show he didn't plan to stay if they didn't want him. After a moment the woman pushed the bottle his way. "You look sober," she said. "Not a good way to see a war. *Rakija*. Smuggled in from Bradina."

"No thanks. They tell me you might want to go to Srebrenica." He pronounced it *Sebreneetsa* too.

She didn't blink. Obviously used to strangers coming up and starting provocative conversations. "Who the hell are you?"

He didn't think it was a good idea to try to cross the Serb lines with a U.S. military ID in his wallet. "I work for a paper in Grand Centre, Saskatchewan."

"Where the heel eez 'Saskatchewan'?" said Ponytail.

"Canada. Western provinces."

The girl said, "What paper?"

He'd been in Grand Centre but didn't remember the name of the paper. But probably she didn't either. "The *Record*. How about you?"

"I work independent. Radio networks, mostly. Jovan here, Jovica, he sells pictures to whoever's buying. Srebrenica? That'd take serious money. And a car."

"I have a little cash." Four thousand dollars, to be exact, which Jonah Freed had counted out, and made him sign for, before he left the Eighteen Acres.

"How much is a little?"

"Two thousand dollars."

"We'd need three."

"I guess I could get my hands on another thousand."

"Canadian?"

"No, U.S.," he said. She smiled, and he realized she'd just blown away his little facade.

"I won't ask who you really are. *Gavorite li srpskohrvatski?*"

"Is that Bosnian?"

"You really aren't going to blend in." She looked him up and down. "Though the stubble helps. But maybe that'll be okay. Maybe that'll even be better."

"So you're going to blend in with the other side? As you put it?"

"At least convince them we're not Muslim."

"You speak Bosnian?"

"*Da, gavorim.* And it's not 'Bosnian,' it's Serbo-Croatian. My mother was from Vlasenica."

"Which is where?"

"Not too far from Srebrenica. As it happens. We had Muslim neighbors. Serb neighbors."

"So you're a Croat?" Dan asked her.

"Yes. But I can pass. And Jovo here, he really *is* a Serb. One of the good ones. So we should be okay. If we don't run into the wrong people. Keep Jovo company while I go talk to somebody."

Dan looked at the guy again—she pronounced his name *Yoh*-vo—wondering just what kind of war it was, when not even the participants could tell enemy from friend.

"We've got a ticket through the tunnel," she said when she came back. "But that's the easy part. Getting through the mountains, that'll be hard."

"All we can do is try," Dan told her.

"You sure you want to do this?" she said, twisting a lock of hair so dark it was blue-black, looking straight at him. "They kill strangers here. Journalists too. The JNA kills them, the Muslims kill them, the Chetniks kill them. Not to mention we could drive over a mine. I don't know your business in Srebrenica. And I don't want to. But it'd be smarter for all three of us to just stay here and finish getting drunk."

"That's not how you get the story," Dan said.

She grinned, not too enthusiastically. "That's right. That's not how you get the story." She stuck out her hand suddenly. It was small and very, very warm. "Zlata Kovacevic."

He stopped in the basement of the house, at the dark entrance that opened like a hatchway to a lightless engine room. Tasting fear like stale crackers. On the way here, trotting across an intersection, someone had taken a shot at him. With a heavy weapon, a fifty-caliber at least, that had whiplashed past his head and blown chunks of brick and mortar off a wall.

He'd ducked and kept going, suddenly a lot more alert. But now, crouching, watching his breath puff out white in the cold air blowing from somewhere ahead, he felt even more vulnerable.

Past that door, he was on his own space walk. Beyond the protection of the military, his orders, beyond what Sebold or Gelzinis or Clayton probably expected him to do. Into a Heart of Darkness where no law prevailed. He hesitated, thinking this probably wasn't smart. Then thought, Fuck it. What did he have to go back to anyway? Without Blair?

He ducked his head and went in.

The tunnel, which Zlata said did not officially exist, was unlit and only five feet high. It would take them under the Serb lines to a BiH-held area on the other side. BiH meant Bosnian and Herzegovinian Army, the part-Croat but mainly Muslim side in this turmoil of a disintegrating country. He followed them, bent, feeling the rough concrete ceiling brushing the back of the stocking cap he'd bought, along with a field jacket with a ripped lining and a worn Yugoslav Army sleeping bag and some well-used boots.

He'd left everything that could identify him—uniforms, luggage, military identification, red passport, class ring, wedding ring—at the Holiday Inn, to be delivered to Buddy Larreinaga. He'd asked Zlata if he should buy a false ID. She said dollars would work better. They'd bullshit, bluff, and bribe their way through. He'd also asked if he should try to get a gun. They'd shaken their heads. Jovan had held up a battered Exakta. "Camera best weapon," he dead-panned.

Zlata said the tunnel ran for a kilometer to Mount Igman. It started in the basement of a shelled-out house not far from the airport. Dan guessed it went *under* the airport, might originally have led to the fuel storage, from the smell of kerosene. He'd had to pony up 450 bucks to go through. He suspected that was for the three of them, though Zlata had insisted it was for him alone. Others were trudging through coming the other way, dragging heavy soft things or bent under bulky pack-frames. Also slung AKs and ammo boxes. Each meeting involved muttered negotiations and twisted contortions to squeeze past.

Jovo went first, then Zlata. She said to keep his head down. There were iron crossbars in the ceiling that would rip your scalp open. Also to not touch the wires that ran along the sides. "They are high tension and will kill you. Stay on the boards and keep going no matter how bad it gets." He

sucked bad memories in with the close, fuel-stinking air,
breathed over and over by the parade of smugglers, or mer-
chants, whatever their fellow Morlocks were.

Some minutes in he was splashing through liquid up to
his ankles. The water, if it was water, was ice cold and stank
of sewage. A pump was running somewhere. His heart was
hammering. He blinked, sucking air but not getting much
out of it. He kept trying to calculate how long it should take
to walk a kilometer. But Jovo kept running into people coming the other way. He had the only flashlight but didn't use it
much. Probably saving batteries.

Dan stood bent in the dark listening to the muttered, im-
penetrable exchanges. The sweat ran down his face and
plopped in the water. He kept telling himself it was better
than pulling himself backward through a wire conduit under
the Tigris River.

It got deeper before it got shallower. But then he was back
on duckboards again. Not long after, the air got a little
fresher. Then he looked up and there was the sky, glowing
faintly, and way up there a light moving against the stars.

He had maps, from Naples. They were xeroxes of UN
military maps, with the boundaries of the enclaves
and estimates of the current front lines inked in.
Zlata had shown him her own treasure, a tattered, flimsy
road map that looked as if it dated from about 1960. What
she now demanded was more money. Another five hundred
to rent or buy, the exact nature of the transaction was
opaque, a Fiatish wreck that had once been blue but now was
mostly rust. It had no doors or trunk lid, and a replacement
hood had been hammered out of roofing iron by some
shade-tree mechanic. The front tires were bald, but the back
ones were oversized and had the knobby tread he was used
to seeing on military vehicles.

Jovo said it was a "Ficho" and that it would get them
there, if they could get there at all.

Though it took up most of the rest of his rapidly shrinking sheaf of twenty-dollar bills, they were on their way not long after midnight, running with the one working headlight, on sometimes and off sometimes according to a mysterious protocol worked out in the front seat. According to the road map it was only seventy kilometers, crow's-flight, from Sarajevo to Srebrenica. Zlata said the roads should be decent for most of that way. The trouble was, it was all through Serb-controlled territory, or worse, past or through the outskirts of the zone of Muslim enclaves being imploded by the new Serb offensive: Gorazde, Zepa, Srebrenica itself. He huddled in the back and pretended to sleep as they approached the first checkpoint.

"JNA," Zlata said tensely. "National Army. They might turn us back, but they probably won't shoot us."

Jovo said something and she replied; the car slowed. Raising his head, Dan saw oil drums, men in uniform carrying AKs, Soviet-style jeeps, a flag fluttering in the headlight over a sandbag-emplaced machine gun. Jovo reached behind him and got a bottle out. He drew the cork with his teeth as Dan pulled the blanket over his head.

Past the roadblock they waited for a long time as a column of trucks ground by, very slowly, with enormous noise and choking diesel smoke. The trucks hogged the road and there was no way past till they were gone. They were stenciled with the red cross. The canvas covers were snugged tight so he couldn't see what they carried. Then the night was empty again. The little car's motor whined. Something in the transmission knocked wildly whenever they went over thirty-five, but Jovo pushed it along a road that looked like the ones where Dan had grown up, except there were no guardrails, no center lines or white lines or reflectors. But the creeks down in the hollows were the same, and the trees too. Even the little towns they went through looked like Pennsylvania seventy years ago: little wooden and brick stores, little houses, dirt tracks leading off the highway instead of paved streets.

He saw only one signpost that whole way. It said Srebrenica, but someone had scrawled over it *CMPT*.

"What's CMPT?" he asked Zlata, thinking it was an
acronym for some military force or political party.

She said tightly, "That's Cyrillic. *Smrt* means 'death.' "

H e was jerked awake by a burring growl from under
the chassis. Which he recognized, but apparently
his companions didn't. They were arguing. Finally
Jovo took his foot off the gas and coasted to the roadside.

Dan threw the blanket back. "It's tanks," he told them.

"Tanks?" Zlata sounded worried.

He explained that unless the treads were fitted with rubber pads, heavy armor made waffles out of asphalt roads.
That was what they were hearing.

"Hmm, tanks," she repeated. Then she and the Serb fell to
arguing again. Maybe over whether they should turn back.
Dan didn't get into it. They knew how dangerous this was
better than he did. Meanwhile Jovo started up again. They
kept going downhill, through heavy pine woods. He told
himself that if tanks had rolled down this road, at least
they'd be safe from mines.

Then the woods opened out to fields. A smell like burning
and rot sucked into the car. The stink of war.

"Srebrenica?" he said.

"Not much farther," Jovo said. His voice was high. The
pitch of a frightened man.

"I remember this town," the girl said. "The Muslims here
were doing well. The fields were good. There was a factory
that made screws."

Dan could hardly tell it had been a town. Not one house
stood. At the crossroads each shattered concrete-block wall
was scarred with bullets. Below a daubed cross with C's on
either side more scrawls flashed in their passing lights. JNA.

"What's the cross mean?"

"The C's are Cyrillic S's. *'Samo sloga Srbina spasava'*—

Only solidarity will save the Serbs. First they shell a village. The tanks blast down any walls still standing. Then they throw hand grenades into any places they think people might be hiding."

Dan didn't ask where those people were now. He was afraid he knew. But then—where were the bodies?

They left the valley and twisted along hills, through hairpin switchbacks that left him nauseated. The smell came back as they passed burned homes, wrecked vehicles pushed or blown to the side of the road. Aside from that the blackness was total. No lights. No movement. Anything left living had hidden. Meanwhile Zlata was telling him about the rape camps. He could not believe what she said. It had to be propaganda, atrocity stories. Even the Nazis had not thought of such things.

They managed five more miles, he guessed, before Jovo slowed again. This time the headlight showed civilian trucks. A group around a fire. Dan ducked again as they unslung weapons, moved toward the car.

He listened to a palaver that didn't take long and ended with shouting. Then the Ficho began backing up. Fast.

"They said there's fighting ahead," Zlata explained. "And not to come back or they'll take us for a walk in the woods. These are Mladic's extremists. The Tigers. The Dragons. Psychos, killers out of the prisons. Not people we want to discuss things with, okay? Jovica says we're not getting any farther."

"I'm getting that feeling too," Dan said. In the middle of a war zone, unarmed, he was ready to admit it. This hadn't been a good idea.

"If you run, you hit the bullet. If you walk, the bullet hits you."

"What's that mean?"

"It means there's no place we're going to be safe. Not in Bosnia. Out here, back in Sarajevo—same thing."

While he was thinking about that she said, "One more thing we can try. Backtrack a couple of kilometers and check out the road to Brloznik. Jovie thinks he knows a way to get from there back to Zedanisko. That'd get us inside the Srebrenica enclave. If that doesn't work, we'll give up."

But five minutes later headlights came over the hill behind them, moving fast.

They sat in what seemed to be a combination café and tire-repair business. A gas lantern hissed on the table. They hadn't been beaten, yet, but there'd been a lot of gun waving and yelling when the militia or paramilitaries or whatever they were, Serbs anyway, Zlata whispered, had pulled them over. They'd jerked them out and shaken them down, taking money, watches, press cards, and the maps. Then ordered them to follow their VW Golf. To this hamlet, this office smelling of rubber and glue and stale beer, the only light on in town. The guy on duty had made a phone call when his buddies pushed the captives in. Where they'd waited since, wrists lashed behind them with plastic zip-ties.

Until a balding man with a large head strode in, followed by two bigger men carrying Kalashnikovs. He snapped at the guards, who scurried to place chairs. He placed a pack of cigarettes on the table. Lit one. Then threw a pistol on the table too. He looked them over.

"They tell me you're spies," he opened. In English, for some reason. Dan was about to answer when Zlata said, "We're journalists. Going to Belgrade."

"Same thing. Where are you going in Belgrade?"

Jovo said something in Serbo-Croatian. The guy slapped his face so hard his head snapped back. Then put out a boot and kicked him off his chair. "Spies, journalists, same fucking thing," he said again. "Stay down there when I kick you. What paper you write for?"

"I'm with Tanjug," Zlata said. "Your own news agency, you fool."

"I don't believe you. How about him?" He jerked his head at Dan. "He's a fucking American, right? What is he doing with you?"

"He told me he was a Canadian."

"Yeah, I'm American," Dan said, just to clear it up. "I told her Canadian. You can let her go. Like she said, she's on your side."

"I'll decide who's on my side." The bald guy smiled, and it wasn't nice. "The Muslims are using journalists to get NATO to bomb us. What are you doing on this road?"

Dan said, trying to sound calm, "We're trying to find out what happened in Srebrenica. We want to talk to Serbs, not just Muslims. Find out the truth. Too many rumors going around right now. And they don't make the BSA, if that's who you are, look good."

The commander didn't seem disturbed by the prospect of bad PR. "We're fighting your battle," he said. He tapped ash and pointed the cigarette at Dan. "You don't understand. Or you'd rather look away. Serbia has been the front line before. Over the centuries. We stopped the fucking Turks here. Kept them out of Europe. Stopped the Nazis too. Well, the Dutch left. They didn't have the *yahyahs* for the job. Another few weeks and we'll have everything cleaned up. Then you won't have to do anything but cry for the poor Muslims."

One of the men outside came in. He placed something in front of the bald guy. Dan tensed as he saw they were his maps.

"Whose are these?" he said after a time.

Dan swallowed with a dry throat. "Mine."

He felt the barrel of a Kalashnikov against his ear. Another, banging into his other temple.

"These are military maps. Why don't you tell me the fucking truth now," the man said gently. "Who are you spying for? It's the Germans, isn't it?"

"Come on, *droozhe,*" Zlata coaxed. "There are no spies here. We're all on the same side here."

But Big Head said there was somebody else who would want to make that decision himself.

They were on the road an hour this time, but blind-folded. So Dan couldn't have said where they ended up. Only that when the blindfolds came off they were in another room, this one sweltering, heated by a hissing pressure stove. Now and then came the grunt of heavy motors outside, the crunch of tires on shattered brick and crumbling asphalt.

This door revealed at last an older man, heavy, gray-haired, with small, very pale blue eyes and the peaked eyebrows and slab cheeks you saw in the States in pictures of union leaders in the coalfields. He was in utilities, a soft hat, black leather gloves. A brandy smell came in with him. No gold on his uniform, but from the way the others sprang to their feet Dan figured him for a general. And from the way Zlata sucked in her breath, one she feared.

He seemed to be in a jovial mood, though. He boomed out Serbo-Croatian. She answered, forcing a bright voice. Then he gave an order. The soldiers jerked Zlata and Jovan up and pushed them out an exit Dan hadn't noticed till then. Leaving him alone, facing the guy.

Who banged the table suddenly with his fist, and shifted to English. "Okay, I know who those two are. But I don't know who *you* are"—glancing at Dan—"other than you're an American traveling with Ustasha agents. You're out here where the wolves fuck. You carry military maps and you say you want to see the Turks. So what do I do with you?"

"I'd say let us go," Dan said. "Those two aren't spies."

"Maybe not. They're still traitors. But what about you? To me you look like professional military. Yes? Maybe we are the same, you and me."

"Sure," Dan said. Professional to professional sounded better than captor to spy.

"So let's get to business, my Yankee friend. First we will shoot this Jovan. Then Miss Kovacevic. Who does not work for Tanjug, by the way. You will tell me then what you're doing here, I think."

"There's no need to shoot anybody. I'll tell you right now," Dan said, feeling unreal, because it was too much like Iraq. The same old script, played out in another war-torn asshole of the world. But different, too.

He'd faced terrorists. He'd been interrogated by Iraqi secret police. But he'd never felt the aura of sheer evil coming off this heavy-cheeked, dough-faced man. Who sat like a sack of potatoes, a silent, hard-faced bodyguard behind him. He said he was professional military. But the feeling Dan got was "professional" the way Adolf Eichmann had been.

So he made it short: where he was from, what his orders were. It wasn't a secret, or at least not one he wanted the others to die for. The Serbian blinked, processing it against politics and ideologies Dan had no idea of. "Your president wants to know what happened in Srebrenica."

Dan didn't bother with the distinction of Clayton versus De Bari. "That's right."

The Serb pondered, then turned his head. Spoke to the guy behind him, and hoisted himself to his feet. Started to leave, then turned back. "It's not a crime to defend your people," he said quietly. "That's all we're doing. Someday you'll understand that."

Dan didn't answer. For a moment no one spoke. Then the general did.

"You want to know what happened to the Muslims in Srebrenica," he said. "All right. I, Ratko Mladic, will show you what you have come so far to see."

The jeeps jounced and swayed, bottoming out with jarring bangs on the rocks. His was in the lead, Zlata and Jovo's trailing. The troops with them said nothing. They'd gone uphill, then down, over drops and ruts that made Dan wonder if they were on a road or a streambed. He couldn't see, because they didn't use headlights. One of the drivers had a tubular object he kept raising. He figured it was a night vision scope. So they suspected surveillance, or attack, from the air. He sat on his still-pinioned hands, trying to roll with the lurches.

Finally the tilt smoothed into valley land, soft soil under the tires instead of rock. They turned sharp and brakes ratcheted and the motors cut off. He caught the creak of frogs—it seemed late in the year for them but there they were—and the chuckle of a stream. The troops levered their legs over the side and fanned out, forming a perimeter.

"Izidji iz auta," said a voice out of the darkness. Hands jerked him out of the seat and set him on his feet.

"How about taking these uh, cuffs off?" he said, but no one answered.

He smelled it before he saw it. At first he thought it was a poultry plant, some kind of animal-processing facility. The long line of a peaked roof against a graying dawn.

"Dan?" Zlata, sounding terrified. He dragged back against the hands of his guards. They resisted, then relaxed as the men from the other jeep pushed the journalists up.

A trooper kicked open the door. The smell came strong. The creek was deafening in the quiet. The Serb gestured inside with his rifle. Dan hesitated, then went through.

He stood bent over, hands behind him, looking out over what the metal-gray predawn coming through the bullet-shattered window frames revealed. Behind him matches scratched as the soldiers lit up.

From one end to the other, perhaps a hundred yards in all, the concrete floor was covered with corpses. Fat flies rose sluggishly, then settled again on open eyes, on crosses carved into foreheads, on gaping groins, on the stewmeat bullets and bayonets and grenades had made of human bodies.

Behind him Zlata was gagging. Dan felt only the detachment of utter horror. He'd seen corpses before. He'd witnessed what explosives and fire made of human flesh on the battlefield, and what the sea and its creatures did. Death, and the dead, were not new to him.

But he'd never seen hundreds jumbled together three and

four deep like some bizarre and monstrous lasagna. Old men, young, bearded, boys, some half naked, others in worn suits and gray hats. Their cheeks were sunken. Their bodies elongated. As if they'd been starved. He began to grasp what had been done to many of them. He hoped it had been after they were dead. He glanced at the roof, knowing now why the drones had seen nothing.

Which meant he was dead too. If they'd gone that far to hide what they were doing, they'd never let them return to testify.

"You wanted to see the Muslims," one of the men said, working the bolt of his Kalashnikov. "Now you can be with them."

Zlata began screaming as the men jerked her out of the building. Her screams continued for a long time before a shot clapped back in the trees.

Jovo stood white-faced, panting and looking sick. A Serb grabbed his ponytail and put a knee in his back. Dan felt them grabbing his own shoulders. Forcing him down. He struggled, but there seemed so little point to it that he stopped. He tried to commit himself to the unutterable God or Being he'd felt near now and then, in times of sorrow or danger.

An automatic clatter bounced off pocked walls, bloated faces. Jovo pitched violently forward onto the other corpses. He writhed, hands rictused behind him, the plastic cutting into his wrists. Then relaxed. Smoke curled up from the torn burned cloth of the back of his jacket.

"He was traitor," someone said. "But *shto si ti*? What are you?"

Dan waited, bent, looking at the photographer's face. Jovo was staring at him. As if saying, *You brought me here. Aren't you coming with me?*

A second went by. Then another. The flies buzzed around as if bored. One landed on his open eye. He shook his head. It buzzed off.

The creak of rusty hinges. A door shutting. Footsteps, headed away.

Laughter. Another burst of gunfire, longer, rattling off the boles of trees.

Motors starting.

He knelt in the presence of so much death. He looked inside himself. He looked at Jovo's motionless face.

He looked at nothing.

12
WASHINGTON, D.C.

Don't get me wrong. I'm glad they did! But why on earth would they ever let you go? After showing you that?" said Sebold, squinting in an expression Dan had never seen before from him.

He said slowly, hunched forward a little in his seat, "I don't know. Maybe just Mladic saying 'Fuck you' to NATO. I hear he does things like that."

"Then what happened?"

He took a deep breath and went on. Perfunctorily, because he'd already cabled back a report before flying out of Macedonia.

He'd trekked alone through the woods, across deserted fields crisp with late autumn, hearing the thunder of artillery in the hills, the distant fry-crackle of small arms. He headed west, the immemorial direction of escape. He tried at first to avoid roads, then realized he'd never make it out alive if he tried to do this cross-country. Remembering what Zlata had said. *If you run, you hit the bullet. If you walk, the bullet hits you.*

Somewhere in that lonely trek, he'd come to understand what she'd meant.

"I kept coming across bodies," he said. "Nearly all men. Not as old, or as young, as the ones in the warehouse. And these were armed."

The fighting-age men in the doomed pockets had tried to break out, either in some sort of last-spasm assault or, more likely, simply trying to escape. He hadn't understood it then and didn't now. Surely the fighters should have stayed with those they defended, their families, their homes. None of the bodies he'd come across, ambushed and machine-gunned in the fields, carried any food. But he'd picked up a rifle, a blanket, matches.

"You walked out?"

"Picked up on the way. A German helicopter."

He'd heard it the second day. Had knelt quickly, pulling up handfuls of dried hay, scrambling to build a fire. He'd thrown the blanket on it to make smoke. Jumped and waved as it circled, gradually dropping as the pilot saw he was alone.

"Well, we're glad to get you back," the director said. "You haven't been home yet, have you? But this might be something—don't go yet. Will you be in the building? Where can I reach you?"

Dan said his office, and left.

He wasn't sure how he felt about being back. He felt as if he were still back in the silent hills. He kept thinking that if he hadn't gone into a bar in Sarajevo, two brave, even heroic people would still be alive. He kept telling himself he hadn't killed them. Mladic had. But he couldn't convince whoever in his heart was keeping score.

If you run, you hit the bullet. If you walk, the bullet hits you.

He stopped in the cafeteria and got the largest black coffee they sold. Staffers stepped out of his way as he headed for the cashier. Conversations died. He realized it was his clothes. He was still wearing the jeans and field jacket, since he'd left his own stuff in Sarajevo. The Germans had given them a cleaning, taken out the dirt and bloodstains, but the jacket was still worn, obviously foreign, and scorched where he'd got too close to the fire.

Postponing the office another couple of minutes, he stopped in a restroom. Washed his hands, making the water as hot as he could stand. It felt good, so he kept doing it. He stared at himself in the mirror. Could this be the same asshole who'd worried about anything else but being alive?

Why him? Why so fucking many others, and not *him*?

He hesitated at his door, unable for a moment to recall the code, then punched it clumsily into the lock. Bloom, Harlowe, and Lynch were solicitous and welcoming. He brushed off their questions. Instead he asked what was going on. Lynch said Ihlemann was still on maternity leave. They might not see her for a while; the Army was sending someone over from the temp pool until they found out. Meilhamer was over on the Hill, talking to staff about the upcoming HIDA hearings. Bloom said he'd been doing the advancing for the Bogotá conference. Dan said he wanted to see the plan, maybe talk with the Colombian and U.S. security people.

Lynch was reaching for another paper, starting to tell him something about airplanes, when the phone rang on the office assistant's desk. Dan was closest, so he got it. "Counterdrug."

"Lenson? Mrs. Clayton here. In my office, please."

"Right now? I'm not in a proper—"

"I understand you've been through a lot. Sorry. My office."

He said he'd be right there.

He got there as Clayton came striding out. "Come with me," she snapped. Dan followed her down a narrow corridor, no more than three feet wide, past the vice president's office. They turned at the chief of staff's and the hallway widened. The curved wall of the Oval Office came into sight. A couple of protective service agents watched them approach. One was the round-faced African American who'd stared at Dan that first time he'd met the president. Clayton turned into a reception area. Two more agents stood there, and a somber-suited group of older men. She nodded to the secretary, and said to the suits, "I'm sorry, gentlemen.

A national security matter. If you'll give us a few minutes, please."

Dan followed her into curved spaciousness. He seemed to glide across the floor, as if on slick tires through wet clay. He was surrounded by whiteness and light, as if he were approaching God. A marble mantel. Shell-shaped moldings above the bookcases. The only touches of color were the banners behind the desk, the Stars and Stripes and the deep blue presidential flag. Those, and to the left and right of the fireplace, two paintings. One was a brilliant Georgia O'Keeffe of sunflowers, too bright a yellow to look steadily at. Dan remembered reading that Letitia De Bari had donated it from her collection. The other, an oil of a little girl holding a black kitten and giggling in the sunlight. The daughter the De Baris had lost years before to leukemia.

The president hung up a phone as they approached. He shifted in a high-backed chair, eyes flicking to Dan, then back to the poised little woman whose heels tapped across the parquet before falling silent on a beautiful oval carpet.

The man, Dan thought, who was probably sleeping with Blair. For a second hate flared. Then it guttered away, like a candle flame cupped by an inverted glass.

"Mr. President," the national security adviser said. "Something you ought to hear."

"Make yourselves comfortable." De Bari waved to a couch, started to get up, to move over there to sit with them.

"We'll stand," Clayton said, and Dan caught an edge to her voice.

She summarized Dan's cable, updated with what he'd told Sebold half an hour before. It was a crystal-clear recapitulation of everything he'd tried to put across, but more concise; what he'd spent hours trying to write and say, given in ten sentences not one word of which he could have improved on. She finished by nodding his way. "I've brought Lenson in. So you can hear this for yourself. He hasn't even been home to change."

"All right, Doris . . . That pretty accurate, Dan? Gosh, I'm glad we got you back. That must've been hell."

"No, Mr. President," Dan said. His mouth felt as if he hadn't used it for years. He took a breath, trying to be where he was, not somewhere far away. "I was only there a few days. For the people who have to live there—that's hell."

The president spread his hands. "Tell me what you saw. In your own words."

Dan told him in unadorned sentences. He came to the events in the warehouse, and stopped, looking past the man who waited. Out the windows behind him. At the bare trees of the South Lawn. At a gardener pulling burlap over the pampas grass for the winter. Then he took another breath, and told about his escape and the dead he'd seen in the fields, lying in windrows like the old pictures from the Somme.

The man with the blow-dried hair swiveled back and forth, thrusting out his lower lip. "What are the numbers?"

"*Numbers,* Mr. President?" Clayton said.

"For deaths in that conflict. The trend line."

"The trend line. In Bosnia—they're down."

"Well, that's good. It's not spreading. Like we thought it might. Though, the collapse of the safe areas—that's bad news."

Dan thought he'd better try again. "Mr. President, those figures don't reflect what I witnessed on the ground. There had to be four hundred bodies in that warehouse. More, many more, in the fields and in the woods. The UN doesn't have a handle on this. I don't think NATO does either. And just containing it isn't going to stop the slaughter."

Clayton said, "We've spent months on this. So did the previous administration. This is not an American problem. We support the UN. But basically, it's a European responsibility."

Dan told her, "No, ma'am. With respect. Genocide is not somebody else's problem. And these are Muslims we're talking about. The whole Middle East is going to judge us by how we respond."

"Dan, I hear what you're saying," De Bari said. "But we've sent Mokey Revell over. Worked with Mitterrand and Kohl. Believe me, I'd like to stop this horror. But committing troops is a big step, in a direction I'm not sure we're ready to go in."

"What about air power?" asked Clayton. "Air strikes, or Tomahawks? We've got to do something to get out in front of this issue. Can we turn the situation around without ground forces?"

"Not with that command setup," Dan said. "They've got some kind of UN-NATO-national triple-key approach that just doesn't work. And the terrain, the forest cover . . . you need boots on the ground. To really make a difference."

"We've just finished troop reductions in Europe," De Bari said, shaking his head. "And we took a hell of a lot of heat for it, too. I have to tell you, Doris, I don't feel much like going back now and saying, 'Hey, boy, were we wrong on that one, let's ship them all back.'"

Dan saw Clayton's brow furrow. The same expression she'd had putting down the phone in the Situation Room. When the man before her wouldn't commit to Eritrea, either.

"Then give them arms," Dan said. "If we can't defend them. Lift the embargo."

"Arm the *Muslims*?" De Bari said. "The French will never agree. Neither will the Germans."

"Then we just leave them to be murdered?" Dan felt his mask slipping. He knew what he said wasn't fair, maybe wasn't even true. But he was losing it. The room was too elegant. These people, too detached. "This is the worst thing since Hitler. In Europe, anyway."

Clayton told him, "Well, the president may be right. We could put troops in, tamp it down. But for how many years? What's our body count? And what's our exit strategy once we're in?"

Dan couldn't believe how quickly she'd put her tiller over, trimmed to match the president's wind. Was this the vaunted loyalty the political staff valued above all else? He muttered, feeling each word like a piece of glass working its way out, "So the Holocaust didn't teach us anything."

Clayton said, "No one likes to say this. But some things can't be stopped."

"If you run, you hit the bullet," Dan started to say, but stopped after "run." The room was silent.

"I assure you, no one's 'running,'" Clayton said, angrily now. "All right, that's enough. This is over—"

"No, no, Doris, dial it back a notch. This guy's been through a lot," De Bari told her. "You sent him to get a first-hand look, didn't you? And he did. He really came home with what we needed to know." His tone was so compassionate, Dan almost bought it. Then he thought: This turd fucks my wife, and pretends he cares about me?

"We'll get you a written debrief, Mr. President. I'll prepare a list of options, and my recommendation."

"Do that," the president said. He too gave Dan a harder look. "And include the option—I know how you must feel about this, Dan, but this is what I want—include the option of continuing with just what we're doing now."

Clayton took his arm. She pointed to the door as De Bari picked up his phone again.

When Dan looked back he was already talking, grinning up at the ceiling, his voice booming, hearty, jovial.

He was ready to go home. But he couldn't find his car. He had to call the Metro police, then take a cab to the impound lot. Someone had scratched the paint, all the way down to raw steel. The tow company insisted they'd found it that way. Even though he left the White House before lunch, he didn't get to Arlington until it was dark.

Her car was in the drive. He sat in the street for some minutes, the engine ticking over quietly, before pressing the accelerator and surging up to park beside it. Looking at the flaking eave he'd intended to scrape and paint, and not gotten to before it got cold. Remembering when he'd cared about things like that.

"Dan? Is that you?"

She was in the bathroom. He stood in the living room, not wanting to go in. On the TV Larry King was interviewing the vice president. They were talking about the designated-hitter rule.

"Yeah," he muttered.

When she came out and clicked the TV off with the remote and hugged him he thought for a moment how nice this might have been, if it had been a normal homecoming. She'd changed out of her work clothes. Out of suits and heels, into what she wore around the house: loose cotton pants and sweatshirt, striped socks and backless clogs. Her hair was pulled back, careless, even untidy, but he'd always liked that. That was what hurt, that he still loved her.

He just didn't trust her anymore.

It must have been his look that made her step back. She searched his face. "Bad, huh?"

"Yeah."

"Meilhamer said they sent you to Bosnia. Then I didn't hear from you—"

He said that was right, and detached her fingers and went into the kitchen. Mainly because he couldn't meet her eyes. He opened the fridge. There were the expensive dark ales that she liked to have maybe once a week, with dinner. He could have one. The trouble was, he couldn't have just one. But he wouldn't have to feel so betrayed, so furious, so empty.

He got a diet Coke instead and let the door suck closed on a cold breath.

Her arms came around him again, from behind. He closed his eyes against her warmth. Her scent. "Well, now you're home. I'll make dinner. We can just stay here."

For a moment, even knowing what he knew, he wanted to hug her back. Pretend nothing had changed. But he couldn't. Even if the truth hurt, he wanted it. He sucked air. It would have torn him apart a week ago.

Now, though, all he had to do was remember a room full of gray light and corpses. And his personal problems seemed to lose their importance.

"Okay, I give up," she said. "I don't have time for games, Dan. Is it something you saw over there?"

"You're right. I don't have time for games either."

"Then why don't you tell me what's on your mind."

"So," he said, not looking at her but out the window at the house next door. Then, harshly, "So, how was it with De Bari?"

"How was what?"

"When you got it on with him? In Russia. And wherever else it's happened."

When he took a look she was staring at him, as if he were something broken, or malfunctioning, that she was trying to figure out.

"Are you serious? You come back from Sarajevo—Srebrenica—and that's what you want to know?"

"Am I serious? What do you think?"

"You seem to be. It's the question I'm having trouble taking seriously."

"That you banged him? He's not that fat."

"He's—wait a minute. That I *banged* him? Is that what I just heard?"

"I guess not." He went past her into the dining room and looked at the table. The glassware. The dishes they'd picked out, with the hand-painted birds. Something shifted in his heart. He wanted to break everything, destroy everything, wreck the room. Then he didn't care again. "No, that couldn't be it. Could it?"

His voice sounded weak. He knew that was what sarcasm was, weakness, but Christ it hurt. He just wished this was over.

She pushed past him. Dropped into a chair, kicked off her clogs, curled her legs under her. Getting ready for a discussion. Which he for one did not intend to have. "You must have seen some ugly shit over there."

"I saw a lot of dead people. A country coming apart. A policy that's not a policy."

"You let them know? At the NSC?"

"In the Oval Office. This morning."

"You briefed him?" Just the way she said "him" hurt.

"Yeah."

"And he said?" She cocked her head in her let's-think-about-this gesture.

"It doesn't seem to be a priority. Like a lot of other things this administration should be putting effort into." He cleared his throat, feeling anger pushing up. It was there. It just took time. "I don't want to talk about that now. How about we talk about you and him."

"Me and Bobby-O."

"That's right."

"Wait. Before this goes any further. Go over to the china cabinet. Look in the mirror."

"What?"

"Please. Look in the mirror."

When he looked in the reflective glass he recoiled. The white of his left eye was sheened with blood. As he pulled down the lid to examine it she said, "Let me put this as clearly as I can. Are you listening? I have never been sexually involved with Robert De Bari."

It looked *Night of the Living Dead* horrible, but it didn't hurt; it seemed to be limited to the sclera, the white of the eyeball; just a broken blood vessel. "You never had sex with him."

"That's what you meant, right? No, I don't think 'banged' leaves much room for misinterpretation." She said precisely, in her appearance-before-Congress tone, "I have not banged the president; I have not screwed the president. I have not fucked him, or blown him, or even given him a hand job. Now, does that take care of whatever's eating you? I hope so, because you're scaring me, Dan. Maybe you should see that doctor again."

"Never mind her. You were never alone with him?"

She glanced away, and that was when he knew he was right. The knowledge tore apart parts of himself he'd thought were healed. She scraped her nails along the arm of the chair. The zipping noise raised the hairs on the back of his neck.

"Well?" he said, in a voice he barely recognized.

"Have I ever been alone with him. Well—actually I was. Once."

He waited.

"I told you I was on his transition team. After the speech to the Guard Association. Well, one day he wanted a briefing. I forget what. Personnel issues, probably. I was in there with Holt, and Gino Varghese, and Charlie Wrinkles. The Christmas help he brought in from Wyoming. We had a suite at the Sheraton. We were there about an hour. Then Tony and the rest left."

She looked at the carpet. "I should have told you. But I figured it would upset you. Anyway, he was on me before I had time to think about it. I pushed him away. Said I was in a relationship. He did his little-boy-caught-in-the-cookie-jar act. Said it wouldn't happen again. Asked me to forgive him. There hasn't been anything since."

He had to admit, it was a good act. But now he knew how things worked inside the Beltway.

She was ambitious. Political. She worshiped De Bari.

"You were never with him after that?" he asked her again. Giving her one last chance.

"Never."

He hadn't wanted to give her the details, tell her how he knew. She'd argue, obfuscate, make him sound stupid and petty. That was the way they worked, and they all screwed you in the end; there was as much chance of finding one who was honest and faithful as picking a buttercup in hell.

"I can see I'm not getting through. There's something in your head. The torture thing. Losing your ship. And now whatever you saw in Bosnia. But snap out of this. Believe me, you're making up something that's not there."

It felt like someone else picked up the serving dish. The sound of it crashing into the mirror, of everything shattering, was the most satisfying thing he'd ever heard.

"Dan. *Dan!*"

He said in a thick voice, "Then how about in St. Petersburg. At the Pribaltskaya. That night, in his suite. How about that?"

She'd jumped to her feet when the mirror exploded. Now she turned for the bedroom. But paused, looking back. "It

180 *David Poyer*

was business. But I see I can't convince you of that. You can't even control your actions. So I don't see any point in continuing this conversation."

He heard the snap as the lock went home. Leaving him clenching his fists. Looking at his bloodshot, crazy, shattered reflection in the shards that littered the sideboard.

Maybe it didn't matter in the great scheme of things, the way a massacre in a distant land mattered. Or maybe that didn't make any difference either.

The guilt, the rage, the shame, hammered through him. He wanted to smash more things, smash everything.

He was mad enough to kill.

S he was already up when he lurched into the kitchen the next morning. The couch had been stylish but uncomfortable. She was dressed, made up, and was eating a toasted sesame bagel. They didn't have much to say. Just the "Did you want coffee?" and "There's more of those in the freezer" nonconversation of a couple who didn't want to talk, didn't want to be near each other.

At the door she said, "This house is half yours. So I can't exactly ask you to leave."

"You want me out? I'll get out."

"Let's talk about it later. I've just got too much going on to deal with this right now," she said, and was gone. Leaving only her scent, and the lingering smell of toast.

Meilhamer was in when he got to the office. "Jeez," his assistant said, looking at his eye. "You have that looked at?"

"It'll go away," Dan told him. "Let's get to it."

"Okay." Meilhamer fitted himself like a puzzle piece into the window chair and unloaded a sheaf of correspondence folders onto Dan's desk. The first alone was an inch thick. "We got catch-up to play. First off, this GAO report on automated information-systems management. The counterdrug systems inventory. Here's their draft report and recommendations, our draft response."

Dan sat with chin on his fist, looking at page after page as

the assistant ground through why NSC-CD could not agree
to this obscure recommendation for this or that arcane reason, but on the other hand, how the working-group reports
could not be considered in the final IRM draft documents.
He was into pointer index systems and the National Counter-
Narcotics Information Protection Architecture when Dan
broke in. "Can we move ahead on this, Bry? Kind of give me
the one-pager. Or we're never going to get through it."

"Sure, boss. Bottom line's that the draft National Drug
Control Information Resource Management plan, as currently configured, should not receive support from within the
NSC-CD staff. Without a major redrafting, it'll end up in the
"too hard" box. This eventuality is underscored by the problems we're having getting letters of promulgation signed for
the TMP and the DETIP. Even if it comes back in a more be-
nign form, it's too expensive. Half a billion my little birds tell
me isn't going to be in the budget."

Dan cradled his skull. "But I understood—the president
went on record in Cleveland saying we were going to improve information sharing, get the various resources and
centers talking to each other better—"

"That's right. We can't shrink from implementing this
project. So we need to remassage these documents so they
are professionally presented, provide recommendations ac-
ceptable to the budgeteers, and reach conclusions that are
not blue-sky like GAO's."

Dan gave up. He signed letters to Sam Nunn, John Warner,
and Charlie Schumer saying how important information-
resources-management leadership was to the War on Drugs,
and a long letter back to the GAO that took apart its propos-
als and regurgitated them in even more obfuscatory bureau-
cratese. This, Meilhamer explained, would serve the purpose
of NSC-CD appearing to cooperate while postponing actually having to do anything into the next budget cycle. Dan felt
sick, but once it was done there was another file, another
smooth explanation by his rumpled, slovenly assistant.

Meilhamer was leaving when Dan called, "Wait. Give me
back that letter to GAO."

The assistant didn't move. "That was the right decision."

"No it wasn't." Dan held out his hand. "We owe them a better response than that. I might not get to it today, but I'll take it home tonight and think about it."

He went through the e-mail, the intel summaries. The first interesting thing was a report from Belize that had located the Baptist in Morawhannä, on the coast of Guyana. The silt Bloom had talked about was settling. Unfortunately, by the time the extradition paperwork got there, he'd left. Dan remembered his suspicions about a leak, but didn't come up with any new ideas about who it might be.

He read the *Early Bird,* then flicked through the cables and messages the Sit Room watchstanders had filed in his queue. One was based on his request for anything about air cargo. It looked like there was going to be another airline strike. Since freight volume had been falling, due to the recession, the companies had been trying to circumvent the baggage handlers' union. The union was going out, just to remind them who was boss.

Message traffic about Bogotá, arrangements for the conference. He started an e-file on that, figured he'd probably be going. Major busts were going down in Colombia. Tejeiro was on the warpath. On the other hand, interception rates through the Bahamas were back up. A single factoid told you nothing in this business. It had to be part of a tapestry before it made sense. And even then, two people could use it to back up opposite conclusions.

What was the point, anyway? When marijuana got scarce everybody went to crack. If they stopped every gram of coke at the border, the Hell's Angels would cook up more meth. If that dried up there was still alcohol, the most destructive drug ever. He wondered what they'd do when it went digital, when you just clamped a headset on and downloaded the latest buzz.

He jerked his mind back to what was in front of him. A

message from the CIA feed. A raid on a Mexican power plant. He made himself read it.

He read it again.

Then went downstairs, trotted across West Executive in a cold drizzle, and let himself into the Sit Room. He stood at the director's cubicle, looking out her window. Dead pansies thrashed in the window box, whipped by the wind.

Captain Roald glanced up. "You look terrible. What's wrong with your eye?"

Dan dropped the printout on her blotter. It was marked "Secret," but it hadn't been out of his hands, and if the Sit Room wasn't a secure space, what was? "See this, Jennifer?"

"The Laguna Verde break-in. We got the first cables at zero-six. They wrecked the place. Shot three guards."

"But didn't take any of the nuclear materials. What was that about?"

"Made me wonder too. I had the watchstanders make some phone calls. See if it was worth passing up the line."

Roald said they'd finally decided it wasn't immediate action, though she'd phone-notified the deputy NSA, and it would go in the daily summary. Took place on foreign soil, no U.S. forces or interests involved; and it hadn't succeeded. She gave him the facts.

Laguna Verde, Green Lagoon, was on the Gulf of Mexico fifty miles north of Veracruz. The Mexican government ran two nuclear reactors there, for power and production of isotopes. Ninety percent of nuclear isotopes used in the U.S. for diagnostic X-rays, nuclear medicine, and radiation therapy were imported. A sizable percentage, Roald said, came from Laguna Verde. They included iodine-131, technium-99, cobalt-60, iridium-192, and cesium-137.

According to the police command center in Mexico City, two vanfuls of armed men had crashed the gates. They'd shot down the guards, then been taken on in a firefight by more security personnel from deeper in the plant.

The security force held its own, dropping two attackers while losing one man to fire, and eventually drove the intruders back outside the perimeter fence. But meanwhile, using the gate action as a diversion, another team landed from a boat flying a huge Greenpeace flag. There were often demonstrations on the gulf, and Greenpeace often crowded the security zone. So no one had thought much of the boat until it ran up on the beach, disembarking six men who blew the seaside fence and penetrated the complex.

Only the timely arrival of a Mexican Army helicopter drove them out. The helo machine-gunned the boat and set it on fire. Both parties of intruders had left in the vans, abandoning one dead man. None of the reactor pressure walls, waste pools, or isotope storage areas had been breached.

"This time," Dan muttered.

" 'This time'?"

"There are three valuable things in that plant. Fuel, waste, and isotopes. They couldn't steal the fuel, not if the reactor's operating. The waste, pretty much the same, as I understand it. But the isotopes: small, light, and valuable. They were after the isotopes."

"Well, that'll juice 'em to beef up their security," Roald said.

He ate at his desk, a plastic sandwich from the cafeteria. Trying to ignore the abyss that beckoned whenever he thought about doomed things. Condemned, surrounded Sarajevo. Slumped bodies . . . when his mind recurred to that vision blackness shaded his sight, his stomach teetered between terror and nausea.

By early afternoon he'd gotten through his callbacks. He even wrote a little on his white paper, the one he'd been doing on the Threat Cell. Thinking about Laguna Verde, he added a section on radioactive materials.

Which reminded him, in turn, of *Horn*. Even now, with a Yankee White clearance, he couldn't access certain files on the incident. Al Qaeda had modified that weapon, in some not-yet-comprehended way, to generate an enormous fallout.

Detonated in the right place, dispersed by the prevailing winds, it would have made hundreds of square miles uninhabitable for years.

He closed the file—didn't want to leave something like that glowing on his screen—and went out to Major Lynch's cubicle. Rapped on it. "Ed."

"Holy smoke. I've heard of riding the red-eye—"

"Everybody's got to make a joke. Remember that thing about FedEx? The guys who were trying to import empty containers?"

"You mean UPS?"

"Yeah. The relief organization. Ever come up with anything more on that?"

Lynch told him he'd followed up as directed. "That's what I was starting to tell you about yesterday, when you got the ring from Mrs. C. Transport security put out a closure bulletin on it. They didn't find anything illegal, and the outfit's clean."

"Where were these containers going to, again?"

Lynch told him L.A., there was a big hub airfield near there. Dan nodded. "Okay . . . Where's Miles these days? I meant to ask Bry this morning, but . . ."

Lynch said the DEA operative was at a forward location in Ecuador, where the Colombian, U.S., and host militaries were setting up a combined surveillance center. Dan thought this over and asked if DEA could forward a message. Lynch thought so. Dan sat at the agent's desk, logged in, and typed a message from his account. He queued it and logged off.

He was headed back to his office when Gil Ouderkirk, the sergeant the Pentagon had sent to replace Ihlemann—a big taciturn guy with a shaven head that looked strange with a sport coat—said, "Commander? Call for you. State Department."

It was a staffer responding to Dan's inquiry on the stuff he'd left with Buddy Larreinaga. His uniform, wallet, passport, and so forth. Dan especially wanted his class ring back. It had gone too many places with him, bore too many dings from the ships he'd served on. The staffer said he'd located it, but it wasn't in State's system. It was coming back through a UN pouch. So it would go to New York, not D.C.

A round five he finished the report on Bosnia that De Bari had asked for, then wondered whom he should turn it in to. Sebold? Gelzinis? That would invite delay, maybe second-guessing from CIA and State. Dan wanted his words read unvarnished. Maybe it was futile, but he was trying to separate the president, the chief executive it was his duty and obligation to counsel, from Bob De Bari. For whom he was starting to cherish a real loathing.

Normally anything from NSC staff went through the executive secretary, in a nook off the Sit Room spaces, and from there to the president's staff secretary. This could take anywhere from a day to a few minutes. He'd noticed anything political got a higher priority than national-security matters. Everything that went into the Oval was monitored. Even the scrap paper the president doodled on was accounted for. He'd gotten back copies of two of his counter-drug reports with the red "President has seen" stamp. Copies only; the originals of everything that went before that sanctified sight came back to the Sit Room, thence into the classified archives.

At last he decided the most direct route was through the chief of staff. If he could get it past the dragon's guardians, into the Secret Cave. He printed off a clean copy and put it in a regular file folder. Holt's office would slip it into one of the blue leather presidential jackets.

T he west wing again. The chief of staff's space was past the vice president's. The usual reception area, then Holt's office off to the right. Neither was large, but the upholstery and carpet were of such luxurious-looking dark blue cloth, with small gold figures on them, that the effect was incongruous, as of infinite power compressed into a shoebox. He told the receptionist that he had an NSC report the president had requested. She held out her hand. "You can give it to me."

"It needs a verbal introduction."

"Mr. Holt's in conference. I'll get it to him." She glanced toward a partition. Dan hesitated. A door opened, and he heard a once familiar voice.

Then he remembered *whose* voice it was, and caught his breath. Holding the folder like a weapon, he pushed past the staffer.

The inner office was bigger than Sebold's or even Clayton's. The polished glass of an enormous desk was covered with knickknacks, golf trophies, stuffed toys, union mugs, souvenirs, presentation globes. The right-hand window framed the south end of the Old Executive, but the one to the left had the long view: down the South Lawn, across the Ellipse, to the white bubble of the Jefferson Memorial against a sky just waiting for an excuse to snow.

Holt, looking startled, was leaning back in a recliner, hands behind his neck. A slim, freckled man sat across from him. Bright red suspenders peeped from beneath a dark blue pinstripe, bracketing a pale lavender silk tie like Donald Trump's. He wasn't as young as he'd been ten years before, but his features still had a pixieish cast. His long hair was still reddish blond, his eyes more sun-crinkled. He looked very much at home in the red leather chair, twiddling a gold fountain pen. They regarded each other for a moment before Dan said, "Tallinger."

"You know each other?" Holt said. "Dr. Martin W. Tallinger. Dan Lenson, on our staff."

Tallinger dropped both hands to the chair arms. The pen hit the carpet. Dan, too, could not speak. Then his astonishment was obliterated by the same red rage as when he'd spat mingled blood and saliva in the face of the man who'd sold secrets, betrayed his country, and in the end helped kill, knowingly or not, a woman who'd cared only for peace.

"What's this asshole doing here?"

"I beg your pardon?"

"This guy's a lying influence peddler. And a spy. Still

running your ring, Tallinger? Still selling the Chinese our technology?"

"Now just a minute." Tallinger was still braced, but he was below Dan, looking up at him from the chair. He probably figured that if he got up, Dan would punch him. He glared at the chief of staff. "Tony. Call him off!"

"I'd like to know what's going on," Holt said.

Dan said, "What you have here's the guy who tried to sell the Tomahawk terminal guidance to the Chinese. Check with the D.C. police. Call the FBI. Mention Operation Snapdragon."

"Which I cooperated with, and which cleared me one hundred percent," Tallinger said. "Tony, here's the picture. This . . . officer holds me responsible for a personal loss, years ago, that I had nothing to do with. I'm surprised to see him here. Surprised to see him still in government service, actually. The last I heard, he'd resigned under a cloud."

"The cloud's yours, you fucking murderer." Dan stepped forward. Tallinger shrank back and raised his hands.

Holt knocked over a whittled figurine of a New England sailing captain as he stretched for his intercom. "I want Garner Sebold in here," he said. "Lenson—outside."

"I have a report for the president. I'll drop it on your desk. Then I'll leave." Dan looked at Tallinger again. "But you can't trust this son of a bitch. He works for the other side. The *real* other side."

"I told you, this guy's a loose cannon. It's well known in his own service, Tony."

"This isn't about me, sir. Just having him here is wrong."

Another voice cut in. "I have a lot of confidence in Dan."

Sebold looked put out, and out of breath. He'd probably heard the last exchange, which had been pretty loud. "But I agree he has strong opinions. And he's seen some things lately no one should have to. Let's go, Dan."

"The chief of staff needs to know who he's dealing with, General."

"He knows that before anybody sets foot in his office, Dan. Don't you think? One last time."

Dan knew the next step was calling in the Secret Service.
He couldn't believe it. Tallinger, next door to the Oval Office. And *he* was the one being hustled out. "All right," he
said. "I've warned you." He stared again at Tallinger, and
followed Sebold out.

In the corridor the general said, "What the fuck was that
about?"

"He's an agent of influence."

Sebold said mildly, "If that's true, I'm sure Tony knows it.
I heard part of what you were putting out in there. I know
tempers get close to the surface in politics. But that was really
over the line."

Dan looked down the hall. He should go back. This time,
get his hands on the traitor. But Sebold was gripping his biceps so hard his arm was going numb. Muscling him down
the steps, to the ground floor. Passing staffers glanced at
them, then away, snapping back to their own concerns. "I
want you back in your office. Stay there till you hear from
me," the general said.

"I've got some—"

"*In your office.*" They were both in civilian dress, but it
was the tone of command.

He said unwillingly, "Right."

The call came after the windows had turned black and
the lights had come on in the quadrangle. The assistant NSA wanted to see him. Dan said to Lynch, to
Harlowe, "Ed, Marty, I'm off to see Gelzinis. If I don't come
back, carry the torch. Keep Bry focused. And keep pushing
the Threat Cell idea."

"Will do." They nodded. Looking, he was encouraged to
note, worried.

The assistant's office was on the third floor. He went
down the cool echoing hallway feeling as if he were going to
his execution. He pushed the gloom away. Martin W.
Tallinger and his kind didn't belong here. To acquiesce in
that . . . he just wasn't going to do it.

"Dan. Come in."

Sebold was with Clayton's second in command. Gelzinis shoved aside a pile of folders and laced his fingers. "Commander Lenson. I'd ask you to sit down, but you've seriously embarrassed us today. I just heard about this from Holt. What the hell was that performance about?"

Dan explained whom Tallinger had represented and what he'd done. The two senior staffers exchanged glances. "That was a long time ago," Gelzinis observed.

"He never paid for it. And I have no doubt in my mind he's still raking the same shit pile."

"Maybe you ought to remember something. You're military. Not in the inner circles of this administration."

"I know that. But it's part of my job, if I see a mistake being made, to point it out. Associating with scum like that is not going to make the president look good."

"So you had his best interests in mind," Gelzinis said with that dry tone he was the master of. "That's good to hear. Because it so happens Dr. Tallinger ran one of the biggest political action committees supporting his campaign."

"Representing who?"

"That's not yours to ask. The point is he's a friend of the administration and we treat him as such."

"You let pricks like him dictate policy? Because they donate money?"

Gelzinis said in a flinty tone, "He dictates *nothing*. I shouldn't have to explain basics. There are a lot of interests who have access, or have to be reassured they have access. Who have to be listened to, but who don't necessarily affect policymaking. That's a given. The point I'm making is, we expect the military staff to stay out of that loop. Force yourself into it and you'll be on the way back to your service before you can log off."

"What I'm saying, sir, is that any face time you're giving this fucker's direct access for the Chinese government."

"Let me set you straight on a couple of items, Lenson. We've got the biggest national debt this country has ever had. Thanks mainly to the previous administration, but we've done our part. Who do you think bought our securities? If the Chinese want a word with us, they've paid the going rate. We need to forge linkages, not perpetuate cold war enmities."

Dan recognized the same weaseling bullshit Tallinger had given him once. "Building trust." "Profitable linkages, not competing interests." The rationale he'd used to steal information to pass to China, and through China to North Korea, and Iran, and the other rogue regimes that were metastasizing into a new generation of threats around the world.

"Are we clear here, Commander?"

Dan stood with fists clenched. He saw the military-civilian divide, all right. But dipping yourself in shit for campaign contributions wasn't right. He said in a tight voice, "I guess that's where I belong. Back at sea. Believe me, I'm ready to go."

"Now, Dan," Sebold said.

"Don't make the mistake of thinking you get fired out of here, you go back to any kind of decent assignment," Gelzinis said. "Remember who approves military promotions. The president. Or his responsible staffer."

"That's exactly the kind of low threat I'd expect from a pandering weasel like you," Dan told him, and was happy to see the assistant choke and splutter, caught wordless.

Which seemed to be Sebold's cue. "Now, Dan, Brent, let's calm down. We're saying things in the heat of the moment. Things we don't really mean. Okay? Dan's going to apologize. Then we're all going back to work."

"I'll apologize to Tony," Dan told them. "But not to the asshole with the suspenders. He should be in prison. They only let him walk because he was the first to turn state's evidence."

But Sebold's intercession seemed to have given the assistant national security adviser a chance to regain his composure. "An apology would be a start. What were you doing in with Holt in the first place?"

Dan explained about the report. Sebold and Gelzinis exchanged glances. "Dan, that should have gone through me," the general said.

"The president asked me for it."

"Again, you're not in the loop," Gelzinis told him. "You think you see what you think you see and that's all there is. But it's not."

"I saw people being killed."

"And you think due to inaction on our part."

"Damn right."

"While what you're actually perceiving is the Pentagon fighting us tooth and nail to avoid having to commit troops. And a certain lack of . . . traction on our part vis-à-vis the Joint Chiefs and others."

"De Bari's the commander in chief. All he has to do is give an order."

The two men exchanged the looks of adults dealing with an unreasonable three-year-old. "It's *not* just a matter of giving an order. Especially with Stahl as chairman. That's not how things work at the higher levels. More of a—a collaborative process—"

"Last time I looked, we still had civilian control."

"I'm afraid in practice that control's situational. A directive they don't care for can be modified. Circumvented. Even ignored, if the Chiefs and the combatant commanders don't agree."

"Then fire them! Lincoln and Truman did it. You mean he's afraid to play hardball."

" 'Afraid' is too strong a word. We've got our problems with the Pentagon, sure."

Dan thought that had to rank as the understatement of the century, given the open ridicule from senior officers, the open disobedience, the way midgrade people were hemorrhaging out of services that couldn't seem to make up their mind either to move ahead or stand pat, that instead whipsawed back and forth, bewildering the rank and file. But he didn't interrupt as Gelzinis went on. "But there are other ways to address the issue. . . . What's actually happening is, we're giving certain parties the green light to ship arms into the region. To redress the balance, so to speak. We have to do it quietly because our European allies, that's contrary to their policy. But it's the only way we'll get the combatants to a state of exhaustion, where we can step in and broker a peace."

Dan felt as if he'd stepped through the looking glass. Hadn't De Bari told him in the Oval Office debriefing that he wouldn't permit arms shipments? "A state of exhaustion . . . *Who* is shipping in these arms?"

"That's not important," Gelzinis said, at the same moment Sebold said, "The Iranians."

"We're letting the *Iranians* ship arms into Bosnia?" Dan clutched his temples, unable to comprehend the piling up of ever more catastrophic idiocies. "And who's training them? The Iranians, are they *training* them too?"

"That's classified and you won't discuss it," Gelzinis said. "You don't know what you're doing, and you'd better shut your mouth. Garner, we need to talk about this—"

"No need," Sebold said equably. "I'll tell you exactly what's happening here, Brent, and don't get all huffy on me, okay? You're talking past each other. Because each of you thinks the other guy's like he is. Okay? But you're not.

"Dan, you're talking to a guy who's been throwing elbows in politics a lot of years. He knows that most of the time, if you take the high road, you end up going over the cliff. And maybe because of that, he tends to expect the worst out of the people he deals with.

"Brent, you're talking to professional military. A guy who still has a functioning sense of honor. He doesn't like what he's seeing. Like they say, politics and making sausage, right? He's telling you that, up front, but that's as far as it's going to go with him. Because he *does* believe in the Constitution, and taking civilian direction. He's not going to leak a word about arms shipments. Or Tallinger. Or about anything else that takes place inside the fence. This may strike you as quaint, but he'll keep his word. It's not going to be like dealing with the rats over at State, or the Hill."

A pause. Finally Gelzinis sighed. Turned away.

"Dismissed," the general said in Dan's direction.

* * *

He stopped in the corridor. Above his head the nineteenth-century light-globes glowed. Staffers were leaving. Brushing by him, carrying briefcases and rolled-up newspapers. He leaned against antique plaster and rubbed his eyes till stars burst. The enemies were gathering. Like buzzards above some wounded thing trailing its guts on the asphalt. Didn't anyone care about the country? About anything beyond his own interest?

He smiled grimly, remembering how Sandy had laughed at him once when he'd asked that. In ten years, it had gotten worse. Much worse.

But until they *did* shitcan him, he didn't plan to stop doing his job. What could they do—send him back to sea?

He only wished they would.

The house was quiet when he let himself in. He paused, listening. No Larry King. No *Crossfire*. Blair snapped on the set as soon as she got in. She was a news junkie. But it wasn't on now.

He found the letter on the dining-room table.

Dan,

I was very angry after our last talk. I tried to write off your unjust accusations to what you went through in Srebrenica. But I find I can't let it go. You need to call your doctor. Get some meds or—something. Maybe you can't see it, but you are getting really unbalanced. I won't stay in the house with someone who might turn violent. And sleeps with a gun by the bed.

What is happening? I still care about you. We're so much alike. But I get the feeling there's a wall where a door used to be. And I have no idea how to break through it, or if you're even still there, on the other side.

Anyway, rather than ask you to move out, I have. If you want to talk, you can reach me on the cell, or at the office, though we have a lot of travel scheduled this month. Or at Fort Myers—I'll be in a suite there. When I'm in town.

I'm sorry. I really thought this could work out.

Blair

He fingered the note for a few seconds, looking at his reflection in the black windows.

He didn't feel like staying at home, with beer waiting in the fridge. He hadn't seen his daughter since school started. So he called and suggested he take her out to dinner. She sounded glad to hear from him. That raised his spirits a little.

He was on I-66, driving west in a chill drizzle, when his pager vibrated. When he checked the number it wasn't familiar. Not even a D.C. area code. He debated not answering it. Then pulled off at the next exit and found a pay phone that worked outside a convenience store. It began to rain harder as he listened to the call go through. There wasn't any overhead shelter. He flipped up the collar of his coat, hoping this didn't take too long.

"JIATF West, how may I help you, sir or ma'am?"

"This is Dan Lenson, NSC counterdrug."

"Whom did you wish to talk to, sir?"

"I'm not sure. I'm returning a call."

The duty person asked him to stand by, and a few seconds later Miles Bloom came on. "Dan? That was me paging you. Returning your call."

"Huh? I didn't call you, Miles."

"I mean, your message askin' me to check out what happened at Laguna Verde. Slid in from Ecuador last night. Stopped here, got your e-mail, made a couple calls."

A car lurched into the lot and squealed to a halt, catching him in the headlight glare. He turned his back. Then, feeling vulnerable, faced it again. Several men piled out of a battered Citation and filed into the store. They left the lights on, illuminating him as he stood in the now-freezing rain.

Bloom said, "Talked to a *federale* I know in Mexico City.

He told me under the counter as it were some things about that raid that didn't make it into the papers. Where are you, anyway?"

"At a 7-Eleven in, uh, Falls Church."

"Should be secure. The dead guy the attackers left behind. Guess what. He was shot in two places: the gut and the back of the head. What's that tell you?"

"Oh. That . . . they killed him themselves. Rather than taking him along."

"Which is the way who operates?"

"The cartel. Nuñez." Cold rain ran down his collar. He shivered.

"Bingo. This is all off the Mexican government record, by the way. No journalists within five miles of the plant. They're hoping to make this all go away rather than admit how flip-fucked their security was."

The men had come out with bottles and cans and were joking and hooting, opening them on the concrete pad in front of the store. Dan said, "Miles, let me ask you something. What they were making. The radiologicals. Why would the cartel want them?"

"I don't know. You might want to ask Luis that. He keeps closer tabs on what they're up to per se than I do."

"Okay, but is there any market for that stuff?"

"You mean, like black market pharmaceuticals? Resell to hospitals? Be a hard way to make a buck. Way I understand it, there's only a few places use this stuff, cancer treatment centers mainly. It's way too hot for diagnostic tracing."

Dan knew the difference between the low-emission isotopes used for tracing and the high-energy particle emitters used to zap cancers. He'd picked up quite a bit of that information after *Horn*'s contamination, making sure his crew was being taken care of. Holding the phone, he watched the men from the Citation drinking and shoving each other. One kept glancing his way.

"What's all that hollering?"

"Just some locals blowing their paychecks. Look, I've got

to get back on the road. When are you getting back?"

"Gonna take the weekend off and head back Monday. That cool, boss man?"

"Sure. See you then."

The men started Dan's way. He got into the Escort and pulled out. He watched for the on-ramp. The rain was coming down so hard he had the wipers on as fast as they would go. He merged with inches to spare as a tractor trailer roared and blared behind him. Traffic was insane, seventy-five, eighty, bumper to bumper and no visibility.

Why would anyone want to steal radioactives? Enough to put together a major, coordinated, obviously rehearsed raid?

Only the cartel killed their own wounded. But medical isotopes, however valuable in monetary terms, weren't something they could sell on the street. Why would they want high-energy neutron sources? He was no nuclear engineer, but he was pretty sure you couldn't use medical isotopes to make a nuclear bomb. The way he understood it, the only metals that would actually chain-react were uranium, plutonium, and thorium.

He tried putting it together with the idea of shipping containers going across the border to a humanitarian assistance organization. He smiled. It'd make a great premise for a thriller. It even locked in with that remark the Baptist had supposedly made, on the way to Haiti, before the Marines and the DEA had crashed their party.

Say the cartel had stolen the isotopes. Certainly they had the muscle, the money, the arms. They could get inside any organization they wanted. They send the isotopes, small, high-value packages—just like drugs, so much like drugs— across the U.S.-Mexican border, either in air freight containers, or by "mule," ignorant peasant smugglers, or in small, low-flying aircraft—the way most coke traveled now.

Then, when they're across, pool them at some location federal agents wouldn't want to go. Like a religious compound. After Waco, nobody wanted to touch a religious compound.

He liked to drive, even in the dark, in the rain. The enforced idleness, the half attention you had to pay, let the back of your brain play with fantasies, idle reveries. Such as, if somebody wanted to make trouble with what had come out of Laguna Verde, what he'd do.

The bomb that had shattered *Horn* hadn't been intended to wipe out Tel Aviv with blast and fire, but with a deadly cloak of radioactive cobalt. Cobalt wasn't a common material. One of the techs who'd interviewed him after the blast had suggested sheep feed. It sounded off the wall, but the guy said the stuff was rich in cobalt compounds, and certainly common enough around the Middle East.

What if you spread some radioactive iodine around? Technium? The other isotopes Roald said Laguna Verde made? It wouldn't have to be aimed at a specific target. A radioactive plume was the ultimate area weapon. It would sicken and kill thousands. Like Chernobyl.

There'll be a hot wind in Washington this spring. What Nuñez had chuckled over in the plane with his financier. Say "Spring Wind" meant an isotope release. Say Washington really was the target. Something like that could make the Mall, the White House, Pentagon, Congress, uninhabitable for years. Maybe generations. Depending on the isotope mix, the laydown density, the half-life.

He was glad they hadn't actually gotten their hands on any of the stuff.

He picked Nan up at her residence hall. Despite the weather she was in an off-the-shoulder blouse and a short skirt. He had to remind himself she was eighteen, old enough to choose her own wardrobe.

"So how's the White House?" she said, once they were in his car and headed for the restaurant.

"Keeps me busy."

"You look awful tired, Dad. Don't take this wrong. But

you look older than when you started." She touched his temple. "Like, gray. And your eye's all bruised."

"Guys don't complain about their hair. They're just glad to still have it."

He looked at her profile, the fall of dark hair, the button nose. A wave of gratitude swelled his heart. No matter what was wrong with the world or his life, she was in it. He surreptitiously touched his eyes, ashamed at getting so emotional. She gave him a conspiratorial smile and patted his hand.

They were into the second course when his pager hummed. "Damn, not again," he muttered.

"What's wrong?"

"Got to call the office. Sorry."

He found a phone in the front lobby. Had to use his AT&T card. Same area code as the last time, but a different number.

"New news," Bloom said. "I made a couple more calls on that last issue we talked about? And guess what? The bad stuff got away."

"I'm sorry?" His mind was elsewhere. "Uh—what bad stuff?"

"You know what bad stuff. The shit they make there."

He was back in the picture, despite the agent's elliptical references. "You said *they* said they never got to it."

"That's what their honchos put out. Right. But it isn't what happened."

He tensed. Cupped the phone to his ear. "Okay, I know this isn't a secure line. But can you—"

"They flew off with the pixie powder," Bloom said. "Enough to turn a whole bunch of folks into pixies."

"Shit!"

"Where are you now?"

"In Fairfax."

"Pay phone? Picked at random? Okay, what I'm hearing is, they got away with thirteen hundred pounds of encapsulated isotope."

"Thirteen hundred pounds?" A woman lighting a ciga-

rette a few steps away looked up, startled, and he lowered his voice. "Is that what you said?"

"Yeah, but that's not isotope weight. Far from it—most of that's going to be the lead shielding. But it's two months' output. And hot, *hot* stuff. Cesium, mostly. Fresh out of the reactor. They hit the plant the day before shipment. Obviously had inside intelligence."

His head was going at about sixteen miles a second. So the fanciful scenario he'd developed on the road might be more than that.

And in that chilling moment he understood that no one else, no other site or agency in the whole edifice of government, military, the intelligence community, had the information to put together that he, Bloom, and Ed Lynch had. Each agency would know a bit. This fragment or that. But nobody else had enough pieces to show a picture that had been jigsawed apart by someone more cunning and patient and inventive than any other adversary he'd ever faced.

The downside was, he had no proof. Only supposition.

It was exactly the kind of event he'd thought the Threat Cell might pick up. The trouble was, there was no Threat Cell yet. So there were no procedures to put out an alert, get other agencies involved, the way there were for an imminent military attack or an impending natural disaster. He felt sweat break along his hairline, and dragged his sleeve across it.

At the same time, he might be wrong. He was already walking a narrow line. If he cried wolf on this one, and no wolf was stalking the flock . . .

"I don't like the sound of this," he said. "With what Ed dug up about the UPS flights, and what that other guy, the one we caught, said the cartel was planning to do—"

"Thinking the same thing, boss. So where do we go with it?"

He looked at his watch, knowing there was no way he could go back in now and eat a quiet dinner with his daughter. "There's only one place we can do anything from. I'm on my way."

"Sit Room?"

"Call me there in an hour. Get hold of Marty and Ed and tell them to come in. And find out as much more in the meantime as you can."

"How about Alvarado?"

Dan remembered his suspicions about the Coast Guard lieutenant commander, that if anyone inside his own office was the leak to the cartel, it might be Luis. Or was that prejudice, just because the guy was Hispanic? And worked his tail off, and stayed late? He said reluctantly, "Yeah, Luis too—but don't tell him what it's about, okay? Just tell him to get his tail in to the Eighteen."

"You're really gonna bust the glass on the red box, huh?"

"You don't think I should?"

"Hey," Bloom laughed, "I don't know. But it's about as good a way to go down in flames as any."

He gave his daughter money for a taxi and told her he was sorry but that he really had to go. He didn't like the disappointment in her eyes, but didn't see anything he could do about it but promise to get together again soon.

The roads were slick and there were accidents working, strobes searing the mist, so it wasn't until midnight that he actually got to the Ellipse. He stalked head down through the blowing rain to the West Wing. The marines weren't out, even in rain gear. That meant the president wasn't in residence. Dan wondered where he was, but dismissed it as something he didn't care enough to wonder about.

As far as he was concerned, the asshole could be grilling in hell.

Lynch and Alvarado got up as he came into the admin staff area. "Marty's on her way," Ed said. "But it may take her a while, there's flooding in her neighborhood."

Dan said fine, looking past them to where the duty officers and comm techs sat in the brightly lit, always flickering-live intensity of the watch center. The night crew here got just as much action as the day people, since night in Washington was day in Asia and the Middle East. He was glad to see Roald's helmet of dark hair in the director's cubicle. First he'd see if he could convince her. He'd already resolved on the drive in that if he couldn't, he'd let it go. He was supposed to interdict drugs, not terror attacks.

On the other hand, he couldn't just look away, wait for somebody else to notice. This had nothing to do with Dan Lenson's job description or counterdrug's lines of command. But compared to this, they faded into unimportance.

If there really was an attack impending, he had to stop it.

He took Lynch and Alvarado into the director's cubicle with him. Making it crowded, but it was a quick way to get them backgrounded. He still wondered if he should be including the Coastie in this. He'd have to keep an eye on his phone calls.

Roald listened with her too-pointed chin propped on a finger, gaze locked on his. Questions darted behind those blue windows. But she didn't voice them. Till at last he ran down and stood listening to the murmur of a desk officer checking a comm channel to some distant corner of the empire. He eyed Alvarado, wondering why he didn't look surprised.

The captain's first question, soft and low-toned: "Why would you think this might be aimed at the Washington area?"

"The cartel second-ranker we turned after the Haiti raid. He didn't know what it was. Or when. But he said it was aimed at D.C."

"Right. The spring wind thing." Roald cut her eyes at the cold rain, actually sleet now, lashing the windows. "But this isn't spring. Not by a long shot."

Dan hurried on, realizing this must sound less than convincing. "Actually the specific target doesn't matter, does it? Something like that, it's an area weapon. They'd target it against a city. The important thing's to catch them on the ground, stop them before they take off."

The Sit Room director swiveled her chair, frowning. "Who else have you shared this with?"

"Just my own people. Bloom. Lynch. Marty Harlowe's coming in."

"Your boss? General Sebold?"

"No . . . not yet."

"Don't you think you should?"

"I wanted to run it past you first. A reality check. If we're jumping out without the 'chute on this."

Her gaze flicked from her screen to the overhead clocks. "It might make sense, but . . . only if you accept a lot of hearsay at face value. What makes you think it's going to happen soon?"

"It's not all hearsay. The documents we found at the Haiti conference. Then the thefts last week from Laguna Verde."

"I understood all that. Though the Mexican authorities are still saying nothing was taken. What I asked was, why the big rush?"

"I don't know . . . it just occurred to me . . . the strike's going to start the day after tomorrow."

"The strike? What strike?"

Dan nodded to Lynch, who said, "The air cargo baggage handlers' union is going out day after tomorrow if the airlines don't sign. And the *Wall Street Journal* says they won't. They say this could be a long strike. Meaning air cargo won't fly."

Roald shrugged. "So what? They just wait until it can."

"They can't just sit on their hands. Every day they keep this stuff in the U.S. is a day more they can be discovered," Dan told her. "Plus think about this. This material they've stolen has what's called 'inherent security'— meaning it's dangerous as hell to be around. Even if they're just in the same building with it, hiding it, or guarding it, they'll be getting neutrons through the walls. They might not have figured on that. They might know, at least the higher-ups, but not have bothered to warn the foot soldiers. But once you start getting radiation sickness, you know it. I've seen it. It's not something you ignore. And it happens fast."

She tried to interrupt but he hurried on. "Okay, dying might not stop them. If there's the jihadist connection we suspect, from this Blessings organization. Or they might just shoot the first people who go down, if the guards are cartel. But if they all get sick, they'll be useless, and it'll be too late. Ed says the last air cargo strike lasted for three months.

"So my call is they'll do whatever they're going to do just as soon as they can turn the isotopes around, just as soon as they can get them into whatever dispersal mechanism or packaging they plan to use. And then—they'll go. They won't delay a day, not an hour. Because they can't afford to."

Roald thought about that. Then swung to her terminal. Her fingers danced. Dan saw she was accessing a Los Alamos National Laboratory site. Then a list of classified papers. Finally, a monograph on medical radiological sources. She scrolled down, speed-reading at an impressive rate.

" 'Uses range from radiation treatment of cancer, to well testing, sterilization of food, seeds, and medical equipment.' What's the isotope again?"

He told her what Bloom had told him, from his unnamed source: that it was mostly cesium.

"Cesium-137." Roald pulled up another screen. " 'Most often employed in the form of cesium chloride . . . product of uranium fission . . . millions of times more radioactive than uranium . . . 'Chemical treatment is required to extract the cesium,' " she read off.

"That'd be the process at Laguna Verde."

"Let's see, this says . . . 'Cesium chloride. A fine, talcum-powder-like precipitate.' God . . . yeah." She ran her hand over her hair, the same self-comforting gesture, Dan noticed, he used sometimes himself.

"What is it?"

"The half-life's thirty years. After area contamination, it takes six half-lives for decay to safe levels."

"Six times fifteen's 180 years," Alvarado said behind them.

"And you're sure this was what was actually stolen?" she asked them.

Dan explained that was a weak point. All they had was cop-to-cop liaison, anonymous background—nothing in writing. "But Miles, my DEA guy, says the *federale* he got this from, he's a good source."

"You say you think the cartel, this Baptist guy, was behind the plant hit. But the people who were into air cargo were a charity foundation?"

"An *Islamic* charity foundation. Out of Pomona. They were shipping cargo containers across the Mexican border. Empty, but that could have been a rehearsal. And you know NSA's been reporting back chatter between the terror boys and the drug people. They're starting to work together."

She looked doubtful. "This is all pretty thin, Dan. We could get burned if we take this seriously, and it turns out to be nothing."

"I know it's thin. But look at the downside, too." He tried to make his voice earnest. "Captain, prudent mariners don't wait till somebody comes out of the fog at us. If we hear something out there, we stop the engines. All I'm saying is, let's call the skipper. Put Transportation, the FBI, and Customs on alert. Maybe they've heard something too. Maybe they've got a piece we're missing."

She thought a bit more. Then, with a quick gesture, flipped open a binder and ran her finger down a list. "Put one of your people on finding out if there's actually anything going on in L.A. At the charity. See if they can persuade the local FBI to go over and check them out again. I'll call a couple of people on the alert chain. I also want to know how big a threat this thing would be. Whether cesium chloride would disperse in a brisk wind, the effect of precipitation on dispersion, and so on. Get me some numbers. Get me some facts. Then maybe I can help you."

Dan said he'd do that, and went back out into the admin area. Alvarado and Lynch trailed him to one of the vacant terminals. The same one he'd sat at during the futile run-up to the Eritrean retreat. He logged in, wondering again what he was supposed to do if Alvarado really was dirty. *Somebody* inside the counterdrug establishment was leaking. But who?

He finally told himself it didn't matter. It might even work to their advantage. If Luis was their leaker and passed the word to the other side that the operation was compromised, they might abort.

Which would be fine with him. They might lose track of the conspirators, but if they stopped whatever was going on before it got off the ground, he'd settle for that. In fact, that might be the smartest thing he could do.

"Okay, let's split this up. Luis, I want you on the phone to anybody and everybody you know in Santa Cruz and Mexico City. Use that excellent Spanish. Find out if what Miles got is the straight skinny. Anything they've uncovered. How much material's missing, if you find anybody who can drill down to that level of detail. Call in all your chips and don't be afraid to beg. Tell them something wicked might be coming our way, and we need the facts."

"I need to go back to the office to do that."

"Why?"

"All my phone numbers are there."

Dan hesitated, then said that was all right.

Marty Harlowe came in, shaking wet off her raincoat. She hung it carefully. Underneath she was wearing black slacks and a lacy, clingy white blouse. "Miles said you needed us."

He explained again. Midway through she said, "The dirty-bomb concept. A radiological-dispersal device, like we used to think about for area denial."

"That's kind of our sense of what we're looking at. Yeah. Ed's working the airline end. Luis's backtracking with his contacts south of the border, trying to confirm what Miles heard, get specifics on the isotopes. We need hard data for Captain Roald to pass up the alert chain."

"Hard data, meaning what?"

"Exactly what got stolen. Where it is, and what they're planning to do with it."

The marine said, "I can't help you with the first two. But maybe I can with the third."

"Yeah?"

She looked toward the back of the admin area, where a beige steel workstation with a small wire-gridded screen stood. Red-striped burn bags bulging with shredded paper lay stacked against it, on it, adding to its air of dusty neglect.

"Let's go back to the Wimmicks," she said.

W WMCCS, the Worldwide Military Command and Control System, was a late-sixties-era forerunner of the Internet. Dan knew it as a secure data exchange system that had linked the Pentagon to the old Strategic Air Command and the rest of the country's military headquarters. It kept tabs on every unit in the defense establishment; you could use it to access or generate operational plans, to communicate and pass orders, supposedly even during a nuclear war—though that had never been tested, of course. The Global Command and Control System had replaced it years before. But Harlowe's fingers flew over the grubby, worn black keys of the Honeywell Datanet 8 like an accordionist playing a polka. Roald, seeing them, came out of her cubicle. "What are you doing with that thing?"

"Accessing the NORAD mainframe. If they haven't gone to distributed processing."

"Can't you use Geeks? I've never even seen that thing turned on before."

"Do they have fallout models on GCCS, Captain? I don't think they do."

The answer must have been no, because Roald went back to her cubicle. She returned with a worn ledger bound in green cloth that she said her predecessor had left in the desk.

Harlowe punched in the personal ID, project code, and password ballpointed inside the front cover. An old-fashioned amber-on-black screen swam up.

She muttered, "I used to be a RECA puke. Residual Capabilities Assessment. Meaning what we'd have left after a nuclear strike. They axed the specialty after the Wall came down. But I think the templates are still on the system . . . and here we are."

Engineered long before Windows, the little screen, phosphors etched with the ghosts of decades, pulsated the color of orange marmalade. Harlowe palmed a trackball, hunted through special-function keys. Pressed one. Then banged it, cursing. The screen blanked, then came up again with a menu. She trackballed RADFO and banged the key again. "Can you get me a wind speed and direction?" she said over her shoulder as they waited some more.

One of the desk officers came back with the local weather printout.

Leaning over her shoulder, noticing her perfume, Dan saw an outline. No detail to speak of. Just an amber-glowing drawing, angular and stylized. A flickering square tipped on its side, with a crooked Y laid over it.

"District of Columbia. The Y is the intersection of the Potomac and the Anacostia. Ever work with FM 3-3?" Harlowe asked him.

"What's that?"

"Fallout prediction. I thought you might have, when you guys got hit on *Horn*."

"We used radiological tables, but they weren't computerized."

"Well, this is the same, only faster. When it works," Harlowe said to the screen. "Assume the point of release is over National Airport. Surface wind's southeasterly at ten knots. Wimmick's used a modified Gaussian plume equation to generate the footprint. It'll show you the hazard zones, normalized dosage rates, a lot of info, depending on how deep in the program you want to get. But remember, I haven't thought about this stuff for years. After the cold war, it just dropped off the radar."

"It might be coming back on," Dan told her. "But that's for a fission burst, right? The materials and decay rates are going to be different for a radiological dispersal."

"Not a problem. I just select the smallest possible weapon yield and change this fission product table."

"What about the point location?" Lynch said. "They can dump this stuff out anywhere, right?"

Dan told them he didn't think they were limited to a dumping or spraying scenario. "If these people are part of the group that bombed *Cole* and *Horn*, they don't mind suiciding. They can get wind data as easily as we can. They'll position themselves, if they're driving the plane, upwind of the city. What Marty's giving us is the footprint; they can orient it any way they want."

Harlowe said, "What have you got on the source?"

"Cesium-137, finely powdered."

"And how much?"

Dan got on the phone to room 303.

Alvarado answered after five rings. "I'm on the other line with him now," he said.

"With who?"

"The security director at Laguna Verde."

"Good. That's real good, Luis! What's he say?"

"Just hold on." The rapid clatter of Spanish. Alvarado sounded angry. Then a staccato series of phrases. Dan realized he was counting down, or up.

"He still won't say."

"Fuck."

"Said he'd lose his job. I said okay, he didn't have to tell me shit. I'd start counting up from ten kilos. All he had to do was listen. He just stopped me. At eighty kilos."

"Holy shit," Harlowe muttered. "And it's 137?"

"It's cesium?" Dan asked Alvarado.

"Cesio radioactivo. That's what he said. Eighty kilos—without the lead packaging."

Harlowe sucked air, looking at the screen. Then started typing again.

She coded the powder as base surge, the finely milled earth and dust thrown up by a near-ground blast. She hit the Enter key. The distant mainframe, under some mountain in Colorado, cogitated for several seconds.

Its output appeared as a funnel-shaped, pulsating amber wedge. They stared at it. "Can you print that out?" Dan said at last. Harlowe pressed a button and a wet-paper printer off to the side, huge, old, grimy, hummed suddenly, as if startled out of a long sleep.

A duty officer, holding up a handset: "One of you Lenson?"

It was Bloom. He started off too fast, and Dan had to slow him down. Finally he got on sync. "I talked to the lieutenant governor of Veracruz—the state, not the city. He confirmed material is missing. But he can't say that officially."

"Well, look, Miles, that's just not good enough. We're getting confirmation through Luis too, but it's still unofficial. We need someone to go on the record about this," Dan told him. "I don't mean to the press; just to us, here in the Sit Room. Call your guy back. Work the 'White House is calling' angle. I want a faxed statement. Promise him a medal from the president. A job this side of the line. A date with Sharon Stone, she's always hanging around at De Bari's parties. Just get it."

It was starting to roll. He felt as if he were riding a snowboard on the crest of an avalanche. He left them all working and went in to see Roald again.

B ut she motioned him to wait. He hovered as she said into the phone, "Yes . . . yes . . . not yet. No."

When she hung up she looked pensive.

"What is it?"

"The team leader at NORAD doesn't think he can declare an alert."

"We don't need to launch interceptors. Just click the readiness up, in case we have to." But even as he said this it occurred to him that it was conceivable, it was just conceivable, that if what he was guessing at was taking place, a plane with those isotopes aboard could be in the air right now. No reason it couldn't be.

For the first time, he really felt afraid.

Roald was saying, "The bottom line is there's no confirmation from the Mexican authorities. And we're not the initiating authority for alerts for most of these agencies. Not for FEMA. Not for NORAD. I can't even get anybody at Transportation. They're supposed to have a duty officer but there's no answer."

"Well, who's the initiating authority for an alert if not the White House? Presidential emergency authority—"

"Whoa, there. Don't get the Sit Room confused with the national command authority, Dan. Remember, we just answer the phones here," Roald said mildly.

"Okay, okay, I know. . . . But how about NMCC? The Pentagon's got to have the authority to get the Air Force moving, and maybe the FBI."

"The National Military Command Center has no link with the FBI. But they could get interceptors up, yes. If they believed there was an imminent threat."

"How about calling the FBI direct then?"

"They're in the crime-fighting business, not round-the-clock command stuff. They don't have a 24/7 operations center." Roald considered it. "I could probably punch the book and get somebody's pager, or contact a phone watch. Ask for a callback. But I doubt we're going to get any live people to talk to this late on a Friday. Let alone somebody who can order a raid in California. We'd do better to wait till eight or eight thirty in the morning, catch people as they open for business—no, then it'll be Saturday."

"How about the CIA?"

Roald bared her teeth. "Believe me, you want somebody to actually do something, Dan, you do not go to Langley. Just trust me on that one."

Dan stared at her, then reached for her phone. Her hand closed over his. "Hold on, Commander. I've presented the issue where it needs to be presented. They're doing the notifications according to their lists. If they think it's worth going to general quarters for, they'll go."

"But how long will that take?"

For answer he got his hand back. "I don't know. But I'll keep pushing the other buttons. Maybe try the Los Angeles Police Department."

"Call the Pentagon again. Damn it, let me talk to them."

"*No.* I have a call in to the deputy assistant. If she thinks we have something worth pursuing, she'll call Mrs. Clayton. Who will then, if she agrees, be the one to really light things off. That's how we're going to do it. By the book."

He was about to burst out that while they were playing Mother May I and making sure no one got offended, terrorists might be loading an aircraft with the most dangerous payload since Nagasaki. But then he remembered how deftly Jennifer Roald had handled a call from Eritrea. How she'd defused that situation, and probably saved a general officer's career. If she thought he was getting tunnel vision, maybe he was. He took a deep breath. "All right. We'll do it your way. Until I see that's not working."

He felt her cool gaze brush him. As if about to ask: And then what? But she didn't, just picked up the phone and tapped a single button.

"This is the White House Situation Room," she said. "I need you to call me back just as soon as you hear this message."

B ut no one did. Roald left other messages, left her number on pagers. Still no response. By 4 A.M. Dan was getting nervous. Where was the CIA? The FBI? He couldn't believe no one else had picked up these clues. Or maybe they weren't clues, and he was seeing mirages.

He was sitting with eyes closed, worrying, when Ed Lynch shook his shoulder. "I'm awake," he snapped.

"I called the UPS hub office in Los Angeles. Told them I was the warehouse manager at International Blessings, and wanted to check on our shipment."

"That's underhanded and brilliant, Major. What did they say?"

"Three containers. That's a big shipment, apparently." He read off the back of a phone message form. "They're marked for Sudan. Flight 3913. I got the shipment number."

Once more Dan thought of the empty containers air transportation security had noticed being shuttled around. He was starting to see what that must have been about. Getting familiar with the air carrier's procedures, schedules, maybe even doing a dry run. Smoothing out any snags, so the final operation would go smooth as silk.

"Routing?"

"Ontario, California—that's near L.A.—to Washington, D.C., via the UPS national hub in Louisville, Kentucky. Container transfer at Washington International for the overseas flight to Sudan."

"Great work, Ed." He slapped the major's shoulder and walked the info back to Roald, realizing on the way that Washington International Airport, more commonly known as Dulles, was only about thirty miles from the White House.

A man with slicked-black hair had his head bent together with the captain's. When Dan tapped a knuckle on glass Brent Gelzinis looked up, annoyed even before he saw who it was knocking. *Uh-oh,* Dan thought. Roald beckoned him in.

"What are you trying to do now, Lenson?" the assistant national security adviser snapped.

This wasn't going to be easy, trying to deal with the man he'd called a weasel only yesterday. He laid the printout in front of him, trying for professionalism. "Trying to abort a terrorist strike, sir. Flight 3913 from Los Angeles to the Sudan, via Washington International. Taking off at 0130 local time, that's 0430 Washington time. This morning. Carrying three containers from International Blessings, an Islamic charity based in Pomona, California. That's a suburb of Los Angeles. The containers will transfer at Dulles. If we're right, you'll find enough radiocesium in them to contaminate most of the District of Colombia."

Gelzinis didn't look impressed. " 'If we're right'—what does that mean? Who reported this? CIA? FBI?"

Dan didn't answer. Neither did Marty Harlowe, whose presence Dan sensed behind him by her scent. Roald cleared her throat. "Commander Lenson's people have put together some indicators. Pretty strong ones, I think."

"Confirmed?"

"We're checking them out. But we don't have confirmation yet."

"What about the intelligence agencies? Did you bother asking them?"

Roald said quietly that she'd tried, but couldn't reach anyone. Gelzinis snorted, made a pushing-away motion. "Which means they have no indicators. Or they'd have someone at the airport."

"Not necessarily. They may have no idea—"

"I'm surprised you called me, Jennifer. Not that I mind coming in, but . . . obviously our counterdrug people, Lenson here, they've picked up some rumor. He's to be . . . complimented for bringing it to your attention. But if you've done your best to check it out with the proper agencies, left messages for action in the morning, as far as I can see, our responsibility ends there. And you have the morning summary to prepare."

Dan saw Roald stiffen. Gelzinis waited. Then added, when neither responded, "Don't you agree?"

"Yes, sir," Roald said.

But Dan didn't leave when the assistant did. He couldn't. The others stayed too. They didn't say much. Just watched him until he went back to Roald and asked if there was any other way they could get that aircraft looked at before it took off. Get someone to check it out. Confirm what he suspected, or prove him wrong.

"Brent made it clear he's not going to wake Mrs. C."

"Right. But damn it, he's assuming the CIA knows everything. You and I both know, Jennifer, there have been times that wasn't true. Not to mention that we can't get them to actually do anything in the middle of the night."

"Well, there's the DOMS route," Roald said.

"What's that?"

"Director of Military Support. Another way to get Defense to react if NMCC won't."

She explained that the secretary of the army was the executive agent for military support to civil authorities. "We use DOMS a lot when U.S.-Mexico border issues crop up. Which I guess this might fall under, in some sense . . . But we can't just tell active-duty forces to go do this, go do that, inside the U.S. That's just not our bailiwick."

"How does that work? And how long does it take?"

"Well, that really should go through channels too. I convince Mrs. Clayton. She calls the secretary of defense, Weatherfield. And he—"

"And that's faster . . . how?"

"Point taken. Maybe, considering it's off-duty hours, I could just get her verbal authorization to call the DOMS contact in the Pentagon. I can almost always get hold of him, even at night. He's the one who can ask the governor out there to authorize whatever's needed." Roald paused. Then her voice changed, and he heard an edge. "Of course what we should *really* be doing is our *important* work—like getting the morning summary ready. Did you hear that one?"

Dan drummed his fingers. It wasn't that he didn't see the need for the national security adviser to approve alerts, or that the armed forces couldn't go into action on U.S. territory without getting the permission of the civil authorities. But it seemed like the whole system had been designed a long time ago, when things moved a lot slower. "Do we *have* to go through all that? There's no way to declare an emergency?"

"If we want to use active-duty forces inside a state, we have to get the governor's permission."

"How about his state troops? The National Guard?"

"We don't have access to them until they're federalized," Roald told him.

Dan had been looking at the clock as they talked. Now Lynch put his head in. "Excuse me. That flight's taking off in ten minutes."

"Call and do your shipping-manager act again. Tell them you want to hold the takeoff. You forgot something. Under no circumstances do you want it to go out tonight. Or you'll sue them. You'll never send another thing UPS."

Sweat broke under his armpits and ran tickling down his ribs. He hoped they were right, the people like Gelzinis who had to check off every block before they acted. Who thought if the intel agencies didn't know about a threat, there was no threat. "Damn it—we've got to stop that plane!"

"Tell me how to do it legally, and I'll be the first to help you," Roald said. "You'd better ask yourself if you're not getting too excited, though."

"You think I'm too excited?"

"You *do* seem awfully fired up."

Lynch, holding the phone's mouthpiece against his chest: "No good getting them to kick the shipment off. She said it's all loaded and my people are already aboard."

"Your *people*? What's she mean by that?"

"I asked her. She said, didn't I know? There's some techies riding along, accompanying our shipment."

Dan knew then beyond any doubt this was not what it seemed. Whoever they were, they were there for no good purpose. And probably armed to the teeth to boot.

Lynch was on the line again. He rolled his eyes. Slapped the phone back down and blew out. "They're gone. They're in the air."

"How about fighters, Captain? We can't use active forces on the ground. Can we use interceptors in the air to force that flight down?"

Roald hesitated, then picked up the phone again. Dan and Lynch waited as she talked to a duty officer at NORAD, the North American Air Defense Command center.

She put her hand over the mouthpiece. "They won't scramble without orders. And they can't scramble on a civilian jetliner. The desk guy turned me down flat on that. Posse Comitatus Act. Maybe on a direct presidential order, he said. But of course the president's not here."

Dan stood blinking. The whole machine, immense, powerful, and expensive, was too slow. And somehow the people who were supposed to look out for things like this had missed it. Oh, they'd probably had hints. A little here, a little there. But no one had pulled it all together. Because that wasn't anyone's job.

Maybe he should call the Pentagon himself. No . . . why bother? He'd get the same stonewall, stall, runaround that Roald had.

He turned abruptly, bumping into Harlowe, and went back out into the watch area. Stood behind one of the desk officers, fingering his lip as incoming cables streamed across the screen.

Infinite information, and blindness to the essential. Instant communication, and total paralysis.

"I'm back," said Alvarado, coming in carrying a cup of what smelled like bouillon.

"You don't know anything else about this?" Dan asked him, distracting himself from the tragedy he saw coming but was impotent to prevent.

"What?"

"Nothing else, Luis? Nothing else about the cartel's plans?"

"If you don't trust me for some reason, say it."

He looked away. Caught Roald's concerned glance through the glass.

She got up and came toward the little, wilted group. "Your UPS flight. Where's it land?"

"Washington. Dulles."

"I mean—there was an intermediate stop, right? Didn't you mention one?"

Lynch said, "A fuel stop. In Kentucky."

She looked at her watch again. Then at Dan. "I guess I was wrong."

"Wrong?"

"We're not going to be able to do this by the book."

He nodded, not really understanding.

"Come back in," she said, and turned on her heel.

◆ ◆ ◆

She had a screen of numbers on her monitor. Dan saw it was the emergency contact numbers of the National Guard adjutant generals for each of the fifty states.

"I'm thinking of something Colin Powell told me once," she said.

"Which was?"

"You never know what you can get away with until you try. Now look. Before we do this . . ."

"Yeah?"

"I can run interference for you. But I can't carry the ball. Understand? The Sit Room has no authority to initiate action."

"Well, neither do I."

"Neither do you. Exactly right. But you're the one who believes there's a critical situation here."

Dan nodded, remembering what they'd told him when he reported aboard: Staff did not command. They coordinated. But there had to be a limit, when no one could be reached; had to be a time for *someone* to make a decision. Accepting too what she hadn't said: that she still didn't quite believe him enough to put her own career on the line.

That was okay. She might still have a future in the Navy. Probably even stars, considering where she was sitting now. Whereas he'd written that off a long time ago.

"Deal," he said.

She nodded and reached for the mouse. Ran the cursor down a column, highlighted a number, double clicked.

They looked at each other as she waited, handset to her ear. "Hello? Major General? Sorry to disturb you, sir. Take a moment and wake up if you need it.

"This is the director of the White House Situation Room. Yes, sir . . . the White House . . . That's right. Not so good, sir. We have a possible problem developing at uh, Standiford Field in Louisville. I'm going to put the man on who knows the most about it. Going to the speakerphone."

Dan found himself leaning toward the console as a man came on who sounded as if he'd just been awakened. He cleared his throat, reminding himself neither to give his own rank, nor to call the man on the other end "sir." "Good morning. We—I—have grounds to believe an air freight shipment of stolen radioactive material will be landing in Louisville about"—he pulled Lynch's note toward him—"1012 local— wait a minute—"

"That's central time," Ed Lynch said behind him, and he turned and saw them all in the doorway. Harlowe flashed him a thumbs-up.

"Yes, central time. There are people accompanying it. We believe they may be armed and should be considered dangerous. We need you to—"

The distant voice interrupted, asking who else had been notified. Dan told him, not untruthfully, that the relevant authorities were being informed, but warning time had been too short to prevent the takeoff. The only chance of stopping it now was the Kentucky Guard and State Police on the ground, as it refueled in Louisville.

Roald cleared her throat. "General, we realize we are not in your state chain of command. We recommend you notify your State Area Command on an emergency-response basis. You are not officially federalized. We will just have to catch up to that after the fact—we don't have time to do this officially and still catch that shipment."

"I've got an Air Guard unit there. At Standiford Field. An airlift wing."

"The choice of units and forces is yours, but we strongly recommend you take this aircraft on the ground with the best assault team you can lay your hands on. I would also recommend you call in your state police counterparts and whatever radiological emergency-response team Kentucky has available. My next call will be to your governor's office, letting them know we have passed the ball to you."

The general wanted to know again what and who were aboard. Dan told him, as closely as he could, hearing hoarse breathing and the scratching of a pencil on the other end. No doubt on a nightstand, a sleepy wife looking on. "That's UPS flight 3913, coming in from Ontario, California," he said again.

"I'm on it," the general said, and the phone slammed down. Leaving him staring at it. Eyebrows raised.

"He went for it," he said, sounding, even to himself, rather stupidly surprised. "Are you really going to call the governor?"

But she was already punching more numbers. He leaned back, realizing only then that there was no way they could separate his involvement in this, and hers. Whatever she said, she was laying her ass on the rail along with his.

He only hoped they were wrong. That they'd lose their jobs for raising a false alarm. That there really weren't people who hated America enough to dump radioactives on a sleeping city.

But he was afraid there were.

Five hours later, exhausted, drained, he was back in the counterdrug office, untouched coffee in front of him, CNN on the office television. He'd watched with Mary, Ed, and Luis as smoke rose over the terminal buildings and shots crackled. Now wavery telephoto images caught clumsy figures in masks and hoods circling a smoking aircraft in the brown-and-gold UPS livery. A fire truck was laying curtains of dirty foam. Behind it response trucks and an armored personnel carrier—not a Bradley, an M113, he thought—stood off.

"A team composed of local and Kentucky State Police SWAT teams assaulted twenty minutes ago. We are still waiting for some indication as to exactly how much of this dangerous material, thought at this time to be radioactive waste, this aircraft contains. Preliminary indications are that the hijackers were members of an armed terrorist group. The destination of the aircraft has not been released."

The camera cut to a woman in a dark suit. Dan thought at

first she was a news anchor, then saw that she stood at a podium, the FBI seal behind her.

"Regional Director Claire Bruffi announced the plot had been uncovered by a joint team from the FBI and the CIA. The aircraft's takeoff was earlier than expected. This morning FBI raids are being launched in Pomona, California, where the explosives and other materials involved were stored prior to loading the aircraft."

The voice-over stopped and the woman said, "It is simply fortunate that we managed to catch the aircraft on the ground, before explosives could be rigged for detonation. We owe thanks to the valiant officers of the Guard and the Kentucky State Police who boarded the plane, once it had landed to refuel, and to the patient and dangerous investigative work by Bureau agents that resulted in the disclosure of the plot."

Lynch, Alvarado, and Harlowe growled, glanced at Dan. They looked outraged. He said nothing. Just swirled his coffee, feeling a strange amalgam of relief and anger. Relief that they'd managed to foil the threat. Anger that ass-covering and lies would prevent his people from getting any credit. What had Sebold said? About how much of what went on inside the iron fence never went public? Now he understood.

"Those fuckers," Lynch said. "They had *nothing* to do with this. We put it together. *You* put it all together."

Dan said, "You really think they can say that? That a bunch of field-grade bozos in White House counterdrug stapled this together in their spare time?"

"They should give us credit—"

"You know what the media'd do with that," Marty Harlowe said. "They'd say: Why do our wonderful intelligence agencies need so much funding if they missed something this big?"

Alvarado said, "It's a good question." They looked at him and he said, "Well? Isn't it?"

The phone rang. The slick-headed admin sergeant answered it. Ouderkirk's eyes flicked to Dan, who started to get up. But the receptionist held up his hand. Said, "Yes, ma'am. Right away, ma'am," and hung up.

To Dan he said, "That was Mrs. Clayton, sir. She just got in. She'd like to see you in her office."

III
EAST WING

031331Z JAN
SCHOLAST:
//Logging on. See Amicable, Hellgod, Blue Danube here already. Thanks for promptness. Welcome Seaward to the group. Gents, I've already placed Sea in the picture regarding both security and aim of our enterprise.

031331Z JAN
AMICABLE:
//Welcome, Seaward.

031331Z JAN
HELLGOD:
//Welcome to the history behind the history.

031331Z JAN
SEAWARD:
//Hope to be able to contribute. Any way I can.

031332Z JAN
SCHOLAST:
//BD, your report.

031332Z JAN
BLUE DANUBE:
//The candidate is motivated and moving into position. Actually there were some lucky breaks in this regard. Unplanned by us, but I'd be happy to take credit.

031333Z JAN
HELLGOD:
//My question same as three-four sessions ago. We can create conditions, but how do we make him move? What exactly is your hold on this guy? Who we need a name for. Not real name, but some kind of handle.

031332Z:
SCHOLAST:
//Call him Forthright.

031332Z JAN
BLUE DANUBE:
//OK. The point is, HG, not so much to make Forthright do what we want as to make it believable afterward that he did. See the diff? We'll put him into position where it would be perfectly credible that he does what he does. If he doesn't, then we go to Plan B, but he still remains the presumptive actor.

031333Z JAN
HELLGOD:
//BD and I have discussed this between us & with one other interested party. That is, how to make it happen if our buddy doesn't operate as planned. Don't trigger off, Schoolboy, the other party was not made privy to any of the rest of the enterprise & is just as security conscious as we are.

031333Z JAN
SCHOLAST:
//Not happy to hear you discussed any part of this outside

the group. But trust your judgment. Wd like to hear more on this between us, let's meet.

//Reminder for everyone: close hold, close hold, CLOSE HOLD.

031333Z JAN
AMICABLE:
//It's still only a contingency plan. Right?

031334Z JAN
HELLGOD:
//Nobody seems to be listening, but I'll say it again: it's past time to retire this player. Don't poll me when G wants to execute, you know where I stand.

031334Z JAN
SEAWARD:
//What happens to Forthright?

031334Z JAN
SCHOLAST:
//Okay, everyone has his piece of the pie to work. Let's get to it. Out here.
LOGOFF

031334Z JAN
AMICABLE:
//Off.
LOGOFF

031334Z JAN
BLUE DANUBE:
//Out.
LOGOFF

031334Z JAN
HELLGOD:
LOGOFF

031334Z JAN
SEAWARD:
//Scholast? You still there?

031335Z JAN
SEAWARD:
//Signing off.
LOGOFF

16

The first thing he noticed was how much quieter it was. No tourists, no journalists, no camera crews shouting and trailing cables and pointing lights. There wasn't much going on in the hallways. The doors stayed closed. The carpet was the same dark blue, the walls the same marigold cream, but it seemed like the far side of the moon after the West Wing. He hesitated at a double door of polished mahogany, then pushed through.

To a small front office, a desk, but no one at it. In a back room, neither large nor very well appointed, two uniformed men sat on a sofa that was obviously a retread from some other part of the White House. One, hunched forward till his uniform jacket hooded over his bull neck, was a buzz-cut, broad-shouldered Marine lieutenant colonel. His large yet startlingly delicate fingers held pages from a loose-leaf binder. The other was Mike Jazak, the Army officer Dan had met jogging with De Bari. They exchanged nods.

"They tell me I'm going to be working over here," he said, extending his hand as the light colonel got to his feet.

The buzz cut grunted. "I just wish not as the Wusso's replacement."

Dan nodded. Moncure "Wusso" Pusser had been the president's Navy aide until two days ago, when a hit-and-run driver had connected in the lower level of the Pentagon City

Mall parking garage. Now he had a broken hip and might not, Bethesda said, ever fly F-18s again.

If not for that, Dan thought, he might be off the Eighteen Acres entirely. First the Nuñez and Tejeiro affairs. Then Srebrenica, news the administration hadn't wanted to hear. Last, but not least, the way he'd gone through the guardrails about what was already being called the Louisville Incident, the subject of intense attention in Congress and the media. He figured pigeonholing him in the East Wing was part of Holt's spin. Stopping the terrorists had been a last-minute save by the intelligence agencies and the Guard, protecting America at a discount under the inspired leadership of Robert L. De Bari.

"I'm Chick Gunning," the marine said. "Senior mil aide. Let's go on down to the PEOC, and we'll start your briefing-in."

The fact that the potentially disastrous consequences of your glory hunting did not occur can't excuse operating outside normal procedures," Gelzinis had said coldly at the termination interview. They were in the assistant's eight-by-ten office adjoining Mrs. Clayton's. "We've had our differences, you and I, but this is beyond personal. Procedures are there for a reason. They reflect statutory limits on the executive side and, most particularly, on the executive staff. General Sebold briefed you, first day you were here, on our standards. Did he not?"

"I was warned," Dan said.

"Well, when a member violates those—the reason, good, bad, or indifferent, that's beside the point—he's violated the trust Congress and the people placed in us. You've been cautioned before. Failed to exercise restraint. Therefore—" He finished with a symbolic handwashing.

Dan was thinking that if he'd exercised *restraint*, they'd all be glowing in the dark right now. But he didn't say anything. He didn't expect a sea command anymore. A training billet, recruiting duty in the Midwest—he didn't care. As long as he was out of this cesspool.

"Well, he has the Yankee White clearance. He's the right rank," said a man beside Gelzinis's desk. One Dan hadn't been introduced to, though he'd seen him before in the hallways, usually deep in low-voiced conversations. A short, fiftyish guy with a gnomelike head a couple sizes larger than it ought to be. Thin hair the color of wet sand. Khaki pants and a Navajo-style bolo tie with a clasp the shape of a thunderbird. Just now he was slouching in the chair with one hand-tooled western boot propped on a knee. The stick of a lollipop protruded from his jaw. He was examining Dan, but not talking to him, as if Lenson were livestock he wasn't sure he wanted to buy. "The congressional, at photo ops—that could offset some of the criticism about the military relationship."

Dan turned to squint at the little guy. What was this? The gnome winked at him, but didn't say who he was or what he wanted.

"The president's relations with the military are excellent," Gelzinis said, with utter and outraged conviction.

Dan wondered what universe the deputy adviser was living in. He sat back, trying to relax. He'd tried, maybe too hard, and it hadn't worked. Well, he'd already lasted longer here than he'd thought he would.

They were both studying him now. "I'm not sure what we're talking about here," he told them.

Gelzinis frowned. "Garner hasn't told you?"

"I came up here as soon as I got your note, sir. Should I have seen General Sebold first?"

"Of course, he's . . . oh, never mind. There's a requirement over in the East Wing."

The little guy said around the lollipop, "Garner's the one who said you might be the square peg. And since I took over the military side . . ."

Dan started to ask what requirement, the "military side" of what, but before he got a word out. Gelzinis said, "You won't be there long. They'll move the guy's replacement up. All you need to do is fill the hole a month or two. Then you'll be on your way."

A tap at the jamb. Sebold came in, apologizing for being late. He nodded to the little guy. "Charlie. How you doing?"

A piece fell into place. Charles Ringalls, "Charlie Wrinkles," one of De Bari's aw-shucks cronies from the oil business he'd started, after the firefighting but before the governorship. A special assistant, one of the expediters and behind-the-scenes fund-raisers. Ringalls had moved up to director of the White House Military Office, the uniformed support group that ran comms and other operations around the Eighteen Acres, on the strength of a few years as a National Guard noncom. The word was he'd smile, then rip your balls off.

"Good enough. How're you, podner?"

"We were bringing your lad here up to date. On his transfer." Gelzinis ran his fingers through his hair. "If you want him, that is," he added to the gnome.

"His clearance good?"

"Oh, his clearance—you won't find any problems with that," the deputy said, with one of the most finely crafted smirks Dan had ever seen.

"How about uniforms? He got all that ready to go?"

"Dan's an Annapolis man," Sebold said with proprietary pride. "A thousand percent performer. Meticulous attention to detail. You'll be very happy with him."

With that, Dan understood. Leaving the West Wing in the evenings, he'd seen the uniformed aides greeting the glamorous, the famous, and the powerful. They took their wraps and escorted the guests through the endless marathon of formal dinners, parties, teas, receptions, and entertainments that took up so much of the Residence permanent staff's time. They greeted arriving heads of state on the South Lawn. Guarded catafalques at state funerals. They were tall, good-looking young officers in full dress and white gloves, selected for poise, resourcefulness, and charm. No doubt it was important, and more onerous than it might seem . . . but.

"Sorry. I don't dance," he told them. "Back problems. And I'm not so good at small talk."

Sebold chuckled. "Those are the *social* aides. No, I don't think you'd fit in there either, Dan."

"Then what are we talking about?"

"We're *talkin'* about the military aide position," the little westerner said, cowpoke-astonished, as if it had been evident the moment he walked in.

Dan sucked in his breath.

Whenever you saw the commander in chief in public, one instantly recognizable figure was never far away. He carried a black briefcase, his expression giving no clue what was in it. Dan dropped his head, trying to organize his objections. He had not the slightest desire to follow the man he hated around with Doomsday handcuffed to his wrist. "I didn't screen for that," he told them.

"You screened for White House duty."

"It's a high-visibility position," said Gelzinis, sounding as if that were above all what counted on this earth.

"I don't want to work on the Eighteen Acres any longer," Dan said, finally losing patience. "And I definitely don't want to serve in that capacity."

"Can I have a word with him?" Sebold said. Gelzinis waved his hand in annoyance, fanning them out of his office. The little guy smiled again, and Dan saw where the "Wrinkles" nickname came from.

In the corridor the general pulled him close. "I had a tough time getting them to consider you for this. Two agency heads called Tony direct about that crap you pulled in the Sit Room."

"If you mean Louisville, I'd do it again. Gelzinis keeps talking about how us staff pissants mustn't poke a toe outside the chop chain. If Jenny Roald and I had followed the flow diagrams, a lot of people would be dead."

"So you're exempt from those rules?"

"That's not what I was saying."

"Then what *were* you saying? Exactly?"

"That occupying a position of responsibility means knowing when to bend those rules."

"I've noticed that before about you Navy people," the general said, pursing his lips in disapproval. "And I want you to know just how far out on a limb I've gone covering your ass around here. You owe me. And you're still in the military, Commander."

Dan said, feeling his lips draw back from his teeth, "I realize that, sir."

"And you're going to take this position and do an outstanding job until we can organize somebody else."

And once again, as so often since he'd put on a uniform, he said, against his desire and better judgment, but that was what taking orders meant: "Aye aye, sir."

He'd heard of the Presidential Emergency Operations Center. Rumor said it was so deep beneath the East Wing you had to ride down on an elevator. It was much less well known than the Sit Room. In fact, few outside the Eighteen Acres knew of it, and Dan hadn't heard it or the agency responsible for it, the Contingency Operations Office, discussed much even in the West Wing.

And in fact there was an elevator. Gunning said that both the mil aides and the uniformed detail were allowed to use it, but that at the moment the cables were being checked. So he followed the colonel down a steep, dimly lit, musty, poured-concrete stairwell whose white paint didn't look as if it had been touched up since the Cuban missile crisis.

At its bottom Gunning tapped a code into a keypad. From the way Dan's ears popped as they went through one heavy steel door, then another, he figured the space was under positive pressure. Like the new destroyers, which maintained a higher air pressure inside the skin of the ship to exclude gas or biological agents. He signed a shelter log, then followed the colonel into a brightly lit air-conditioned warren. He hadn't realized how big it was, or how many people worked down here.

Gunning started with the comm spaces, introducing him

to the duty dudes and the shelter maintenance guys. They
didn't wear uniforms, but they were military. Air Force,
most of them. The displays showed they had connectivity
with the agencies that mattered. Gunning said that if an aide
was with POTUS when a short-fuze alert came down, or if
there was any armed intrusion, it would be Dan's responsibility to get him down here into shelter.

"Uh, what degree of hardening have we got? What kind
of hit could we take?"

"Pretty much anything conventional, but a nuclear attack—
well, you don't want to stick around for that. If we get
enough warning, we'll bring in *Marine One* and airlift out of
D.C. Go out to Mount Weather, out near Berryville. Or if
you're at Camp David, you'll go to Site R, if you're not already in the air."

Gunning went on outlining the warning and evacuation
procedures while showing him a stark little bunkroom the
military aides used. They stuck their heads into the Emergency Boardroom. It was larger than the one in the Sit Room
complex, but with an even more ominous feel. The ceilings
were higher, the walls white instead of dark paneling.

The rooms were actually bigger than West Wing standard. But he still felt oppressed, as if he weren't just underground, but slowly being crushed. This whole side of the
White House was military, hidden beneath the tourist-
friendly infrastructure like some huge, deeply buried foundation. It felt secretive, menacing, like . . . the Bat Cave. The
Skull Cave. The Death Star.

"We'll come back later," Gunning told him. "Ready for
lunch?"

Climbing the stairs felt like ascending from the depths.

They picked up Jazak back at the aides' office—
upstairs in the East Wing, at the end of the hall on the
Treasury side—for a quick sandwich. Then Jazak
and Gunning showed him the secret underground tunnel that

went under the Treasury to emerge at a screened exit on the far side. Then they all went back down to the PEOC, to the classified-materials vault.

Dan recognized the alarm wiring and two-man entry procedures. The placarding inside, when the door at last swung open, was DoD standard for nuclear controlled material. Yeah, the codes and permissions to release hell on earth, that'd be worth locking up. But everything looked dated, faded, like things you'd find at a not-too-trendy antique store. The light fixtures and the exposed conduit wiring were 1960s. A torn poster headed REMEMBER—CONELRAD IS THE KEY looked even older. One wall was lined with binders and references. A table with its veneer separating at the corners stood in the middle of the vault.

Gunning flicked an overhead on, did something to the lock, then tugged on the door as Jazak flicked open folding chairs like switchblades and set them around the table. The door sealed with a reluctant thunk. The air instantly became stuffy, fusty, like a wet basement. Dan couldn't hear anything that sounded like a fan.

Gunning said that since Dan already worked here, he could skip the basic orientation. But he'd still have to train on the comm side and database management. He'd need an IT security briefing. He'd have to touch base with "Carpet," the White House Transportation Agency, out at the Anacostia Annex, since a lot of the presidential comms were managed from there. And he'd meet the other players the mil aides did business with: the social secretary, the first lady's people, chief of protocol, press secretary, and so on.

"All right," the colonel said, "let's get to the meat. How up to speed are you on nuclear release procedures?"

"I've served on nuclear-capable ships," Dan told him. "So I'm familiar with the authentication system. Past that, just what everybody knows. You carry the football. The go codes."

"We do a lot more than stand around with that thing," Jazak told him. "We coordinate what the president needs from our respective services. The White House mess and the valets—the Filipinos, the enlisted who help him get dressed and so forth—that's always been a Navy responsibility. I hear the yacht was too, back when we had the *Sequoia*. Once he leaves town, we take on a lot of other responsibilities: comms, codes, transportation, though the advance party and so forth help. Speaking of advance parties, you'll be on one of them—probably Adamant Black."

Gunning said, "But the football's what everybody thinks of first, right? So let's open with that." He pulled a binder off the shelf. "It's all designed out in these pubs. You know what the SIOP is, right?"

Dan said, getting more tense by the moment and hoping it didn't show, "The single integrated operational plan. What weapons are assigned to what targets."

"Originally, yeah. But it's a lot more complicated now. I expect you to know these cold," Gunning said, giving him a close look. "I mean, till you can recite every page verbatim. Plus explain the underlying strategy for each option."

Dan thought about explaining how he felt about the whole idea instead, but didn't. A month or two, and he'd be out of here. "I understand."

"Good. Mike'll give you the once-over now, but once isn't enough. Take a couple days. You can look at the binders out in the conference room, but they stay in the vault when you're not working on them. When you're ready, I'll give you the quiz."

Dan nodded, and Gunning looked at Jazak, who reached under the table.

"The Presidential Emergency Satchel. Or PES," Jazak said.

It was bigger than a briefcase. More like a salesman's sample case. It was made of some light metal, covered with black leather and set off with silver-toned hardware. Dialing numbers into a beefy combination lock, then popping the latches, Jazak said, "Item one: No one but you and the prez gets to look inside this. I don't care if the SecDef wants a peek, he's out of the loop. Chick reports direct to Charlie Wrinkles, but Little Big Man's not allowed in either. There are actually two complete satchels. So if somebody ever steals one, or we lose it, we've got a backup. The vice president's mil aide, he's got one too, for obvious reasons. Total: three."

Gunning tapped Dan's wrist to emphasize the point. "About losing it: It's never happened yet. Don't let it on your watch."

Partitions divided the satchel's interior into compartments. Dealing each object out on the tabletop, Jazak showed him a security wristlet, a black-bound custody log, an inch-thick handbook with red plastic covers labeled SIOP DECISION HANDBOOK 7D, two other booklets with black plastic covers, and a flat card, sealed in metal foil: the autheticator itself. A sturdy-looking transceiver with flip-up antenna and handset was the bulkiest item. Last came a nylon-holstered nine-millimeter Beretta service automatic, with two loaded magazines.

"This handbook's the big deal," Jazak told him, flicking the one with the red cover. "Everything else we could replace. If the bad guys get their hands on this book, though, they'd know exactly what we know about them, and how we'd respond to an attack. That's what the pistol's for."

"You'd better tell me exactly what you mean by that," Dan said.

Gunning said, "He means, your printed orders—we'll get you a copy to sign—authorize you to use deadly force to protect these codes."

"Licensed to kill," said Jazak, smiling.

"But only if somebody makes a grab for it," Gunning cautioned. "The Secret Service didn't like us carrying. But it is what it is."

"Who's this transmitter connect me to?"

"Secure UHF voice, uplinks to Defense Sat Com. You have to be within fifteen miles of the uplink, which will be in the Roadrunner van most of the time." He showed Dan how to punch in numbers from the comm handbook. "There's a recharger in our office, another in the van. Let's say the daily schedule shows Mustang in the District that day. Before you go on duty you pick up two fully charged batteries, showing the green light here. When you go off duty, plug the old sets back in the charger. If you go overseas, there's adapters for foreign outlets. Do a comm check each time you relieve.

"If we ever get word an attack's on the way, it'll give you a warbling alarm. That notifies you to get next to the president, open the case, and go on the air. All the call signs and procedures are in 7D, the red book. Select your options and get the word out before their strike lands. Launch on warning's been doctrine for a long time now. It doesn't say that in print anywhere, but it's no secret."

"Okay, the book." Jazak flipped through plastic-coated pages. Dan saw they were printed in red. There were drawings, almost cartoons. Large print. It was designed to be used by terrified men in the moments before they died.

The colonel said, "Going through this you'll see the first part is who has the capacity to hit us—how many delivery vehicles, where based, times of flight. Then there's the info on our own forces. How many, where, and what countries they'd have to overfly to hit a specific target. That's important because they might think we're attacking them if they see our missiles on the way."

Jazak flipped over more glossy cardstock. "The heart of the Decision Handbook is the options section—here. The president gets to choose. Like from a Chinese menu. There's LAOs, limited attack options. MAOs, major attack options. Regional options, against North Korea and China. Special options: launch on warning, launch under attack, preemptive strike."

"Give him the book, Mike, so he can see," Gunning said.

Jazek shoved it over, but Dan didn't want to touch it. He said slowly, just to say something, "What happens if he can't make up his mind?"

"You'd think nothing, but actually it cascades to the next decision level. The whole thing used to be just greased to go, but it's gotten a little less so—I think."

"How up to speed on this is De Bari?"

"Who? Blow-dry Bob? That dumb son of a bitch doesn't

know jack about any of this," Jazak said witheringly. "Or care. He got a fifteen-minute briefing the day he moved in and hasn't said word one about it since. He's supposed to get refreshers, but he's never had time for that. We issue him a new authenticator card—the one you have to match with the one in the case—every month. Half the time, when Chick gives him the new biscuit, he doesn't know where the old one went. We have to go to the dry cleaner's and get it."

They told him stories that sounded like they'd been passed down through many hands and improved along the way. About Haig locking Nixon's codes away during the Watergate hearings. JFK's mil aide carrying condoms in the case as emergency reserves. Lyndon Johnson pissing on his aide's shoes. Another aide who'd ridden around Reagan's ranch with the PES in a saddle bag, and had to shoot a rabid coyote with the pistol.

Until Colonel Gunning cleared his throat. "Let's finish with the release procedures, Mike." And to Dan, "Funny stories aside, you're gonna be the ball carrier. That's what we call this thing: the Pigskin. The Ball. Or, the Ball and Chain. Don't kid yourself. There are still missiles pointed at this country, no matter what anybody says. You're the guy who's going to have to explain this to De Bari, if he ever has to use it.

"Once he makes up his mind, you write down the code for that option here, with this pen. Next you both break your biscuits. You pick up the phone."

The colonel laid his pianist's fingers on Dan's wrist again. "Meanwhile, there's going to be a major monkeyfuck. Everyone's going to be screaming. The protective detail's going to be trying to get him on *Marine One*. You have to make sure this gets done, no matter how bugshit everybody else goes. Just say your call sign. Then the option number, and say, 'Presidential execute authorization.' Follow that with the codes. Your card first, then his. His card's gold colored, which is why they call that the Gold Code."

Jazak chanted, as if he'd droned it for years in a Tibetan monastery, "Flash flash, all stations this net, this is Prehistoric Corona. Authorization to follow. Option number. Presidential execute authorization. His authenticator. My authenticator. Prehistoric Corona, over."

Gunning said, "They'll read it back. Confirm, and you're good to go. They have emergency action messages prewritten that trigger the launches. After that, just stay with him when they take him to Mount Weather or wherever."

Dan tried to imagine it. The confusion, the panic, while he tried for a rational conversation with Robert De Bari about the end of the world. "Monkeyfuck" struck him as an understatement.

"What's so funny?"

"Nothing."

"Yeah, there's some emotion tied to this thing," Jazak said, apparently assuming he'd been smiling so he wouldn't do anything else. Which was not far from the truth. The irony weighed. The guy who hadn't wanted to work on nuclear weapons, who'd lost men and women to a nuclear blast, would be carrying the detonator for the Armageddon the world had dreaded for half a century.

"Just do the best you can and *don't lose the fucking thing*. Use the security strap. Eat with it, jog with it, pee with it. But whatever you do *it doesn't get out of grabbing range* until your relief signs for it."

Dan said he understood.

"Okay, here's some tips we pass down. If you don't want to miss the ride, stand between the president and his transport. You lag behind, you get left behind," Gunning said.

"And don't *ever* get between Bad Bob and a camera," Jazak said.

Dan said, "What about personal services?"

This struck a sore spot; they exchanged grimaces. Gunning said yeah, sometimes the aides got tasked to carry luggage or do other personal tasks. The president and first lady both had personal assistants, but when they weren't immediately available or had too much to do, the aides would be expected to step in.

"When he's in the Residence, the duty dog can take

things a little easier," Gunning said. "Just keep your eye on the daily schedule, and track his whereabouts on the monitors. And kind of respond to his staff—you'll get to know them. Now, there's different gangs. There's Holt's people—you know them already. And our boss, Charlie Wrinkles, the guy who's always got a lollipop stuck in his jaw—"

"Yeah, I met him."

"Charlie's getting bigger every year. Director of the military office, the guy who controls all the perks for the staff—that swings weight on the Acres. Then there's Varghese's gang, the original Nevada Mafia. Steer clear of them. And the first lady's people, keep them at arm's length too if you can. We pull twenty-four-hour duty days. I showed you the bedroom. Or use the sofa in the office. You can work your collateral duties—like Mike said, the mess, or the valets, or the planning for the next overseas trip, whatever.

"When he has an event outside the compound, say Kennedy Center or the Gridiron, most of the planning for that, the pol staff and the Secret Service take care of. We just hop in the motorcade and go along.

"It's when he travels it really picks up for us. We schedule seating on *Air Force One* and do the transport and comm liaison. There's binders on that, too."

"What uniforms will I need?"

"*Good* question. Official events: class A's, with the aide badge, and the aiguillette on the right shoulder. Unofficial events: sports coat and tie, usually. And this pin." Gunning pushed a Secret Service pin across to him. Dan fingered the tiny gold star and blue shield. "There's a walk-in closet where you can keep your uniforms and your civilian combinations, like for quick changes. There used be an enlisted guy to help out, but he's long gone.

"Now, close up to POTUS and FLOTUS, in the personal entourage, it's different from being over in the West Wing. Certain things you will hear, and not repeat. See, and not recall. Even after you leave here, or retire, you will never talk or write about them. Never."

"FLOTUS?" Dan said.

"First lady of the United States," Gunning said. "Code name Tinkerbell, but Pit Bull would fit better. Okay. Over the next few days, I'm setting you up with briefings from the other staff agencies. We'll go over what to do in case there's a transfer of command authority—like last year, remember when he had that gallbladder operation and the vice had the stick for eight hours when he was on the table. Then you'll do hover tours, looking over the shoulder of the guy who's on duty. Or gal—we got Francie Upshaw, too. Next week you can go out to Camp David with Mike. The rest, you pick up on the job." He stretched, joints cracking, then heaved himself up. "Any more questions?"

"Hundreds."

"Sure, but that's enough for today. Zero-seven tomorrow, here. And we'll start getting you read in."

"One last thing," Dan said. "Maybe I should have asked it before. It might be a dumb question—"

"No such thing," the colonel said. "Shoot."

"What if there's an attack, and he freezes? The president can't make up his mind?"

"And the missiles are coming in?" Gunning and Jazak looked at each other. The colonel glanced at the sealed door of the vault.

"We've discussed that," the marine said, voice so soft that even if some electronic device had been listening, it wouldn't have picked it up. "Considering the pussy-ass we've got in the driver's seat right now."

"And?"

Gunning murmured, "In that case, Commander, you're going to have to do what Blow-dry Bob isn't man enough to. You grab that card out of his hand, before we're all vaporized, and you send that fucking go message all by your fucking self."

17

MARINE ONE

The satchel crouched at his feet like a black mastiff to which he was unwillingly leashed. Jazak was crammed in beside him. The sofa bench, upholstered in light blue cloth, ran along the starboard side of the compartment. Facing them, in comfortable-looking armchairs, were the president and the Distinguished Guest, and opposite Dan and Jazak, on another sofa bench, the secretary of state and the undersecretary for African affairs.

Dan couldn't keep his eyes from going back to De Bari. Was she still seeing him? He couldn't help imagining the president and Blair together. And when he did, it was hard to stay in his seat and pretend he didn't know, or didn't care.

What sort of man could do that to someone who worked for him?

Then they were aloft, to the muffled howl of twin turboshafts and five rotor blades. *Marine One* banked deliberately, so as not to cause its passengers to lose their breakfasts. The gentle hills of Maryland emerged from the roseate haze of a hundred thousand cars stalled on the Beltway.

The radios had snapped out "POTUS departing" at eight that morning. When Barney McKoy—head of the protective detail, the round-faced black agent

Dan had noticed before, always next to the president—had nodded, he and Jazak had taken off jogging across a lightly snowed-over South Lawn, clutching their hats. And of course the satchel, which Jazak had security-wristleted to Dan's wrist "to get you used to it."

HMX-1 flew the Sikorsky VH-3D Sea King helicopter out of Naval Air Station Anacostia. Up close *Marine One* had loomed huge and loud and sparkling, auxiliary power unit whining, the glossy green-and-white finish waxed bright. Even the tires, which squatted so nearly flat on the blocks that Dan deduced internal armor, looked new. A marine in full dress stood at attention. The metal stairs were polished rhodium-bright. In contrast to naval tradition, where the highest-ranking boarded last, the aides boarded after the VIPs, along with the Secret Service. Other agents kept a cordon around it till the door thunked closed.

He'd noticed one other thing. As De Bari and today's guest, the president of Chad, had boarded, a dark-skinned man in an ill-cut summer suit had come rushing up. The Secret Service had closed in; then, seeing all he wanted was to make sure his boss got a leather portfolio, accepted it from him. McKoy had opened it. Leafed through the contents. Then assured the African it would be handed to his president.

Dan and Jazak were next up. A Secret Service agent reached for the emergency satchel. But McKoy stopped him with a shake of his head. Dan followed Jazak up the steps as the rotors began turning. "Remember, nobody else touches it," the major yelled, squinting into the cold wind, thick with the smoky lamp-oil smell of jet exhaust. "Or even looks inside. You and the president. That's it."

"Got it," Dan yelled back.

He looked around as they settled in, clicking seat belts embossed with the presidential seal. He'd flown in "Sea Pigs" before, but this was different. No sonobuoy racks. No antisubmarine warfare consoles or search-and-rescue winches. Instead it had reading lights and map tables, and was separated halfway down with comm consoles, one of which Jazak was plugging into. The protective detail guys were in windbreakers instead of blazers. Also on the bench seats were the president's personal assistant, "Haz" Nosler, a self-effacing young man who had something to do with the first lady's family; and the senior White House physician, a Navy captain, Dr. Shigeru "Shiggy" Yoshida.

These were people you didn't see much in the West Wing. He had a sudden sense of the presidency as a faceted jewel, with rays that shot off this way and that, into realms unknown to one another. But he no longer thought of it in terms of overawing power.

The hearty man who sat gesturing with un unlit cigar had the trappings of it. The helicopters. The staff. But did De Bari truly captain the ship of state? Dan was beginning to wonder if he did, if he wanted to, or even if he could. Because Washington didn't seem to work that way. There was no plan. No leadership. Only different circles that schemed and leaked and betrayed, who fought desperately to be *in the loop*. There was no concern for the country. Only interests, and what favor or appropriation or regulatory exemption they could buy.

Democracy? Maybe. But it seemed squalid and wasteful, compared to the service. Or had Sebold been right with practically the first words he'd said when he arrived. That he shouldn't assume things didn't make sense just because they didn't to him. That there *was* a big picture.

He hoped so. But the longer he played this game, the less he believed in it.

The president was talking to the Distinguished Guest. The Chadian president's bald scalp was covered with dark-complected bumps, like a plucked turkey. He gripped the arms of his chair, squinting out a picture window at the city below. De Bari sprawled in a gray suit and light blue tie. He'd yanked his collar open as the door slid closed. Dan stared, not caring if his contempt showed. The U.S. president rolled his cigar in the remaining fingers of his right hand. His gaze kept flicking to a locker. Dan guessed it held liquor, which of course he couldn't help himself to in front of his Muslim guest. The translator bent between them as De Bari held forth. The secretary and the under-secretary huddled in too, expressions intent. De Bari gestured again with the cigar, delivering a punch line Dan couldn't hear.

The Chadian had come in the night before, slept in the Lincoln Bedroom, and now was accompanying De Bari to meet with other heads of state and representatives from central Africa. The *Post* had run a piece that morning about the deteriorating security and ecological situation there, the drought, the growing famine.

The winter-stripped woods below slowly grew into the Catoctin Mountains. Dan couldn't help remembering Bosnia. He shifted, recalling the antiaircraft guns, the shoulder-launched missiles. An SA-7 would make short work of them at this altitude. Wouldn't *that* be a great way to assassinate the president. You could armor a helicopter all you wanted, but if a fragment hit the blades, everybody would die.

Somehow, watching the blue mountains slide closer, he couldn't bring himself to care.

N aval Support Facility Thurmont, the official name for Camp David, consisted of rolling hills, pebbled trails, and cabins with shake roofs scattered under chestnut oaks and pitch pines. Dan and Jazak cooled their heels outside the largest, perched on a rude log bench on a flagstone terrace, looking out over the valley in the fresh cold air.

The opening meeting broke around four. The Secret Service and the Africans' bodyguards emerged onto the terrace. Dan caught McKoy's eye, and the baby-faced agent nodded. Other teams fanned out through the wooded trails, scuffing through frozen leaves.

With heads together, the participants straggled out. A photographer hovered, trying to work in the view. Dan watched as the now-familiar photo op took shape, the leaders stepping up one by one for the grip and grin. De Bari beamed, obviously enjoying himself. The others looked stiff, even tormented. Or maybe they were just cold. A few yards away a tall woman, shawled against the chill, was sitting in a golf cart with another woman. After a moment Dan recognized the first lady.

Jazak saw her too. "This might be a good time to meet the missus."

"Sure. Uh . . . how do we address her? 'Madame President'?"

"No, that would be for a woman president, if we ever got one. It sounds informal, but just 'Mrs. De Bari' or 'Ma'am.' "

The winter sunlight dappled the ground as they strolled over. Jazak was careful, Dan noticed, to keep the president in view between the oaks.

Mrs. De Bari looked vacantly past them as they reached the cart. She was facing in the general direction of the president, but it didn't seem as if she was watching someone she loved or even had much interest in. Her eyes were dark and her chin was firm. Her hair was covered with a green silk Hermès kerchief. Her profile was elegant, with the nose of an Italian aristocrat. But up close she looked older than her husband, even haggard, with rouged cheeks and a fold at the edge of her mouth that suggested constant pain. Raising his voice above the wind in the treetops, Jazak said, "Ma'am? I'd like to introduce Commander Dan Lenson. The new naval aide. Dan, Mrs. De Bari."

Dan bowed slightly, but didn't put out his hand until she extended hers. Her fingers were icy cold.

So he and this woman had a secret bond. What if he should mention it to her? Tell her about her husband and his wife?

It probably wouldn't surprise her. Everyone knew De Bari's weakness. She must have given permission at some point, overtly or tacitly. Or at least decided to look away. Thinking this, he must have held her hand a moment longer than necessary, because she frowned and withdrew it, the thin fingers slipping his grasp.

"Notice anything?" Jazak murmured as they strolled back

toward the president, who was laughing heartily and miming a golf swing. The Africans looked as if they wished they were somewhere warmer.

"She looked tired."

"It's the big C. But you never heard it from me."

Dan glanced back. When he followed her gaze, he saw the group was dispersing, the golden moment under the trees at an end.

A s Chick Gunning had said, the rings of staffers and social aides that orbited the first family fell away out here. He and Jazak helped Nosler carry the luggage into the presidential cabin, a rustic sprawler of pine logs and split shakes. Inside, its pine floors, knotted rugs, and hand-laid stone fireplaces, stoked and roaring with oak splits, were no more pretentious than a luxurious bed-and-breakfast, though Jazak showed him a discreet door that revealed an elevator to regions beneath. Dan fetched dinner for Snorrie, the first dachshund, then decided to check out the mess arrangements under his naval aide hat.

The chief was eager to show him around, as Dan would be writing her evaluation. She took him through noisy steamy kitchens, detailing the food-preparation precautions. Everybody down to the guys who unloaded the food trucks was Yankee White cleared. Everything was spotless. He was telling her to pass his "bravo zulu" on when one of the female agents, smooth and detached as a positronic robot, looked in. "*He* wants to go for a run. We need another runner."

He had no desire to go jogging with this guy. He wanted out of this job just as quickly as he could. But meanwhile . . . the old story . . . it was his duty. So: he'd just get through it. Then, out of this septic tank and back to sea.

He changed in the aides' cabin. Pulled on his sweats. Did a few stretches, concentrating on back and calves, and put on a headband to keep his ears warm. Then looped back to the presidential cabin. Jazak handed him the satchel and tapped off a salute.

Dan jogged off, the dread weight of nuclear retaliation pulling him off balance at each step.

The compound was quickly out of sight, erased by the leafless branches of mountain laurel and wild roses that became screening-thick as they left the hilltop. Dead leaves crunched underfoot. Their breaths panted out in white steam. Six runners: four Secret Service guys, all male, in blue track suits to cut the chill; the president, in a dark green University of Wyoming sweatshirt and the same blue pants as the agents; and Dan, in his gray Academy-issue sweats. He wondered if anyone had invited the Africans. They hadn't seemed like the jogging type, but you never knew.

De Bari looked heavy today. Maybe it was the sweats. He set a good pace, though, on the initial downhill. Dan figured they were doing about a twelve-minute mile. But as soon as they were out of sight of the cabins he eased off to a lazy bear-shamble. His cheeks mottled red. He pushed his hair back and coughed. "Damn, colder'n I thought out here," he said to no one in particular. The detail guys didn't respond. Glancing at them Dan wondered suddenly how they felt about the man they so intimately guarded. Whom they were with every minute of his day, save for when he closed the bathroom door.

Or the bedroom. Which brought the shriveling memory of facing these same men—had they been the same ones?—in the freezing-dim corridors of the Pribaltskaya . . . Their flat returning gazes gave no answer. Did they pass around the story of his shame? Did they think of the man keeping pace with them, loping steadily if slowly down into the valley, was an impotent cuckold?

"What about that new guy? What's his name—Kubicki, Kubicka? Something like that."

He flinched. De Bari had slipped back, still cocooned by his human shields, but measuring his pace to Dan's.

His mind hunted, then made the connection. The Naval Academy team had broken out of its decade-long doldrums. De Bari was talking about a new quarterback, a half–Native American who was the biggest ground gainer any of the service academies had seen since Staubach. He said unwillingly, "Uh, I hear he's something, Mr. President."

"Seen him play?"

"I keep meaning to make it to a game. . . ."

"I'm thinking of going to Army-Navy next season," De Bari said between breaths. "If they invite me."

"I'm sure they will, Mr. President."

"You think so? I keep trying, but I just can't seem to make any progress with your people."

Was it his imagination, or was the guy trying to be *chummy*? His fists tightened. Fuck a guy's wife, then stroke him . . . but what else could you expect from the premier politician of the age? Everything America wanted she'd found in Buckshot Bob. The television presence of a superstar. The Dr. Atkins of the federal budget. Pulling U.S. troops out of country after country. And now, some sort of Mideast peace deal he was supposed to be putting together, along with central Africa, a Medicare catastrophic-expenses cap—

He cleared his throat, fighting to keep his tone neutral. "What 'people' is that, sir?"

"Your military folks. The top brass. Stahl, Bornheiter, Knight, those shirts. The CNO. The retired four-stars, like Skip Froelinghausen. What's your call, Dan? Any way I could turn them around?"

A fallen log lay across the snowy trail, powdery rot spilling out like dirty cinnamon from its hollow core. It had to have just come down; he couldn't imagine the detail letting the president run a trail they hadn't swept. McKoy waved, and two of the earpiece boys sprinted ahead. The president took a breather, arms akimbo, as they looked it over, then kicked it out of the way.

He couldn't believe this. De Bari knew his name. Had to know he was Blair Titus's husband. He was either totally oblivious, or totally shameless. Could he really believe a few flattering words could make him a Buddy de Bob again?

They eased back into a slow pace. "Ah, I couldn't tell you that, sir."

"We've got to cut back. Tokyo's hammering Detroit. We're losing textiles and computers to the Chinese. And Social Security, tax reform, we can't let those go another year. Who've we got left to fight anyway?"

Dan said, still incredulous, "Sir, I'm way too far down the chop chain to give you any insight on that."

"And you wouldn't tell me if you knew." De Bari hit him, a fairly painful jab to the shoulder.

He didn't like this man. He grated out, trying to keep his timbre short of actively savage, "I would if I could, Mr. President."

"Then give it a shot."

Dan tried to focus. McKoy and the other detail guys were eyeballing the passing woods. "Well, my opinion—"

"That's what I want."

"Shit flows downhill. But so does everything else."

"Like what?" De Bari was riveted. Again, as if his total attention were on Dan. Once it had been mesmerizing. Now it nauseated him. What had Congressman Freck said about the guy—that he'd never known a human being De Bari really cared about.

"Uh, I don't know how it is dealing with other organizations. But with the Pentagon, whatever the guys at the top think, that flows downhill too. Everybody takes his cue from them."

"I figured it was the conscientious-objector thing."

"That's just a rag to smear you with," Dan told him. "The admirals, the generals, used to at least say it didn't matter to them which party had power. Now they don't even bother to pretend." He almost added that was the most ominous trend he'd seen in his years in the service, but didn't. Spilling his guts to De Bari wasn't going to change anything. And why should *he* even try to help him?

The snow was slushy down here out of the wind. Water

stood in depressions as they came down off the saddle, making them weave among shining puddles of sky. De Bari panted, "I'm going to keep cutting. If the country wanted to keep a big military, they'd have elected the other guy."

"They don't like backing down around the world, sir. Leaving places we've been for years."

De Bari chuffed along frowning. "They think I'm retreating."

"Yes, sir."

"Know how I see it?"

"No, Mr. President."

"We went into those places to keep the Soviets out. Right? Now they're gone. You wanted me to put troops into Bosnia. But it just ain't our fight. We're not all-powerful anymore. Is it better to start moving back, on our own? Or wait till somebody decides to kick us out?"

Dan saw what he was getting at. Like shortening a defensive perimeter. But you could argue just as well that if you had to fight, it was better to do it as far from the homeland as you could. Or that if you abandoned one ally, why should the others trust you? And you could say Bosnia wasn't America's business . . . like Czechoslovakia hadn't been Britain's business in 1938.

It was like looking into a hall of mirrors, where you couldn't see which was a wise choice and which a foolish overstepping. Maybe the historians could, in a hundred years. Or maybe not even then.

"See what I'm sayin'?"

"I do. But I don't know if you're right."

For answer he got a bark of laughter, then wheezing as De Bari made up lost air. "So there's nothing I can do to get them on my side."

"They're never going to *like* you, Mr. President. To them, you're the enemy." He ran a few paces, then added recklessly, "So I guess—you've just got to decide where you want to go, and lead the way."

De Bari gave him an ironic smile. "You find out fast, in this job, you can only lead people where they already want to go."

"Then get out front, and see if they follow you."

De Bari didn't answer. He seemed to be laboring to keep up even this slow pace. Dan shook his head as if flinging flies off. Despite everything, he felt just a little sorry for the guy. He was taking so much flak. The insults and innuendoes, the smears and outright contempt.

But De Bari was just so false. All the bonhomie, the sham compassion he oozed on television with some poor bastard who'd lost his house in a tornado, *everything about him* was a lie ... even the way he *made* you like him. It was like fucking a whore. As soon as it was over you hated yourself. Even the policies Dan had once liked he saw now as just what made the guy's donors—including, no doubt, Tallinger and the Chinese—happy.

Bad Bob was no different from any other politician. Out for themselves and what they could get away with. And Lincoln, Washington, Roosevelt? All just shyster politicians, canonized by a people so starved for heroes they closed their eyes to the fact they had none.

"Aw, shit. Here it comes."

Dan saw it. The trail branched, one fork leading down into the valley, the other around the mountain again, back toward the hilltop. The sky was clouding, taking on the ominous leaden hue that presaged more snow. The lead runners glanced back, gauging which direction they'd take. Agent McKoy looked at De Bari, then waved: Go left. The long way around, Dan figured. That left two protective agents, Dan, and the president. They shuffled slowly up to the fork.

But instead of making the downhill turn, De Bari shambled to a halt. "I better get back," he grunted. He bent for a few seconds, hands on knees, coughing. Then straightened, turned right, and started to walk, swinging his arms and wheezing as if he'd run a marathon. Dan figured all told, they'd gone half a mile.

Right then, almost from nowhere, Dan knew he could kill him.

They were alone on the trail. All he had to do was grab a fallen limb and brain the lying, adulterous son of a bitch. BS

Bob, as the opposition called him, their commentators hammering it over and over into their programmable listeners. Or go for the pistol in the satchel. Getting even—wouldn't that be worth dying for?

He stood rooted, sick and trembling.

De Bari turned his head, as if he could sense his thoughts. Their eyes met. Then the president looked away, and resumed the climb.

Dan hiked after him, feeling sweat break all over his body. Feeling as if he could not stand one more hour of breathing. Why didn't anyone notice he was losing his grip, running off the rails, going just plain bughouse? He tried looking away. Lagging back. Thinking about how the shadowing sun embossed every bole and twig with cold pewter light.

Finally the shakes eased. He took a deep breath of cold air. Pulled it in slowly, so he could taste it around his tongue. Mint. Pine. Melting snow. Then let it out. Another. That was better.

He didn't really want to kill the man climbing laboriously ahead of him, panting, his once-white Adidas coated and slipping in the mud.

But he couldn't take much more of this either.

18

ASMARA, ERITREA

The familiar parching heat, glaring sun, pale dust of the Middle East. He stood watching the huge white-and-blue aircraft float down toward a runway he'd paced for hours that morning, inspecting for potholes, rocks, foreign objects, or anything suspicious.

The wheels touched, and kissed up smoke. And the chest-shaking roar of the immense engines reversing into braking thrust was met by an even greater thunder from hundreds of thousands of throats, a surging sea that broke and recoiled, walled from the heat-shimmering tarmac by lines of troops and armor, weapons pointed at the hungry and desperate.

As desperate, in a different way, as the De Bari administration, now trapped in a firestorm of criticism. The major indexes had hit new lows. A scandal was brewing in the Department of Education. Even the vice president was speaking out against Bob De Bari now, whose poll numbers had dropped into the thirties.

Dan had followed it on the BBC, and what little he'd heard through staff channels. But he couldn't say he did so with any interest. It felt distant, or *he* felt distant. He really couldn't say he cared.

◆ ◆ ◆

Colonel Gunning had put him on the advance party for Adamant Black. "Adamant" was the code word for a presidential foreign visit. Since *Air Force One* would be taking off in less than a month, that meant he was playing catch-up from the start.

In his first meeting with the Air Mobility Command at Andrews, they'd told him a presidential visit was the equivalent of a medium-sized military intervention. The numbers were staggering: a thousand people, 180 airlift and aerial refueling missions, maintenance support teams, medical evacuation units. Actually it *was* a military operation, run by the Defense Department according to an order that included all the concepts of operations, logistics, command and signal sections, and minute-by-minute schedules he was familiar with from other operations. It would have struck someone who hadn't operated in a joint planning environment as insanely complex, anally specific, and neurotically over detailed, down to the thickness of the railings on the reviewing stands, ground loading for the helicopter dome shelters, and specs for the plugs on the microphones. But he'd plunged in, sleeping on the cot in the PEOC, pulling work over him like a sheltering blanket.

Along with the two 747s, *Air Force One* and *Two*, Adamant Black included three C-5 Galaxy heavy lift air transports carrying two presidential limousines, the Road-runners, the command vans, a specially equipped ambulance, and hordes of other vehicles for staff and support. One airlifter carried *Marine One* and its escort aircraft. There was medical staff. Press corps. Comm staff. Valets, negotiators, advisers, stewards, area specialists, hairdressers . . . nearly two hundred security people, both uniformed and plainclothes. "Blacktop" alone, the Secret Service foreign mission personnel, consisted of fifty agents and four vans of equipment.

The advance party left at D minus six. Dan kept in constant phone contact with Charlie Ringalls. The little westerner was the go-to guy on presidential travel, though Dan had to consult with Holt and the first lady's people too, as she was coming along.

The chief of staff sounded peremptory and harried these days, no doubt because of the coverage a knot of demonstrators was getting. They'd camped out in front of the White House, demanding action on jobs. Their numbers were growing. So was concern about the president's polls. Holt kept emphasizing that the press secretary would call the shots on this tour. He kept mentioning "the Moment," which Dan had at first taken as shorthand for the now-familiar De Bari photo op. But when the press secretary's people used the phrase, it sounded mystical, an iconic encapsulation in one unforgettable image of what the trip was about. When he asked them what the trip actually *was* about, one guy said that was it: the Moment.

At which point he gave up. This was just another bubble from Robert De Bari's content-free shipwreck of a presidency. He took that futility or reassurance out with him onto the dusty roads of drought-ridden East Africa, riding in rented Land Rovers with the press and protective detail through village after village. These people had *real* problems. He only wished he had even a little power, a little money. Even the smallest bit of what was being wasted . . .

And here he was, "Mustang," arms lifted triumphantly heavenward as he posed atop the exit stair. De Bari descended to embrace President Afwerki. Then, ushered ahead, he preceded his host between ranks of troops at present arms. (Dan had personally inspected each rifle to make sure none was loaded.) The crowd-roar grew as they ducked into a limo with the Stars and Stripes and the green, red, and blue Eritrean banner.

Pushing through local officials, spitting windblown grit, Dan finally got to the command van. The door cracked to his hammering. Someone groaned; it was already over seating capacity with perspiring, crumpled USIA and USAID people, Nosler, and the press secretary. He wedged himself in with a sense of rejoining civilization.

He caught up to Gunning, who was carrying the football, in front of the Governor's Palace. The Raj-era building was surrounded by palms and gardens. The colonel nodded as if he'd seen him yesterday, and asked for the plans for the next stop. Dan looked around for shade, and punched the schedule up on his new personal digital assistant.

"Four countries in eight days, then Jerusalem," the senior aide said in disgust. "And what countries. Who signed him up for these shitholes?"

"I get marching orders from Wrinkles, but I don't know who gives them to him. The press secretary? Holt?"

"Yeah, sounds like a Tony Pony. It's a good time to get Bob out of the country, though. People are talking impeachment, and not just Freck's gang. Since Louisville—"

"What about Louisville? Nobody got hurt."

"I figure it's not for Louisville, it's for what hasn't happened since Louisville. And what's not happening on the stock market. And what's not happening, period."

"What do they want him to do?"

"The fuck should I know? I'm not the president. He should do *something*. Fire some missiles. Invade somebody. Shit, like they're saying on the radio, even Edwards would be better than this guy."

Dan had thought the FBI *was* doing something; rooting out the organization in California that had planned the radioactive dispersal and sheltered the terrorists, trying to find out who'd financed and armed them. But he didn't argue. The people he worked with at Mobility Command were still eager to do a good job. But even they were outspoken about their growing hatred for Robert De Bari and everything he represented.

From Asmara the tour headed up into the hinterlands. Ringalls had suggested they visit Kerkerbit, where the battle had taken place, but Holt vetoed that when Dan pointed out it was still in an unsecured area. The compromise was Camp Keaney, the base in the highlands Task Force Cougar operated from.

Dan had flown there to look things over, and have a talk with General Wood. He was relieved to find the man didn't recognize his voice as the staffer he'd spoken to at the Sit Room. Wood wasn't happy about playing host, but after some cutting remarks he'd nodded acknowledgment of Dan's point that even a president who'd decided not to support his offensive was still his commander in chief.

150900: MARINE ONE LANDING CAMP KEANEY

150900–0915: BRIEFING BY COMMANDING GENERAL TASK FORCE COUGAR

Marine One landed two minutes ahead of schedule, escorted by three Army Black Hawks, for what Dan had scheduled as a two-hour visit. The weather was clear but cold, due to the altitude, and the wind boiled up the dust into a sandpaper fog. The landscape was sand and rock, with eroded mountains barring the western horizon.

Dan jumped off the chopper after De Bari, clutching the satchel and worrying about the distance to the UHF uplink. Since this was a combat zone, he'd borrowed a pistol belt from the marines at the embassy and clipped the Beretta to it.

He didn't enjoy being back in battle dress. Just the smell of the cloth reminded him of Iraq. He jerked his mind out of that groove, which spiraled down first into fear, then panic so extreme he'd hyperventilate himself nearly into a blackout. The president was dressed as if he were at his ranch, in jeans and snakeskin boots and a camo flak jacket that looked out of place over a plaid shirt that probably came out of the L.L. Bean catalog. At least he wasn't wearing his white Stetson.

Dan trailed him into a meet and greet in the command tent with Wood, his staff, and some locals. The general said little, just offered everybody bottled water and went into a map brief on the situation on the border and the composition of the Sudanese and militia forces opposite. The staff officers, though, were glowering and muttering in the back. Standing with them, Dan could hear everything they said.

150915–0930: MEETING WITH TRIBAL ELDERS
AND LOCAL MILITARY REPRESENTATIVES

The tribal elders bowed repeatedly when they were introduced, holding cans of Coca-Cola. Their unwashed stench
filled the tent. The smell didn't seem to bother De Bari,
though. He was sympathetic and amiable, asking what they
needed, how they got their news, how the U.S. could help.
Wood stood silently by at parade rest, participating only
when De Bari asked him a direct question. A State guy Dan
didn't know translated, conspicuously taking notes every
time one of the graybeards mentioned something his tribe
wanted.

150930–1000: TOUR OF CAMP KEANEY, INTERAC-
TION WITH ENLISTED

Wood handed De Bari goggles and led him out into the
wind again. The rest of the party shuffled after, those who
didn't get protective eyewear shading their eyes against the
blowing grit. The press secretary had announced that since
the task force was conducting operations, the president
would forgo the usual chat with the troops and just do an informal walkaround.

The clatter and whine of the gunships Dan had set up to
orbit came—now loud, now distant—from the tan sky. The
press staff worked the camera crews, pointing out shots of De
Bari joking with the Eritrean liaison, lending a hand sand-
bagging a position, inspecting a Hummer's transmission.

Head down, staying ten steps behind the gaggle, Dan
meditated on the divergence of aim between the press staff
and the media itself, noisy, fractious, and determined to get
a story out of one of De Bari's increasingly rare visits to a
military post. When a cornered Ranger submitted to a handshake, the reps dragged the crews over to film it. When on
the other hand a working party turned its collective back on
the president, the reps waved the media off like cops waving
traffic past an accident. POTUS moved on, and the crews fell
in again behind him, the plastic wrappings on their video-
cams flapping in the cold wind.

A large tent, with a line of dusty, tired troops standing

outside, took shape from the fog. M-4s were slung muzzle down over their shoulders. Their boots were caked with dirt. De Bari lifted the flap, grabbed a mess tray, and joined them.

Not a bad move from the PR point of view, Dan thought. Unfortunately, the president decided to join on not at the tail of the queue, but at the front. And since his protective detail went with him, the net effect was to push the hungry, tired troops in line back on their heels.

The beefing got loud fast. Dan looked for a noncom, but didn't see one. He didn't see Wood either. Finally he raised his voice. The objections dropped in volume, but didn't stop.

One of Wood's staff officers, with the railroad tracks of an army captain: "What's the trouble, Colonel?"

"Commander. These troops are talking in ranks."

"They aren't in ranks. They're in the mess line." The captain told them, "Keep it down. I don't like this prick any more than you do, but military courtesy, okay?"

Dan blinked. Validating the troops' feelings wasn't the way to handle this situation. But they weren't his men. His responsibility was security—banded to his wrist. Moreover, they were now the focus of three camera teams.

But when he turned back, the flap was falling closed. The captain had *left*.

"Son of a bitch just pushes in front," one trooper said tentatively, and the beefing caught fire again.

"Left us hangin' in Ker-ker. Now the fucker wants his picture taken with us?"

"Conscientious objector, my ass."

They kept getting louder. Worse, they began crowding into the tent.

Dan pushed in too, using the satchel to bulldoze soldiers out of the way, and saw as the flap lifted De Bari being backed against the serving line. The protective detail closed up. But within seconds, in the close, food-smelling, near-dark confines of the tent, the result was a struggling knot of muscular bodies behind which the president was just visible trying to say something amid rising shouts and the clatter of mess trays on rifles from outside. Gritty dust milled, beaten off uniforms, scuffed up from the dirt floor. A stack of cups collapsed with a deafening clatter.

Dan wedged into the scrum, yelling at the troops to back off. Elbowing men out of the way, he came face-to-face with McKoy. The head of the protective detail grabbed him by the shoulders and spun him around. Now, facing out, not in, he felt himself propelled from behind, the satchel gripped like a shield in front of his chest, like the front hoplite in a Spartan phalanx. The rest of the detail had their feet braced and were shoving, turtled around De Bari. When Dan glanced back, the president's cheeks were flushed. He'd never seen the guy mad before. Or was it fear?

When he looked around again he was face-to-face with an angry-looking soldier with a dark complexion, black mustache, and stubble on his cheeks. He was shouting in Dan's face, but with a foot or two still between them, when someone behind him shoved the trooper forward.

Dan grabbed with one arm, missed, but McKoy was ready. Big palms wide in front of him, when the soldier crashed into him the agent pushed back so hard the thump of his hands against the man's chest echoed through the tent. Staggering back, the soldier made a sudden involuntary movement. One hand went, perhaps by chance, to his combat vest.

Dan saw his fingers close around a grenade.

Without even appearing to move McKoy had his pistol out and leveled at the trooper's head. With a simultaneous dip and thrust all the Secret Service men—they were all men on this forward-base visit—had theirs out too. Everyone froze, staring at the weapons. Somebody muttered, "Oooh . . . *shit*."

A light blazed on at the tent entrance. The glare of a videocam flood limned shocked eyes, gaping mouths, capturing them all in a suddenly frozen tableau.

"Clear the tent. Clear this fucking tent!"

General Wood, as pissed off as Dan had ever seen a human being. The troops recoiled. Cursing noncoms grabbed at uniforms, web gear, hauled them out bodily. Within seconds the tent was empty, except for the panting Secret Service men, Wood, Dan, and the president.

Dan lowered the satchel to the scuffed dirt, breathing hard. He couldn't believe what he'd just seen. He'd never seen American troops act like this.

He remembered the hate-filled eyes, the hard, tanned faces. The legionaries of the Border. Would the first emperor come from among them?

19

KHARTOUM, SUDAN; GOMA
REFUGEE CAMP, EASTERN ZAIRE

H e'd expected a feeding frenzy when the video hit, but to his surprise only a couple of outlets mentioned the incident. He watched it in *Air Force One*'s pressroom twenty thousand feet above the North African desert. It came across as a confused scuffle in a dark tent, not as the mass and open disrespect he'd experienced. Somehow Ringalls, Holt, and the rest of the president's men had put the well-known De Bari spin on the story.

He didn't believe the troops would actually have used their weapons. The one who'd grabbed the grenade had done so by reflex. But what they'd been *saying* was another matter. He couldn't believe American troops would express open contempt of the commander in chief like that. He had to go back a lot of years for anything like it. To when officers were getting fragged in Vietnam.

K hartoum was a chaotic, run-down sprawl that smelled of paranoia where *khawaja*—foreigners—were concerned. Dan advanced the visit with a sinister-looking colonel who described himself as an "aide." Lenson suspected he was more likely head of the secret police. The streets reeked of diesel exhaust, shit, and an ancient dry dung-stink that seemed to come from the very bricks.

He helped Gunning set up the comm relays, then carried the PES for De Bari's first meeting with "President" Omar Hassan Ahmed el-Bashir. Dan, the Sudanese colonel, McKoy, and the rest of the protective detail drank cardamom tea in a corridor while the Sudanese bodyguards scowled at them. That afternoon he went along with the first lady and the president for a boat trip on the Nile— which was short, as the river was low and the black mud stank horribly. McKoy had vetoed the visit to the Souk Arabi, fearing anyone could run out of the market crowd, fire a shot at close range, and disappear back into the thousands of beggars, refugees, day laborers, tribesmen, and women in black chadors and leather masks who thronged the juice stalls and spice shops.

The state dinner that evening was at a palace on the river that had once been "Chinese" Gordon's headquarters. Dan thought he'd seen the grand staircase before in some film. He vaguely remembered Gordon being speared to death on it by a howling mob of the Mahdi's fanatics. Islamic uprisings, jihad, massacre, were old stories here. He stood by in an anteroom. The power went out during the performance, which was children doing traditional dances. Guards brought in torches, and the show went on. The effect was exotic and frightening; strange whining music, guttering torchlight, the fixed expressions of the dictator's staffers-slash-henchmen.

The De Baris retired early, but the State people stayed at the palace for a night session. Dan overheard enough to get the feeling this wasn't the fact-finding jaunt the press people had made it out to be.

The second day a huge, grizzle-bearded black man arrived, surrounded by bodyguards. Now three gangs of guards, all heavily armed, including the Secret Service's SWAT people, glowered and elbowed each other outside the carved doors of the conference room. He wondered what would happen if one of the Sudanese decided the Mahdi had been right about Christians after all.

The highlight was the photo op, when the session finally

broke. No, the Moment. Garang and el-Bashir were both
bald, fat, ugly thugs whose suits did not fit at all. A beaming
De Bari shepherded them into a reception room with the
pontifical bonhomie of a don brokering a gangland truce. He
announced they'd just signed a cease-fire. The Sudan People's Liberation Army would end twelve years of civil war,
and Garang would join a coalition government as el-Bashir's
vice president.

The two shook hands like tranquilized grizzlies as the
press teemed and shouted questions, which they ignored.
Dan noticed el-Bashir looking at him. His heavy-lidded eyes
examined his uniform, then dropped to the satchel. As soon
as the handshake was over Garang left, his security crowded
so close he could not even be seen.

It was probably a historic occasion, but he was busy trying to rejuggle the seating arrangements on *Air Force One*
for the next leg, to Zaire. He'd have been more impressed if
he hadn't also seen the oil company executives with the
State people the night before, and heard them discussing ex-
ploration blocks, probable reserves, and a pipeline to the
Red Sea. He recognized these men now. They were De
Bari's golfing buddies, his intimates and presumably his
donors. Not only that, one of the companies was the China
National Petroleum Corporation. A reporter told him the
deal was that the Nuer and Dinkas wouldn't attack the oil
fields, in exchange for a third of the revenue.

The more he saw of politics, the better he liked the Navy.
It had its share of assholes and incompetents. But being
ready to step in front of a bullet, or face a hurricane, sheared
away at least some of the greed and ego.

But the next moment he answered himself. Who *cared* if
the Dinkas got paid off? If this thug or that lobbyist got rich?
Wasn't ending a civil war a good thing?

He stood with the satchel between his boots, pistol under
his jacket, watching the smiling men congratulating each
other. The president's back was to him. He stood rigid,
struggling again with the demon that whispered, *Do it. You
fucking coward.*

❖ ❖ ❖

The next day, in Zaire. He'd located a marginally navigable road out to the camp, so they took the motorcade. In the command van, enjoying air-conditioning while he had it, he rode in silence across from McKoy. Dan thought after a time: Maybe I should tell him. Or somebody.

He envisioned it. "I'm having thoughts about killing the president." Yeah right . . . or maybe, "I'm having doubts about my fitness for this job." That might be better. But phrase it how he might, it'd still put the last nail in his coffin.

If he could *just finish,* he might still get back to sea. It was possible, with the medal, with his record . . . not that it was such a great record . . . too many damaged ships, too many dead, too many internationally inconvenient episodes swept under the carpet. Still, he'd done his duty. There were those who disagreed. But you couldn't please everybody.

But *could* he go on? Being in this situation day after day . . . More pressure wasn't what he needed. His neck hurt. He had flashbacks. He didn't need this.

But if he couldn't handle it, he'd never get another ship . . .

"You're deep in thought," the lead agent said.

"Just going over the schedule."

"One more country, then we can head home."

"Well, I'll be ready."

But to himself he wondered: Home? And where was that? An empty house? A wife who'd left? He looked out at the ash and patches of tortured volcanic rock that got larger and more frequent, the vegetation more sick and stunted-looking, the closer they got to the Goma Refugee Camp.

The tents started dotting the gravelly, wasted terrain half an hour before they turned off the road. The van lurched. Rocks screeched along the pan and whanged in the wheel wells. Some were cloth shelters, military surplus, but most were nothing more than sticks propping up blue plastic tarps with the letters UNHCR on them.

He looked at the briefing sheet again. A million dead, hacked apart with machetes. A million and a half refugees, fleeing rape, militia rampages, looting, and tribal terror. Their hovels were crammed campfire to campfire all the way to distant green mountains streaked with mist, or smoke, or maybe even volcanic vapor. Supposedly the last mountain gorillas lived up there. Or had, until hungry humans had invaded their domain.

When they got out the humid, cloying heat closed down like a sauna at full blast. A distant murmur surrounded them, and a stink like smoldering matches. The volcano had burned this whole valley out only a few years before. It still smoked on the horizon, chuffing out sulfurous gas and a fine gray fog. That fog was a choking-fine powder of ash, and the gas turned to sulfuric acid in the lungs and eyes. The briefing sheet said that the volcano could explode again any time. Fumes, clinkers, and a gritty black dust like hard, shiny little particles of fly shit permeated everything.

The UN resident commissioner was waiting on a little drab hill of what looked like frozen mud. Dan, following the president's party across it, realized it was a mixture of volcanic rubble and some sort of petrified or vulcanized dung, human or animal he couldn't tell.

Following the commissioner, handkerchiefs to their faces, they trailed the president and a slowly walking Letitia De Bari down into the valley. Under the equatorial sun, as if developed by the fumes, colors grew feverishly vibrant as they drew closer over the dead black ground. Traces of strangely too-green grass lay trampled and scorched. The refugees' visages were inky holes under their scarves, clothes a fluorescent riot of cheap oranges, sick blues, hot pinks. They milled slowly, coughing, on the far side of a bright yellow webbed-plastic crowd barrier. He coughed too, feeling the acid bite into his lungs, as the administrator began, "They call this the Valley of Death."

The president and first lady looked uneasy as Ericssen gave them the rundown on the refugees. "As you can see, this is wasteland, avoided and dreaded before they arrived. There are no wells; this is lava mantle beneath us. No water and no drainage equals epidemics. Typhoid. Dysentery. Malaria. Blackwater fever. The mass graves are half a mile east of here. We lost twenty thousand this summer to cholera."

Empty eyes followed them as they picked their way downhill. A female staffer turned an ankle and went down. When she lifted her hands blood trickled from all-but-invisible lava cuts. The commissioner droned on in a digital voice, hands in his pockets and a gaze blank as those of his charges. He spoke of rations. Transport. The hostility of the indigenous population. The destruction of the gorillas. The denuding of the mountains to feed the greenwood cookfires that Dan realized were responsible for as much of the haze as the volcano. Each sentence he formed, each shack they passed, each group of huddled, vacant-looking human beings, was more hopeless. From inside one tent, as they drew near, a woman was screaming and crying.

"This is just horrible," Mrs. De Bari interrupted at last, voice high and breaking-brittle. "All these people. Somebody should do something."

"We're trying our best," the commissioner said. "HIV infections have jumped elevenfold this year, due to rapes, prostitution, and lack of both condoms and an understanding of the disease . . ."

Under the plastic sheeting the woman came into view, rocking and hugging a wrapped bundle. Dan looked at the president. De Bari's face shone with sweat. Dark half-moons bearded the armpits of his golf shirt. He looked poleaxed, like one of the steers on his ranch.

His wife asked to be taken back to the limo. De Bari looked longingly after her. Dan waited, clutching the football. He kept checking the barrier, noting the thousands of bodies on the other side. If they decided to swarm, was he really going to shoot to keep some starving refugee's hands off the SIOP? He decided he wasn't. Nobody here was going to call in an option on encrypted UHF.

When he looked back toward the president he caught his breath and began hurriedly picking his way over the sharp ground after him. A thin wailing chorus came from the fog-smoke ahead. POTUS was not walking back, toward the motorcade, air-conditioning, and safety. He was headed up one of the lava-strewn hills that rose into the haze. Maybe to see better, but not pleasing McKoy. Dan heard the lead agent shouting, but didn't catch De Bari's reply.

The keening grew louder as they climbed. He couldn't imagine what it was. Then, as he crested the hill, he came to a stop where the president had already halted, looking down into a pit over which the choking haze hung low.

It was filled with forms that took him a moment to identify. Wasted, small figures lying on blankets and on the omnipresent blue tarps. These people might lack everything else, a horrified corner of his mind wisecracked. But they had enough blue plastic sheeting.

They'd been lying motionless, but when they noticed the group watching from above, they began to stir. They sat up. Left their games of tossing stones at bushes. Gradually a crowd gathered.

"Who are these kids?" De Bari wanted to know.

"Orphans," the commissioner said. "Their families have been murdered. Or died of AIDS or cholera. When the children have no remaining family, we concentrate them. For their own protection."

Dan looked at the open sky, the sprawling horror all around. But for some reason this seemed more appalling. These small withered creatures, huddling into groups out of the simple child's desire to be close to someone.

A translator shouted something. The children hesitated. Then kept coming, stumbling up the hillock. Some were crawling. Individually they were just smudge-faced kids. His gaze went from one to the next. But there were hundreds, and more were getting to their feet and beginning to wander their way. The translator shouted again, but they didn't stop. The air smelled of shit and smolder and something almost coppery, like blood.

"Let's move back now, Mr. President," McKoy said. He hand-signaled to the detail. The agents pincered out, taking positions between De Bari and the advancing tide. "Time to get back to the motorcade."

The president didn't move, so Dan moved up beside him. The kids were thirty yards away. Two spindly boys had the lead. One was wrapped in blue plastic. The other had found a man's T-shirt somewhere. Stained and ragged, it flapped over bony knees swollen to the size of softballs. He led an even smaller girl by the hand. She looked up as they climbed, barefoot on the flinty hot ground. Her eyes were huge and very white against dusty skin.

"There should be shelter," Dan heard the president say. "Not just these fucking tarps."

"We've had to allocate all our transport space to fuel and food."

"Why do these people need fuel?"

"They don't, sir. We do. To transport the food to them."

"Let's move back, Mr. President." McKoy again, insistent, as the children flowed to right and left, boxing them in now on three sides. A throng whose only sound was the shuffling of bare feet in cinders, and weeping sniffles from the smallest.

The smoke and dust parted to a hot breeze. When Dan lifted his gaze it went out over hundreds, no, *thousands* of children. It was like a battlefield, except that these still or slowly wandering forms were ridiculously small, absurdly thin, incredibly heartbreaking.

Now all the agents and even the UN people were moving to place themselves in front of where De Bari stood, somehow looking alone for the first time. No trace of the glad-handing politician now. Nor of the gangland don. He stood coughing, shoulders slumped, staring at the oncoming tide.

"Mr. President, we should go back," the UN rep suggested.

"Sir, he's right," Dan put in.

He glanced back to make sure the way back over the lava and trash was still clear. Even the press people were backing away, though they were still recording, telecams intent. The press secretary looked apprehensive. The Moment, Dan thought. It might be here. But what kind of Moment would it turn out to be?

He took De Bari's arm. But the president reached down and brushed his hand off, gaze still on the advancing throng.

The translator shouted again. But the children, fascinated by the strange beings they'd discovered, didn't even slow. The smells of their bodies and clothes and diseases came up on the hot wind. A strange, dry, inhuman stink like a herd of dying animals. But close up they were not a herd. Just a boy in a ragged T-shirt. A girl with a dirty bandage around her head. Others carried sharpened sticks over their shoulders. Dan could not imagine what their lives were like, locked in this nightmare valley without food, or water, under the white relentless sky.

McKoy said, "Sir, you have to go back. This is dangerous."

"They're just kids." De Bari's first words since they'd started up the hill.

"If you don't leave we'll have to drag you back."

"No," De Bari said, so softly Dan almost couldn't hear him. "Let 'em come."

The agents and Dan looked at one another. Now, having completed the ring, some of the children were approaching De Bari. "Stop that one, with the stick," McKoy shouted. An agent lurched forward, shoes crunching into the ash. The children separated slowly, like sleepwalkers, as he plunged through them.

Then they reached them. Surrounded them. De Bari looked down as they fingered his clothes and gazed at his boots. Some murmured pleas, holding out hands, begging. Others just stared up. A little girl spun in a circle, kicking up the ashy dust in some childish dance. Despite her wasted face, sticklike legs, she was laughing. De Bari seemed transfixed by what she was doing. "They're just kids," he said again.

The technicals from the comm van, the Secret Service limo drivers, the camp staff, came straggling up, panting, spitting, slipping on the loose black scree. Yoshida carried his doctor's bag. The techs hefted tools and lengths of conduit, as if they'd rallied in the last ditch to defend the president. "What the hell's going on?" a potbellied older guy in a maroon windbreaker asked Dan.

"I'm not sure." De Bari had been staring at all the kids, yeah. But hadn't his attention been riveted by the girl?

Hadn't De Bari lost his own daughter when she was five?

"Jesus, look at this," the tech said. "My God. Doesn't *this* suck."

"Yeah. It does."

In a lower voice, glancing at the president: "What the hell's *he* doing? Is *he* okay?"

The president was kneeling. Speaking to the little girl. Fumbling in his pockets. Then turning angrily, cheeks mottled, hair hanging over his forehead, De Bari shouted in a choked voice to bring the lunches and drinks from the cars. He seemed to be crying. He *was* crying.

Dan wiped his own cheeks. Like the president's, like those of every man and woman on the hilltop, they were wet with angry tears.

20

WASHINGTON, D.C.

B elow-zero temperatures were a disorienting shock after the bitter heat of Africa. De Bari escaped them by
flying to his ranch, then to Managua for a meeting
with the heads of state in Central America. But it was another mil aide's turn to accompany him, Major Francie Upshaw's, and Dan stayed on in the East Wing.

Jazak was doing the postgraduate course at the National
Military Command College. He asked Dan if he wanted to
sit in. The Greater Washington chapter of the Naval Academy Alumni Association called asking if he wanted to attend
a talk by one of his classmates who'd just completed his second trip as captain of the space shuttle. Sandy Treherne
called about a reception she was hosting.

Instead he bought a VCR. In the evening he made dinner,
then watched movie after movie. Snow blanketed the city,
heaping dirty white outside the fence. Blair was in Taiwan.
He saw Nan for dinner again, but they didn't seem to connect. She sent him an e-mail afterward telling him he had to
cheer up, she was worried about him.

He drifted in a zone where he did nothing, wanted nothing, felt nothing. He wondered if he was getting depressed.
He slept a lot. That was supposed to be one of the symp-
toms. Wasn't it?

But he really couldn't say he cared.

• • •

The president came back the last day in January. When Dan went in the next day the Eighteen Acres was bustling again. De Bari had lost weight. He looked serious. He closeted himself in the Oval Office as senators and ambassadors, speechwriters and cronies went in and out. The first week in February loomed.

Then it was here. The State of the Union address. Dan picked up his service dress blue at the dry cleaner's. In the aides' office, he toothbrushed the seams of his shoes, slid fresh ribbons onto his ribbon bar, snapped on a new white cap cover. He pinned on the gold "water wings" of a surface warfare officer, then, centered on his right breast pocket, the presidential service badge. The coat of arms of the president: the gold eagle against dark blue enamel, arrows in one claw, olive branch in the other. He looped and pinned the aiguillette. The routine was reassuring. Like inspection at the Academy. Be on time, in the right uniform, tell the truth . . . Annapolis and reality had never seemed so far apart.

At 1400 the phone rang. Sebold wanted to see him. The staffer who called didn't say why, and Dan couldn't think of any reason his former boss would need him. But you didn't ask a general that. He hung up that evening's uniform, sheathed in transparent plastic like the immobilized prey of some alien predator, and went down to the colonnade, intending to take the ground-floor corridor across to the West Wing. But when he reached the Residence for some reason climbed upward again, toward cold daylight.

The high immaculate rooms of the state floor echoed to the whispers of their unending stream of visitants. He paced slowly, hands behind him. The State Dining Room, with Healy's quizzical Lincoln above the mantel. The Red Room, intimate in mauve and gold, with the portrait of Angelica Van Buren that Dan thought was the most human touch in the whole Residence. The Blue Room, its great gilt-and-blue oval looking out onto the Portico. Its shape reflected, one of the docents' fluting voices echoed, President Washington's first levees in New York, and was reflected in its turn by the Oval Office. He left her well-bred murmur for the exquisite, spare Federal furniture of the Green Room. And grandest of all, the parqueted perspective of the East Room, where Stuart's Washington gazed out, hand outstretched in renunciation or blessing.

With De Bari back the corridors of the West Wing were filled again with bright-eyed youngsters. The contempt and distance of the political staff didn't bother him now. Nor the shell games to cover up how much of the staff and budget were actually supplied from across the Potomac. Like so much else about this building, this government, about his country, he was beginning to suspect, it was blue smoke and mirrors.

Across West Executive, his shoes crunching in an inch of fresh snowfall. The corridors of the OEOB felt as chilly as the outdoors. The old heating system just wasn't keeping up, and the cold radiated up off the stone flooring.

Sebold was standing at his window when Dan knocked. An electric heater whined. Music seeped from a CD player. Sweeping, melodic strains . . . a waltz. The senior director for defense was wearing what looked like the same gray suit and scuffed wingtips as when Dan had met him a year before. The white bristle cut was the same, but now he wore plastic-framed glasses. "Dan. Sit down. How's it working out in the East Wing?"

Dan said all right. Sebold asked about his workload, whether he was getting any time off.

Finally he said, "I understand, hear, you've been having some . . . marital problems. Blair, by the way, is one of my closest friends. Since we worked together on the cheating scandal. That was a while back. But we've stayed in touch."

Dan lifted his head. Despite everything, he wanted to see her again. It didn't make sense, but there it was. "Has she asked you about me?"

"No. No. I just wanted to . . . see if there was anything I

could do. Since I was the one who brought you here in the first place. And we hadn't talked since you went over to the far side." Sebold was up again and pacing, whirling the glasses between thumb and forefinger like a propeller.

"Well, sir, no, there isn't."

The general hesitated. "This is a tricky issue to bring up. And it might not be any of my business. I'm talking about rumors I've heard."

Dan said tightly, "What rumors?"

"About your wife and the president."

He couldn't believe the man would call him in and say something like that. "I haven't heard anything like that, sorry," Dan told him.

"Well, I have. Not only that. I've heard an even nastier one. That you know about it, but put up with it."

"Put up with it." His voice rose. "Jesus *Christ*. Why would I *put up* with it?"

"Exactly; I spoke out at once that it was impossible, unthinkable."

"What are they saying? I *let* him fuck her?"

"Clearly that's not what was meant—"

Dan said, so furious his voice shook, "Clearly it *is* what was meant, and clearly it's malevolent bullshit. Targeted at her. The assholes who never accepted a woman at Defense. As far as our marriage goes, that is our own damned business, General."

"Of course it is. Only I—"

"It's our business, and there's nothing you or anyone else can do. Or has any reason discussing."

"I was afraid you'd take it that way. But I had to ask. Same as you'd feel if one of your men, on your ship, say, was having problems."

"Yes, sir," Dan told him, but he didn't buy it. It wasn't the son of a bitch's place even to mention it. That was all.

Sebold paced, letting a pause establish distance from the last topic. Dan tried to compose himself.

"I heard some things about your naval service that were pretty impressive. Things I hadn't realized before. I knew about the congressional, but I hadn't heard about the rest. You strike me as a patriot."

"A *patriot*, sir?" Where the hell was he going with *that*?

"In the old sense. You've put your butt on the line for this country. More than once."

"I've tried to do the best I can."

Sebold was looking out the window now, hands locked behind him. Talking to Dan, but at the same time, it seemed, to himself as well. "Somehow that flag means more to you once you've seen combat. Or sent good men out. Telling them to take an objective, knowing they won't all come back. That's the hardest thing."

Dan nodded. He'd sent troops back as rear guard in a fire-fight in Iraq. Sent teams out onto a deck contaminated with radioactivity, down into a flooding, burning engine room.

Sebold peered out. The snow was falling again. "Have you given any thought to where you want to go next? Whether you want to stay in government? A lot of people who've served here as junior officers find they have a taste for it. Scowcroft. Powell. Haig."

Dan was astonished. "Sir, what *is* this? The last time we talked, you were getting me reassigned. You said I'd only be there till they could come up with somebody else."

"I had to fight Brent Gelzinis to get you another chance. But I did."

"Well, I have to say, I truly wish you hadn't. I thought my reassignment was being worked."

"So you don't care to stay."

"No, sir. I don't have much taste for politics."

"Probably a wise decision. Sometimes I doubt I have, myself."

"You've got as good a rep around here as anyone I know," Dan told him, not as a compliment, just as a fact. But it seemed to make Sebold uncomfortable. He looked away, prodded his lips with his glasses.

"Anyway . . . you've done a good job, both here and then over in the East Wing," the general said. "I just wanted to say that."

The guy still wasn't meeting his eyes. Dan thought this was all very curious. As if Sebold were cleaning out his desk to leave, or Dan himself were being let go.

The general didn't seem to have anything else to say, though. He cleared his throat again and said that would be all, thanks for stopping by. When Dan rose, Sebold put out his hand. Dan hesitated, then took it. The director's grip, as they parted, was very firm.

A s long as he was in the Old Executive, he stopped by counterdrug. Ouderkirk looked surprised to see him, then angry. Dan almost asked the sergeant what was going on, then didn't. Just nodded and slid past.

His former assistant, Meilhamer, looked up from a littered desk. "Commander Lenson," he said, with what sounded like gloating. "Back to the old stand?"

"Just wondered what's going on. Anything?"

"Just the usual. Everybody's out on travel but Bloom. Want to see him?"

"In a minute." Dan couldn't help glancing at his old desk. Empty and clean.

"Nobody yet," Meilhamer said. "I'm signing as acting director."

Bloom put his head in. "Hey, Dan. Thought I heard you out here. On our Colombian friend? The trail went cold after El Salvador. But one interesting thing. You might have seen it in the papers. The Baptist put out a contract."

"On who?"

"Actually a bunch of contracts. He's always been a fan of economic incentives." The DEA agent slipped a newspaper clipping from his wallet and pointed to the bottom. "That's in pesos, but it works out to twenty million dollars U.S. for De Bari. Ten million for Tejeiro. A million for a major drug enforcement official of either president. Doubt that includes us—he probably means cabinet level—but there it is."

Dan shook his head. Putting a price on two presidents' heads . . . "Well, we put out a reward on him. Didn't we?"

"Hell yeah. Turnabout's fair play." Bloom grinned. "I'm just trying to figure out how I can collect."

Dan asked Meilhamer, "How's the Threat Cell idea going, Bry?"

The civil servant turned over a piece of paper. Past him Dan saw Ouderkirk talking on the phone. He glanced toward Dan, and their eyes met. The sergeant looked away as Meilhamer echoed blandly, "Threat Cell?"

"You remember. Trying to outguess the terrorists. I was pulling the money together to staff that. I thought maybe, after Louisville, Mrs. Clayton might think it was worth pushing."

"Oh yes, Commander. I always thought that was a wonderful idea. Very far-seeing. Though I wasn't sure this was the desk to implement it from." His former assistant smiled. "*You* know how things work around here. If somebody stops pushing a project, there are always other fires to put out. Other priorities."

Dan said between clenched teeth: "Yeah. I know."

A glittering blacksnake slithered out the South Gate, past the demonstrators—their numbers had grown, he noted, and they shook their signs angrily from behind police barricades—and turned its nose east. Up front was a District patrol car, followed by a comm van. Then two identical heavily armored limousines, one of which carried the president and Mrs. De Bari. Next came the CAT truck, one of those he'd looked down on so often from his office in the Old Executive, with its heavily armed team hidden inside. The black control van the mil aides rode in was next. Then came the press van, and last another set of District wheels, to guard against surprises from the rear.

He was riding with three of the protective detail guys; another security type, apparently from the Capitol; and Dr. Yoshida. McKoy rode across from him again, knee to knee.

Dan knew all the Secret Service guys now. They looked bulky because of their protective vests. They didn't play cards. They didn't talk unless he spoke first. Just now they'd taken their sunglasses off to see out the tinted windows. Well, maybe they thought as much or as little of him, in brushed dress blues, cap on his lap, the omnipresent satchel between his shining Corfams. All of them, agents, aides, doctors, acolytes at the altar of power.

McKoy's eyes went distant, as if listening to God. He brought his arm up and spoke into the sleeve mike. Dan waited, then leaned forward. "Ever think about putting the mil aides on that net?"

The dark eyes turned his way. "On the Motorolas?"

"Maybe just listen-only. You know—'Mustang and Tinkerbell are proceeding to Trail Breaker.' Just to give us the picture."

"I don't know if the director would go for that."

One of the other agents said he'd heard it had come up before, but didn't know how it had turned out. Obviously it hadn't been approved.

Then silence rode with them again, interrupted only by the hiss of the tires.

The motorcade rolled down Pennsylvania and turned at the ring road around Capitol Hill. The glass walls of the Conservatory slid past shining in the night like a cathedral of ice. Then they were climbing, the lawns, covered with patches of snow, sliding by.

Elderly men in dark suits waited under the portico of the House wing. They greeted De Bari with handshakes. The protective detail was out in a ring, none farther than ten feet from their charge. Around them strolled uniformed Capitol cops. Dan and the personal assistant, Nosler, tagged behind De Bari, outside the inner and inside the outer circle, as they moved through a crowd of Capitol Hill workers, staffers, and the press. Eyes moved past him, then slid down to the black burden on his security cuff.

The Capitol felt icy and cavernous. The presidential party trailed out down a long ground-floor corridor. The floors were glossy slick. Occasional words floated back, echoed off marble. Then a door closed. McKoy and his boys halted and faced out. Dan looked around for a seat, but didn't see any. He checked his watch. Eight forty, with the address scheduled to begin at nine. At least they wouldn't have long to wait.

He stood wondering where he was supposed to be during the address itself. Finally he went over to a solemn older gentleman in old-fashioned tails, who bowed gravely as Dan approached. "May I be of service, sir?"

He introduced himself, and asked. Said he needed to stay close, but not necessarily up front.

The old man said gravely, "In this House, sir, the president does not make the rules. You will remain on the House floor, standing, during the address. Behind the dais and out of sight of the television cameras."

He felt like a Christian entering the Colosseum. First the narrow corridor. Then a portal, and waves of sound like the crashing sea. Gold-and-blue carpet, polished mahogany, an expanse of warm air. The audience were already on their feet. Party stalwarts. The Senate and House leadership. The Joint Chiefs, standing in the front well. Behind them stood rank after rank of the Senate, the women members' suit dresses like flowers amid the dark tones of the male majority. The galleries rippled with the flutter of clapping hands.

Light ignited. He blinked as blurs of lambent fire pulsed across his vision. Thirty feet ahead De Bari beamed, lifting both arms in his trademark missing-fingered salute. Then followed the Speaker up the multitiered ziggurat of the podium.

Dan found a place where he could watch both the exit and the president. He unsnapped the security bracelet and went to parade rest.

De Bari's opening words rolled out over the waiting faces.

"We meet here tonight at a time of challenge . . . and opportunity.

"America is great because it is free. It is strong because it desires not domination, but peace.

"For the first time since World War II, a president can report to Congress on the state of a Union that is threatened by, and threatens, no other nation of the world. Because of this breathing space after great exertions, we have a historic opportunity. A chance, given only once in two or three generations, to shape the century to come."

Dan tuned out the next few minutes. For some reason this chamber seemed even more august and solemn than the Oval Office. Maybe he'd spent so much time around Bob De Bari, knew him so well by now, that neither the man nor the office impressed him anymore.

But here was the sovereign the founding fathers had envisioned, rooted in storefront offices and Rotary dinners and voting booths across a continent. Maybe it wasn't as wise as they'd hoped. Not as farsighted. But was anything human perfect?

His thoughts were broken by applause. But not the storm that had greeted the president's entrance. This sounded doubtful, half voiced. And some were not applauding at all.

He began to listen again.

"America is safer, more prosperous today, with more opportunity for more of its people, than ever before in our history.

"But we cannot remain at peace while a third of the world—disadvantaged, famine-stricken, largely illiterate—is a breeding ground for war.

We must extend the helping hand of America to those peoples who have been left out of our century's progress toward development and democracy. Nations and regions unable to cope with drought, disease, famine, civil war—the Four Horsemen of the oncoming Apocalypse. I call it Plan 21—America's plan for the twenty-first century."

Dan felt a prickle run up his spine. De Bari was flinging the words past his murmuring audience, into the cameras.

"There are two types of states in the developing world. One, though not wealthy yet by our standards, is on the road to democracy and development. These nations act responsibly in the world community. The others lag behind, cursed by capricious dictatorships, lack of human rights, but above all, by poverty and ecological stress. These are the havens for terror. They will be the source of war and unrest in the century to come. For strangely enough, it is when human beings have nothing . . . that they act as if they have nothing to lose.

"We can react to crisis after crisis, piecemeal and without making real progress—or we can take a giant stride.

"We must work with other nations to forgive the debt that asphyxiates development in so much of the Third World.

"We must strengthen the capacity of local governments to provide basic social, medical, and economic infrastructure, and build a robust international effort to address such growing risks as drug-resistant malaria, tuberculosis, and HIV.

"We must address the impending disaster of global warming, with its concomitants of drought, rising sea levels, and weather disturbances. This gradually accelerating catastrophe will first destroy those peoples already on the brink. But make no mistake: Unaddressed, it will reduce us all to a desperate struggle for shrinking resources. Till our children's children, heirs to all our greed, wander starving under a burning sun, and curse us for what we took from them forever."

Now Dan saw the puzzlement on the faces before him turning to something else. In some, to delight; in far more, to open anger. But De Bari kept on.

"As part of Plan 21, we must also resolve that dispute that has for a long time now been the most dangerous reality in the Mideast: the conflict between Israeli and Palestinian over the land both claim, both with justice, as their birthright.

"The time has come to permanently settle the problem. To this end, I have acceded to requests from both sides to post American troops as a peacekeeping force between Israel and the new Palestinian state. This will be followed by a level of aid aimed at bringing the Palestinian people to a standard of education and living fully equal to their Israeli neighbors."

The buzz climbed, then fell away. Dan had never seen a group of human beings so breathlessly attentive. Though he could not tell yet what they thought of what they heard.

"I have prepared a comprehensive message recommending the legislative measures necessary to meet the requirements of Plan 21. I urge that this be made the first priority of this Congress."

Dan could not believe it. De Bari was proposing a massive aid program. To Palestinians, Sudanese, central Africans, Bangladeshis. And some unspecified but also no doubt massive program to combat greenhouse warming. But where would the money come from? The speechwriters, of course, had anticipated that very question.

"Plan 21 will be funded by further reductions in military, space, and intelligence establishments still bloated by cold war–era requirements. It may be said this will leave us unready in a dangerous world. I believe it will not. The world's peace, as well as our own, depends on our remaining strong. But neither can we depend on military strength alone."

Dan couldn't help glancing at the Chiefs, in the front row. Stahl and the others listened in somber concentration.

"It may be said that this task is too big for us," De Bari said. "That it's too idealistic. Or just too hard.

"But as we look back, those years that stand out in our history are those in which the administration and Congress, working together, had the foresight to seize those initiatives for which the nation was ready—and in which they *acted*.

"This is such a moment. Perhaps the *last* moment in which we can realize the age-old dream of a world without widespread and recurrent famine. War. And ecological degradation."

The murmur that rose reflected Dan's own questions. *Was* it too much? Could such a self-indulgent and complacent country as theirs had become still rally to sacrifice and resolve?

De Bari's voice rose. "A great American once said, of the generation that made our Revolution: 'We have it in our power to begin the world again.'

"Have we been doing what America, and the world, expected of us? Have we looked further ahead than the next election? Above all, have we been *acting*? For far too long, we have not. And I bear the responsibility for that, as much as any. I too thought of myself first. I too lost sight of my duty. I too forgot—even with these to remind me—"

And he held up his hand, splayed, so that they all could see the missing fingers—

"That it is our duty, our trust, it is our *job*—that when there's a fire, we get all the people out of the building that we can. And put that fire out.

"But it is not yet too late. With the help of God, who has blessed us so richly, we can and will build lasting peace in the world, with security and freedom for all."

The vast chamber remained hushed after he finished. Then the applause began. Many sat in disapproving silence, arms folded. Others surged to their feet, shouting wildly, clapping as hard as they could. It went on and on.

De Bari appeared at the bottom of the rostrum, his big flushed face covered with sweat. He looked vacant and shocked and exhausted. Dan picked up his burden and followed him.

In the limo someone turned on a radio. A commentator was saying, "You have to applaud the president for a powerful and visionary State of the Union. But the issues he raises are more complex than they may seem. Is it really in our best interest to give billions to countries who hate us, countries we've been giving money to for decades now with no result other than making the ruling parties richer? And then, throw billions more at a global warming 'problem' that may not even exist? Especially when average Americans are watching their stocks dwindle, in a market that seems to have no bottom?"

Another station, another speaker. This one, on the left wing, assumed a cutting tone as she pointed out De Bari's proposal was far from selfless. The provisions for tax benefits for participating businesses would transfer millions of jobs to low-wage countries. Plan 21 was a corporate give-away, subsidizing the export of American jobs.

"So much for lack of an issue," the doctor said, to no one in particular. Dan nodded. He was still trying to organize his own thoughts. It was as daring a proposal as the New Deal, or the Great Society, or the Apollo program. One that would line everybody in the country up, either pro or con.

But he didn't have to make up his mind. What was he? Only a horse holder. A spear carrier. At most, a temple dog. It all would be decided at a level far above his. And for rea-sons that had nothing to do with his welfare, or that of the millions of others who believed as blindly as he did that all was for the best, that everything would turn out well.

Sucking in his breath, trying desperately to stem his de-pression and fear, he gazed out at the passing city.

2 1

THE WHITE HOUSE

Dan spent the night on the sofa in the aides' office, and got up still seething. His depression had been converted, by some mysterious alchemy, to rage. He could have understood if Blair had called it quits. He wasn't easy to live with. And neither the Navy nor Defense gave you much chance at a normal life. But why couldn't she just have told him. Instead of moving on to someone else?

Even if he was the most powerful man in the world.

He found batteries ripe in the charger, ready lights glowing, and plucked them. Next he checked the monitor, updated from the Secret Service office in the subbasement that located POTUS on the Eighteen Acres. Just now it showed him in the Oval. Unusually early, Dan thought.

Looking out the window, he saw the demonstration had grown again overnight. Now the protesters surrounded the building. Signs bobbed. Someone was shouting through a bullhorn, though Dan couldn't make out the message. Maybe it didn't matter. Now more than ever, you were either for Bad Bob or against him.

The schedule showed De Bari in the Residence that afternoon. No doubt working on his upcoming speech to the UN, to explain why he was sending American troops into the Middle East after pulling them out of everywhere else. Trying to bring peace to a place that hadn't seen any in a thousand years. Or ever, if you took the Old Testament's word for it.

Dan found Major Upshaw next door to the Oval Office, on the chair reserved for the mil aides in the secretary to the president's office. The football was under her chair. As he came in she stood, hand coming up briefly to smooth the front of her jacket. Dan recognized the gesture. Francie liked to carry the Beretta in a shoulder holster, to lighten the satchel. She said it was so heavy it gave her a backache. "He's about to leave. Ready to take it?"

He said he was. She glanced around, then drew the handgun with a quick nervous gesture and handed it over. He checked the safety and tucked it into his belt. Later he'd find a restroom and strap on the holster. Or just stow it back in the case.

Upshaw set the case down on the chair. Keeping her back to him—no doubt out of habit—she dialed in the combination. The lid unsnapped. She moved so he could see, and took out the battery set. He handed over the fresh ones, and heard a click as one seated in the transceiver.

She held out the clipboard with the custody form. He ran his eye over the open case. Spare magazine. Backup charged battery. The radio, its top visible and the stub of its antenna, folded but still capable of receiving the alert signal. The red plastic spine of the SIOP manual, the black spines of the others.

He took the pen and scribbled his initials. "I relieve you," he said, and saluted. It might look silly to a civilian, but all the aides did it. Then she was tapping off down the corridor. When he took her chair the seat was still warm.

As ever, the detail was first to appear, the agents rolling out ahead of the oncoming Presence like altar boys before a monstrance. The press secretary, then the secretary of defense's Taftesque bulk nearly plugging the hallway. Ringalls, looking shrunken between the overweight SecDef and the none-too-small De Bari. But then they halted. The president's voice was peremptory, cutting. "Don't give me that bullshit, Charlie. Just make it happen."

Dan was getting to his feet, ready to follow, when he saw Ouderkirk, the shaven-headed sergeant from the counterdrug office, beckoning from the Roosevelt Room. He pointed to his chest: *Me?* The staffer nodded. Dan went to the door. The sergeant gestured again, urgently.

He crossed the corridor. Ouderkirk muttered, "You on duty right now?"

"Yeah. I am. What do you want?"

"We need you to come by 303 once you get off."

"Counterdrug? Why? What's the problem?"

"No problem. Just that we need you to sign the debrief forms. You went over to the East Wing so fast we never got you signed out."

Dan said he'd be off in six hours and would come by then. Ouderkirk nodded and turned away.

The president was still outside the Oval Office, talking loudly to Ringalls, Weatherfield, and now his other old Nevada buddies too, Gino Varghese and Happy Harry Hedley. De Bari sounded angry. Looking to his left, Dan noticed a man in a gray suit heading down the corridor away from him. The corner of a large file box he was carrying was just visible. But he couldn't quite tell who it was, and the man didn't look back, so Dan went back into the secretary's office.

Then they were coming toward him, the same way he'd first seen De Bari, months before, flanked by the agents of the protective detail. He was still chewing out his cronies as he came. Weatherfield looked sick. The president's gaze slid past Dan as if he were greased. By now, so did the Secret Service's. Only Barney McKoy nodded. Dan hefted the satchel and fell in at the rear.

He was fastening the security strap when three hands rose simultaneously to three left ears. McKoy said, gaze darting down the corridor as his hand slid inside his jacket, "Anarchy. Anarchy!"

Dan went taut too. "Anarchy" meant an assassination attempt was under way. The detail contracted like the spiny shell of some primitive animal around the man they protected. Whose voice rose, demanding to know what was going on.

McKoy: "The control room says someone just called the switchboard, Mr. President."

"You get crank calls all the time," De Bari shouted. "What's the big goddamn deal all of a sudden?"

"This didn't sound like a crank, Mr. President. He had a strong foreign accent. He said truck bomb. Now. Headed for the West Executive gate."

De Bari's tone changed. He asked where his wife was. McKoy, brow furrowed, was listening to his radio. He made a hand signal to his team. To De Bari he said, "We're going to evacuate you both, sir. Then everyone one else on the Eighteen. This way. Through the Residence."

"Why not just out the—"

"If it's coming in West Executive, sir, we need to get you as far away as we can."

All this time they'd been hiking along. Now the retinue broke into a not-quite-in-step trot along the corridors. Dan kept up. The case jolted his arm. It seemed heavier than usual. Probably just because he was trying to run with it. But the unsecured pistol was working its way out from under his belt. He grabbed it just as it started down his pants leg, and wedged it under his belt, rather than his waistband. They hurried down a flight of stairs, then turned into the mansion.

"A truck bomb?" De Bari wheezed. "Can't you stop it at the gate?"

"They go right through gates, Mr. President. And if it's a truck bomb, it'll be big."

A group of donors, or maybe just better-dressed-than-usual tourists, were having their pictures taken in front of the Library fireplace. They gasped at De Bari's sudden appearance. Cameras came up as the president, ever the campaigner, waved and grinned without breaking stride. McKoy made a hand signal to the docent. A moment later she was herding the tourists out, disregarding their protests that they'd not yet seen the whole White House.

Under an arched entrance into the ground-floor corridor. The parquet floor creaked as they hammered over it. The agents' faces looked ever more grim. Dan wondered what they were hearing through those flesh-colored earpieces.

He felt his heart skipping beats, and not just from running. A truck bomb. Of course. How else to get through the pat-downs, briefcase scanners, bomb-sniffing dogs, metal detectors, uniformed security. A truckload of explosive would take out the whole West Wing and half the Old Executive. McKoy was probably heading for the PEOC. That deep in the ground, even tons of explosive would be just a rumble overhead.

But the protective detail had other plans. McKoy led them up a flight of marble steps toward the South Lawn. As they emerged onto the portico the marines were falling in to line the path.

Marine One had landed. Its turbines whined hot smoke as it squatted. Another party emerged from the East Wing. Dan caught a glimpse of Letitia De Bari. Not far behind came a scramble of photographers and videocam crews.

He kept following the man who was the nucleus of that moving circle, that self-sacrificial wall of flesh. In public view, they'd slowed to a brisk walk. With his free hand, the one not locked to his responsibility, Dan put his cap on and tugged his service dress blouse down over the pistol.

The scrum reached the landing pad and parted, falling back to let the president and first lady board.

De Bari ushered his wife inside. Then turned on the topmost step, the presidential seal behind him on the gleaming fuselage. He lifted a fist to the cameras, looking stern and resolute. The crowd noise swelled as the protesters caught sight of him. Bottles and cans bounced on the grass. Dan caught the flash of annoyance on De Bari's face.

Above him, in the cockpit window, the commanding officer of HMX-1 was looking down anxiously at the boarding ladder, headset clamped to his ears. The engine noise rose, like an impatient cabdriver gunning his engine.

De Bari ducked inside. Dan glimpsed him at the big side window making his way aft. The secretary of defense was still with him, and by the way he was moving his hands, still talking.

McKoy stood by, hand to his ear. His gaze examined Dan, dropped to the satchel. He gave the briefest of micronods: *Go on, board.*

Dan went up the ladder, turned right, and found himself alone with the De Baris and Weatherfield in the passenger compartment. He slung the satchel under the bench seat as McKoy and another agent, the female one, the minimum protective detail, pounded in after him. They dropped into seats opposite Dan and buckled in.

Through the window he saw photographers falling to one knee, aiming lenses like snipers. Past them, more trash was sailing over the fence. The video crews were getting that as well, then panning to the helo. Zooming in on what was probably Robert De Bari's frown, framed in the big window.

The blades had been revolving. Now he heard the transmission whine and then the chop of the blades going to positive pitch. The lift pressed him into his seat, harder than usual. Dan wondered who exactly had called about the truck. "A strong foreign accent." It didn't seem logical to go to all the trouble and risk to build a bomb, then phone in a warning.

As the ground dropped away he caught a glimpse of the roof. A countersniper looked up from the balustrade, rifle lowered, shielding his eyes from the sun as the helo climbed into it. The gardens and lawn spread in the tentative green of late winter. A nimbus seemed to hover amid the treetops, and below them glowed the bright yellow buds of the first daffodils.

It looked so grand. Again he felt the glory and power, gazing down at the sheer classic beauty of this building, knowing all it meant to the country. For all the tawdry doings and the failed men who'd passed through its doors, it was the stage of history. Whatever else happened, he'd remember the time he'd served here. From this height the crowd might have been festive, tossing not debris but brightly colored flowers. The walls and columns shone in the sun.

The horizon tipped and wheeled. A heaving sea of car glass, car metal, glittered Ellipseward. The white shaft of the Washington Monument rammed into the sky. The Tidal Basin shone like just-poured lead. Beyond it a speedboat unzipped the Potomac's gown. They were headed south, but he didn't know where. There were no plans for travel this afternoon, so they couldn't just advance the schedule.

He leaned to see past McKoy, who looked more relaxed now they were off the ground. Weatherfield was still talking, wincing and jerking his shoulders the way the guy always did. Dan wondered what they were discussing. The concerted refusal of the Joint Chiefs to make plans for the Palestinian occupation, most likely. You could argue that as a good thing or a bad thing. He wasn't sure himself which way the truth lay.

He suddenly wondered, the question coming from nowhere: Why had *Marine One* been waiting, if no travel was scheduled?

They droned over the Potomac, still gaining altitude. Above them passenger jets chalked contrails on blue velvet. Once again, as he had on the flight to Camp David, he thought how easy it would be to assassinate the president in the air. Any of the light planes that were probably all around them, in the crowded airspace of northern Virginia, could fly into them. It would be suicide, but there seemed to be more and more fanatics these days. He looked at McKoy again, then at the other Secret Service agent. Her name was Lee, Leigh, something like that. Blond. She looked back from behind dark wraparounds, expressionless as a death mask.

The PES crept out from beneath the seat, walked across the floor by an invisible hand. Despite meticulous maintenance, *Marine One* still had a chopper's inherent vibration.

He stretched out a shoe, hooked it, and pulled it back. Looked up to find Leigh's eyes still on him. He gave her a smile but got only that flat stare.

He dropped his gaze. Looked at the satchel again.

Had it really felt heavier than usual?

Yeah, right. He grinned at himself and sat back. Amusing himself with the idea. If you wanted to get something aboard *Marine One* or *Air Force One,* what better way than to give it to the mil aide?

Sure. Who was the only guy the Secret Service couldn't search? Couldn't touch? And wouldn't even suspect? The dude who carried the football.

He sat there for a few minutes. Felt his smile fade, like the Cheshire cat in reverse.

Christ, he *was* getting paranoid. Upshaw had opened the satchel in the secretary's office. Gone through it while he'd looked over her shoulder. Nothing there that hadn't always been there.

He glanced at the agents again. Neither McKoy nor Leigh was looking at him now. The lead agent was gazing out and down to where the Beltway, like a Robert Heinlein roadcity, lay flashing and streaming across the Wilson Bridge.

You are so fucking nuts, he told himself savagely. You really ought to turn yourself in. He'd fought it for too long. Self-loathing overwhelmed him.

He looked at the satchel again. Pulled it out with the toe of his shoe. Bending, he fiddled with the catch, trying to look casual. He set the combination, and popped the first latch.

Only it didn't pop.

He pushed harder, but it didn't move. He frowned. Checked the combo. The numbers were lined up dead center on the indicator marks. But neither latch was opening. He spun it, set it up again, pushed the latch again.

Nada.

He cleared his throat. Glanced at the agents. They were ignoring him, lost in the vibration and noise. De Bari and

Weatherfield were in their own world, arguing. Mrs. De Bari stared into eternity somewhere above all their heads.

Why would they change the combo without telling him? The duty dog had to be able to get to the radio. And the handbook, if the warbler went off. Plus the other stuff in there. There wasn't much room, but Jazak sometimes left Power Bars and the small-size Gatorades in there. When he found them Dan had no qualms about drinking the juice, though he drew the line at the Power Bars.

You're around the bend, he told himself. Nutzoid. The lock's jammed, that's all. Or Upshaw had reset the combination by accident.

Only he didn't see how. All she'd done was spin the dials, as they all did when they closed the PES, so that even if it was stolen it'd still be locked.

Son of a bitch! What if that warbler went off right now? Or the president asked to look at the manual? He broke into a sweat, glancing toward De Bari and Weatherfield as if they could read his mind. But the next minute he thought: They don't care. What had Jazak said? Bad Bob didn't have a clue. Had sent the Gold Code to the dry cleaners in his pants.

But even as he thought that, he knew he was skating around the truth and his duty. Because if Robert De Bari didn't give a shit, that was no excuse for Commander Dan Lenson to cut corners or look away.

Moving as casually as he could, he leaned to look down through polished bulletproof plastic. Now forest bordered the gleam of river, and the glowing mercury of the Chesapeake broadened ahead.

He snapped open his seat belt. Took a step forward, toward the cockpit; then, as if he'd forgotten, came back and bent and took the satchel along, and set it casually on the step up to the pilots' compartment. He rapped on the sliding port. A face glanced back. The port slid open.

"Anything from the White House?" he shouted up into significantly louder noise.

The marine shouted back, "Nothing yet."

"No truck bombs?"

"Not that they've told me about."

"Where we headed?"

"Oh, we're just flyin' around, down toward Pax River. Looking for a recall any minute, unless they want me to shoot for Thurmont."

Dan looked past him, into the cockpit, and saw what he'd hoped to. "Can you hand me that?" he shouted, pointing.

"Hand you what? The fire extinguisher?" the pilot yelled, twisting in his seat. The copilot, who had the stick, glanced back too, eyebrows raised.

"No. No!" He didn't dare look back at the agents. "The extraction tool."

The colonel followed his finger to a steel crowbar-and-cutter on the bulkhead. "What do you need that for?"

Dan patted the satchel. "Fucking latch is jammed."

He saw the marine's lips purse as he took it in: who Dan was, what he was saying. "*That's* not good."

"No kidding. I got to get it open."

"I heard that thing's set so it goes off if you fuck with it."

"I heard that one too," Dan said. "But there's nothing in here but a manual and a radio."

The colonel unclipped the crash bar and poked it through to him. Dan tried to keep his body between the case and McKoy and Leigh. The less he had to explain, the better. There was professional pride involved, too.

For a second, as he put the bar to the latch, he wondered: Am I going off the deep end? Then he shrugged. If he couldn't get it open, then it'd be time to go to general quarters. Though all he really had to do was have the pilot call back and explain the situation, and have Gunning meet them with the spare.

The latch was stout. Brass-coated steel, and hardened to boot. It was even difficult to get the tip of the crash bar in position. When he exerted force it slipped off suddenly, gouging a rip into the top grain leather.

"Shit," he muttered. But the pry bar was hardened too,

sharpened and tempered for getting jammed hatches open, not just briefcase latches.

The first latch popped, but it took all his strength. The second broke, leaving the catch jammed in the lock. But finally he got the lid open. He peered in, with the sun pouring through the window plastic lighting everything with perfect clarity.

Well, he thought. That was a lot of angst over nothing.

Everything was there. The black plastic of the radio case. The spare battery. The red plastic of the Decision Handbook. The Beretta, in its nylon holster. The other notebooks, with comm data and the rest of his essential knowledge.

He was closing it up when he froze.

He *had* the duty Beretta. Stuck into his belt. Where it had been since he took over from Upshaw.

There hadn't been any pistol in the satchel he'd inventoried with her. He called back the picture, and saw it clear in his mind. No. The gun compartment had been *empty*.

So why were there suddenly *two* pistols?

Son of a *bitch*! He felt for the gun under his blouse. Making absolutely sure he wasn't forgetting something. But there it was, steel-hard against the bone of his hip. Right where he'd wedged it when they were running through the Residence.

Yet here was another one. He pulled the holster out just to make sure there was a gun in it. Yep.

At his shoulder McKoy said in an unfriendly tone, "What are you doing?"

"Barney—I'm still trying to figure this out—but I think somebody switched satchels on me."

"What are you talking about?"

The woman agent was unbuttoning her jacket, moving to put herself between him and the still obliviously arguing De Bari and Weatherfield. Dan said, glancing at her but speaking to the lead agent, "I'm seeing something funny here, Barn. I have a handgun in my belt already, from the aide I relieved, from the case she turned over to me. But here's *an-*

other one. The only thing I can think, somebody switched cases on me."

"Why would they do that?" said the baby-faced agent. He was watching Dan narrowly. Flicking a warning glance at the woman.

"Look, relax. I'm not doing anything threatening. Here. Take it." He held the holstered pistol out. McKoy hesitated, then shook his head. Dan thrust it back into the satchel's fitted compartment. Then swung around and put the case on the sofa bench.

"What's he doing?" the woman said. Her jacket was open, her hand within.

"I'm inventorying the PES," Dan told her. "Making sure everything's okay here."

Both agents were standing now, between Dan and where the president, the secretary of defense, and the first lady sat. They swayed as the aircraft pitched. He cleared his throat, a little nervous, though he still didn't think he had anything to be nervous about. He was more puzzled than anything else. He started lifting things out and lining them up on the seat. Red handbook. Black handbook. Another black handbook. Transceiver.

His fingers halted. The radio, with its handset and little stub UHF antenna, hadn't come all the way out. A black wire led from it to the spare battery beneath. He blinked at it.

Beside him McKoy said, "Everything okay?"

"I don't know," he muttered. "Wait a minute."

Then he understood, not wanting to, but comprehending nonetheless. And the knowledge felt like a rush of cold descending air.

He stood cradling the thing. Trying not to move anything else, to jiggle anything. Trying to think of some other way, *any* other way around it. But he couldn't.

There'd never been any *wires* between the spare pack and the transceiver.

If this was really what he was beginning to think it was . . . the battery pack, compact yet heavy as a brick, could hold three or four pounds of plastique or RDX. That might not sound like much. But it would be enough high-energy explosive to turn *Marine One,* and everyone in it into an enormous fireball, peppered with very small parts.

Beside him McKoy was frowning at the transceiver. Dan was still holding it, a few inches above the open satchel. "What's going on? What's wrong?" he said.

"It's a fucking bomb," Dan muttered. "We've got to get this thing out of here."

"What are you talking about? An explosive device?"

Of course McKoy didn't see it. The protective detail had never been allowed to look inside the PES. As far as the lead agent knew, this was how everything was supposed to look.

Yes. It was very clever.

"This wire isn't supposed to be here," Dan said. "The black one, looks like a power cord? It isn't. And this isn't my satchel. Somebody switched it. This thing's a bomb."

The agent's face went still. "Don't touch anything," he said. Dan glimpsed the female agent over his shoulder, face so pale she might have just patted it all over with flour. Behind her De Bari guffawed, at something Weatherfield had said, apparently.

McKoy put his face close. Said, just loudly enough to carry over the engine noise, "You sure about this, Lenson?"

Dan had to admit it didn't look dangerous. What they could see of the cord looked like part of the set. Only if you were familiar with the equipment would you know it didn't belong.

Doubt wormed into his brain. Could the Military Office comm people have upgraded the radio without telling him? Put some kind of improved rig in there? But damn it, there was already a battery in the transceiver. Why wire *another* battery to it?

"Yeah . . . well . . . pretty sure," he said, but his voice wasn't as certain as it might have been.

McKoy caught that undertone. "You mean it might not be?"

"I think it probably is. But no—I can't be sure. There's something funny going on here, though. I'm sure of that much."

Shit! If it *was* a device . . . he glanced at the window. The smart thing would probably be to just pop a window or the door and chuck it out. But looking out now, he saw to his horror that they weren't over forest anymore. The pilot had taken them back over civilization. He didn't know where— Annandale, Alexandria—but it wasn't woods down there but houses, streets, people. Plus, if it *was* just some upgrade they'd forgotten to tell him about, then throwing out the secret transceiver, with encryption and release codes for the nation's nuclear command structure, didn't sound like a brilliant idea.

Another possibility slammed into his brain like blunt metal. Wired to a radio, a bomb could be command detonated. Like the way Israelis killed terrorists with cell phones. Which meant it could go off *any second*.

His thoughts darted like a trapped sparrow, but met a wall wherever they flew. He couldn't cut the cable. It was perfectly possible, no, probably *likely*, that something this sophisticated would be booby-trapped.

"We've got to get on the ground," he told McKoy. "Like, ASAP. Right now."

And it looked like the agent had come to the same conclusion in the same fragment of time, because he was already charging between De Bari and Weatherfield, banging on the pilot's door. The two men regarded him with amazement. When the colonel slid it back he yelled up. Dan saw the marine's eyes flick to the open satchel. To him.

Then the elevator went down. Fast.

Suddenly a lot was happening at once. He was grabbing for things as they floated up off the seat. Then, forced to his knees by g's going the other way, felt his trousers tear as they snagged on something. The woman agent was hanging on to a strap, shouting into a small radio that had appeared from nowhere. Weatherfield was shouting too.

He clung to the seat, weightless, as they fell again, this time in a long, endless, terrifying drop, like Lucifer banished from heaven. Realizing in those seconds that if whatever they'd packed his satchel with went off, he'd never feel it. Never realize he'd just stopped living.

But much worse than that, for who could object to painless and instantaneous death, he understood in those screaming seconds that if it did, *he'd* be known forever as the assassin.

Someone had switched satchels with him. That was the only possible conclusion. And he suspected now it had been whoever had gone into the office while he'd been talking to Ouderkirk. Remembering that glimpse of a back, walking away. Gunning? Sebold? He couldn't swear to either. But whoever it *had* been, he'd been toting a cardboard box.

The luggage switch. A classic. The guy carried in Bag A, in the cardboard box, and set it down next to Bag B. Swapped them out, bent over to mask the switch, and walked out.

But no one had seen it. So he'd be blamed. And he had a motive! The president was boffing his wife!

John Wilkes Booth, Leon Czolgosz, Lee Harvey Oswald. All loners, misfits with a grudge. That was how they'd paint Dan Lenson. . . .

Turbine whining, transmission making tortured noises, the huge machine dropped like a meteor, the slanted ground rushing up so fast it seemed impossible they could ever stop.

No more than a minute could have passed since he'd told McKoy they had a problem. Each of those seconds had been filled with so much terror and noise it had seemed ten times longer than its objective existence. Just now, the fingers of one hand digging into the seat fabric so hard he felt his nails breaking, he was helping the agent stuff things back into the satchel with the other. His hand shook as he very cautiously slid the radio and battery inside. McKoy held out the red book. Dan shouted, "You keep that. I'll get off with everything else."

"Oh no. I'll take it."

"Who's staying with the president?"

"She is." McKoy jerked his head, and Dan saw Leigh crouched and braced, pistol pointed, between him and the De Baris. She looked ready to use it.

Out the window he glimpsed cars and box buildings, the storefronts of a megamall. They flared out over a traffic-crowded highway, barely missing a web of power lines. He saw the pilot's intent: to set them down in a sprawling lot ahead.

Unfortunately it was packed with vehicles. Glancing up, he saw the colonel speaking fast into his throat mike. The copilot was stabbing his finger earthward with great emphasis.

The elevator dropped again. Asphalt rushed up with sickening velocity. The roofs of individual SUVs and minivans took shape out of the glitter. Dan didn't know where they were. Somewhere in northern Virginia, but from the huge logos on the great brick fronts, Goodyear, Applebee's, Barnes & Noble, Circuit City, they could be anywhere from Maine to California.

They touched down a hundred yards from Sears on a ring road. He was braced for a hard landing, but at the last minute the colonel flared again and they settled with hardly a bump. A station wagon skidded to a halt, tires smoking. A woman dragged two children back by their collars. Faces stared openmouthed up through windshields. A crewman dropped the door and sunlight flooded in.

McKoy whipped around. Before Dan could react, he'd snatched the satchel from his hands. "Stay here," he bawled. His feet hammered down the ladder.

Dan followed without hesitation, even as the engines wound up again and the wheels lifted. He leaped off the rising steps, ignoring the woman's shout behind him. Stay here? Right. *He'd* brought the thing aboard. *He'd* be the prime suspect. Was McKoy in on this? What if he disappeared with the case?

He fell ten or twelve feet and hit the asphalt so hard it slammed the breath out of him. He sprawled forward, feeling, though not yet accompanied by any pain, the rough pavement plane the skin off his outstretched palms, hearing the seams rip in his uniform.

If there really was a bomb in that satchel, a lot of things that had happened lately might not have been what he'd thought they were. His transfer to the East Wing—the previous Navy aide's accident in the parking garage—

He ground his teeth, trying to get his feet under him. Maybe even what he'd thought, or been *led* to think, about Blair and De Bari.

Someone had gone to a lot of trouble to set this up. If the PES disappeared—and how easy that would be, in this chaotic swirl of cars and shoppers—they might never find out who'd rigged it. Who'd tried to kill the president, and everyone else aboard.

McKoy had his ID folder out, his badge. Flourishing it, he was screaming at what was becoming quite the little gathering of suburban rubberneckers, pushing shopping carts and baby strollers. It wasn't every day *Marine One* touched down at the mall. Everyone within a quarter mile was headed their way.

The satchel sat on the asphalt not far from a branch bank. Customers stared from the ATM line. Behind Dan the turbine-howl grew again to an earsplitting roar. He looked up to see the huge machine passing over them, a few hundred feet up, blowing down hot smoke and rotor-wash.

Dan hesitated, looking at McKoy. Then at the satchel. It looked lonely, sitting deserted between the painted lines of an empty parking space.

Swallowing the bitter metal-taste of fear, he took a step toward it.

McKoy hollered over his shoulder at him, cheeks distorted with rage. The engines were howling overhead, so Dan couldn't make out the words. He figured the Secret Service agent was telling him to back off. Leave it alone.

He took another step, feeling the wind tearing at his uniform as the helicopter made another low pass. The rotor-wash whipped up paper cups, fast-food wrappers, discarded receipts.

Turning his back on the wind, forcing his reluctant legs into motion, he lurched the last few yards and sank to his knees.

S quatting in front of the satchel, he tried to fight down the terror. His throat was so dry he couldn't swallow. He could barely think. But he had to. He might have only seconds left.

The warbler circuit. They'd use that for the detonator.

In that pressurized moment he realized that though his body was on the edge of animal panic, he could still think. Still act. As he'd always been able to when decisions had to be made.

If it ended here . . . better than in an abandoned factory in Bosnia.

If you run, you meet the bullet . . . .

"Keep those idiots back!" he screamed at McKoy.

"Get away from it!" the agent howled back, face mottled dark. Past him the spectators milled. Dan couldn't believe it. They were pointing cameras. Chattering on cell phones.

Dan nodded, but for reassurance, not to acknowledge an order. He switched his attention back to the blackly waiting satchel. Reviewing his options as McKoy shouted again, swore, voice cracking raw. As *Marine One,* blades clattering with a hellish racket, banked and headed off, rotor-chop fading into the honking of stalled traffic. At least the president was safe. Whatever that was worth.

He put out fingertips and brushed the leather surface.

Maybe he should back off, as McKoy was telling him to. But screw McKoy! Once the president was safe, the protective detail wasn't in charge anymore.

He was the military aide. This was *his* responsibility.

He rubbed his face, trying to focus. This . . . thing was no crude homemade, strapped in duct tape and pushed into a mailbox. This was professional. He didn't even want to think about by whom. Not right now.

He remembered the guy who'd carried the briefcase into Hitler's bunker.

Somebody had tried to motivate him. Make him just like von Stauffenberg. Make him *want* to be a killer. An assassin. Or at least to look exactly like one, after the fact.

The honking had stopped. McKoy wasn't shouting anymore either. The quiet felt eerie after the tremendous racket from the helo.

He could almost hear the case ticking. Though of course it wouldn't *tick*.

Forcing his hands to function, he unsnapped the broken latches once more. He lifted out the "device," as McKoy had called it. Then glanced around, judging the crowd that now entirely surrounded them. McKoy, assisted now by a rent-a-cop from the mall, was trying to move them back. But the public wasn't cooperating. They kept edging in. Didn't they have any fucking police here? Or any sense?

He couldn't just cut the cord. Whoever had put this together would have anticipated that.

The smart thing would be to just leave it. Retreat, call the D.C. bomb squad, help McKoy keep the crowd back. But it might go off then. And whoever the conspirators were, they'd flee, or go to earth.

To try again. And maybe, next time, succeed.

It might explode. And kill him.

Last chance here, he told himself. You really should do the smart thing and back off.

But if it exploded . . . they might never find out who'd made it. Where it had come from. And who had made him the patsy.

And that, at the end of everything, made it his problem. To figure out, or die trying.

Taking a deep breath, he lifted the plastic case in both hands. The battery pack came up with it, dangling on the cord.

Leaving the satchel behind, he carried the bomb toward the bank. The crowd at the ATM edged back. Remembering the Beretta at last, he pulled it out of his belt and held it up. A gun: that they understood. Shrieking, they scattered, dropping purses and checkbooks and Dillard's bags.

He set the thing down near the wall of the bank, hoping the brick, and whatever reinforcement they had around the vault, would stop any flying debris from the blast.

He cocked the pistol, and aimed.

THE AFTERIMAGE ARLINGTON
NATIONAL CEMETERY

The grass, as green that spring as grass ever grew. The breeze, soft as any had ever blown.

On the hillside overlooking the river men and women in uniform stood at attention. Civilians in dark suits and black dresses stood with bowed heads, self-conscious amid the military ceremonial, the funereal ritual.

The crack of rifles, three times three, shattered the air and echoed from the serried rows of stone.

When the last note of Taps died away, the gathering broke up. The participants, subdued, came back along the wending paths two by two or in straggling groups.

Dan, in a new set of blues, paced alone, hands locked behind him. He blinked now and then, caught up in his thoughts rather than the bright day.

They'd found Garner Sebold's car parked by the Tidal Basin. A presentation .45 lay on the passenger seat, and a bloody blossom bloomed against the driver-side window. The media had speculated endlessly. The fringe pushed their ever-more-bizarre theories on talk radio and the Web, aimed, as usual, at the administration. They said De Bari's Mob contacts had planted the bomb, to rally the public behind an unpopular chief executive. They opined darkly that Sebold had been murdered, to pin the blame on a distinguished public servant. No, another said; De Bari had had him killed when it looked like they were closing in on Don Juan Nuñez, who worked for the first lady's crime family.

Others whispered that the heart of the plot had been the army. Disgruntled senior officers. A small cabal, "a few bad apples"—but then it only took a few. Dan knew that Sergeant Ouderkirk, Major Upshaw, and others were in FBI custody. Ulrich Stahl, Knight, and two other Joint Staff generals had submitted their resignations. Geraldo B. Edwards had announced his retirement from politics. Medical reasons, his spokesman had said. He was too ill to handle the pace of the vice presidency, and wanted to spend more time with his family.

Yet others speculated on more obscure forces. The shadowy Islamic organization that had underwritten International Blessings. The cartel, whose technique—radio-detonated explosives aboard an aircraft—had clearly been borrowed from the Tejeiro assassination.

But in the end, the only wholly truthful thing anyone could say was that the investigation was in progress. Where it would finish, what its findings would be, and whether they'd be made public in his lifetime, Dan could not even guess.

He knew he didn't understand all of what had just happened. Sometimes he suspected he didn't understand *any* of what had happened, close to the crux of history though he'd been. Revenge, corruption, misguided patriotism, institutional loyalty—any and every motive might have been involved. If Sebold and other high officers had been the movers behind the plot, no doubt they'd thought themselves justified. But they'd needed a tool. A violent loner. A loose cannon.

Enter Dan Lenson.

He could not believe his own blindness. He'd been manipulated. Used. His distrust for authority, his impatience with procedure had made him the all too obvious choice. Move by move they'd advanced him across the board, toward the castled king. Programmed him, like some half-sentient weapon, to make his final mission credible to those who would peruse it for generations to come.

How many other assassins over the bloody course of history had been fashioned as he had? How many Booths and Brutuses, Montholons and Cordays, had struck at the behest of those who stayed in the shadows, to profit from the crimes they'd set in train?

He trembled when he thought how close he'd come to infamy. And how close even yet he was to condemnation. The questioning had been hard, and lasted for days. Even now, men still followed him. Whether for his protection, or his doom, he did not know.

When he raised his eyes a figure in a black coat barred his path. They looked at each other without speaking. Finally he nodded to her, and bent his head. They fell in together, her heels clicking on the bricks.

Beneath a shadowing oak they stood together, looking out over the sunlit downhill and the white city beyond. If he turned his head Dan saw two men some distance away. They wore ties and light topcoats. They stood before one of the headstones, not quite looking in their direction.

"Your friend called me," Blair said. "From the Secret Service. McKoy."

"Yeah. Barney."

"After what he told me, I had to talk to you. To see how much of this was my fault."

"None of it was *your* fault, Blair. It was all mine. My . . . stupid and unjustified suspicion. Of you. Of others. But it was also just very, very cleverly done."

"You really thought I was . . . sleeping with the president. In Russia."

"Somebody told me you were there. In the middle of the night. I saw the Secret Service outside his suite."

"But you wouldn't believe me when I told you it was work."

"No," he admitted. "I didn't. And I'm sorry."

Who had called him that night in St. Petersburg to tell

him he needed to check on his wife? He didn't know. Maybe the investigation would reveal it. Most likely, he suspected, it would not. He was on leave now, stripped of official duties. He didn't think he was going to get any medals for this tour. In fact, depending on how far up the conspiracy reached, he'd be lucky to stay alive.

He knew now his wondering about the next threat had not taken into account the most dangerous quarter of all.

The greatest menace to his country had never been terrorists, or assassins, or even hostile ideologies. It was those who worked not for the common good, but for their own power.

"So how are you doing now?"

He cleared his throat. "Well, it's damned lonely. Out here in the cold."

"Is the Navy going to take care of you?"

"I talked to some people I know." He laughed. "I do have friends. They're not exactly De Bari fans either, but they're not part of this. They say the smartest thing for me would be to get as far away as I can."

"I think they might be right. At least for now." She touched his sleeve.

"That's what I figured too."

"And how about us, Dan?" She took his hand, but didn't meet his eyes. "Okay, it's time for me to say it. When you needed help, I was ready to point it out. But I wasn't exactly there for you when it got rough, was I?"

"You tried. I wasn't a very good listener, though."

She nodded soberly. "Okay. We were both assholes."

"Well, that's what we still are. In a lot of people's books."

"Something in common?"

"I guess."

"Well, for what it's worth, I'm still not happy you could think that about De Bari and me. But I'm sorry I didn't see what was happening either, and try to help." She bit her lip; he saw this wasn't easy for her, either. "Uh—shall we try it again?"

He didn't have to think about that. "I'd like to," he told her. "I'd like that a lot."

"Then let's do it."

"I always loved you. And I still do."

"I love you too," she said. She coughed, and rubbed her eyes, and he saw she was weeping. He'd never seen her cry before. It didn't seem like her. "I'm sorry. I'm really, really sorry. And I'll try not to be such a fucking asshole this time. We're both tough to live with, I guess. And we're both so fucking *busy*. So maybe we deserve each other. Oh—damn it—I'm crying. God, I hate that," she said furiously, looking around as if afraid someone would take a picture.

"It's not a problem," he told her. "I feel that way myself sometimes. Maybe you should just let go more often."

"Just let go, huh?"

"Not in meetings, though."

"No, not in meetings," she said. "Not in this town, anyway."

He tilted her face up and wiped the corners of her eyes gently with his thumbs. She closed them and took a shuddering breath, and laid her face against his shoulder.

Holding her, pressing her against him with his still painfully skinned palms, he looked past her, down on the alabaster city.

He thought of what Washington, and America, had been when he was young, and of how much had changed. From protest to conformity. From openness to secrecy. From confidence to carefully inculcated fear.

Sometimes he thought the dream of democracy might be ending. As it had for Rome long before. Bringing a new imperial age. Dictatorship. Slavery. And unending war.

If the choice was empire, then the threat was clear. The threat would be America herself—her power, her violence, her blind, crusading arrogance.

But he couldn't allow himself to believe that. Not yet.

A crippling fear lurked deep in his country. It always had. But then, so did courage.

And so far, courage had always won.

KOREA STRAIT

The smooth-surfaced sea heaved slowly under a cloudless aramanthine sky. It was just before dawn. There was no wind. Not a ripple marred the ever-changing, everlasting interface between water and air. But it rose slowly, then fell away along the worn steel of the hull, all but imperceptibly, as if the sea were breathing.

One- to two-foot swells at most, Dan judged, leaning over the side to gaze down into bottomless turquoise. Every hundred feet or so, a wave broke with a quiet splatter. It left a patch of ivory froth rocking, slowly melting, till the clear blue welled up again from far beneath. Small silvery fish hovered in the hull-shadow, fluid rippling commas poised tensely between quiescence and alarm.

Beside him a Major Zach Carmichael, U.S. Army, who was beyond any reasonable doubt Defense Intelligence, was telling him about the Maritime Department of the North Korean Reconnaissance Bureau. "That's who's most likely running it. The most elite of all NK special forces. Disciplined. Tough. Sworn never to surrender. They caught one before, in a fishing net. When they got it to the surface, they were all dead."

"Drowned? Hull breach?"

"Shot each other, far as we can tell. Last one used a grenade." Carmichael sounded as if he admired this.

On the flight out, on a ROK helo, he'd looked down to see the lights of fishing boats setting out, nodding their way toward their salty crop-fields from the flickering yellow lights of hamlets that clung to blackened zinc cliffs. Rocky islets dotted the coast. As first light rose, the pilot pointed out North Korea in the distance. Dan gazed out on a hazy,

featureless sweep that gave no hint that anything human had
ever existed. Save, far away, the contrail of an MIG patrolling the Northern Limiting Line, the naval extension of
the DMZ out to sea.

They'd droned out till the land fell back and vanished in a
nebulous mercury blurring. Gradually a ship emerged from
the rosy haze. From her anachronistic, towering masts, her
dented gray steel sides, she'd slid down some Stateside ship-
way during World War Two. They'd circled, the copilot
barking into his throat mike in abrupt Korean, then moved
over the bluff bow for the transfer. He'd dangled, rotating
slowly on a sling, till Koreans crouched against the rotor-
blast reached up, receiving them like gifts from Heaven.
First Dan, then Shappell, then Carmichael.

Now they stood aft on the main deck, looking out on a
wide rounded counter. The stern was flat and almost featureless except for two large centerline hatches, a towing chock,
a stanchion with the stern light, and bitts spotted to port and
starboard. The black steel underfoot was scarred and dented
with decades of dragged chains and dropped shackles. So
many layers of old paint scabbed it, it looked like the Black
Hills seen from above. A canvas awning reminded Dan of
The Sand Pebbles. But wherever she'd been built, she was
Korean now. They swarmed over the fantail. The divers just
now lifting their helmets above a gently heaving froth of
bubbles, slowly making their way to a rigged-out platform
and boat-ladder, were Korean, too. She was at diving stations, with hoses and lines flemished out across the deck.
Tanks, weight belts, suits, regulators were lashed to the gun-
wales or laid out on canvas. Beyond them, patrolling the
horizon, prowled the low wolf-gray silhouette of a destroyer.

"She was once USS ship," a junior officer told them.
"USS *Grasp*. Now *Chung Won*."

"So what exactly you people got down there?" Carmichael
asked him. He fiddled impatiently with the Nikon around
his neck, glancing at the divers clambering awkwardly up
the ladder.

"Enemy submarine," the ensign said.

Shappell muttered "Aha." Carmichael focused his telephoto and snapped a couple frames of the divers.

"How deep?" Dan asked. The guy cocked his head, considering, then called to a squat man in slacks and a blue windbreaker. His face was leathery, like that of an old tortoise.

"Kim Baksa nim!"

"Ke miguk sa ram del yi yo? Yi chok ue ro de rigo o si yo."

Dan bowed and shook hands. The man in the windbreaker said he was Dr. Kim, in charge of the salvage operation. Carmichael asked again what they had.

"It appears to be a Sang-o," Kim said, choosing each word. "Which means 'shark.' It is most likely either embarking on, or returning from, a reconnaissance mission. They come out of Toejo-Dong, and transit south across the Tongjoson-man. Sometimes they attempt to land agents."

"How'd you find it?"

"It broached, we are not sure why. Perhaps an accident. We did not detect it until then. Our units fired on it. Then it either sank, or was scuttled when they realized we had detected them."

"Wicked," Carmichael said. He advanced the film and took a picture of the Korean, but at the last moment the doctor turned away.

Dan had memorized everything the U.S. Navy knew about the Sang-os, which wasn't much. The North Korean People's Navy operated three classes of submarines. Sharks were the middle rung, small diesel-electrics built in-country to a native design at the Nampo or Wonsan shipyards. Naval Intelligence estimated their operational depth between three and four hundred feet. They carried a crew of twenty with torpedo and mining capabilities. Their max speed was about nine knots at snorkel depth. They came in two variants, attack and infiltration. Even that was a guess . . . which meant it would be an intel coup to get their hands on one, or even get a close look.

Carmichael said, "Is the crew aboard?"

Dan, at the same moment: "How deep is it?"

Kim shouted a question to the divers. One shouted up, his answer half cut off by a wave that jostled him into the ladder. The doctor turned back to them. "The crew is dead. The sub is lying on the bottom of sand thirty-five meters down. The salvage divers have blown one compartment clear."

"About a hundred and ten feet," Dan said. "That's in air range."

Kim glanced at him. "You are a diver?"

"I sport dive. SCUBA."

"You have done this in wrecks?"

"Wrecks? Sure. Now and then."

"Then, of course, you will want to see for yourself. If you are willing."

The Korean held his gaze, and Dan realized it wasn't an invitation; he was being dared. "Sure," he said. "Suit me up. I'll take a look."

Carmichael and Shappell traded glances. "Hey, now," said the commander. "I don't really think you need to go down there yourself—"

But the Korean was smiling, and Dan also very much wanted to have the first U.S. look at a Sang-o class sub, if that was what it was. He glanced over the side again, then off to where the destroyer hovered. Storing the information, in case he should need it.

"All right then," said the Korean. He called to one of the tenders, who came over, running a critical eye up Dan's height. "He will help you suit up."

T he water was very cold. The wet suit was heavy black rubber, the biggest they had aboard, but still too tight, which wasn't good; he'd take some serious heat loss by the end of the dive.

Twenty feet down, he clung to the thick yellowing braided nylon of the descent line, sucking gas with a hissing click. His mouth was already parched and the moistureless gas didn't help. What the fuck had he gotten into? He gazed up at the black wedge of the salvage ship's stern, the motionless, cruel-looking screws. Golden rays flickered around it. They slid through the blue down into an inky twilight that yawned beneath his slowly kicking fins. The fish he'd watched from above undulated slowly between him and the light.

Dropping his gaze, he finned himself horizontal and slowly pivoted round the line, searching the sea to the accelerated thud of his heart. He was encased in lightfilled sapphire, surrounded by a circular wall of blue-gray haze. About thirty yards visibility. No sharks yet. Some yards away red and black hoses and safety lines dropped away into the black, losing their color as they receded from the sun. The helmet divers were working down there. His free hand roved over the regulator, checked his mask, tested the buckle of his weight belt. The gear wasn't that different from what he was used to. Solid quality, but not exactly the latest technology.

A plunge of bubbles, and his partner fell through the silvery rocking roof. A pudgy fellow who'd made comic faces when they told him Dan would be going down with him. He hovered, adjusting his buoyancy, then jack-knifed and headed down, jabbing a questioning finger to his head.

Dan pointed to his own ears and nodded. He thumbed the exhaust button of his buoyancy compensator and felt himself go from weightless to heavy.

He kept his right hand out, letting the line drag through it as they dropped into steadily darkening blue. Flecks of organic matter drove past them like a slow snowstorm. Pain jabbed inside his head. He grabbed his nose through the mask and cleared his ears. Again.

He grinned around the regulator, remembering Shappell's warning that he shouldn't go. They were here to observe, not participate. And the naked envy on the intel officer's face, his begging for a written report afterward.

But he'd never enjoyed standing around and watching. And the Koreans who suited him up had slapped his back, grinning and nodding. These people operated on face. And strapping on a tank with them had earned him some.

He checked the depth, then his Seiko. Sixty feet already. The light from above was dimming away. He looked down, but didn't see only blackness. His partner was swimming down the line headfirst, fins kicking turbulence toward him. A backturned mask flashed the last of the sunlight. Dan was content to drop slowly, staying vertical. He'd check out the hull, maybe swim along it, then come up. Punch his ticket and surface.

Was he really being foolish? Stepping beyond what a full commander ought to be doing? To hell with it. He could push paper anytime. Carmichael wanted a report, didn't he?

Eighty feet, and sinking faster as the pressure squeezed the buoyancy out of vest and suit. His stay time would only be fifteen minutes at a hundred and ten feet. Longer than that would require decompression stops. He'd have to pay attention. That deep you could get fuzzy, disoriented—the famous rapture of the deep. He reminded himself he was short on sleep, and the cold wouldn't help. He'd better stay on the conservative side of the dive tables.

When he looked down again, the sub lay below him. It was obscured by the dim and the blowing silt, but the surprise stopped his breath for a moment before the hiss and click resumed. The descent line was gray now, all yellow sucked away in the dim light. It was tied off on what looked like a rudder pivot. The afterbody was smoothly curved. The craft lay stern, or perhaps bow—he couldn't quite tell yet—down in soft-looking brown muddy sand.

He dropped a few more feet in the bubbling silence and realized he was looking at the stern. The whole picture dim and fragmentary as it was snapped into place. The craft was much smaller than he'd expected. It was dead black, dotted here and there with pale specks of barnacles. The tail planes and rudder were rigged with struts. He wondered why. Then realized they were antifouling guards, to keep fishing nets or mine cables out of the prop.

A ridge ran the length of the hull, with port-and-starboard swellings that had to be side-saddle ballast tanks. He couldn't see the bow, but a small sail, or conning tower, loomed dimly through the murk. It was denser down here, blowing past at the rate, he remembered from the briefing, of the knot and a half's worth of slow massive current that was hanging him out along the descent line like a slowly flapping flag. He noted carefully that the sub lay crosscurrent. He didn't want to let go of this line and not know which way led back.

His dive buddy had already released it. He was finning forward just above the hull, toward a silvery gush of bubbles. They rushed wavering up into the vague brightness like a silver escalator. Dan saw he was following the air hoses. He bled air into his compensator until he hovered. It was colder down here, as if they'd passed through some chill barrier that blocked any emanation of the sun. His hands, even in gloves, and feet were going numb. He fumbled for his watch and ratcheted the elapsed-time bezel to fifteen. Then let go the line.

His buddy eased over the hull and disappeared into the darkness below. Dan followed, clearing his ears again as he descended. Brown rippled sand rose up through the milling murk. The bow was clear of the bottom. The hoses led under it. He started at a flicker in the obscurity, then realized what looked like black flames was the flutter of fins, *under* the hull. He hung back, wary of overhanging black steel. Then forced himself forward.

The other diver hung on what looked like a hatch-rim. Dan caught dark eyes studying him. A finger pointed up.

He nodded, and the Korean turtled his head and chinned himself up into what must be a lockout chamber. Fins kicked, then disappeared. Dreading the mass looming above him, Dan herded himself farther under it. When he looked up, he saw only a vibrating green-golden gleam, trickling and twisting like melted light.

He checked his watch. Three minutes. He got a grip on his breathing and finned slowly upward, arms raised, fingering along smooth cold metal for some handhold.

His head burst through into an echoing ullage crammed with darkness, splashing, a deafening hiss of releasing gas,

hollow shouts. A flashlight strobed across a circular empti-
ness above that mirrored that below.

"You come up," a voice gonged. A pudgy figure filled his
sky. A gloved hand grabbed his wet suit. "Set tank in that
rack. Give me your hand."

They were in what seemed to be the control
compartment—or more accurately, a combined control, berthing, and torpedo area. The upper hemi-
sphere of the lockout module took up most of the space. It
left a short, extremely cramped tube maybe twelve feet
across, so crammed with equipment they had to worm their
way through an aisle that touched Dan's shoulders on either
side. Dive lights beamed glares that left most of it in shadow.
A discarded glove huddled like a small dead animal. The
cold air was thick, dense, humid. It stank of the heavy oil
that coated every surface and a bleachy sting he realized
must be chlorine from the flooded batteries. The incoming
air hissed so loudly from its hose fitting, clamped to one of
the hull ribs with a red C clamp, that communication had to
be in shouts.

Compressed air, he reminded himself. So they were still
pressurized. He looked at his Seiko again. Still building up
bottom time, taking on nitrogen, though he was out of the
water. Seven minutes gone; eight remained.

The Koreans glanced at him as they worked. Four occupied the space, three hose divers and the stocky guy who'd
come down with him on tanks. The chubby diver belted out
aggressive-sounding Korean, gesturing at Dan. They reached
through piping to shake hands, grinning and nodding. "Welcome," one said, "Thank you," said another. He waved and
smiled, feeling he was intruding.

He stepped on something soft, and instinctively lifted his
bootied foot. An oil-smeared, startled, wide-cheekboned
face appeared. Its features were strangely delicate. It looked
up at the curved ribs of the inner hull. The left side of its
skull was missing. Brain was visible, but no blood. Dan

stared. Then made out a shoe nearby. It was oil-stained dark, but bore a familiar boomerang-shaped logo.

"Nikes."

"*Muarago?* What did you say?"

"I didn't know they had Nikes in North Korea."

He followed a flaccid leg to another corpse wedged face-down behind a motor-generator. The barrel of an AK-type rifle poked out. He couldn't tell what had killed this second man. He had on a red windbreaker with a red-and-white patch. The Marlboro logo.

"Three dead," the pudgy diver said at his elbow.

"I only see two."

"Another there." He pointed into the shadows forward.

"Who are they?"

"North Korea, like commando. Like SEAL."

"Who shot them?"

"They shoot each other. Do not give up."

"Huh."

"*Yichoyero!* You come, see this," called one of the others. "See what we find."

He gave the bodies a last glance, and followed the beams of their lights.

A few feet aft the diver slapped what Dan recognized as a fairly unsophisticated-looking periscope stand, then pulled him to a little fold-down wooden table. Either a captain's station or a navigator's chart table. Dan blinked at it: cheap plywood, complete with knot holes. Everything in the space looked crude, hastily finished and covered, where it was shielded at all, with flimsy metal banged together with machine screws. He bent closer as a paper caught his eye. Someone had unfolded it carefully, so as not to tear the sodden, oilstained fibers.

It was a chart. Shivering as the cold crept deeper, he stripped off a glove and traced a coastline by the beam of a flash. Curving away, small islands . . . a larger island offshore. The Hangul characters conveyed nothing, but he gradually made it the Straits of Korea, if the long island was Tsushima.

He dug in with the spot of light till the lens touched the cheap shoddy paper. Was that a pencil-trace? A dead reckoning line, an advanced course? He let the chart sag where it lay. Fished in what looked like a wire wine-rack and came out with another. This was in English. *Approaches to Pusan*, it read. Next came a small book that hefted astonishingly massive. When he opened the lead covers, each soaking page was filled with tiny handwritten characters.

An exclamation from the far end of the compartment brought him back to where he was. He squinted at his watch. Twelve minutes gone, out of fifteen. He had to get out. It'd take a few minutes to get back to the bow, no, the stern— anyway back to the ascent line.

A louder gabble from the divers. He glanced their way, then back toward the black toothless maw of the chamber. A hatch at the top, another at the bottom. The inner hatch opened upward, the lower, downward. Obviously to lock out divers while still submerged.

Since it left no room for torpedo stowage, this must be the infiltration version of the sub. But what were they doing here? Trying to tap submerged cables? The U.S. Navy had pioneered it, but that didn't mean nobody else could try.

And they were almost to the DMZ. Why charts for Pusan, the southernmost port on the Eastern Sea? And why was the crew wearing clothes that must have been purchased in South Korea?

Maybe the logbook held an answer. He unzipped the top of his suit and tucked it inside, against his chest, figuring he'd turn it over to Dr. Kim when they surfaced.

The unmistakable clack of a pistol slide slamming forward snapped his attention up. He wriggled toward the others. As he reached them, his pudgy friend held up a hand. His mouth hung open. They were as far aft in the compartment as they could get. His ear was pressed to the steel bulkhead beside a heavy watertight door.

"What is it?" Dan murmured.

The diver made walking legs with his fingers. Jerked his head at the bulkhead. At the closed door.

He sucked an astonished breath. Someone still alive? A flooded forward compartment this big would take them to the bottom. But if they'd sealed off the boat in time, they could still have a bubble in there. It was just barely possible.

Only . . . weren't they supposed to commit suicide?

One of the divers lifted a pistol. It gleamed darkly with grease. They'd come armed. Apparently not as paranoid a precaution as one might think. But now what?

He looked at his watch again and felt fear crawl over his skin like ticks. He was into decompression time. But he wasn't sure he had enough air in his tank to get through it.

His pudgy friend slammed a wrench on the bulkhead. *"Kechokye itneonjadeol. Tohanghameon sal su yitda!"*

The only answer was silence. His guy, who apparently had rank, pointed to the dogging wheel. Two divers seized it, one on either side. They braced themselves and threw it over.

"Shit," Dan muttered. He scrambled to where the corpses lay and fumbled the AK out from under a thin arm. Oily water pissed out of the action, draining from the barrel as he pointed it down and jerked the bolt back. A cartridge flipped out and pinged away. He let go and the bolt slammed closed. But he couldn't remember which way the safety lever worked and it was too dark too see any markings.

"Yeolligoit seom ni da," Pudgy shouted. He aimed at the door. The others were straining at the wheel, faces going dark with blood. The dogs crept back from their locking lugs, screeching faintly, as if under terrific strain.

He realized with horror that the reason might be a pressure differential. "Goddamn it, you're going to bend us," he shouted. "Or flood us, if that's water on the other side."

They didn't even turn their heads.

The door slammed open with a bang like a bank vault being dynamited. His ears popped violently.

An object flew in through the opening, trailing smoke. Before his stunned mind had time even to register what it was, Pudgy scooped the grenade up and threw it back in. It exploded almost as it left his hand. The blast was deafening in the steel-walled tunnel. Fragments clanged into equipment cabinets. Explosive fumes filled the air, then thinned, pushed by the steadily inrushing compressed air toward where the air bubbled out through the open lock.

Leaning into the hatchway, Pudgy emptied the pistol through it, firing rapidly as he could, then dove in after the bullets.

A rapid, roaring clatter from the far side of the bulkhead. He had a bad feeling his stocky friend was history. The others cursed frantically. One pulled a dive knife from a thigh sheath. The other spun around and jerked the AK out of Dan's hands.

A wiry, black-haired, lithe little figure in black shorts flew through the door headfirst, as if bounced off a trampoline on the far side. It hit the deck and rolled, agile as a gymnast, and came up holding a commando-type knife that it instantly backhanded across one of the divers' face. The South Korean staggered back, shouting and pawing at his eyes. The enemy crewmember whipped the blade back to guard and faced Dan, not four feet distant. His instinctive hesitation at what he saw was almost fatal. Held at arm's length and lunged with incredible quickness, the blade drove in straight as an arrow and slammed into his chest.

The North Korean gaped, taken aback, as the point slid off, gouging black rubber with a tearing sound. Deflected by the soft lead cover of the logbook tucked against Dan's chest under the wet-suit top.

Dark eyes dropped to the AK's muzzle just as the other diver pulled the trigger.

The rifle blasted twice, then stopped, either jammed or out of ammunition. Both bullets struck the North Korean in the chest. The knife went flying. The small face contracted in pain and shock. An arm clutched small nude breasts, welling now with dark blood. She gasped, struggled to speak; then crumpled.

The diver worked the bolt frantically, watching the open hole of the door. He aimed the rifle at it and pulled the trigger again, but got only a dry click. No light on the other side. But when Dan aimed a flashlight in, something fluid gleamed back.

The water licked at the lip of the hatch like a black cat testing a treat. Then edged forward, elongated, and began pouring in. They must have cracked a valve, yielded their one unflooded compartment to the sea, when they realized someone was aboard who shouldn't be, on the far side, in the control compartment.

He couldn't fault them for guts. Or was it something darker, not heroism, but the unconscious reactions of automatons? He started to shake with the aftermath of terror. The wounded diver moaned, holding his gory face in one piece with the pressure of both hands. His buddy threw the rifle aside and grabbed him by the shoulders, asking something in a concerned tone.

That was when the last North Korean slid through.

She was larger than the others, more muscular than wiry. Short hair, matted with oil and sweat. Pistol in one hand, knife in the other. Smooth thick arms. Panting, with a craving for death lighting black eyes. She squinted past the flashlights. They must have dazzled her after the utter dark. Maybe that was why she didn't see Dan, standing to the side of the access. Why she focused on the South Korean bending over his wounded buddy.

Barking something hoarse, she brought the pistol around.

Dan tripped the buckle on his weight belt. The heavy nylon strap studded with cast lead slid off his hips, and he continued and altered the motion and whipped it around into the side of her head. Lead impacted bone like a sledgehammer hitting a hollow log. She went down at once. The gun hit the deck with a clattering splash. The others were on her in a moment, kneeing, shouting, kicking, punching, until he screamed at them over and over again to stop.

He hung on the line, only checking his watch when he couldn't help it. Decomp time passed so slowly. Shudders writhed through him. His suit leaked cold water through the rip in his chest. He yearned up at the surface. Only fifteen feet away now, a silvery rolling through

which now and then shot a hot golden vein of sun. He'd
spent an hour hanging on the line. Two safety divers hovered
near. They'd brought down the extra air he needed.

They'd found eleven more bodies in the after compartment, all shot in the head at close range.

He twisted to look behind him. The last one alive, the
woman he'd knocked out. Her hands were wired behind her.
The South Koreans gripped her by the arms. They'd bundled
her into the suit Dan's buddy, the dead diver, didn't need
anymore, and wired her ankles and wrists together. She'd re-
gained consciousness dangling on the ascent line. Struggled,
glaring at them through the helmet port, before accepting
captivity. Now she sagged in the water, slowly turning in the
tidal current.

What had the Sang-O been doing? Why were they carrying charts for the Strait? Why had they surfaced? According
to Dr. Kim, they'd been almost to the DMZ and safety when
it had broached.

Lots of questions. Maybe she'd have some answers.
Which was part, at least, of why he'd stopped them from
killing her.

He checked his watch one last time. Gave it a few more
seconds, just to be sure. Then valved air into his vest.

Shivering, gripping his captive's arm spasmodically, he
lofted toward the shivering light. Contemplating what had
startled him so much, there in the sunken pressure hull, that
he'd almost lost his life. He'd only belatedly recognized it,
so strange it seemed to a Western eye.

Every one of the submarine's crew had been a woman.